THE LEGACY OF AL CAPONE

*Portraits and Annals
of Chicago's Public Enemies*

THE LEGACY

Portraits and Annals

Also by George Murray

THE MADHOUSE ON MADISON STREET
NEW HORIZONS

OF AL CAPONE

of Chicago's Public Enemies

by George Murray

G. P. Putnam's Sons, New York

Contents

Illustrations will be found
following page 188

Foreword

A friend asked me seriously if the incidence of crime in Chicago had not been decreasing since the death of Al Capone. I turned to the nearest newsstand, bought a copy of the Chicago *Sun-Times* for November 27, 1974, and read: "In the first ten months of this year, Chicago had 866 reported homicides. This compared with a total of 863 in all of 1973."

The story went on to tell of similar increases in the incidence of rape, robbery with a gun, aggravated assault, and other types of crime against the person.

The story cited the uniform crime reports compiled by the Federal Bureau of Investigation. They indicated that what was true of Chicago was true of all other American cities and suburban communities.

Most of these crimes are not committed by members of the organized crime syndicates. But they go unpunished, for the most part, because of the presence in the communities of the crime syndicates.

Some years ago Mayor Martin H. Kennelly of Chicago told this writer: "They accused me of being a reformer. I was not. I never sought to run a Sunday School town. But after I had been in office a few months I closed down the Chez Paree, which offered Las Vegas-type gambling and entertainment.

"I did so only after I learned that eighty-one cents of every dollar of profit at the Chez Paree went for payoffs to police and prosecutors. I knew that policemen accepting payoffs to permit gambling would not be free to investigate other types of crime."

Kennelly knew what he was talking about. It was true then and it is true today. It was true in Chicago and it is true in any other community where the profits of crime are sufficient to justify its rational organization into a syndicate.

The policeman who accepts payoffs to permit one type of illegal activity will almost always go a step further and free any criminal who pays enough. What is true for the policeman is true for the prosecutor. What is true for the prosecutor is true for the judge. What is true for the judge is true for members of the parole board.

5

Once officialdom begins to differentiate between types of laws which will be enforced, it ends up enforcing none. Once the police and prosecutors and politicians who become judges begin to go lightly on those accused of gambling and prostitution, they cannot get tough with those accused of rape and murder. One man's money spends just as well as another's.

Any rookie with sense enough to graduate from the police academy knows the laws are not enforced equally against all. He knows the richest men in the country pay no income tax because they are in a position to control Congressmen who write tax laws as well as the appointment of Internal Revenue Service directors who enforce them.

As long as the upperworld millionaire can buy immunity from the law, the underworld millionaire will also be able to do so. As long as the barons of organized crime can get away with murder, the casual robber in the streets and alleys will be able to do so. The incidence of violent crime will continue to grow until it is forcibly stopped.

The one man in the United States who might be expected to know most about organized crime syndicates is Henry E. Peterson. For more than a decade he headed the organized crime section of the Department of Justice as an Assistant Attorney General. He said: "So far all efforts to destroy this multibillion-dollar crime industry have been pitiful."

Peterson might have added that in a democracy any effort to destroy organized crime by organized politics is likely to go on being pitiful. For organized crime is tied in with organized politics at the community, county, state, and federal levels.

This is true with the single exception of those rural communities so small that the profits from crime have not so far justified its rational organization into a syndicate or corporation.

In a democracy the candidate for public office needs funds with which to campaign. The man who makes such funds available need not advertise himself as the representative of organized crime. After the election the successful candidate treats his financial backers more generously than he does others in the community.

This does not mean organized crime cannot be fought successfully. In New Orleans in 1891 the citizens by vigilante action bypassed their politicians and courts to break the back of the Mafia for a generation.

Benito Mussolini ran Italy as a dictatorship, not as a democracy. He put the Mafia on the run in its home territory for the first time in its history. It did not regain power until America's military leaders joined forces with Sicily's Mafia leaders against Mussolini.

Attorney General William Saxbe recently hinted, according to *The*

Wall Street Journal of November 1, 1974, that Americans might emulate Brazil's vigilante methods "if the terror of crime becomes too strong." Not enough Americans know the work of the death squads (*Esquadroes da Morte*) of the Brazilian policemen.

Brazil is a nation only slightly smaller than the United States. Ten years ago some of its policemen got tired of seeing thieves, rapists, and murderers freed by politicians who had been paid off. The police formed their own vigilante squads and began killing known criminals who had been turned loose by the courts.

Brazil's politicians disapproved. The chambers of commerce of Brazil's most populous cities disapproved. The preachers and the teachers and the newspaper editors disapproved. Everybody disapproved but the ordinary people who wanted to live unmolested by criminals.

In 1970, 40 percent of those queried in a public opinion poll—including 60 percent of those queried in São Paulo, the nation's most populous city—said they favored the activities of the Death Squads.

Less than a year ago two of the deputies from Rio de Janeiro described the vigilante groups as an evil necessary to fight the *marginais* (outlaws or gangsters) with their own tactics. Not all of Brazil's policemen are vigilantes. Death Squad membership represents only a tiny minority of Brazil's 225,000 policemen.

Brazil's lawless elements, like those in the United States, began growing more emboldened after World War II. Through the first four months of 1974, Sao Paulo—with a population of about 6 million —recorded 395 homicides. This compared with 545 during the same period in New York City with a population of 7.8 million.

In 1973 Rio de Janeiro experienced 741 homicides among a population of 4.5 million, as compared with 1,680 in New York City.

The first Death Squad appeared in 1964, when Rio policeman Milton Le Cocq was killed by a criminal. For six years, Le Cocq had commanded a special police unit in charge of ridding the state of Guanabara of criminal activity. Le Cocq was said to be a rare blend of efficiency and compassion, not only arresting gangsters but finding jobs for many and trying to help in their rehabilitation.

Le Cocq's colleagues, already frustrated by judicial coddling of criminals, swore to avenge their chief's murder by killing ten gangsters for each policeman killed. They cornered Le Cocq's killer, who had taken refuge on a farm, and shot him to death. Then they filed past the body and each fired several shots into the corpse.

Before long the bullet-riddled bodies of thirty more gangsters were found in abandoned fields, along deserted roads, and in darkened streets and alleys of the cities.

Indictments were brought against sixteen policemen, but the governor of São Paulo went on television to tell his audience that any talk of Death Squads was "sensational fiction."

Perhaps one reason the governor took this position was because several of São Paulo's best known and most popular policemen were involved, including Sergio P. Fleury. This was the detective who commanded the police ambush which killed urban terrorist Carlos Marighela.

Among other things, Detective Fleury was said to have helped take nine prisoners from their cells and execute them to avenge the murder of a fellow policeman.

A jury in Bahia recently acquitted Manoel Quadros, a former police chief accused of several killings. In October, 1974, spectators in a São Paulo courtroom cheered when a jury acquitted two policemen accused of executions.

Prosecution of policemen accused of such executions is difficult. Prosecutors have resigned without explanation on the eve of trials. Indicted Death Squad members are sometimes returned to active police duty while awaiting trial in such cases. Incriminating records are mislaid, destroyed, or simply disappear from police files.

During the last ten years more than 2,000 persons, most of them big-time gangsters, have been summarily executed by the Death Squads. Late in 1973 a dozen were put to death by policemen in Rio. In July, 1974, the bodies of five were found in the Rio suburb of Nova Iguaçu. Each corpse had been shot several times.

Affixed to the corpses were hand-lettered signs proclaiming I WAS A NARCOTICS DEALER or I ROBBED AND THIEVED with the initials E. M. for *Esquadro da Morte.*

Most of the messages bore a skull and crossbones, replica of the "Le Cocq medals" that Rio policemen were awarding to fellow officers for exceptional bravery.

The Death Squad idea caught on quickly in the major cities. A Death Squad chief in Vitória killed eleven. Another in Bahia was accused of killing eight but was acquitted when his police files disappeared. In the first six months of 1969, when Death Squad executions were approaching 400 a year just in the states of Rio and Guanabara, forty partially decomposed bodies were found buried in the mud beneath the Macacu River.

Most of the dead had been shot in the back of the neck.

At first anonymous spokesmen regularly telephoned newspapers to tip them off as to the location of the corpses. The tipster in São Paulo called himself "White Lily." His Rio counterpart called himself "Red Rose." The Death Squads now rarely bother to publicize their executions.

In the Rio suburb of Nova Iguaçu, where in 1973 a hundred such executions were credited to the policemen, the bodies were commonly dumped in shallow graves, doused with gasoline, and set afire.

Church officials often condemn the Death Squads. Former President Emilio Médici all but demanded that states form inquiry commissions to investigate the vigilante groups. But of late the newspapers and politicians have been playing down the idea.

The Death Squads are composed almost entirely of state civil police, plainclothesmen responsible for investigating crime. They know the gangsters in their jurisdictions as well as the gangsters in Chicago are known to the police department's organized crime unit.

I told my friend that the incidence of crime against the person has been increasing in Chicago every year since Capone's death. The incidence of such crime has been increasing every year in every American city under the control of organized criminals and their lackeys holding political office.

Once the Mafia, and the crime syndicates of which it is a part, get power in any geographical area all crime increases in that area. If the syndicate chieftains can openly buy immunity from laws governing vice, gambling, narcotics, usury, and murder, such immunity will be sold to any casual strong-arm thug on the street.

Crime, like inflation, will increase until the people put a stop to it.

Casual crime obviously will never disappear so long as one man covets the goods of another. Killing will be a fact of life as long as one man covets another's woman. But organized crime is something else again. This type of crime can be eliminated in any American community whose citizens cease to be squeamish and handle it the same way their pioneer forefathers did the problem of horse thieves and cattle rustlers.

Chicago, Christmas, 1974   GEORGE MURRAY

1 "The Church never condones . . ."

Shivering in the piercing cold of that bleak February day, the chief lieutenants of the old Capone army of Prohibition years stood by as the body of Scarface Al was lowered into its grave.

Virtually all the survivors of that mob of the twenties—at least those who were out of prison at the time—were grouped around the Capone family lot in Mount Olivet Cemetery on the Far South Side of Chicago.

Those who felt themselves closest in life to their dead leader crowded under the gaily colored canvas canopy. The others stood in twos and threes outside, hunched against the wind and talking in low tones to one another. Occasionally one or another looked around.

There were nowhere near the 600 estimated at one time to have borne arms in the service of the multimillionaire liquor king. But the reputations of those present gave them stature far above the rank and file of the muggers and sluggers and killers.

These were the tested and proven of Capone's crop of criminals. No more representative group could have been put together anywhere on earth. These were the survivors of the bloodiest street wars ever seen.

Outside the periphery of this inner circle the police herded the throngs of curious. Despite the bitter weather the crowds had been waiting since dawn to watch the burial. Now it was midafternoon and the watchers stamped their feet in the snow to stimulate circulation.

From time to time dumpy little Jake Guzik turned to stare in the direction of the crowd. Murray Humphreys, slender and handsome, would make some comment that brought a smile from Guzik. The other gangsters appeared to gossip. From time to time, in their conversations, their faces lit up at some recalled incident.

Gangsters, as any newspaperman knows, are the greatest gossips on earth. When among their kind, or when talking off the record, they tell and retell old tales of their exploits.

Tough Tony Capezio, in his derby hat, dark sunglasses, and Chesterfield greatcoat, snarled something to Guzik. He was told, "Forget

11

it." Capone's cousin, Charlie Fischetti, told news cameramen, "I'll kill any son of a bitch that makes a picture."

At 2 o'clock the caravan of automobiles had begun arriving. From their green sedan stepped the Cicero contingent: Willie Heeney, Joey Aiuppa, Joey Korngold, Bob Ansonio.

Then came Sam Hunt, called "Golf Bag" because in the twenties he had carried a shotgun among his niblicks and mashies. Then Nick De Grazio. Then Capone's cousins, the Fischettis: Charlie, Rocco, and Joe.

Here were the biggest names of the postwar underworld. All turned and removed their hats at arrival of the three women: Capone's mother, sister, and widow. The widow, attractive and blond, was the former Mae Coughlin. With her was Capone's grown son, known to all as "Sonny."

The women were among the last to arrive. Their coming was a signal for the hearse from Rago Brothers' funeral home to back up to the temporary vault in which Capone's body had been kept. The coffin, draped with a huge blanket of gardenias and with dozens of orchids, was lifted into the vehicle and transported a hundred yards north to the yawning grave.

When reporters sought to edge close, the dead gangster's brother, Ralph, stepped out from beneath the canopy, and pleaded, "Why don't you leave us alone?" The reporters and photographers, with a job to do, stolidly held their ground and the coffin was brought to its proper place.

The simplest of ceremonies was presided over by Monsignor William J. Gorman, chaplain of the Chicago Fire Department and pastor of Resurrection Parish on the West Side. He handed his overcoat and hat to an attendant, kissed his stole before draping it about his neck, and opened a prayer book. Before starting, he said, "The Roman Catholic Church never condones evil, nor the evil in any man's life. But this ceremony is sanctioned by our archbishop in recognition of Alphonse Capone's repentance, and the fact that he died with the sacraments of the Church."

Father Gorman went on to say that a few hours before his death on Saturday, January 25, 1947, Capone had recovered consciousness briefly. He asked for a priest and was attended by Monsignor Joseph Barry of the Florida diocese.

At these words, Capone's mother, Mrs. Theresa Annunzio Capone, wailed aloud and succumbed to a new burst of tears. She was comforted by her daughter, Mrs. Mafalda Capone Maritote, and by Tony Accardo, chief among the dead emperor's heirs apparent.

Father Gorman looked at Capone's mother as he went on. "I never knew Alphonse Capone in life, but during the years that I was pastor of

St. Columbanus' Church on the South Side, I knew and respected his mother for her unfailing piety. So far as I know, she never missed mass a day of her adult life or missed communion of a Sunday. She asked me to conduct this service today."

Father Gorman then opened his missal, read a few passages in Latin, and knelt on the priedieu provided at the graveside to lead the mourning group in prayer. With his words and their responses, there were several Our Fathers, Hail Marys, and Acts of Contrition said. The women fingered their beads. Most of the men simply bowed their heads, but a few—such as Willie Heeney and Tony Accardo—spoke the responses loud and clear.

Father Gorman obviously cut the prayers short because of the cold. He signaled the pallbearers and cemetery attendants to begin lowering the coffin. He said a brief prayer for the dead, then stooped to pick up a clod of earth.

He crushed the piece in one hand, and with a scattering motion, tossed the bits onto the coffin at his feet. "Dust thou art. . . ."

The little ceremony was over. Twilight was already falling in the cemetery, and the weeping women were led away. Father Gorman, his overcoat draped over his shoulders, accompanied Mother Capone to her car.

The confusion around the cars settled down, and one by one they drew away. The police, who had been out in force for the event, urged the curious: "Go home; it's all over now." The cemetery workers began to fill in the grave quickly, to get it done before dark, and Father Gorman came back to talk to the newspapermen.

"The Church forbade a requiem mass either in Florida or here in Chicago. But several of Capone's friends and acquaintances, who had been in Miami and Miami Beach for the winter season, arranged for a quiet little mass at St. Patrick's Church near Capone's home."

Father Gorman said the $2,000 coffin bearing the body had been brought by motor from the Philbrick funeral home in Miami Beach to the Rago Brothers' funeral home in Chicago. The coffin had been kept closed to all except members of the immediate family, since Capone had been in ill health for seven years before the stroke and pneumonia which brought on his death at the age of forty-eight.

The cemetery workers gathered up the flowers for delivery to the poorer wards of the city's hospitals and orphanages. Other workers took down the canopy and packed it away, cleaning things up while they still had enough light to work. The afternoon was waning fast as the headstone, already cut and waiting, was put into position. It bore the words:

QUI RIPOSA
ALPHONSE CAPONE
NATO: JANUARY 17, 1899
MORTO: JANUARY 25, 1947

As newspapermen made their way to their own cars, the cemetery workers used rakes to blot out the ruts and footprints in the snow. All hurried now, as gray dusk blotted out the short winter's day, and more snow began to fall. Capone's first interment was ended.

A few years later, with no fanfare at all, Capone's body was moved from the South Side cemetery at 111th Street and California Avenue to Mount Carmel Cemetery on Wolf Road in the western suburb of Hillside. There were persistent rumors, neither confirmed nor denied by the Church, that his first grave had been in unhallowed ground, in a section of the cemetery not blessed by the bishop, but that his later resting place had been duly sprinkled with holy water and granted benediction.

Capone shares space in the new plot with his parents, his sister, and his wife. Chiseled into the granite headstone which marks his grave are the words MY JESUS MERCY.

The paucity of mourners at Capone's first burial in 1947 was decreed by Tony Accardo, known throughout the underworld as "Joe Batters" or familiarly as "J.B." He had become operating head of the Chicago Crime Syndicate with imprisonment of Paul (the Waiter) Ricca. Accardo had named those of the gang considered too hot to appear in public, and had instructed them to pay their respects at the wake held in one of the chapels at Rago Brothers.

The graveside ceremony was reserved for the Capone family and for those of the gangster's lieutenants who over the years had become family friends rather than simply business associates.

Hundreds of Capone's old associates had asked permission to attend. Judges and aldermen had volunteered to act as pallbearers. The word came down from Accardo: "We gotta draw the line someplace. If we let 'em, everybody in Chicago will crowd into the cemetery. Al had no enemies."

Accardo's sense of humor showed. Nobody knew better than he that Capone's enemies were mostly dead and that few had died natural deaths. Capone, one of the greatest practical politicians of his time, went out of his way to win over his enemies. If he could not convert them into friends, he at least sought to neutralize them. Only when nothing else worked did he kill them. By 1947, as Accardo said, Capone had no enemies.

Capone had friends beyond number. During the years when he was top man in Chicago and most of northern Illinois and Indiana, he cultivated people.

He was naturally gregarious, a social animal. He talked boxing or baseball to the sports-minded, political speculation and vote-getting techniques to the judges and Senators and governors, profits to the merchants and industrialists.

Capone saw to it that the poor got baskets of groceries. He opened soup kitchens for the jobless, scattered pennies to children playing in the streets, and largesse among their elders drinking in speakeasies. Any man with any kind of problem could stop Al Capone on the street and talk to him. More often than not Capone, like any other politician, would make a note of it and try to straighten it out.

Accardo did not want the cemetery overrun with worshipers. He told important politicians their presence would not be wanted. Many of Capone's old friends were in prison.

Besides Ricca, those of Capone's old and close associates in prison at the time included Frankie (Diamond) Maritote, Phil D'Andrea, John Roselli of Hollywood, Charles (Cherry Nose) Gioe, and Louis (Little New York) Campagna.

The Campagna family, which had changed its name to Champagne, was represented. The Annunzio family of Capone's mother was represented. Some of Capone's family had come out from New York, still spelling their name "Caponi" as had Al Capone when first arrested in Chicago in 1922.

The reporters identified as many of the mourners as they could, getting names from Monsignor Gorman, from the police, and from each other.

They wanted as many facts as they could gather about this burial, knowing it would be of interest to their readers. When they had cleaned up the story, they made their way to the nearest tavern with phones to turn it in. Their job done, they began to yarn.

The old-timers among the newspapermen recalled Al Capone when he first had come to Chicago at the age of twenty. He was a husky, brawling youngster who had to get out of Brooklyn until the heat died down after he had beaten up a politician's son. That was in 1919, the year after World War I ended.

Young Capone, born in Castellamare, near Naples, had been brought by his parents to Brooklyn as a child. He had been a thief from earliest boyhood, a pimp by the time he attained puberty, a strong-arm robber, a lookout for waterfront dice games, a bouncer in the rough saloon run by Frankie Uale, alias Yale, Brooklyn chief of the Unione Siciliane.

When Capone needed sanctuary, he was brought out to Chicago by Johnny Torrio, who ran the First Ward vice empire for his uncle, Big Jim Colosimo. Torrio put Capone to work in the Four Deuces, a brothel so called because of its address at 2222 South Wabash Avenue. Capone was supposed to be the bouncer but he quickly became its manager.

As a precaution, just in case the police were alerted by authorities in Brooklyn, Capone used the alias "Al Brown." The front of his brothel bore a sign which fooled no one: NEW AND USED FURNITURE.

Capone had business cards printed up for himself, identifying him as manager of the furniture store. He would laugh as he said he sold "any old thing a man might want to lay on."

Newspapermen of Chicago were not above visiting the Levee dives once in a while. Some of the older reporters early got acquainted with Al Capone and rather liked him as an open and talkative youngster, despite the trade which made him a pariah. Newspapermen might visit whores, but no decent reporter would ever knowingly shake the hand of a pimp.

Maybe it was hindsight, but the older reporters who had covered Capone's funeral said that from the first he seemed the kind who would have done well at whatever he turned his hand to. He had a friendly way about him, never bullied the people who worked for him, was quiet and efficient and businesslike in his management of the brothel.

In those days, Colosimo was courted by the politicians who wanted to be elected aldermen or judges. His friendship was sought by the men who dreamed of some day holding the office of mayor or governor or Congressman down in Washington.

Although Colosimo's empire seemed to be centered in the First Ward, his influence was felt throughout the city. Torrio was his chief lieutenant and seemed to be brilliant where Colosimo was plodding, modern where Colosimo was old-fashioned. From the first, it was clear that Capone was one of Torrio's brightest young aides.

The newspapermen talking at Capone's funeral decided that his rise to the heights, like the rise of Adolf Hitler or Franklin Delano Roosevelt or Winston Churchill, could be attributed to his being the right man in the right place at the right time.

Capone barely had time to settle into the underworld of Chicago when Prohibition came along.

The Volstead Act was approved by Congress on October 28, 1919, following ratification on January 16, 1919, of the Eighteenth Amendment to the Constitution. That amendment, as ratified by the states, declared that all liquors with more than one-half of one percent of alcohol were intoxicating. The amendment ordered that the manufacture, transportation, or sale of such liquors be prohibited throughout the nation. The Volstead Act, providing the enabling legislation by which such a prohibition might be effected, was to become law at midnight on January 16, 1920.

The men and women who favored the prohibition of alcoholic beverages expected everyone in the country to quench their thirsts in future with coffee, tea, milk, and soft drinks.

But in every city of the land there were men such as Big Jim Colosimo and Johnny Torrio, men who had grown rich as provisioners to the general public of things denied by law. They had always dealt in prostitution, sometimes legal and sometimes not. They had always engaged in the interstate exchange of prostitutes. They had always given the public, for a percentage of the wagers, the high-stake poker games and high-rolling dice games and off-the-track horserace betting which so much of the public seemed to demand. They had always acted as brokers in the provision of mayhem and murder for hire.

Their services as brokers for threats, bodily injuries, and cold-blooded murder had always been in demand.

Individuals for one reason or another had always been willing to pay for the deaths of others. In Chicago since the 1871 fire such services were more than ever sought by the labor unions which needed an edge in organizing and by employers who wanted to prevent or break up labor organizations.

In every city in the land the Colosimos and the Torrios saw new opportunities in the law intended to deny beer, wine, and strong spirits to the American public. Within weeks after ratification of the Eighteenth Amendment, underworld operators in Chicago began buying up breweries.

In the spring of 1919, Johnny Torrio bought the Malt-Maid Company at 3901 South Emerald Avenue, and put Lou Greenberg on the premises as manager. When the Volstead Act took effect a year later, Torrio changed the name of the business to the Manhattan Brewing Company.

The Malt-Maid was only one of Torrio's purchases. He took options on several breweries whose owners sought to divest themselves of businesses in which they could see no future legitimate profits. The breweries were sometimes as far away from Chicago's First Ward as Joliet to the southwest, Waukegan to the north, and southeast across the state line in Hammond, Indiana.

Torrio talked with the heads of Italian families who had always made wine in their homes. He arranged for huge sugar purchases, so they could vastly increase the output of their home wineries. He arranged for the distillation of much of this wine into homemade brandy.

One of the reasons Torrio saw a need for Al Capone and others he was simultaneously hiring from outside the city was as overseers.

Torrio anticipated a vast new industry and recognized his need for lieutenants with brains and muscle.

Al Capone listened carefully as Johnny Torrio told him of the potential of his new job. Many others were being hired at the same time. Apparently none of the others had the imagination to see the opportunities through Torrio's eyes. Capone promptly sent to Brooklyn for his brothers. Within months a whole Capone clan was on the scene. Capone was a budding emperor before he attained his majority.

Colosimo was Torrio's uncle. In the underworld, as in the upperworld, nepotism has much to do with history. Capone indicated years later that he found Jim Colosimo parochial in his outlook. Colosimo had done well with his Black Hand extortions, his many houses of prostitution, and his restaurant and cabaret. He saw no reason to expand. Torrio could not interest Colosimo in the vast new opportunities for wealth which opened with Prohibition.

Capone grasped Torrio's vision at once. He saw, even before Torrio recognized the fact, that Colosimo's day was past. Once Torrio and Capone agreed on a course of action, Colosimo's fate was decided. Capone's old employer, Frankie Yale, was brought out from New York City and at 4 o'clock in the afternoon of Tuesday, May 11, 1920, Colosimo was shot to death in the vestibule of his cabaret at 2126 Wabash Avenue.

Prohibition had been in effect less than four months at the time.

All of Colosimo's wide business interests now belonged to his nephew, Johnny Torrio, with Al Capone as Torrio's chief lieutenant.

A few years later Torrio, having recovered from numerous bullet wounds, departed Chicago to return to Brooklyn in retirement.

Al Capone was only in his mid-twenties when left undisputed master of the Colosimo-Torrio combine, a heady rise to tremendous power and riches. Even so, Capone had a sure grasp of the reins. He knew every nook and cranny of his empire, with its labor unions, police and political payrolls, prostitution and gambling, beer and alcohol manufacturing, liquor smuggling and import, retail outlets in the form of speakeasies throughout the northern part of two states.

Capone was in Chicago only a decade when sent to prison for a year in Pennsylvania. After he got out, he was busy for the next two years fighting the income tax charges which sent him to a federal prison in 1932. His identification with Chicago coincided almost exactly with the thirteen years during which Prohibition was the law of the land. He seemed born to the role in which fate cast him.

This wild youngster radiated the force necessary to control and discipline the worst criminals of his time. He quickly developed to an unusual level his inborn qualities of organization and administration. He found and surrounded himself with the men needed to head great—if illegal—business enterprises. He showed leadership of a kind which won the total loyalties of those around him.

Virtually every surviving gangster who got his start in the Capone years speaks today with pride and pleasure of whatever association he had with "the Big Fellow." Many such gangsters, simple thieves or killers before they got rich enough to buy police and prosecutors and judges, are now semiretired. They are far removed from the mugging and slugging and strong-arm work of their youth. They have sent their children to the best schools and the most expensive universities.

Some of the grown children have entered the semilegitimate businesses of their fathers. Others are now doctors or lawyers or legislators. The children, now grown, absorbed the stories of Al Capone with their mothers' milk. They speak of the legendary Capone as having had a mystique—a charisma.

Along with the empire they inherited when Capone was removed from the Chicago scene, his successors and their children inherited the legend. The empire is easily delineated. It consists of the ownership of breweries and distilleries, of scores of warehouses and office buildings, of hundreds of labor unions and employers' associations, of the most important thing of all—the roster of legislators and judges and governmental administrators on the underworld payroll. The men who inherited this empire have added to it and expanded it. The legend is something else.

While it is easy to explain the empire as being held together in the same way as is any upperworld bureaucratic machine—by loyalty and friendship and jobs—the legend cannot be as simply explained.

Capone's genius lay in part in his ability to organize thieves from back alleys into a disciplined army. They learned to wear custom-made suits but never forgot to have special pockets built in, reinforced for the carrying of pistols.

When Capone came on the scene in Chicago, every neighborhood in the city had its ethnic gangs. That year of 1919 was the year of the greatest race war in Chicago's history. The ethnic gangs fought each other, black against white, Jew against non-Jew, Italian against Irish, Pole against Greek.

All were seemingly undisciplined by anyone, police or their own leaders, financed principally by the politicians for whom they got out the vote on election day. The gangs and the gangsters appeared to live in total anarchy. Capone made of this ragtag and bobtail a cohesive fighting force.

Probably it could not have been done without the limitless funds available ,as a result of Prohibition and the underworld's stake in the business. But it was done.

The individual ethnic gang leaders sought and failed to build their own armies with those funds. One by one they turned to Capone's banner as his empire came into being. He won them in the same way upperworld emperors brought together kingdoms and principalities, by the sharing of profits, the granting of fiefdoms, by marriage and diplomacy, and—when all else failed—by war.

These men of the ethnic gangs, the Jews and the Irish and the Greeks and the Poles and the blacks, are as much a part of the Capone story as the Italians and Sicilians. They were the contemporaries of the Big Fellow. They fought with him or against him as the tides of battle changed. They gave the city of Chicago the reputation it bears today—the city of cooperation between the underworld and the half-world of politics and politicians.

Some of these ethnic gang leaders were helping shape the character of Chicago before Capone ever heard of the place. And while his name will forever be the touchstone of the legend, these men were almost as responsible as Capone himself for creation of the legend. They are part of the legacy and their roles should be recorded.

Capone was to say of justices of the United States Supreme Court, "They are nothing but precinct captains in long black robes."

But it was not Capone who began the practice of buying politicians at every level, right up to and including the highest court in the land. That practice dated back to the earliest days of the Republic. The practice was not even originated in the underworld, as the records of the Jackson and Grant administrations indicate.

Big business has always been able to use the chief resident politician in the White House, the nine politicians who have worked their way up to places on the nation's highest bench, the Senators who like to think of themselves as members of the most exclusive gentlemen's club in the world.

Capone broke this business monopoly. Capone's organization could not have taken over the city of Chicago and the state of Illinois without working hand in glove with the black-bag businessmen of the stamp of Charles T. Yerkes, the traction magnate who regularly bought up lawmakers.

The newspapermen of Chicago are not cynics. They are realists. At Capone's funeral they talked of these things and more.

The businessmen and politicians who cooperated with each other in Capone's day have been known to chuckle with delight at the memory of Big Al and some of his contemporaries. They love to tell of the businessman who sought to avoid other predatory extortionists by cutting Capone in for a one-fourth interest in his business and who later said, "No man ever had a more honest partner. If I had it to do over again, I'd do the same thing."

Cash and corruption alone cannot explain the attraction Capone held for the businessmen of his time. Personality enters into it.

Capone's force was never doubted, his dynamic leadership was felt by all who came under his spell, he proved himself merciless when need be. But there were other qualities seldom noted by historians. There was empathy and sympathy and a capacity for kindness and generosity. There was the humor, not always black. There was understanding.

Many of the businessmen and politicians who knew Capone best are still to be found in Chicago and its suburbs. Some are living out their days in Florida, California, Arizona, or New Mexico. Few will acknowledge in so many words that Capone started them on the road to riches and power. But it comes through in their memories.

They delight in reminiscing about those great days of the twenties when Capone was undisputed monarch of a sovereign state, when the Capone family owned and operated Illinois just as surely as the DuPont family today owns and operates the state of Delaware. Whenever they get together, the businessmen and politicians rehash the Prohibition period. Like old men everywhere they relive in memory the adventurous days of their youth.

If you know them well enough they will tell you how Lou Greenberg got his start by rolling drunks and looting junkyards. How he became the multimillionaire owner of the Seneca Hotel on Chicago's Gold Coast and was killed when he sought to cheat Frank Nitti's foster son out of his inheritance.

They will tell you how Dion O'Banion became the first hijacker in history on a sudden impulse. And of how, with a cocked pistol in his hand, this killer of sixty-two men let himself be captured in front of an open safe by an unknowing policeman. "I remembered we had a pint of nitroglycerine, and the shock of one shot would have blown up the Loop."

They will tell you how Frankie Diamond and Murray Humphreys kidnapped a union leader to get $50,000 with which to start their own retail dairy and how that dairy is today one of the biggest in Chicago, still in the hands of the heirs to its founders.

They delight in telling how Murray Humphreys got $42,000, the biggest sum on record for an underworld killing, for the simple hit of an aging and garrulous one-time beer runner. And of how the hit was paid for by an upperworld millionaire.

They love to tell how Al Capone was responsible for protecting Chicago slum children by giving them the first Grade A milk in history. And how through his influence the children of Chicago, for the first time, were assured of getting fresh milk from the grocers' shelves.

They tell of the dated-milk ordinance which Capone's forces rammed through the Chicago City Council over the objection of the upperworld dairies. For two generations the housewives of Chicago could look at a carton of milk and read the deadline date before which it must be sold: a date only seventy-two hours from the time the milk came from the cow.

Capone's influence in this case was on the side of the people. After his passing the upperworld dairies, the legitimate conglomerates of wealth, power, and influence had the dated-milk ordinance removed from the books of Chicago. So now the Chicago housewife has no idea whether the milk she buys is fresh or near souring. A lot of upperworld money and lobbying went into that crime against Chicago children.

The old-timers among the newspapermen told their younger colleagues that "Capone was not all bad." They had all read the Capone biographies but at his funeral they talked of other things, of the things that had never seen print. Their talk was spiced with tales of how Willie Bioff used grated ice to keep his whores in line, of how Red Barker had an uncanny sense for a fat union treasury which could be looted, of how Frank Nitti and Tony Cermak fought a duel by proxy. And how Cermak lost.

They told as though they had been present how Al Capone personally and publicly executed the man who had humiliated Jake Guzik and boasted, "You should have heard the little Jew whine." They told the story that was never hinted at in print in Chicago, of how the Roman Catholic archbishop sent into exile a priest who befriended gangsters.

A good Catholic among the newspapermen present commented, "Every time I see Father Pat I ask him how he enjoyed the company of the headhunters along the Upper Amazon. He always takes my head between his hands, pretends to measure it for length and width, and says, 'To tell you the truth, Eddie, it wouldn't be worth shrinking.'"

A couple of the black newspapermen who had seen Capone buried had a few words to contribute. They told of how Capone's heirs were beginning to muscle into the policy empire built by Edward Perry Jones, Jr.

Every yarn spun on that occasion added to the legend of Al Capone. The newspapermen laughed at the humor of many of the episodes.

They spoke with disdain of the crooked judges, crooked Senators, and crooked Congressmen who made it all possible. One veteran reporter said, "I've got a hell of a lot more respect for Al Capone than I have for those thieving hypocrites in politics."

The newspapermen drinking together on that cold evening agreed that Al Capone left to his heirs an underworld empire, and left to the world a legend, but that his true legacy to the people of America was something quite different from either of them.

They apparently found much to think about in this idea of a legacy. They tried to put it into words. None of them was very proud of it as they considered this legacy, made up of the sum of many things. They thought it more or less started with Lou Greenberg. . . .

2 The richest SOB in hell

Alex Louis Greenberg always loved to tell how he came to the United States at the age of fourteen with only 6 cents in his pocket. When he was shot to death fifty years later, his heirs paid taxes on an estate of $3,328,532.

Greenberg's was a Horatio Alger story to please any man. He started out jackrolling drunks and ended up as owner of the Canadian Ace Brewing Company at 3940 South Union Avenue, selling them beer.

In those fifty years Greenberg had as colorful a life as any of Al Capone's early associates. He went from petty thievery to bartending, from loan-sharking to ownership of a string of saloons. He finally became a banker as head of the Roosevelt Finance Corporation and a boniface as head of the Seneca at 200 East Chestnut Street.

Greenberg was a native of Minsk. He fled Russia in the pogroms of 1905, and was given a home and a job in New York City by an uncle who owned a restaurant. Greenberg did not have to speak English to work as a busboy. But in 1950 he told the Kefauver Senate committee, "Within a year I was manager of the restaurant, which seated four hundred."

Two more years and Greenberg's generous uncle found out where the profits were going. He called the police and the ambitious youth had to give back most of the money he had stolen. His uncle told him, "You goniff, if I ever see you in New York again you'll go to jail."

That was when Greenberg decided to come to Chicago.

Greenberg had learned more than English while working for and living with the family of his uncle in New York. The uncle had taught him the first thing to do when opening a business in any new neighborhood is to get acquainted with the local precinct captains and the local police station desk sergeants.

Each political party has its precinct captain in every block, its ward committeeman in every neighborhood. The local police station not only has patrolmen on every block, but a different desk sergeant for each of the three shifts daily. Greenberg's uncle looked up all these men and asked them to bring their families to his restaurant from time to time for Sunday dinner. It worked wonders.

So when Lou Greenberg got off his freight train in Chicago in 1909, at the age of eighteen, he headed for the garment district, where Yiddish was generally spoken. He got a job as swamper in a workingmen's saloon. The swamper mops the place out every morning, emptying the spittoons, washing the windows and back-bar mirrors, scouring the pots in which the free lunch soup and chili and sauerkraut are made. Greenberg later was to say, "The first place I asked for a job the guy said he had a nigger for that work. I told him I didn't need any money, except the tips the customers might give me from time to time. I could eat the free lunch and sleep on some old sacks the guy had in the basement. He fired the nigger and I went to work."

Greenberg had other ideas for earning a little income on the side. When the place closed up that first night, he had his eye on a man who seemed to have unlimited money and a limited capacity for strong drink.

Greenberg followed this man down the dark side of Van Buren Street east of Market Street. As they passed an alley, he sprang on the man's back, with his left forearm across the man's throat, his right hand clutching his left wrist to exert pressure. Greenberg's right knee was in the middle of the man's spine, pushing forward to cause immediate collapse.

The classic jackrolling position resulted in the man falling to the sidewalk, fearing his back was being broken, and held silent and choking by the tight forearm across his windpipe. Greenberg ground his face in the dirt, making sure his eyes were full of dust so he could see nothing, then emptied the man's pockets of money. Greenberg left in leisurely fashion, certain the man would spend the next five minutes gasping for breath and thankful his life had been spared.

That became Greenberg's pattern at closing hour each night.

The nearest police station was a few blocks north, in the alley west of Market Street and south of Madison Street. Greenberg went out of his way to make the acquaintance of the various desk sergeants as they came on duty. He knew the time might come when he would need an edge with the police.

In those days each of Chicago's wards, or political subdivisions, had two aldermen in the City Council. The two from the First Ward were Michael Kenna, called Hinky Dink because of his short stature; and John Coughlin, as big as Kenna was small. Coughlin had once been a rubber in a bathhouse downstairs on North Clark Street, so ever after he was known as Bathhouse John.

The two aldermen were generally to be found either in Kenna's cigar store and office, on South Clark Street near Van Buren Street, or in his saloon across Clark Street, the Workingmen's Exchange.

Lou Greenberg made a practice of stopping in at the saloon, bringing himself to the attention of the politicians and their lackeys.

Greenberg first came to the attention of Chicago police in their official capacity when caught pilfering from a junkyard on South Wabash Avenue. He was arrested and charged, so the incident is part of the record, but he judiciously spread a little money around and was not convicted.

After that, Greenberg stuck to jackrolling drunks. One night he was just completing his stalk, starting the customary run for the final attack, when a limping figure darted out of an alley and slugged the intended victim. The two attackers saw each other simultaneously, but too late to spare the drunk, who was collapsing unconscious onto the sidewalk.

Suddenly the muggers were in confrontation. Greenberg was a spare little fellow, face deeply lined and eyebrows bushy even in youth. He was not looking for a fight. The man who stood before him, blackjack swinging loosely at the end of a long arm, was a smiling Irishman of stocky build who obviously would welcome a fight or a frolic. He said to Greenberg, "Well, boy, you want to fight or get lost?"

Greenberg was not going to give up his chance at the victim's bankroll without at least attempting negotiation. Trying to adapt his tone to that of the other, he replied, "There's no point in fighting for it, Irisher. Why don't we split it fifty-fifty, or match for it—winner take all?"

They split the take on that one, and then waited in the alley to jackroll the next two drunks who walked east on Van Buren Street, splitting the take from those jobs as well. That was the beginning of a friendship which was to last for the next fifteen years. Greenberg and Dion O'Banion had discovered each other. In the next several years they were to side each other in any number of burglaries of fur lofts, jewelry stores, and liquor warehouses.

Both Greenberg and O'Banion were thrifty. They hung onto the money they stole and talked of their plans for going into business. Greenberg wanted a saloon and O'Banion wanted a florist shop. They felt they were safer working together on jackrollings, rather than continuing as they had been at lone mugging. Usually they split the cash on something less than a fifty-fifty basis, with O'Banion getting the lion's share and Greenberg keeping such jewelry as rings, vest-pocket watches, and lodge insignia worn by their prey. Both felt it an equitable arrangement.

Greenberg's cash hoard in the basement of the saloon where he still slept continued to grow. He looked around for a place to sell the stolen jewelry. That was how he met a little Italian barber who acted as a fence. The man's name was Frank Nitti.

Nitti then called himself Italian. Actually he was a Sicilian and eventually he was to become president of the Unione Siciliane.

Greenberg had graduated in the saloon hierarchy from porter to morning bartender and assistant cook. He had to put the beans to soak overnight and start them boiling the first thing in the morning so they could be served later as part of the free lunch. He had to peel the onions to be mixed with the herring, and to put out the bread and cold cuts and pickled pigs' feet. The workers in the garment district followed no dietary laws when it came to free lunch.

Greenberg was not yet twenty-one when he felt he had enough capital and enough connections to open his own saloon. He looked around and decided on a hole-in-the-wall operation in the garment district.

A minimum of capital was required. The beer and whiskey salesmen had to be convinced that the owner was worthy of credit. This meant they had to have faith in his larceny, convinced that he could and would shortchange customers if necessary so that when the bills fell due he would be able to pay for the liquid merchandise advanced. Beyond that a man needed only his first month's rent. He could sleep in the back room and eat the leftovers from the free lunch.

Greenberg opened his place on Market Street, just north of Van Buren, with the blessings of Hinky Dink, Bathhouse John, and the police captain from the Second District. The cops on the beat were paid off in free lunch and beer, the desk sergeants were on a retainer of $2 a week each, and the two aldermen only asked that Greenberg speak up for their candidates among his customers at election time.

Both Greenberg and O'Banion loved to yarn about their early days.

O'Banion had a friend and constant companion named Earl Wajciechowski, nicknamed Hymie Weiss. On the day Greenberg opened his new place, O'Banion and Hymie Weiss were having a drink with Greenberg to help him celebrate. A free-spending stranger stepped up to the bar and began putting away booze. The stranger was well-dressed and made the mistake of showing a great deal of money. After he had tossed off several drinks, he got to the point where he was almost falling-down drunk.

At this point, O'Banion caught Greenberg's eye. O'Banion and Greenberg together caught the drunk under the arms and led him to a back room. Greenberg told him, "You can lie down and be more comfortable."

Hymie Weiss followed them and took up a position at the door where he could block the view of others in the saloon. Out of sight of the bar, Greenberg held the drunk's arms while O'Banion slugged him. Greenberg, Hymie Weiss, and O'Banion split the drunk's money three ways. After dark O'Banion and Hymie Weiss came back, rolled the still-unconscious drunk onto a two-wheeled cart used by a garment district ragpicker, and pushed him over to the West Madison Street skid row. They dumped him in a gutter and never saw him again.

O'Banion and Hymie Weiss were on the payrolls of newspapers in Chicago by this time. The newspapers were vying for circulation and hiring sluggers to see that they got it. But either O'Banion or Hymie Weiss tried to get to Greenberg's saloon during its busiest hours, after the close of the working day, prepared to follow and jackroll drunks who got too loaded.

Nobody ever had to stop drinking in Lou Greenberg's saloon because he ran out of money. Greenberg was generous. He would lend any customer $5 any day of the week—with the understanding that $6 would be repaid the following Monday. That was the standard rate: 6 for 5.

Greenberg never lost a dollar at this loan business. Not with Dion O'Banion and Hymie Weiss ready to talk to the borrower, offering to break his arms or his legs if he did not keep up the $1-a-week payments on the loan. They told the borrower that it was always possible he would not have $6 on Monday, but he could simply pay the $1 interest due and continue the $5 loan in force for another week.

One borrower did not believe O'Banion would go through with his threat. Two minutes later his right arm was broken between the elbow and the wrist. He became a believer. After he had paid his medical bills he still found enough money to pay Greenberg what he owed. No police complaint was ever filed.

Greenberg never liked to pay for anything he could steal. Since he had a legitimate saloon, and thus an outlet for stolen whiskey or beer, he let it be known that he would act as a fence. For every case he bought at wholesale prices from loft and warehouse thieves, he got a case free. That took care of the whiskey and gin. He made the same deal on beer by the barrel. He had so much merchandise coming to him on this basis that he had to open two other outlets, a saloon at Sixteenth Street and Lawndale Avenue and a second saloon at 4346 Lincoln Avenue (a South Side street whose name was later changed to Wolcott Avenue).

All the businesses prospered, with Greenberg paying off the cops and politicians, until one of the city's leading whiskey distributors decided not to take such losses. His guards caught the ring of whiskey thieves while they were busy loading a horse-drawn wagon at the back of the warehouse. Charges were brought and the whiskey distributor let it be known he intended to go through with the prosecution.

Greenberg had been arrested along with the others. He was charged with larceny and receiving stolen goods, in an indictment reported out by the Cook County grand jury in May, 1919. Among his co-defendants were two brothers whose names were to turn up later in connection with several more of Greenberg's enterprises. They were Harry and Morris Terfansky.

Greenberg had to turn to Kenna and Coughlin, the two First Ward aldermen, to get that indictment quashed. He never went to trial on the charge but later complained that the politicians had charged him too much money for the services they had rendered.

Prohibition was still some months in the future but several of the city's old-time brewing magnates, most of whom then lived on Astor Street in the Gold Coast, wanted to divest themselves of their holdings. Johnny Torrio bought the Malt-Maid at 3901 South Emerald Avenue, a property that goes through the entire block. On Union Avenue the address is that earlier noted for the Canadian Ace Brewery. The place changed names several times, but never locations. When Torrio bought it, he hired Greenberg as resident manager.

Greenberg had been in Chicago only a decade but he had come a long way.

Now he began to make his headquarters at Colosimo's Cafe on Wabash Avenue and to make his reports on the brewery business direct to Al Capone, as Torrio's lieutenant. Greenberg kept his saloons. A few months later, when the Prohibition law took effect, he had the names painted over on the front windows and operated them as speakeasies.

In later years Greenberg gave credit to Torrio and Capone. He said, "They never tried to hog it all for themselves. By 1922 they had let me buy twenty-five percent of the stock in the brewery. I bought more stock in the mid-twenties and then increased my holdings again in 1931 and 1932." Greenberg at the time was testifying before a Senate committee.

With a brewery and three speakeasies in operation, Greenberg was deep in the liquor business as the Prohibition era opened. He spent part of each day at the brewery, but put in a few hours daily at each of the saloons. In each ward in which he operated, the ward committeeman or alderman put a bookmaker into Greenberg's places of business. This not only gave Greenberg a cut of the gambling take, but was a bonanza for his loan-shark operations.

Besides the bookmaker, who worked for the organized gambling ring in the city, Greenberg employed in each saloon a dealer who ran cardgames in the back room. His income from the poker, dice, and blackjack games was always augmented by the *vigorish* from his six-for-five loan business. Just where the term "vigorish" ever came from, to describe the interest on loans, has never been satisfactorily explained. The word came into Yiddish only as it came into the English language. But nobody in Chicago's underworld speaks of loan-shark interest in any other terms.

Very quickly Greenberg realized that busy as he was, the bulk of his income could be accounted for by his loan activities. He considered his gambling operations only as feeders for high-interest lending. He got Capone's permission to open a handbook in the Lexington Hotel, always with his moneylending business.

The Lexington, at 2135 South Michigan Avenue, had been adopted by Capone as headquarters when he began moving up in the Torrio organization. Capone used the Four Deuces as a meeting place for his men, a planning place for various illegal jobs such as burglary and hijacking, and a hideout for criminals on the run. They could rent small rooms upstairs at $100 a week and get girls at half the going rate. But while Capone kept his office at the Four Deuces he lived at the Lexington. He paid a monthly rate for the whole fourth floor, taking rooms for all in his personal retinue. He eventually paid $1,500 a month for the space he used.

Greenberg used Capone's influence with the management to open a cigar stand in the lobby. The stand's manager sold enough cigarettes and chewing gum to pay the rent, but the real business was a handbook at which anyone could place off-track bets on the horses. And Greenberg personally was on hand at 5 o'clock every afternoon to pay off the winnings and make loans to such losers as sought his services.

The loan-sharking business was not limited to this. In the very earliest days of Prohibition, most of the Midwestern thieves had not yet got into the liquor business. They were still working as burglars, or loft thieves, or holdup men, or safecrackers. They planned and executed big jobs.

They needed short-term loans just as does any upperworld business.

When they were planning a big one they had to hire skilled personnel to case the bank or post office and draw the floor plans, other personnel to use nitroglycerine or dynamite, still other personnel to work as "heavies" prepared to gun down any who got in their way. They needed a driver for a getaway car. From three to half a dozen men might have to be put up for three or four weeks at some hideout such as that operated by Capone. Guns and explosives had to be bought.

Just before a big heist, a gang of thieves might need credit to the extent of three or four thousand dollars. Greenberg could and did take care of all needs for proven operators. None ever considered trying to cut off their banker after they got away with the money.

In the years immediately following World War I, Lou Greenberg found his services in demand as a legitimate source of loans. Men coming back from overseas sometimes could not find work immediately. They borrowed from whatever source was at hand. Every policeman in any neighborhood where Greenberg was located passed the word along, "Greenberg lends without collateral."

In 1921 and 1922, the nation went through a financial panic. The history books speak of it as a brief recession. There was nothing brief or easy about it to those who had built or bought homes with insufficient money and had given some bank a mortgage to guarantee monthly payments of installments on a note.

In those days there was no such thing as governmental aid to borrowers. When the bank was ready to foreclose, many a harassed homeowner turned to Lou Greenberg. He would lend without collateral, or at least without anything material. The word got around that a man's body was his collateral. If he failed to pay he would lose the use of his arms, or his legs, or his eyes. Only as a last resort would he be killed. Nobody ever cheated Lou Greenberg.

This part of his business prospered to such an extent that in the early twenties Greenberg hired a bookkeeper to manage the office he opened at 3159 Roosevelt Road. He called it Roosevelt Finance Company.

Like so many of Greenberg's businesses, this one had its name changed several times, but it was always operated from the same address. Greenberg's partners in the original enterprise were Simon Hasterlik and Samuel C. Levin. Then, in 1926, the outfit was incorporated as the Roosevelt Finance Corporation, and among its original stockholders was listed Harry Terfansky, who had been one of Greenberg's co-defendants in the 1919 indictment for stealing whiskey.

Greenberg's name did not appear as a stockholder in the corporation. But the two largest stockholders were his wife and his father.

When the world's fair opened in Chicago in 1933, Greenberg became one of the partners in the operation of the San Carlo Italian Village on the grounds of A Century of Progress. He permitted the Roosevelt Finance Company to be dissolved by the Illinois attorney general. Two years later he went through bankruptcy on the operation.

Then, at the same address, he set up the Realty Management Company, which he owned in toto. This company owned the stock in the Seneca Hotel, as Greenberg acquired an ever growing share in that rich enterprise. He made of the Seneca his home.

A subsidiary of this Realty Management Company was the Building Corporation, which managed Al Capone's hotel headquarters in Cicero, the Towne Hotel. When Capone was no longer around, Frank Nitti—Capone's successor and the same little Sicilian barber who had been Greenberg's first fence for stolen goods—ran the Paddock Lounge in this hotel. The hotel was only a few blocks from the two racetracks, Hawthorne and Arlington.

After a series of murders on the premises left the Paddock with a bad name, its owners incorporated it with a new name, the Turf Lounge, Inc. Greenberg still managed it.

Greenberg's real estate ventures during the twenties took him into the ownership of several neighborhood motion picture theaters. It was to get first-run films for these—so he later told the Senate—that he got mixed up with Willie Bioff and others in the million-dollar movie shakedown. That story will be told in its place.

Greenberg needed alcohol for customers at his three speakeasies. The stuff was offered for sale by Capone and several other manufacturers, but Greenberg had his own way of doing things. He bought some of his supplies from Capone but always kept his channels open in other directions.

Two of the legitimate businesses which use alcohol in quantity are perfume manufacturers and cooking extract manufacturers.

Greenberg inquired about to learn the possibilities for going into the blending of colognes and toilet waters, or for going into the business of making vanilla extract. He found the possibilities limited. Before any new permits to go into such businesses were approved, the federal authorities carefully studied the backgrounds of their owners. Greenberg did the next-best thing. He financed burglary bands which constantly preyed on such businesses in Chicago.

The greatest single users of legitimate alcohol throughout the thirteen years of Prohibition were the hospitals and doctors. Several warehouses in Chicago had quantities of alcohol which could be withdrawn on demand on presentation of the proper certificates from a hospital or physician, just as the warehouses kept aged whiskey which could be withdrawn on presentation of certificates from wholesale drugstore suppliers.

Greenberg felt that what one man can print, another can duplicate. He found printers who could prepare such certificates, properly drawn and notarized by forgers in his employ. This got to be such a big part of his business that he opened an office at 414 West Washington Boulevard to handle the shipments. But Greenberg could not help cheating. He did not want to pay the nominal monthly bribes asked by the judges, prosecutors, federal agents, and government whiskey authorities. They raided his office.

On February 25, 1925, a federal grand jury in Chicago indicted Greenberg among others on six counts charging violation of the National Prohibition Act.

The charges involved 5,176 gallons of liquor withdrawn from a warehouse by means of forged or counterfeit government withdrawal permits.

That was the year that Manhattan Brewing Company, as the Malt-Maid outfit had come to be called, changed its name to the Fort Dearborn Products Company, Inc. One of its incorporators was Morris Terfansky, who had been indicted with Greenberg in 1919 and was a brother of Harry Terfansky of the Roosevelt Finance Company.

Greenberg testified before a House subcommittee of Congress that he bought some of the Seneca Hotel stock from the wife of Charles (Cherry Nose) Gioe before that old Capone sidekick went to prison in the movie shakedown. The Seneca, with a fine address in one of Chicago's best residential neighborhoods, became the home of a dozen racketeers and killers, among them Hymie (Loud Mouth) Levin.

When the racketeers were brought to court for the great movie shakedown, Greenberg was called to identify Gioe for the jury.

At that trial the jurors learned that the bookkeeper who kept track of the shakedown money for the racketeers was Greenberg's brother-in-law, Izzy Zevlin. This was the bookkeeper who manipulated the accounts so as to cover the embezzlement of millions of dollars in union funds. But that story will be told in its place.

Greenberg testified that he had borrowed great sums without security from Frank Nitti, saying that the sum owed at one time totaled $110,000 but that he had paid back $65,000.

The assumption was that Nitti had given Greenberg the money to be used as capital in his high-interest loan-sharking business. Nitti committed suicide in that year of 1943 and Greenberg tried to weasel out of paying what he owed to Nitti's widow and son.

The extortion which formed the basis for the New York indictment had been directed against the Hollywood motion picture industry and several unions by Willie Bioff and George Browne, who ruled the stage-hands' union. Greenberg said he had known both for years.

Greenberg said that when the Prohibition Act was repealed in 1933 he changed the name of Manhattan Brewing to the Canadian Ace Brewing Company and put in as its president Arthur C. Lueder, a wheelhorse of the Republican Party in Chicago. Lueder had been the city's postmaster from 1921 to 1933. He had been Republican candidate for mayor in

1923, defeated for the office by the reform Democratic candidate, Judge William E. Dever. Lueder kept his office at the brewery even after he was elected Illinois state auditor in 1940.

Greenberg was asked if his hiring of a Republican for this front job was not unusual in that the brewery owners were generally felt to favor the Democrats who had brought about repeal. Greenberg appeared astonished. He said, "From the first week I arrived in Chicago" he had taken care of members of both parties at all levels. He said there was no difference between the politicians of one party or the other. "They both want money. You pay them for what you want. Then you get it."

His political friends did not help Greenberg much when on February 29, 1944, he signed a waiver of immunity and testified before a federal grand jury in Chicago which was investigating charges of mail fraud and violation of the Bankruptcy Act. He later compromised civil and criminal liabilities by paying $250,000 in settlement of back income taxes.

Greenberg told how state officials who are on the underworld payrolls can help their backers pick up extra money. Of Arthur Lueder, former president of Manhattan Brewing Company, Greenberg said, "He would appraise real estate in bankruptcy proceedings at a low figure. Several of us would form a pool to buy up these properties. Then we took care of him with a share. That was good for one hundred thousand a year for each of us."

Frank Nitti was known to have a piece of Manhattan Brewing. Just how big a piece came under dispute after Nitti's death and was to lead to Greenberg's violent demise twelve years later.

When Nitti committed suicide on March 19, 1943, his widow, the former Annette Caravetta, said that from 1919 forward Nitti had been turning over cash and securities to Greenberg. She said that by the time of Nitti's death Greenberg had $2,000,000 of Nitti's assets. She said Frank Nitti often spoke of this as an ace in the hole in case anything should ever happen to him.

A year and a half after Nitti's death, said his widow, Greenberg paid the Nitti estate $64,500 and paid $100,000 into the trust of Nitti's ten-year-old adopted son, Joseph.

She said that Greenberg talked her into signing a release, in her capacity as the boy's guardian, stating that all legal claims of the boy's trust had been satisfied. She signed a second release stating that all legal claims against Greenberg by the Frank Nitti estate had been satisfied.

With these two releases, Greenberg had the protection of the law.

All of Nitti's friends and family knew of the two releases. They felt that Greenberg's actions had been something less than kosher. Some of them mentioned the matter to Greenberg at one time or another over the years. But Greenberg knew nothing of the values that govern the Italian and Sicilian communities. To him, only money values counted.

The matter of young Joseph Nitti's trust came to the fore again among Frank Nitti's old friends in 1955 when the boy reached the age of twenty-one. One of Nitti's friends told Greenberg at Thanksgiving time that year that Nitti's widow and son had been grateful for Greenberg's payment of the interest on Nitti's investment, but that at the age of twenty-one they thought the boy ought to have access to the capital.

Greenberg flew into a rage, affecting indignation and anger. "I'm tired of this. I won't hear any more about it. They'll never get another cent from me."

Ten days later, on December 8, 1955, Greenberg was shot to death.

With his second wife, Pearl, he had eaten dinner in the Glass Dome hickory barbecue pit at Twenty-eighth Street and Union Avenue, just north of the brewery.

They left the place when it was still early evening and walked across the street where they had parked their car. Two men stepped from the shadows, dropped Greenberg with four .38 caliber bullets, and calmly walked away. Exit Lou Greenberg.

A footnote to the Lou Greenberg story was provided by one of Frank Nitti's cousins who hung around the funeral parlor to make sure the Greenberg body was properly disposed of. He reported back to others: "Now he's the richest son of a bitch in hell."

3 A protégé of Hot Stove Jimmy

Dion O'Banion became the first hijacker of the Prohibition Era as a result of a spur-of-the-moment decision on a winter's morning in Chicago. The date was December 30, 1919. The Loop was still decorated in festive fashion, with poinsettias in almost every office window and sprigs of holly or balsam on virtually every utility pole.

This was two weeks before the Prohibition law was scheduled to take effect officially, at midnight on January 16, 1920. Every hotel and major restaurant in town planned a tremendous blowout for New Year's Eve. The saloonkeepers were all advertising the coming dry era as a means of whipping up trade for "your last chance to celebrate the coming of a new year in the old-fashioned way."

Since drinking was supposed to be almost a thing of the past, everybody was being encouraged to get drunk just one more time. For liquor dealers, distributors, and wholesalers, this was a bonanza. They had a chance to get rid of warehouse stocks at premium prices. Throughout the Christmas holidays trucks had been out day and night delivering beer and liquor in preparation for New Year's Eve parties.

One Loop hotel laying in a tremendous stock was the Bismarck, at the southeast corner of Randolph and Wells Streets. This famed old hostelry had during the anti-German hysteria of World War I changed its name to the Randolph and its name had not yet been changed back, but everyone in Chicago still referred to it as the Bismarck.

The swaggering Dion O'Banion, boss of the Irish political sluggers who delivered the vote in the Forty-second Ward just north of the Loop, was in a festive mood.

He was limping southward one morning on the east side of Wells Street south of Randolph Street when his path was blocked by a very long flatbed truck. The driver had begun to back into the alley next to the hotel. For some reason he had halted his truck with its nose still out in Wells Street, as it lay athwart the sidewalk.

O'Banion was not the only pedestrian compelled to halt. The wide sidewalk was totally blocked and nobody could walk past, going either north or south, without tramping through snow and slush at the curb to go around the truck's radiator. A few pedestrians came to a stop near O'Banion. Then their number grew until a dozen or more waited impatiently, stamping their feet against the cold and snow.

O'Banion was a laughing Irishman, a cheerful fellow who liked to think he had a great sense of humor. He was a practical joker, the most innocent of whose pranks lay in such fields as giving a friend Ex Lax and telling him it was a piece of sweet chocolate. O'Banion's idea of really thigh-slapping fun had to do with the shotgun challenge.

The challenger would secretly fill both barrels of a shotgun with hard-packed clay and then bet some friend or acquaintance the latter couldn't hit the side of a barn thirty feet away. When the money had been put up, O'Banion would ostentatiously load both barrels, hand the shotgun to the patsy, and scramble back to be out of the way of the carnage.

Then O'Banion would laugh as both barrels were discharged and the victim lost an arm, an eye, or part of his face in the explosion.

In addition to his great sense of humor, O'Banion was a pious fellow never without his rosary, and a natural fighter who would take on all comers with fists, paving blocks, baseball bats, or pistols.

Anyway, here was Dion O'Banion standing in the freezing cold of North Wells Street on a December morning while a truckdriver, obviously cozy inside the warm cab of his vehicle, all but laughed aloud at the plight of the pedestrians whose way was blocked. O'Banion, curious about the cargo, which was covered with a huge tarpaulin, lifted it and saw scores of cases of Grommes & Ullrich whiskey. He made a quick mental calculation of the number and value of the whiskey cases probably carried on that ten-ton flatbed. Having calculated, he acted.

O'Banion stepped up on the truck's running board and signaled the driver to roll down the window. The driver did so, leaning forward so that his head protruded through the open aperture. O'Banion put his left arm around the driver's neck, pulled his head still further through the window, and slugged him twice with a fist holding a dollar's worth of nickels rolled up tight. The driver slumped unconscious.

Now O'Banion opened the cab door, pulled the truckdriver to the sidewalk, and propped his unconscious body against the west wall of the Randolph. O'Banion got into the truck, put it in gear, moved slowly forward and into the southbound traffic of Wells Street, and was in possession of a great deal of somebody else's liquor.

Nobody ever reported what happened to the unconscious driver.

The people of Chicago then as now thought such incidents part of the street scene in any neighborhood. No one called police. With the truck out of the way, each pedestrian went about his or her business.

O'Banion later told what happened to the whiskey. "I had no idea what to do with the stuff. I drove around for fifteen minutes and then headed for Nails Morton's garage out on Maxwell Street."

Just as O'Banion was boss of the Irish gang of the Forty-second Ward, so Samuel (Nails) Morton was one of the leaders of the Jewish gang in the old Twentieth Ward west of Halsted Street and south of Roosevelt Road. Morton, who had become something of a local hero when brevetted a lieutenant as a result of a machine gun action in the trenches of France, operated a hot-car drop. This was a huge garage, employing several auto painters and bodyworkers, devoted to giving stolen cars new color schemes and new owners.

When O'Banion drove in with the truckload of whiskey, he and Morton quickly came to agreement over the split. They both got on telephones and called saloonkeepers. O'Banion said later, "In twenty minutes we had buyers for the whole load. We sold the truck separately, to a brewery down in Peoria." O'Banion said much of the stolen liquor was taken off his hands by McGovern's Liberty Inn on North Clark Street.

The story of this exploit became a part of Chicago's bootleg history. As word got around the underworld, everyone acknowledged O'Banion's cleverness.

O'Banion had been a lifelong thief, burglar, and safecracker, but in recent years had been selling his brawling talents.

His slugging was in demand at election time, along with that of his Irish thugs, throughout the North Side. He had organized his gang in the Forty-second Ward during the ascendancy of the ward boss, Hot Stove Jimmy Quinn.

James Aloysius Quinn, a haberdasher who was city sealer during one of the five terms of Mayor Carter H. Harrison the younger, was a model politician. He got the nickname of "Hot Stove Jimmy" in his youth.

With a few friends, Quinn was engaged in burgling a neighborhood store in the after-midnight hours. They had rented a horse and wagon and had propped the back door of the place open. They had moved out of the store everything that might have any resale value when Quinn's eye fell on the merchant's new stove. He wanted it.

Quinn's companions urged him to leave it. The merchant had banked the fire with ashes, but the cast-iron box still radiated a great deal of heat. None of the others would help Quinn with the stove, so he tried it all by himself. Only when he burned his hands did he decide to go without it. The nickname stuck to the day of his death.

For many years Quinn was boss of the old Twenty-first Ward (now the Forty-second). Control alternated between Quinn and John F. O'Malley, known as the Red Fellow, whose saloon at Clark and Kinzie during the Prohibition years was called the Red Lantern.

O'Malley and Quinn fought constantly, sometimes one winning and sometimes the other. Quinn always accorded O'Malley respect after the latter shot an alderman in his saloon. O'Malley delighted in telling a story on himself. "The first time anyone mentioned to me I could be elected Senator I said the hell with it. I didn't want to live in Washington. They told me there was such a thing as a state senate so I said fine. And I set out to get elected."

O'Malley won the nomination in a meeting of the ward's precinct captains, who ordinarily would have nominated Stanley Kunz. But Kunz lived west of the Chicago River, as did all members of the Kunz faction. On the day of the meeting, O'Malley went around to the bridge tenders with a pocket full of money. He arranged for all the bridges to be kept open from 7 o'clock until 11 o'clock that evening. The Kunz faction could not get across the river to vote.

Anyway, since Dion O'Banion was a protégé of Hot Stove Jimmy Quinn, everyone in the underworld agreed that Dion, like Jimmy, would steal anything that was not nailed down.

The sociologist who wants to learn what constituted the "typical" bootlegger of the early twenties could do worse than study Charles Dion O'Banion. Born in Aurora, a west suburb of Chicago, in 1892, he moved with his father at the age of twelve to Chestnut and Wells streets. His mother had died when he was five. His father was a farmer who became a plasterer.

O'Banion completed elementary school at Holy Name Cathedral and for four years was an acolyte serving mass for Father William D. O'Brien, who received the honorary title of auxiliary bishop from the hands of Pope Pius XII. O'Brien's closest friend was Father Patrick J. Molloy, who later got in trouble for praying at O'Banion's funeral.

O'Banion as a boy was short and stocky. His hips were narrow and his shoulders unusually broad. He knew the heft of his own two fists but early learned never to use a fist if a rock was available. Through most of his life he carried brass knucks as other men might carry a wristwatch.

When he was seventeen, Dion O'Banion was sent to the Bridewell for a robbery. That was in 1909, about the time O'Banion met Lou Greenberg.

Two years later, when O'Banion was working as a waiter in Terry

McGovern's saloon, a rough spot on the northeast corner of Clark and Erie, he was sent to the Bridewell again. This time he got three months for carrying concealed weapons. When arrested he not only had brass knucks and a revolver, but a sheath knife and a leather blackjack.

This was the police record that brought O'Banion to the attention of the Forty-second Ward political leaders as a likely slugger for election days.

One of O'Banion's earliest companions was a Polish Catholic youth named Earl Wajciechowski and together they served mass many a morning in the Cathedral.

Naturally, their friends shortened Earl's unpronounceable family name, but just why he ended up with such a Jewish nickname as Hymie Weiss nobody could ever remember. Hymie Weiss and Dion O'Banion were hired together by Max Annenberg when the latter was circulation manager for the Chicago *Tribune.*

O'Banion had been a tough kid, but he knew he was in the roughest kind of adult company when he signed on as one of Annenberg's sluggers. His companions included Vincent and Frankie McErlane, the four Gentlemen brothers, Jim Ragen, Walter Stevens, Tommy Maloy, and Maurice (Mossy) Enright. No more likely a bunch of plug-ugly killers was ever gathered together on one payroll.

Once O'Banion learned his trade, he switched allegiance and went with the rival Hearst papers in the same capacity he had served with the *Tribune.* He quickly rose through the ranks to supervisory duties.

Meanwhile, O'Banion took up with a gang of safecrackers which was having a good deal of success around Chicago at the time. He learned the arcane arts of cooking nitroglycerine and pulling combination knobs.

O'Banion began to need more money these days. He never had been a woman chaser, but at twenty-nine he met a schoolgirl whose beauty gripped his heart. She was nearly twelve years younger than O'Banion, and he thought her innocent as the Virgin Mother. Her name was Viola Kaniff.

Viola had been attending school in Iowa that winter and came home for the Christmas holidays. For Dion O'Banion it was love at first sight. He bought the ring and asked her to set the day.

They were married two months later, in February, 1921. Like any other young couple, they started out life in a sparkling flat at 6081 Ridge Avenue, and had the fun of furnishing it to their own taste. Strictly for business reasons, O'Banion kept his hideout apartment at 448 Surf Street.

O'Banion found circulation work ideally suited to his temperament, except that it did not provide enough excitement. He wanted excitement and money, in that order. After he married Viola Kaniff he was never known to stray.

His work for the newspapers took him into every neighborhood of the city. His affinity for trouble brought him into contact with the gang leaders of every neighborhood. These were friendships that were to last throughout his brief life.

Two of his earliest friends in the Maxwell Street ghetto area were Samuel (Nails) Morton, and David (Jew Bates) Jerus. Earl Wajciechowski, known as Polack Earl or more frequently as Hymie Weiss, had been a childhood companion. The only Italian he ever got really close to was Vincent (Schemer) Drucci. And then, in late 1917, O'Banion met and fell under the influence of Charles (the Ox) Reiser, the most famous safecracker of the day. This meeting opened a whole new chapter in O'Banion's life.

Reiser was called by knowledgeable police at the time, "the premier safecracker since the time of Eddie Fay." Reiser had been active as a "peterman," as safecrackers who used nitroglycerine were called since the turn of the century.

He fell into the hands of Chicago police for the first time on September 15, 1903, when he was charged with burglary.

While O'Banion made a practice of dealing with police, prosecutors, and politicians in order to go free of any charge that might be brought against him, Reiser had a different method. He always killed the witnesses. When no witness appeared against him on this 1903 charge, Reiser was found not guilty.

Two years later, on September 15, 1905, he was once again charged with burglary. This time the witness disappeared and there was no indictment.

On January 7, 1907, he was found not guilty of a robbery charge.

Two months later, for the only conviction of his active life of crime, Reiser was sent to the county jail for thirty days after being charged on March 30, 1907, with assault with a deadly weapon. Then, on November 28, 1909, he was turned over by Chicago to the police of Seattle to face charges of robbery and murder. The witnesses were killed and the case was dismissed for lack of sufficient evidence.

When O'Banion met Reiser they found they had friends in common, but they did not start working together until years later.

When in late 1917 Reiser was looking around for a few good men to help him rob some safes, he turned to O'Banion, one of the likeliest young men of his acquaintance. O'Banion recommended George (Bugs) Moran, alias Morrissey, whose Chicago police record dated back to

December 28, 1915, when he was nineteen years old; and Hymie Weiss.

Reiser led a Jekyll-Hyde existence. He lived at 1704 Otto Street, where he owned his own apartment building as well as the building next door. To his neighbors he was a friendly sort who was a shrewd businessman with real estate investments. He was known in his home neighborhood by the name of Fred Shopes, an anglicization of the name to which he had been born: Schoeps. To his tenants he was known as the ideal landlord, who never pressed for his rents on the first of the month if a man happened to be a little tardy.

But to police all over the country, Reiser was known as "the Ox," a man so strong that he could single-handedly move a heavy safe from one side of an office to the other.

Now Reiser proposed partnership. O'Banion accepted and learned how the big-time safecrackers operate.

Reiser was a perfectionist. He paid for tips, so that he knew when a company safe might be full of money for a payroll or another reason. When he decided that a safe might be worth hitting, he found some excuse to get inside the office and acquaint himself with the layout. If possible he bought a set of floor plans to the place. He told O'Banion, "I'll pay a hundred dollars anytime to score with a thousand."

Reiser then would draw the map of the whole area he intended to work in, paths of entry and exit carefully marked. He would spend time in his basement at home, cooking up the nitroglycerine from sticks of dynamite.

When he felt he was ready, he would recruit a few helpers and begin rehearsals. He figured just how many men he needed and what part each should play.

This was the type of operation for which he recruited O'Banion and the others. For the next few years the personnel might vary from time to time as to both identity and numbers, depending on the job at hand, but O'Banion and Moran and Hymie Weiss were invited whenever they wanted to take part.

They were active throughout 1918. On January 29 they blew the safe at Western Dairy Company and took $2,000.

So it went for the rest of the year. They took keys from the watchman at Standard Oil Company on September 2, blowing the safe for $2,060; entered Schaeffer Brothers Theater through a coal chute on September 3, blowing the safe for $1,400; climbed the fire escape to the Prudential Life Insurance Company on November 5, blowing the safe for $3,865; used a coal chute again on December 3 to get into the Borden Farm Products Company, where the safe was blown for $594.61.

These were the robberies reported by one of the gang who was caught and decided to give state's evidence in return for leniency. Much of Reiser's history apparently had been picked up in gossip by this man, who wanted to be a stool pigeon. His name was John Mahoney, a brother-in-law of Anthony (Mops) Volpe, who in turn was a gunman on the payroll of Diamond Joe Esposito. Presumably only the fact that Reiser did not use Mahoney on all the gang's jobs kept some of them from being known.

Almost three years after he had worked with the O'Banion-Reiser crowd on these safecracking jobs, Mahoney had gone into business for himself. He was making his own nitroglycerine and blowing the doors off safes just as well as the old master, "Ox" Reiser. His trouble was that he kept coming back to the same place time after time. He was robbing, for the ninth time, the safe in the West Side Masonic Temple building at 10 North Oakley Boulevard when caught.

Mahoney was nabbed on St. Patrick's Day, March 17, 1921. In his pockets he had a revolver and ten bills of $100 denomination. In the grip he carried he had burlgar tools, two automatic pistols, four cartridge clips, two flashlights, three handkerchief masks, and a World War I army shirt and blouse.

Mahoney was thirty years old at the time. Police took him to his home at 3625 Wells Street, where they found thirty ounces (nearly a full quart) of nitroglycerine. The explosives experts called it "enough to blow up the Loop." In addition there were 200 fuses with the wires attached, percussion caps, two spools of steel wire, two jimmies, a lot of safecracker's tools, drills, chisels, jacks, sledgehammers, and Stillson wrenches for twisting the combination dials off safe doors.

The steel wire was identical in type with that used to tie up employees of the Western Shade Cloth Company in a safecracking in which a watchman, Thomas O'Donnell, was shot and killed. In that burglary, one of the thieves had been reported wearing an army shirt and blouse.

The Western Shade offices were at 2100 South Jefferson Street.

Mahoney was told at once that he would be charged with murder. He was taken to the offices of State's Attorney Robert E. Crowe and offered to tell everything about the O'Banion-Reiser gang in return for leniency. Crowe let him talk.

Mahoney told of the safecrackings mentioned earlier. He named Reiser, O'Banion, Hymie Weiss, Bugs Moran, and a Charles Thulis of 7229 South Carpenter Avenue, whose truck the gang used in their alcohol thefts. Before Prohibition, said Mahoney, they had simply robbed safes. But since Prohibition began, they robbed warehouses where alcohol might be found.

Mahoney said that on March 11, just a week before he was arrested, they had broken the glass in a rear window to gain entry to the Northwestern Barber Supply Company at 1400 Milwaukee Avenue and had stolen three barrels of pure grain alcohol.

Then, on March 14, they climbed a fire escape to a fourth-floor window so they could enter the warehouse of the Dr. Price Flavoring Extract Company at 237 East Superior Street. They got away with twenty barrels of pure grain alcohol.

Once Mahoney started talking, nothing could stop him. He said that Reiser had eliminated his first wife, Mrs. May Mulligan Shoeps (later Shopes) when they lived at 1137 West Washington Boulevard in 1912.

He said Reiser had boasted that the woman threatened to "get the law" on him and he beat her to death but the coroner's jury said she had died of asphyxiation.

Mahoney went on to say that one of the groups involved in Reiser safecrackings included Guy Wadsworth, a former policeman. Mahoney said they had accounted for at least a dozen such burglaries. After this, they were all rounded up and Wadsworth gave state's evidence against the others in return for a promise of clemency.

Mahoney said that Reiser always killed witnesses rather than leave behind anyone who might testify against him. He said that Clarence White, an Eighteenth Ward teaming contractor, had participated with Reiser in the Standard Oil burglary and when police phoned White and asked him to come in he promised to do so. But White made the mistake of telephoning Reiser. Then White was found in his home, shot through the heart, apparently a suicide. Mahoney called it homicide, rigged to look like suicide.

Mahoney was permitted to post bond of $2,500 and go free on March 31. Less than a month later, at 11 P.M. on April 30, 1921, he was shot to death and his body dumped from a car in the alley at 1814 South Peoria Street.

This talkative witness eliminated, Reiser was not even brought to trial.

Reiser did not last long after this. At 3 A.M. on October 10, 1921, Reiser fought a pistol duel with Steve Pochnal, the watchman at Cooke Cold Storage Company, 30 North Green Street.

Reiser killed Pochnal but was wounded—a bullet through the lung and a shattered left arm. He was taken to Alexian Brothers Hospital, and he told a weird story of having been assaulted on the street by a stranger.

Detective Sergeant Lawrence Cooney was on guard outside Reiser's hospital room a few days later when it appeared the safecracker was on his way to recovery. Murder charges had been brought against him. The newspapers said that if he recovered, was tried and convicted, his entire estate would be confiscated to make restitution to some of his burglary victims.

Mrs. Madeline Shopes, who had divorced an earlier husband to marry Reiser, thought about the loss of the property she had come to consider hers. She did not like it. At 4 o'clock in the afternoon on October 21 she talked Cooney into admitting her to the hospital room with her husband. In a minute or so Cooney heard "a rattle of shots that sounded like a machine gun." He opened the door and went in, to find Mrs. Shopes leaning over the body of her husband and sobbing hysterically.

Reiser had ten bullets in him. His wife said, "He committed suicide." His brother, Ernest Schoeps of 524 North Lawndale Avenue, said, "He could not shoot himself. His right hand and left arm were both broken."

There was a police charge of murder brought against Mrs. Shopes-Reiser, but it was dropped on December 8 when a coroner's jury ruled Reiser's death a suicide.

His widow came into an estate valued at well over $100,000. The great safecracker was dead at forty-three.

4   "We gave up, like good citizens"

O'Banion was like a juggler in the way he could keep two or more jobs going at the same time. He was running a florist shop, hijacking whiskey shipments, and working as a slugger for one of the city's daily newspapers in the summer of 1921, when he decided to take on the chore of blowing a safe in the offices of the Chicago Typographical Union.

The union at the time had its offices on the second floor of the Postal Telegraph building at 332 South La Salle Street, next door to the Fort Dearborn Hotel. This location is across the Loop, about eight blocks from the offices of the Chicago *Herald and Examiner,* the Hearst morning paper for which O'Banion worked. This fact is important because there was only a forty-minute span between the time O'Banion was seen in the newspaper office and the time he was caught at the safe.

George F. Hartford of 6257 Sheridan Road was circulation manager of the newspaper at the time. He later testified he had seen O'Banion in the office at 2:30 in the morning of June 1, 1921, and had told him, "Stick around; we may need you." O'Banion yawned, said he wanted to take a nap, and could be reached at the Fort Dearborn Hotel.

Forty minutes later, at 3:10 A.M., two watchmen at the Board of Trade building, across the street from the Postal Telegraph building, saw activity in the union offices. They thought it unusual. They halted Patrolman John J. Ryan of the Central District police, who happened to pass at the moment, and told him of the suspicious activity. Ryan got the watchman from the Postal Telegraph building and together they climbed the steps to the second floor and pushed open the door to the union office.

Ryan and the watchman entered to find several men clustered around the safe, from which the combination knob already had been knocked with a sledgehammer. The men seemed to have an assortment of burglar tools. One of them, later identified as Dion O'Banion, turned at some slight sound and raised a cocked revolver which he held in his hand. Ryan later said, "For some reason he let the hammer down easily and said, 'Don't shoot; we give up.'"

Months later, after suitable payoffs to judge, jury, and prosecutor had got the gang released, O'Banion explained, "I was just about to shoot that yokel cop when I remembered the Ox had a pint bottle of nitroglycerine in his pocket. One shot in that room would have blown the whole south end of the Loop to Kingdom Come."

So Patrolman Ryan made a single-handed capture of O'Banion, Hymie Weiss, George (Bugs) Moran, and Charles (the Ox) Reiser. Ryan called for help. Money found in the possession of all four, slightly burned and ragged around the edges, indicated they were the quartet who earlier that same night had blown and robbed the safe in Joseph Klein's feed store at 525 West Thirty-fifth Street.

The safecracking gang had all the usual tools: fuses, yellow laundry soap, chisels, drills, and heavy hammers. They also had fourteen large bed comforters in various states of repair which they intended using to deaden the sounds of the blast. O'Banion later explained, "First we tried to get into the box by knocking the combination knob off and getting to the tumblers inside.

"If that didn't work, we used the chisel to open the hairline cracks where the safe door fits into the safe frame. We hammer these cracks as wide as we can.

"Then we drill a hole at the top of the hairline crack, a hole big enough to pour nitroglycerine into. We use the soap to cover the cracks all the way around the safe door, so that when we pour the nitroglycerine in at the top it will flow all the way around the door but won't flow out onto the floor.

"Then we put a fuse in the hole at the top, wrap the safe in all the blankets and comforters we can find, touch a match to the fuse—and get as far away as possible. When that charge goes off, the door of the safe will be blasted clear across the room."

Patrolman Ryan got a $300-a-year pay raise for his exploit. There was no point in the gang trying to put the fix in with him. They had submitted without a fight and permitted themselves to be taken to the police station.

But at that point the fix began. O'Banion said they spent money "with everybody in sight." They were indicted by the May grand jury, which was still sitting, and a member of that jury told a bit of the story. George Fay, cashier of J. V. Farwell Company at 102 South Market Street, said the case against the four, the charge being possession of burglary tools, was presented by Assistant State's Attorney Edgar A. Jonas.

Despite the fact that the grand jury recommended bail be set as high as possible, the exact amount was left to the judgment of the prosecutor.

Fay concluded ruefully, "They were freed on just two thousand dollars' bail apiece, which meant they each had to put up only two hundred, or ten percent of the total."

Jonas at the time was a candidate for the circuit court bench on "the City Hall ticket." William Hale Thompson was the Republican mayor. Jonas was elected to the bench and remained on the public payroll for the rest of his life, always a faithful machine politician.

Henry Barrett Chamberlin, the ex-newspaper editor who then headed the Chicago Crime Commission, expressed himself "shocked" at Jonas seeking such low bail. On June 4 he went before Judge Frank Johnston, Jr., and asked that it be raised. So the judge set Reiser's bail at $100,000; O'Banion's at $60,000; Moran's at $60,000; Hymie Weiss' at $50,000.

A few days later Matt Foley, an official of the Chicago *American,* the Hearst afternoon paper, posted $5,000 in United States bonds with Commissioner James R. Glass to get O'Banion free on the federal charge of possession of explosives.

The state's attorney of Cook County at the time was Bob Crowe, whose election had been helped by the Forty-second Ward work of O'Banion and Hymie Weiss. Crowe assigned as prosecutor Steve Malato, an assistant state's attorney who had marched hat in hand at the funeral of Big Jim Colosimo to show proper respect for the dead pimp.

When the case was presented in court there was no question raised as to the presence on the scene of the four men Ryan had arrested.

There was no question that $35,000 was in the safe at the time the boys were caught there. The defense lay in the story as to how the boys came to be in the room with the safe just at that time. O'Banion told it, and the rest backed him up. Under oath, he said, "We had all met at about three o'clock in the morning in the all-night Raklios restaurant there on the corner. We were having hot chocolate and chocolate eclairs. We heard a lot of racket, could have been an explosion, in the union office in the Postal Telegraph building. So we climbed the fire escape to see what it was all about.

"Whoever was blowing the safe must have heard us coming. They got away. We stepped off the fire escape through the window and were just looking at the safe when the policeman came in. I always carry a gun in the course of my work. At first I thought it might have been the thieves coming back. But when I saw it was a policeman, I put my gun down and we gave ourselves up. Like good citizens."

The jury wasted no time returning its verdict: not guilty.

The whole crowd, defendants and their families and friends, the prosecutor and defense counsel, the judge and several members of the jury adjourned to the Bella Napoli Café run by Diamond Joe Esposito. That was the night of December 1, 1921, six months to the day since the arrest.

When the Prohibition law went into effect early in 1920, only a few of the best-organized gangs in Chicago saw its potential. If others saw it, they lacked the capital to take advantage of it.

In most neighborhoods in those earliest days of Prohibition, the street gangs simply picked up what money they could by opening speakeasies or finding work delivering beer and alcohol to speakeasies opened by others.

An exception was the Colosimo-Torrio-Capone combine in the Loop and on the Near South Side. Another exception was to be found on the Far South Side, where two O'Donnell brothers—Spike and Walter—had the money and the wit to invest in breweries and provide beer for the speakeasies being opened by neighborhood gangs. On the Near West Side, in what was sometimes known as "the Valley" and sometimes as "Little Italy," Terry Druggan and Frankie Lake had become beer and alcohol distributors.

O'Banion and his friends had early got into the hijacking business. O'Banion was even quoted in the earliest days of Prohibition as saying, "Let Johnny Torrio make the stuff. I'll steal what I want of it." But O'Banion changed his mind. He decided that Prohibition was here to stay and if he wanted to get in on the bonanza he would have to invest some money. He bought the Sieben brewery at 1478 North Larrabee Street and discovered that he had a considerable talent as an administrator.

There were then twenty-nine breweries operating in Chicago alone, not counting nearly as many in such suburbs as Gary and Hammond, Joliet and Cicero, Niles and Waukegan.

These breweries were operating twenty-four hours a day and their trucks were running day and night delivering beer to the speakeasies in Chicago and the suburbs. There was a saloon on every block in business districts and lower-class residential districts. There was a beer flat in every block of the highest-class residential areas. Deliveries of beer were made openly, with little or no attempt at concealment. The police and federal officers were paid off handsomely.

There were outlying gangs, such as the Touhy brothers in the northwest suburbs, but all the city breweries were gradually taken over by four main distributors: Johnny Torrio and Al Capone in the Loop and in Stickney; Spike and Walter O'Donnell on the South Side; Terry

Druggan and Frankie Lake on the West Side; and Dion O'Banion on the North Side.

A few other groups had small beer manufactories, but they never were in the big competition. These included Joe Saltis and Dingbat Oberta on the Southwest Side, Klondike O'Donnell and his brothers on the Far West Side, and Teddy Newberry on the Far North Side.

This was the beer picture by the beginning of 1924.

For the first few years of Prohibition the city depended for its alcohol supply on that which could be illegally imported from Canada, the Bahamas, or Europe; that which could be stolen from perfume makers, flavoring extract companies, or hospital supply firms; and small quantities of alcohol bought from farmers with silos or distilled in outlying areas from corn and other grains.

Then Johnny Torrio set up a cottage industry of alcohol producers who worked at home.

No one is sure today whether the original idea came from the Genna brothers, an Italian family of Black Hand extortionists in the Taylor-Halsted Street area, or from Torrio; whether the Gennas went to Torrio for help in financing, or Torrio went to them with the idea of organizing most Italian families into alcohol production. In any case it became a Torrio-financed but Genna-operated project.

Virtually every immigrant Italian and Sicilian family in certain areas of Chicago, principally the Near West Side, traditionally made its own wine. When grapes were harvested, the Italians went to the South Water Market or sometimes out of the city to the vineyards and bought by the truckload. Before Prohibition this was a gala and festive time for the entire Italian community. Each family made its wine and got the local priest to come and bless it. Then the whole neighborhood participated in a fiesta at which each family sampled the wines made by the others. There was competition for the finest and driest of wines.

With the coming of Prohibition, the families continued making their own wines at home. But some of them saw the advantage in distilling this wine to make grappa, or clear white brandy, and selling this stuff at a dollar a pint to any who would buy. They found a ready market among bootleggers. From here it was just a step to the production of straight grain alcohol. What they could do with grapes and sugar they could also do with corn and sugar.

The Torrio-Capone combine put up $150 a week for each family, in the form of corn and sugar purchases, and the Genna boys went from door to door getting families to accept this money and start producing alcohol. They supplied crocks and barrels in which the mash could ferment, and rudimentary home stills which required little attention.

The Gennas offered a market for all that could be thus produced.

Many an Italian family saw this supplementary income as a gift from heaven. Few thought of it as against the law. They knew they had to keep their operations hidden from the police but did not worry. The Gennas told them that most of the police officers in the Maxwell Street district were in on the scheme, making money from it, and would turn their backs.

Each Italian or Sicilian family that took part in the operation assigned one person, usually an ancient grandfather or grandmother, to sit by the still and keep an eye on it to see that it did not get too hot. The oldster would sit there with his book, or she with her knitting, hour after hour while others in the family were out earning a living at jobs.

This was not the only way of making alcohol. Some chose not to use the fresh grain supplied by the Torrio-Capone combine. These people, peasants from the old country, were accustomed to poverty and to making do. They bought up horse manure from the street sweepers and from livery stables, using this instead of corn or other grain.

They knew that the grain fed horses was seldom thoroughly digested. More than half such grain remains whole in the droppings. While mixed with a little hay or straw and thus two or three times as bulky as the straight grain mash, it nevertheless could be spread with sugar and covered with water and allowed to ferment in the same way.

After a few weeks, when the vegetable matter had rotted to leave a ferment of alcohol, it could be sent through the still like any other alcohol. All impurities would be left behind and the resultant steam, when condensed once again into liquid, turned out to be just as fine and pure alcohol as any other that could be so primitively made.

All this alcohol from Little Italy was packaged in five-gallon tins for ease of transportation. Some of it was sold in those original containers. Most of them went to the Torrio-Capone warehouses for blending, bottling, and labeling before delivery to the speakeasies and neighborhood bootleggers who retailed the stuff.

The alcohol could be cut with tap water from the 180 proof at which it left the cottage industry distillery to the 90 proof at which it would be sold. Then it was mixed with the proper flavoring for bourbon, rye, or scotch whiskey; for rum or gin. The gin was always sold when made. There would be 45 percent alcohol (90 proof), and nearly 55 percent water. To this would be added juniper berry flavoring extract and about half an ounce of glycerine to the bottle. The glycerine made it smooth enough to drink.

Sometimes the bourbon or scotch, after being flavored and colored with caramel or browned sugar coloring, would be put in charred oak barrels to age. Lumps of charcoal might be added. A few weeks of such aging was considered ample. This stuff would sometimes be used to cut the genuine aged bourbon, rye, or scotch whiskey which was imported or hijacked.

In that manner, if a hijacker got hold of 100 cases of pints of Antique bourbon or Old Overholt rye he might cut it fifty-fifty with the genuine and the homemade whiskey, ending up with 200 cases of pints that would bring $6 apiece retail in the drugstore with a prescription.

Anyone could go to a friendly doctor, perhaps his family or neighborhood physician, and explain that he had a cold. The doctor would not even have to examine the patient to know that he needed whiskey as a prescription. The doctor would so prescribe, and would charge the patient $3. With the written prescription in hand, the patient would go downstairs or next door to the drugstore and pay $6, plus the prescription, for a pint of Antique whiskey or some other brand. The total cost would be $9.

The whiskey thus bought in the drugstore might be half genuine aged whiskey and half the locally made and one-week-aged product.

Most drinkers preferred to pay $2 a pint to the friendly bootlegger.

The Torrio-Capone combine could put any label required on the brands of booze they sold, but most of their gin was put up in the square fifth bottles used by the Gordon producers of England. Their bottle, label, and seal were indistinguishable from the original product. The taste of the crystal-clear liquor inside might be questioned. A fifth of gin usually sold on the street, from the speakeasy or bootlegger, at $3. The difference between the speakeasy and the bootlegger was that the speakeasy was like a neighborhood saloon and one could drink on the premises. The bootlegger sold bottled goods only, and if he expected a tip could usually be depended on to deliver his goods.

By 1921, O'Banion had seen the need to deliver booze by the bottle or case. He went into business with Nails Morton and William F. Schofield, opening a florist shop at 738 North State Street. O'Banion genuinely loved to fool around with flowers and had a green thumb. But the florist business gave him a front. He had an office with phones to which people could call in and place orders for booze.

O'Banion's deliveries were made in his florist trucks. From 1921 through virtually the entire year of 1924 he had the Near North Side business for weddings, receptions, luncheons, dinners, Bar Mitzvahs, circumcisions, debutante parties, class proms, parties, and social events of all sorts. O'Banion's liquor, champagnes, and other fine imported wines graced tables in homes, clubs, hotels, and all catered affairs along the Gold Coast.

By late 1923, O'Banion decided to go into the liquor business for himself as he had gone into the beer business. He decided to be independent of the Torrio-Capone combine for his supplies. He bought the Cragin Products Company, a brewery with a tremendous alcohol plant in conjunction, located at 1833 North Laramie Street. His partner in this venture was Dapper Dan McCarthy, who owned the plumbers' union. Now O'Banion had his own source of alcohol and for the first time was in direct competition with the Genna brothers.

At this time O'Banion seemed to be sitting on top of the world. He had a young bride and a comfortable home. He had a business grossing $2,000,000 a year, from which he netted 10 percent tax free. His closest companions were Nails Morton, Hymie Weiss, Louis Alterie, Schemer Drucci, and Dan McCarthy. Bugs Moran was usually on hand and Teddy Newberry was just coming into the operation. O'Banion had heard a few rumbles about the Genna brothers being unhappy with his ownership of Cragin Products Company but had not let them bother him.

There were other rumors he did not like. O'Banion owned half of the Ship, a profitable suburban Stickney gambling joint which he operated in conjunction with the Torrio-Capone gang. Now he heard that the Miller brothers, a West Side Jewish family, wanted to ease him out.

The four Miller boys were Herschel, Dave, Max, and Harry. They had been election sluggers and in the protection racket, had been thieves from childhood, and had early turned to bootlegging.

Hirshie Miller led the gang and held one of the biggest gambling concessions in Chicago during the early twenties, when Mayor Thompson in City Hall was in a position to sell such concessions to the highest bidder. Hirshie Miller's territory embraced the length of Roosevelt Road, the greatest concentration in the city of middle-class Jewish merchants. The gambling concession was rich.

Hirshie Miller let it be known that he intended to take over O'Banion's half interest in the Ship, with or without O'Banion's consent.

Hirshie Miller never hesitated to shoot when he had to, and in 1922 he and Nails Morton had occasion to fight two policemen in the Beaux Arts Café, a black-and-tan joint at 2700 South State Street. Miller drew a revolver and killed both policemen, Patrolmen Hennessey and Mulcahy. By spreading a little money around, and by virtue of the fact that his gang regularly delivered the vote for the Jewish politicians of the West Side, he got off on a plea of self-defense.

Even before the Prohibition years, Hirshie Miller had seen the fortune to be made in the protection racket. He visited the cleaning and dyeing and tailoring establishments throughout his wide Jewish territory and told them all they had to pay him $10 a week for protection. When they said they did not need protection, he broke their plate-glass windows and beat them up. If they still refused to pay, he went into their shops with bottles of acid and ruined the clothing they had just finished pressing for customers. They all began to pay him $10 a week.

So when Dion O'Banion was told that Hirshie Miller intended to take over the Ship, O'Banion acted at the first opportunity. He was in the Loop, walking along West Madison Street on the evening of January 20, 1924, with Dan McCarthy, Hymie Weiss, and Yankee Schwartz, a Philadelphia gunman then registered at the Hotel Sherman. As they passed in front of the La Salle Theater, at 115 West Madison Street, O'Banion saw the Millers emerging. O'Banion turned to Schwartz and said, "Let me have your piece." Schwartz handed him a revolver and O'Banion shot two of the Miller brothers.

The two shot were Davey Miller, who ran a restaurant at 3216 West Roosevelt Road, was the gambling power in the Douglas Park neighborhood, and was a prizefight referee; and Maxie Miller, the baby of the family, who ran a poolroom and restaurant, and controlled several handbooks in the neighborhood. Davey was shot in the stomach and soon was reported doing well in the University Hospital. Maxie had suffered only a flesh wound.

Two taxicab drivers saw the shooting. Both told police they could identify no one. Mrs. Maxie Miller, who had been at her husband's side, told Chief of Police Michael Hughes she was "too excited" at the time to be positive of O'Banion's identification. But Maxie Miller, visiting O'Banion and Hymie Weiss at their cells in the detective bureau, said, "That man [pointing at O'Banion] shot me. He tried to kill me. Then he shot my brother, Davey."

Maxie Miller signed complaints of assault to commit murder. O'Banion and Hymie Weiss were arraigned January 23 before Judge Samuel Trude in South Clark Street police court. He set O'Banion's bond at $40,000 and that for Hymie Weiss at $35,000. They posted the bonds and went free. The Millers later refused to prosecute and charges were dropped.

Two days later, at 11 o'clock in the morning of January 25, 1924, Police Lieutenant William O'Connor was cruising with his partner in their squad car on the Near South Side at Nineteenth Street and Indiana Avenue. An auto passed them, headed north on Indiana Avenue. O'Connor took a second look and recognized as its driver Dion O'Banion, who was, he thought, still being sought for the Miller shooting. The policemen curbed O'Banion's car.

Beside O'Banion sat Hymie Weiss. In the back seat was Dan

McCarthy, who owned the plumbers' union. McCarthy had taken this union from Steve Kelliher by the simple action of shooting Kelliher dead. The shooting had taken place in Al Tierney's speakeasy, the Auto Inn, at Thirty-fifth Street and Indiana Avenue.

McCarthy appeared to be guarding two other passengers in the back seat. They identified themselves as Samuel Baer and Charles Levine. They said they were drivers for the Sterling Transfer Company and that they had been held up at gunpoint and robbed of their two trucks by O'Banion and his men.

Baer and Levine said they had picked up two truckloads of bonded whiskey from the warehouse at 8619 South Cottage Grove Avenue.

They were taking it to the Rock Island Railroad station, whence it was to be shipped to the Corning Distillery Company at Peoria. They said the shipment consisted of 251 cases of Haviland rye, worth $30,000.

Baer and Levine said their trucks had been curbed between Twenty-first and Twentieth streets. They said O'Banion and the others had revolvers in their hands and identified themselves as detectives. Two of O'Banion's boys had climbed into the trucks and driven them off to an unknown destination. O'Banion had told Baer and Levine. "Get in our car. We are taking you to the detective bureau."

At that point O'Banion's car was curbed by Police Lieutenant O'Connor.

As soon as they arrived at the police station they all went free on bail, but on April 25, three months after the arrest, a federal grand jury indicted O'Banion, Hymie Weiss, and McCarthy. The grand jury was told that when McCarthy killed Kelliher to take over the plumbers' union, he got $150,000 in the union treasury.

The boys had to spread some of that $150,000 around. They went to trial briefly on July 7, but the charges were dropped when Baer and Levine refused to testify. The trial was conducted before Judge Adam C. Cliffe in federal court, with Assistant District Attorney Edwin L. Weisl prosecuting. The defense was handled by Michael Ahern, Thomas Nash, and Joseph Merensky.

The trial ended in a hung jury.

One old farmer got down on his knees to pray for a vote of guilty. But prayer could not tip the balance against currency of the realm.

Prosecutor Weisl later said he had been told that $50,000 had been handled by a lawyer to put in the fix on this case.

Even while they were awaiting trial, O'Banion and several others were indicted on May 30, 1924, on charges of illegally removing tremendous quantities of whiskey and straight grain alcohol from the Sibley

Warehouse Storage Company at 1530 South Sangamon Street, and from two other warehouses, Harder and Mayer Brothers.

Among those indicted with O'Banion this time were two brothers of John V. Clinnin, a former Assistant United States District Attorney. The two were Sheridan Clinnin and Walter Clinnin.

The grand jury was told that a powerful ring including police officers and a dozen officials or clerks of the warehouses had used forged certificates to withdraw quantities of spirits over a period of time. The prosecutor presenting the case to the grand jury said the ring had perfected an elaborate organization for the disposal of such stocks through bootleggers all over the United States.

A great deal of money was spent to close this case without convictions.

The O'Banion talent for changing ideas into money did not stop with these few hijackings.

His gang was suspected but never charged with the $1,500,000 burglary of the Werner Brothers warehouses, and with the $2,000,000 mail robbery from Chicago's Union Station.

O'Banion's wide acquaintanceship throughout Chicago gave him uncommon opportunities to learn where the alcohol or whiskey was stored, when it would be on the street for delivery, how it could best be stolen. He told everyone he met, shortly after introductions were completed, "I'm in the market for tips on alcohol or booze. I pay ten percent of whatever I can sell it for. Nobody who tips me off ever gets implicated."

Strangers meeting O'Banion for the first time sometimes thought this an unusual way to do business. But it was O'Banion's way. To his friends, the newspaper reporters and photographers, he said, "For you, it's fifteen percent. No kidding. One of these days you're going to run across a nice bit of news. Just keep me in mind. Give me a call and if I can get the stuff, you get fifteen percent. Meanwhile, drop by the florist shop, identify yourself, and tell them I sent you, and they'll give you a couple of pints of good stuff."

One morning in early November of 1922, O'Banion and Dapper Dan McCarthy were having pancakes and coffee in the Hotel Sherman coffeehouse. Hymie Levin came in, all excited. He was then running a speakeasy diagonally across the street upstairs at the southeast corner of Randolph and Clark. Levin said, "I was hoping I'd find you here. A truckdriver for the Walter Powers Warehouse at 162 West Washington Street is in my place right now, having a quick drink.

"I heard him tell another guy that he is about to deliver a load of bonded booze to some West Side drugstores."

Even as Hymie Levin was talking, Schemer Drucci entered, accompanied by Harry Hartford, a small-time boxer who fought under the name of Johnny Dundee. Hymie Levin's face fell when he saw the newcomers. He said, "I don't know if there's enough to go around." Drucci and Hartford said they wanted no part of the action but would go along for the ride.

O'Banion and McCarthy had scarcely started on their breakfasts. Now they told the waitress they would be back later and to save everything for them. O'Banion, with the police on his payroll, had his car parked in front of the hotel. They got into his car just as the truck, driven by Joseph Goodman, started west.

They waited until the truck had crossed Wells Street and was out of the Loop. When it slowed at Canal Street for a stop, O'Banion and McCarthy sprang out of their car, ran to the truck and, one on either side of the driver's cab, displayed their revolvers. Goodman stopped the motor at their command. He got out and was permitted to leave. O'Banion drove off in the truck to park it a block away.

Goodman made his way to the nearest telephone to report the theft of his truck and its load of whiskey. McCarthy picked up O'Banion as the latter parked the truck and the four thieves returned to the Sherman Hotel to finish their breakfasts.

Hymie Levin had not accompanied them, as he had to finish opening his Loop speakeasy across the street from City Hall.

Detective Sergeants Frank Smith and Thomas Piper were put on the case. They learned that after he had finished his breakfast, O'Banion went back to the truck and drove it to Nails Morton's garage in the Twentieth Ward. They said at the trial that Morton took the load of 225 cases of bottled whiskey off O'Banion's hands for a cash price of $22,500. The aged and uncut whiskey, a full 100 proof and made in the years before World War I, was a steal at $100 a case of twenty-four pints.

The police showed photographs to Goodman, and he picked out the pictures of O'Banion, Drucci, and Hartford. Although neither Drucci nor Hartford were in on the theft, O'Banion paid to have charges against them dropped.

O'Banion later said, "We wasn't away from the breakfast table for twenty minutes all told. My coffee was still hot, but I had the girl bring me another order of wheat cakes. Hymie Levin and McCarthy and me split that money three ways, seven thousand five hundred apiece for twenty minutes' work. You can't beat that."

Morton by this time had come in with O'Banion and Schofield in operation of the florist shop, but he still maintained his West Side garage as a hot-car drop and for handling wholesale quantities of liquor. The

Schofield florist shop on State Street, with its three busy clerks at phones, was the center for retailing into Morton's Near West Side as well as O'Banion's North Side territory.

O'Banion's representatives in operation of the Ship were Louie Alterie and David (Jew Bates) Jerus. Torrio's representatives were Al Capone and (West Side) Frankie Pope. There were two Frankie Popes in the underworld at the time, as well as a third on the police force, so the one who worked for Torrio in Stickney was always identified as "West Side." All were Italian, the name sometimes spelled P-a-p-e.

The Ship was a political plum, a Cook County gambling concession granted by the county politicians, worth $200,000 a month in profits. Besides the roadhouse atmosphere, with beer and liquor available as in an old English tavern, the place offered Las Vegas-type gambling and a dry-screw dance hall. This was really a dime-a-dance palace, operated under the dimmest of lights, in which for five tickets the girl would rub her partner to a climax. The girls also had bedrooms upstairs to which they would retire with a partner for $2 a trip.

O'Banion's representatives in its operation—and he always claimed that he never took a dollar of the girls' earnings—were both union leaders, labor statesmen of the school which Chicago has always provided. Alterie ruled the Chicago Theatrical Janitors Union at 59 East Van Buren Street, and anyone who wanted to push brooms backstage at any theater in town had to pay Alterie $10 a month for the privilege.

No one questioned Alterie's right to rule the union. In the first place, he had started it. He saw a type of labor in Chicago which had not yet been organized and decided to bring to this labor the benefits of organization.

He compelled employers to double their wages and charged the men $10 a month for the service. A fair enough exchange. Some of the men said they did not want to be organized. They were taken into the nearest alley and beaten up. Then they joined the union.

That was the first place. In the second place, Alterie had shown himself always armed and always ready to shoot if he had to. He had once killed a man publicly in a duel in Al Tierney's place, the same Auto Inn where Dan McCarthy killed Steve Kelliher for the plumbers' union. Alterie's killing was not over union affairs. He and the man were drinking in the place and they had a difference over a girl. Both were armed so they paced off the length of the speakeasy, turned, drew, and fired. Alterie killed his man. Alterie favored such "old West" shoot-outs. He owned a Colorado ranch and was a fan of Western movies.

Jerus originally had been one of Nails Morton's gang, along with Alterie and others. They all joined Dion O'Banion's ranks at the same time, but Jerus took on the additional chore of becoming a slugger for Alterie's union. Good union sluggers were in demand, worth $100 a week or better. They were more than plug-uglies. They always tried to talk sense to recalcitrant workers, pointing out the advantages of membership in unions. Only when all else failed did they reluctantly draw a pistol, order the man into the alley, and proceed to give him a sound and professional beating.

Every union since the beginning of time has needed sluggers. All of them still do, since the union's ultimate weapon is the strike, and both sides, employers and unions, hire goons to do their dirty work.

Larceny of one kind or another has gone on since the beginning of time, and as long as one man covets another's goods it will be in style.

Prohibition was really the only new addition to modern criminal civilization. Every dealer in illegal beer or liquor needed men such as O'Banion and the others to give his stocks the protection the police give legal businesses. His competitors needed similar armies of gunmen. And thus vast armies of gunmen came into being to protect a business patronized by every community's social leaders.

5 "Have them rubbed out"

O'Banion's sense of humor, usually of the black type, was never far from the surface. Often it brought him close to trouble. In the million-dollar Sibley Warehouse Company robbery, of which a jury later found him not guilty, he had paid for his share of the booze with a rubber check in the amount of $41,000. This was a certified check, the only kind generally accepted in the underworld.

O'Banion had found a forger who could print the check on a big Boston bank, deck it out with revenue stamps and bank seals, and fix it up—O'Banion said later—so the bank itself would have accepted it as legitimate. O'Banion paid $100 to the forger for the job. What made his colleagues in the theft particularly angry, when they discovered that O'Banion's certified check was no good, was that he had used the same forger who counterfeited the bills of sale and warehouse receipts used to loot the warehouses.

O'Banion's cockeyed sense of humor was blamed again in the Sieben Brewery Company pinch. This great complex of buildings, then at 1478 North Larrabee Street, had been in operation since 1876. The bierstube and outdoor garden had been famous since 1903. After Prohibition came along, O'Banion got control and paid off police and federal agents so it could be operated illegally. He sold the place for $500,000 in the spring of 1924 to a West Side Italian gang. They were to take delivery at dawn on May 19, 1924.

Just at dawn, a few minutes after delivery had been formally made and accepted, the place was surrounded by dozens of squad cars. Everyone on the scene was taken into custody.

This included Dion O'Banion, Johnny Torrio, Louie Alterie, Spike O'Donnell, and twenty-eight others. The cops confiscated thirteen huge trucks already loaded with beer and ready to move.

O'Banion's laughter on this occasion gave rise to the rumor that he had set up the pinch. He had his money, in certified checks, and refused to return it. The West Side gang lost the beer that was confiscated and had to spend a good deal of money with Chicago authorities to have the brewery released so they could go on making beer and earn back the cost of the brewery.

O'Banion said at this time, "There's thirty million dollars' worth of beer sold in Chicago every month and a million dollars a month is spread among police, politicians, and federal agents to keep it flowing. Nobody in his right mind will turn his back on a share of a million dollars a month."

O'Banion was probably in a position to know. It is important to note here that he was speaking only of beer sales, not sales of whiskey, gin, cognac, and champagne.

At this time Chicago had just elected a reform mayor, William E. Dever, on the Democratic ticket. He was given the office solely as a rubber stamp for Boss George E. Brennan, who kept all the patronage in his own hands. As a judge, Dever had avoided taking the heavy money offered by the bootleggers, gamblers, and pimps so he was presented to the voters as a "reform" candidate. He succeeded William Hale Thompson, who had then been Republican mayor for two four-year terms and was to serve the public in this capacity again for four years after Dever's single term.

Johnny Torrio, seeing the handwriting on the wall, had taken over the town of Cicero, a West Side suburb of Chicago, as a base of operations.

This may sound like taking over a village. Actually, Cicero is the sixth-largest city in the state of Illinois. Torrio assigned truckloads of gunmen to guard the polling places of Cicero on election day, April 1, 1924. Al Capone was in charge of the operation. In the course of it his brother, Frankie Capone, was shot and killed by police.

When election day was over, the Torrio slate had made a clean sweep. Either the good people of the town had been too uninformed to vote, too lazy to vote, too scared to vote with a loaded revolver in the hands of guards at every polling place, or their votes had simply not been counted at the end of the day. The election judges and election clerks who counted the votes were the ones directly under Torrio's guns.

So, by the summer of 1924, with his slate temporarily clean—having bought off every single charge against him at the time—Dion O'Banion felt he deserved a vacation. He took Viola with him to Colorado. Louie Alterie, brother-in-law of Johnny Torrio, lived at Castle Rock, Colorado, and was always bragging up the state. O'Banion wanted to see what it was all about. He spent a month vacationing at the Woodbine Lodge in Jarr Canyon, near Sedalia, south of Denver.

O'Banion loved it so much he put up the money for a rodeo which attracted cowboys from miles around.

O'Banion spent freely and the rodeo weekend was a huge success. Everybody was happy. O'Banion paid cash for a 2,700-acre ranch before he came back to Chicago. He left Denver on October 20, 1924, with what police officials there said were "enough guns to outfit a Mexican army." O'Banion had bought a machine gun, several rifles, more than a dozen pistols and revolvers, and hundreds of rounds of ammunition to fit all the firearms.

In Chicago he said he was getting tired of business and thinking of retiring. He said he had "about two hundred thousand dollars cash" and wanted to invest the money and travel through Europe for a year.

O'Banion gave a big party at the Webster Hotel, 2150 North Lincoln Park West, on November 1. His guests included Chief of Detectives Michael Hughes, Cook County Clerk Robert Schweitzer, Colonel A. A. Sprague, a city official, and others of the upperworld who owed their jobs to political preferment. The half-world of local politics and labor unions was represented by Danny O'Connor of the Motion Picture Operators Union, Louis Alterie, Dapper Dan McCarthy, and just about every politician of the Lake Front wards, the Forty-second, Forty-third, Forty-fourth, and Forty-fifth. O'Connor, it should be noted, was patronage dispenser for the county assessor's office at the time.

The Church was represented by the Reverend Patrick J. Molloy, who loved to pal around with hoodlums and gangsters, and whose story will be told a little later.

Everybody laughed when Dion O'Banion told a story on Johnny Torrio. The story, although O'Banion did not say so, pointed up the difference between Torrio, always a businessman, and O'Banion, always a killer.

O'Banion said that he and Torrio were in a limousine loaded with imported scotch when they were halted by two policemen in a squad car. O'Banion was driving so Torrio got out to talk to the cops. Torrio came back to the car and said, "They want to arrest us, but they will drive away and forget it for three hundred dollars."

O'Banion roared. "Three hundred dollars? I can have those two bastards rubbed out for half that much."

Everybody at the party ate well, drank a good deal of fine wine, toasted each other. Among those present were several newspapermen, accustomed to observing and making notes. The records of the party are fairly complete.

Just three days after this party, on November 4, Dion O'Banion and dozens of his hired gunmen helped swing the normally Democratic Forty-second Ward into the Republican column. O'Banion set the pace.

To get everyone into the proper frame of mind to obey his election-day orders, he went from polling place to polling place. Every precinct in the ward got more than a glimpse of O'Banion that day.

In the polling places, he entered with several gunmen and upon leaving would ask two or three of his boys to remain. This was done in the presence of the election judges and clerks. O'Banion would have addressed everybody in the place, declaring his interest in seeing "that the Republicans get a fair shake this time, instead of all you people giving all the edge to the Democrats." Then he ostentatiously checked his revolver to see that it was loaded.

When he left, the judges and clerks looked at each other, too frightened to talk. There were policemen in every polling place and they were just as frightened as the political workers.

From the polling places, O'Banion went to the nearest saloon. This was Prohibition and by law there were not supposed to be any saloons. So there was no legal stricture, as there is today, against drink being sold within so many yards of a polling place.

When O'Banion went into the speakeasies, he ordered a drink for everybody in the house. While they were drinking, he drew his revolver and with easy nonchalance cut loose at anything in sight. His favorite target was the doorknobs on the toilet doors. When he had emptied one or two revolvers, he said to all assembled, "We're going to have a Republican victory celebration tonight. Anybody who votes Democratic ain't going to be there."

Then almost as an afterthought, he would add, "Or anywhere else!"

Everybody got the message. When the Democratic precinct captains came around later, trying to buy votes for a few drinks or a dollar or so, they found no takers. On that day everybody in the Forty-second Ward either voted Republican or went home without voting.

At the end of the day, O'Banion's gunmen were on hand to make sure that the tallies showed 98 percent Republican voting and only 2 percent Democratic.

Dozens of O'Banion's gunmen were arrested that day by rolling squads of police answering calls from polling places. But as soon as those arrested were booked at the East Chicago Avenue police station, O'Banion's lawyers had them out and working once again. From early morning till late at night, O'Banion kept all of them working. The results paid off. He delivered the ward.

Then, on November 9, the Sunday following the election day, all Chicago was shaken by news that Mike Merlo, the president of the Unione Siciliane, was dead of cancer in his home at 433 Diversey Boulevard. Merlo, known as "the Little Guy," was the diplomat who kept peace in the underworld. He it was who calmed the Genna brothers when O'Banion laughed at them publicly and called them "greaseballs." Merlo kept the Italians and Sicilians quiet when O'Banion, who never had taken a dollar from a whore, to hear him tell it, spoke of them as "a bunch of spic pimps."

The death of Mike Merlo removed from the Chicago milieu the one man who might have kept peace among the various factions, the Jews and the Irish, the Poles and the Greeks, the Italians and Sicilians, the blacks and the whites who were coining money in the world of Prohibition.

O'Banion had made many enemies among the Italians and Sicilians. He had quarreled with Torrio over profits from the Ship. He had quarreled with the Gennas over territories in which to sell raw alcohol. And he had a quarrel dating back many years with the Gloriana gang, as the Italians and Sicilians of his own neighborhood called themselves.

The leader of this gang was Dominick (Libby) Nuccio, and in the 1924 election he and his gang sought to do for the Forty-second Ward Democrats what O'Banion and the Irish so successfully did for the Republicans. Early in the day, O'Banion had encountered Libby Nuccio in a polling place at Division and Wells Streets, and had run him out at gunpoint.

Then, five days after the election, Mike Merlo died.

Everyone who knew the seething underworld currents realized O'Banion and the Italians were about to have at it.

On the Sunday that Merlo died, Schofield went to the Merlo home to see about floral arrangements for the funeral. He talked to James Genna, eldest of the Genna clan, and Carmen Vacco, the city sealer. The city sealer in Chicago was the people's representative in the field of weights and measures. This meant every butcher and grocer in town who wanted to cheat had to pay him graft to certify a scale as delivering sixteen ounces when actually it delivered only fourteen. The same arrangement was made at a number of coal yards, gasoline stations, and anywhere else where the consumer depended on weights and measures. The city sealer was frequently the political payoff point at city level, as was the sheriff at county level, and the auditor at state level. This is of course not always true today.

Genna and Vacco, like Merlo, were Sicilians,. They told Schofield they would come to O'Banion's florist shop next day to buy $650 worth of flowers for Mike Merlo's funeral.

Next day, shortly before noon, O'Banion was in the florist shop. Genna and Vacco entered with a third man, Pete Gusenberg. A clerk heard O'Banion greet the trio. Two of them reached out simultaneously to shake hands. One shook and held O'Banion's right hand; the other held his left hand. The third man drew a revolver and put several shots into the writhing O'Banion.

As O'Banion fell, the others let go of him to do some shooting on their own. When his body was examined, there was a bullet in each cheek, two bullets through the throat at the larynx, and two bullets in the right breast.

O'Banion never had a chance to get at any of the three guns he carried on his person at the time.

The three men emerged from the shop, walked south on State Street to Superior Street, there entered a Jewett automobile driven by a veiled woman, and proceeded west. When they left the shop they bumped into three boys who had heard the shooting, knew they were witnessing a gangland execution, and watched the killers as they departed. Naturally, no one was ever charged with the murder.

Within a few months the remnants of the O'Banion gang had killed Angelo and Anthony Genna. Then Mike Genna was killed by police as he fled a North Side gang attack. Gradually the Genna mob ceased to be.

Carmen Vacco went on from his job as city sealer to a seat in the state legislature. He was no better or worse than other politicians.

Pete Gusenberg was one of those who died in the St. Valentine's Day massacre on February 14, 1929. They were mostly old members of the O'Banion gang who had accepted the leadership of Bugs Moran.

The importance of the O'Banion killing is that it marked the beginning of the gang wars of the twenties. These were the wars from which Al Capone emerged triumphant as the greatest force left in the city. Ever since that time the Chicago gangs have been dominated by the Italian-Sicilian element and the Jews who work with them. The old ethnic gangs as such have disappeared. What remains is variously called the syndicate, the Outfit, or the Mafia.

O'Banion's place in the city's history was voiced by Chief of Police Morgan Collins, the reform administrator appointed by reform Mayor William E. Dever. Collins said at the time of O'Banion's death, "Chicago's archcriminal is dead. I don't doubt that O'Banion was responsible for at least twenty-five murders in this city."

That was a somewhat more conservative estimate than the sixty-two killings with which O'Banion had been credited by other police who kept score.

O'Banion was buried on November 14. Since he headed one of the biggest aggregations of underworld slugging and shooting talent in the city, as well as owning his own florist shop, the flowers were heaped as high as a house. Gangsters, like politicians, make a point of attending one another's wakes and funerals, trying to outdo one another in the size and magnificence of their floral offerings.

Judge Henry Horner in probate court was later given papers showing that the O'Banion funeral expenses included a silvered coffin at $7,500, a solid copper box to contain the coffin at $750, fifteen gilded chairs at $150, and music at $125.

Despite the fact O'Banion in his youth had been an altar boy, Cardinal Mundelein decreed that no Roman Catholic church was to be used for the funeral, no requiem mass was to be said for O'Banion, and that he was not to be buried in consecrated ground.

O'Banion had always been vain about his silky brown hair and his soft, long-fingered hands.

The cosmeticians at the Sbarboro funeral chapel, 708 North Wells Street, did their best to accentuate these features for the thirty-two-year-old corpse.

They said the coffin was the best that money could buy. Its designers in Pennsylvania had sent it west in a special express car with no other freight. While silver in tone, the coffin itself was naturally of bronze, but at its corners were solid-silver posts.

At the wake it turned out that O'Banion's full name had been Charles Dion O'Banion. His father said that when they first came to Chicago they lived a block north of the funeral home, at 841 North Wells Street.

Dion's widow was so broken up she had to lean on her father-in-law for support, but she managed to say a few words about O'Banion's habits when not out cracking safes, hijacking booze, or slugging news venders: "Dion was a simple man. He loved his home. He never left home without telling me where he was going. He was seldom out at night. He hated ostentation. He had one small car, a little sedan he bought for me. His greatest pleasure was going to the ranch in Colorado."

Although Cardinal Mundelein had cautioned all priests to stay away, Father Patrick Molloy said a benediction in the funeral home and a few prayers for the dead in Mount Carmel Cemetery when the coffin was placed in the ground.

An estimated 150,000 men, women, and children turned out for the funeral. Twenty thousand gathered in the cemetery. There were 122 autos in the cortege, including the twenty-four piled high with wreaths and other floral offerings. There were 500 cars parked in the vicinity of the cemetery by those who wanted to see the criminal laid away.

All of O'Banion's friends turned up at the cemetery.

Naturally, Hymie Weiss was on hand. He had sided O'Banion in most of the latter's pranks as well as safecrackings. Weiss had been a youthful criminal in his own right. He was only twenty-two in May, 1919, when he had to pay off heavily to assure a no bill from a grand jury considering charges of larceny and receiving stolen property. On September 8 of that same year he was caught in the act of blowing the safe in the American Theater at 1600 West Madison Street. On October 11 of that year he paid off and was found not guilty of larceny.

But Hymie Weiss' best story concerned the time on January 24, 1920, when he was charged with larceny and taken before Judge Robert E. Crowe. Hymie Weiss and O'Banion had been at the jurist's home only the night before, arranging for some election-day violence. When Hymie Weiss appeared before Crowe, neither smiled or in any way acknowledged acquaintance. Crowe heard the evidence and solemnly freed the defendant but said, "There is not enough evidence here to convict, I am sorry to say. I have heard of you, young man.

"The police tell me you are in all kinds of mischief and just laugh at the law. I warn you to straighten up. Society will not stand for this sort of thing. If you ever come before me again, and there is enough evidence to convict, I'll give•you the limit. I hope it never happens. Now think of your mother and try to do better."

Maxie Eisen showed up at O'Banion's funeral. He was one of the old Nails Morton gang and still ran his all-night restaurant at the corner of Newberry Street, Blue Island Avenue, and Roosevelt Road, where every safecracker in town turned up for ham and eggs after a successful robbery.

Anthony (Red) Kissane was there. He had been with John Mackey when the latter was shot to death in a car a few days earlier on election day. Both were political sluggers and members of Terry Druggan's old Valley gang.

Terry Druggan was present. He had been a minor member of the Valley gang on the West Side, on Maxwell and neighboring streets west of Halsted Street, until Paddy (the Bear) Ryan was one day found dead in an alley. Then Druggan became the head man. Some of Ryan's friends grumbled, but nobody wanted to do anything about it. Druggan formed a partnership with Frankie Lake, a gangster come west from New York City.

Two-Gun Louie Alterie, alias Leland Varain, was there. He was Johnny Torrio's brother-in-law. Varain had been a ham-and-egg fighter in his youth in the West, married Erma Rossi when her father, Mike Rossi, was the leader of Denver's underworld, and come to Chicago in 1921 as bodyguard to Melvin Reeves.

Reeves was an international burglar who had been robbed of $30,000 in negotiable securities.

Alterie started running a small gambling operation, teamed up with Nails Morton, Hirshie Miller, and the Jewish gangsters of the West Side, and eventually took several of that group with him when he joined O'Banion. He was born in California, son of Charles Varain, a French immigrant, and had first come to the attention of Chicago police when with Terry Druggan he robbed two women of $50,000 in gems. They were wealthy Jewish women who lived in the Edgewater area, Mrs. Clara Weinberger and Mrs. Joseph Mendelson. They identified Alterie at first, but changed their stories by the time of the trial. They had seen no one.

Alterie had organized the Chicago Theater Janitors Union Local 25. He lived at the Congress Hotel in Chicago, and owned a 3,000-acre ranch near Glenwood Springs, Colorado.

Schemer Drucci showed up to pay his last respects to O'Banion. Drucci had helped O'Banion crack a safe or two, but he preferred to hold a gun in his hand and see the man he was robbing. In July, 1921, he and Mike Geary, along with four others, walked into the Clearing State Bank with guns in their hands and took the tellers for $60,000. Geary and a locally notorious bank robber named "Big Six" Sichs were convicted. Drucci bought his way out. He had been in his shirtsleeves when found wandering in a cornfield near Lemont, a suburb twenty-five miles southwest of Chicago, with some of the bank loot in his pocket.

Drucci came to public attention for the last time on April 4, 1927, the day before the election which returned William Hale Thompson to the office of mayor. That was when, unarmed and in a police squad car, Drucci was shot to death in broad daylight at the corner of Wacker Drive and Clark Street. Patrolman Daniel F. Healy, for no reason that anyone could ever adduce, simply drew his revolver and put four bullets into his prisoner. There were plenty of witnesses, including those in the car with them. Healy never denied or sought to extenuate the facts.

Chief of Detectives William H. (Shoes) Shoemaker said, "I'm having a medal prepared for Healy."

At the coroner's inquest, Healy was represented by Attorney Charles E. Erbstein. He said that Chief of Police Morgan Collins had ordered a roundup of known gangsters to prevent election-day violence. Healy was in a squad car with Patrolmen Roy Hessler and Matt J. Cunningham, and Lieutenant William Lieback. They saw Drucci with Henry Finkelstein, an associate of Titus Haffa, the bootlegger and politician, and of Albert Single, a Peoria bootlegger. The police halted to pick up the three.

Finkelstein testified at the inquest that Healy slugged Drucci twice with his fists before shoving him into the squad car.

Drucci had achieved a certain amount of notoriety when he raced his car north on downtown Michigan Avenue in flight from pursuing police squad cars.

As he approached Wacker Drive the bells were ringing and the lights were flashing to indicate that the Michigan Avenue link bridge was slowly being raised to permit passage of a high-masted schooner in the Chicago River. Drucci never slowed. Rather, he stepped on the gas, broke the wooden gates which had come down across the entrance to the bridge, and jumped his car across the opening bridge. He came down safely on the other side and drove on north to escape.

When O'Banion was laid to rest, Drucci was free on bond in connection with a $300,000 jewel robbery. He paid off and went free.

Drucci was a Navy veteran of World War I, and when it came time for him to be buried, the Harold A. Taylor post of the American Legion provided his body with an honor guard. Entwined in the Schemer's hands, as he was laid out in the coffin, was a rosary. A choir of little girls sang the "Ave Maria" and other hymns he had known in his churchgoing youth. His widow, Cecilia, as they were about to close the coffin, screamed, "My lover, my lover, let me see him just once more!" Exit Schemer Drucci, aged twenty-seven.

Finkelstein will be encountered again in these chronicles. He was part of the bootlegging enterprise of Titus Haffa, Republican committeeman and alderman of the Forty-third Ward, and of Albert P. Bauer, the Lincoln Park commissioner whose memory is honored even today by his political heirs.

Healy, who had joined the Chicago police force in 1925, retired in 1964. He never did explain how he had come to kill Drucci.

But the Schemer was in disrepute with Al Capone at the time of his death and it is worthy of note that Healy after retirement became chief of police of Stone Park.

This was a West Side suburb favored by Capone Syndicate gangsters for their investments in motels, cocktail lounges, and Vegas-type gambling operations.

Attorney Charles S. Wharton had been retained by Drucci's widow at the inquest into the Schemer's death. He later remarked, "We never did find out how an unarmed man in a police squad car surrounded by armed policemen can be shot to death by one of them without the act being called murder."

Besides those mentioned, the O'Banion funeral brought wreaths and floral pieces from every criminal in the Middle West. And among the mourners were such local notables of the underworld as John (Dingbat)

Oberta, (Polack) Joe Saltis, and Julius (Potatoes) Kaufman. The last-named was a member of a family of well-to-do commission merchants on South Water Market, often seen in the company of gangsters.

Kaufman was a compulsive gambler. There are two kinds: the man who runs the games but does not bet on them, and the sucker who bets the games run by someone else. Kaufman was in the latter class. He was a sucker who could not stay away from a table featuring hot dice and cold cards. He spent everything he got on fast women and slow horses.

He got his kicks by being seen in the company of criminals and there were only the vaguest of rumors that he sometimes had a piece of the action. He was never caught at it.

6 Taking over a black union

Early in this century Tim Murphy ran the Street Sweepers Union. That union in Chicago has always been important to politicians. It remains so to this day. Not alone can the union deliver the votes of men and their families in every ward of the city, but the union can absorb a lot of men for whom the politician must find jobs. .

Politics is not quite the upperworld, nor is it quite the underworld. The politician at any level is a member of a middle world in between, a puppet on strings dangled by the Establishment and underworld money.

But the politician's strength, like that of the industrial giant or merchant prince—or the gangster chieftain—is rooted in jobs, friendships, and loyalties. In about that order.

The politician is constantly being called upon to find a job for a nephew or cousin who cannot make it in private industry, for a son or a drinking father or an aging grandfather who lacks the skills in demand.

The Street Sweepers Union, with branches in every ward, was the ideal dumping ground for all such misfits. The politician could make friends of a family, and later cultivate their loyalties, by the simple writing of a note to a ward superintendent. It was this man's job to see to the cleanliness of alleys, to the washing down of the streets, the hauling away of refuse from a front stoop. With such a note in hand, anyone could go to a ward superintendent, get a broom and shovel, and a paycheck every week.

The skilled were easy to place. The unskilled, immigrants from abroad or in-migrants from elsewhere in the country, needed such a landing place as the Street Sweepers Union, which once performed the function that welfare rolls do today. The history of this union, so far as this story is concerned, begins with Mike Carrozzo.

Carrozzo, born in Montaguto, Italy, in 1895, emigrated at the age of eleven and reached Chicago at fourteen. In 1909, just at the time Big Jim Colosimo was bringing Johnny Torrio west from Brooklyn, Colosimo first had his shoes shined by young Carrozzo. Big Jim saw before him a bright-eyed youngster with a mop of curly black hair, a pair of broad shoulders, and a font of shrewd native wit. He took a liking to the boy and made him his boy-of-all-work.

Colosimo then was absolute ruler of the city's red-light district. Both he and his wife, Victoria Moresco, had their own brothels among the scores operated south of the Loop and as far west as Halsted Street. Colosimo was precinct captain for the area, appointed by the two Democratic First Ward aldermen, Kenna and Coughlin. On every election day he delivered the votes of the madams, the whores, the pimps, the liquor dealers, and all the purveyors of groceries and other goods to the brothels. He also delivered the votes of the landlords of the Levee, at least those who lived in the district, and their maintenance men.

Before Mike Carrozzo was old enough to vote, Big Jim had taught him all the things a young man in that milieu was required to know.

Carrozzo had always had a ready smile and a cheerful word for everyone he met. Colosimo taught him the art of doing favors for people. Carrozzo became neighborly with the immigrant Italians and Sicilians, helping them get their citizenship without waiting five years or five months or five days. After all, what else were political connections good for? Carrozzo got all the immigrants registered as voters. He knew they could not read, so he stepped with them behind the curtains in the polling places on election days and filled out their ballots for them. A friend is a friend.

Carrozzo was a believer in democracy. He voted several times on every election day at the different polling places which he controlled. He never permitted any of his friends and hangers-on to miss a chance to vote. If a man was too sick, Carrozzo would cast a vote for him.

If the man died a few days before an election, Carrozzo saw that a vote was cast in his name.

On Colosimo's recommendation, Mike Carrozzo was made a precinct captain. On election days, Kenna and Coughlin would hand him a bundle of currency to help get out the vote. Carrozzo knew the dregs of the Levee red-light district, the worn-out whores who no longer could work in the brothels and who walked the streets to turn a trick in an alley for a dime or a quarter. He knew the winos, the saloon swampers, the newsboys, the hangers-on. He knew the habitués of the opium cellars in the area. He registered them all, between elections, and on election day he passsed among them with a pocket full of bright fresh silver quarter-dollars. Mike Carrozzo saw that every one of them voted at least once.

Like Colosimo himself, Carrozzo's first regular job was that of "white wing." With a broom in one hand and a shovel in the other, Carrozzo followed the milk-wagon horses and draymen through the Loop. He had joined Local 1001 of the Street Maintenance Employees, the union then owned by Big Tim Murphy. Carrozzo's good nature, his shrewd judgment, and the fact that he was a protégé of Colosimo and a politician of rising importance in his own right brought him to Murphy's attention.

Although Murphy ruled the Street Sweepers Union, he could not give full time to its operation. He had dozens of other irons in the fire and he ran the union through a stooge named Hugo Lynch. Murphy realized that Lynch was pocketing too great a portion of the monthly dues and special assessments paid by the members.

He had his eye out for a likely successor to Lynch and after talking to Colosimo he decided on Carrozzo.

Then Murphy waited for an auspicious time to get rid of Lynch.

Hugo Lynch, the incautious union president, had no idea his number was up. He left town for a vacation and in his absence Murphy called a special meeting of the union local. A quick election was held and, in the democratic way of such elections, Mike Carrozzo was installed as president and business agent. Everyone cheered, the union meeting was over, and Murphy took Carrozzo to a saloon for a few words of advice.

Murphy laid it on the line. He told Mike Carrozzo that a position as union leader was a position of trust. He said he had permitted Hugo Lynch to live because of old family friendships, but he told Carrozzo what would happen if the new president sought to give Tim Murphy anything less than a fair split of the monthly take. Carrozzo nodded his agreement and thereafter proved to be an honest partner in the looting of the city's thousands of white wings.

Overnight Carrozzo became in his home neighborhood a man of stature and substance. In the First Ward of 1916 the pimps and the precinct captains were exceeded in importance only by the owners of the whorehouses and the labor unions. Carrozzo's friendliness in the future was tempered with his dignity and the aura of power which surrounded him. He had barely turned twenty-one and was already a man of wealth.

Toward the close of World War I, Big Jim Colosimo's interests changed.

He was no longer hungry, as he had been in the days when he was building his vice and political empire. Now he was fat and satisfied. He had fallen in love with Dale Winters, a beautiful saloon singer, and no longer lived with Victoria Moresco.

Eventually he was to marry the one after divorcing the other.

But meanwhile his affairs were handled by his underlings. Johnny Torrio was the chief lieutenant in operation of the vice empire and upper-level payoffs to politicians. Mike Carrozzo was, under Torrio, chief lieutenant in the operation of Colosimo's various labor unions. Colosimo ruled the Street Laborers Union, and the City Street Repairers Union, two different outfits—but Carrozzo ran them.

By the time Prohibition began, Colosimo had just about abdicated the throne. He was not to be killed until May but, with his new wife, he was like an old man in his dotage. When decisions had to be made, his lieutenants made them without consulting the once-powerful boss. One of the decisions Mike Carrozzo had to make concerned the Chicago Building Trades Council in which Big Tim Murphy was a power.

Murphy was on a collision course with Maurice (Mossy) Enright, who controlled the Plumbers and Steamfitters Union and who had become arbiter for the Pipe Trades Council, an adjunct of that union and its voice in the Chicago Building Trades Council.

Enright, like so many gangsters of the era, got his start in the first decade of the century as one of Max Annenberg's circulation sluggers.

After World War I his horizons broadened and he thought to be boss of the construction industry throughout the city. Murphy's own ambitions paralleled those of Mossy Enright. So Enright became the city's first victim of an automobile assassination.

As Enright's car left the Loop on the snowy winter evening of February 3, 1920, another car followed at a leisurely pace to the Enright home at 1110 West Garfield Boulevard. As Enright stepped out of his car, the second car drew up alongside and the shotgun muzzles were stuck out toward the victim. Enright was hit by several sprays of shotgun slugs.

The curtain of falling snow, great wet flakes that stuck to everything they touched, muffled the sound of the shots. It was the dinner hour and none of the neighbors along this prosperous street raised a window or opened a door to see what was going on.

The four killers—Mike Carrozzo, Tim Murphy, Vincenzo Cosmano, and James Vinci—did not even step out of their car. They opened its door next to the body of the fallen union leader. They paused a moment to study the position of the body and, from their knowledge and experience in such things, to be certain Enright was either dead or beyond recovery. Then they drove slowly westward.

Enright's murder might have been filed away as unsolved had not Jimmy Vinci got an attack of conscience. He made a detailed confession, naming his companions and corroborating witnesses. Carrozzo, Murphy, and Cosmano were arrested, charged with the crime, and released on bond.

Vinci repeated his story to a grand jury and murder indictments were returned. This compelled Carrozzo, Murphy, and Cosmano to look up and eliminate, one by one, every witness Jimmy Vinci had named.

When the case came to trial, Jimmy Vinci's confession was made part of the record. He was sentenced to fourteen years in prison for his part in a murder he never denied. But there was no evidence against the others. Simply the unsupported word of a confessed killer. No jury in the land would convict on such slender testimony. The other three went free.

When Big Jim Colosimo was killed on May 12, 1920, Mike Carrozzo became one of the owners instead of simply the operator of Colosimo's labor union holdings. And he began adding to his labor empire the unions of garbage wagon drivers and of section and dump foremen. All his unions up to this time were of workers on city payrolls, those most important to city politicians.

With the notable exception of a few dissidents, every Italian and Sicilian family in the Chicago area looked upon certain men as their friends in high places. These men included Big Jim Colosimo, and by extension his nephew, Johnny Torrio; Mike Merlo, president of the Unione Siciliane; and Diamond Joe Esposito, who ran the Bella Napoli restaurant at 850 South Halsted Street and owned the Hod Carriers International Union. Esposito was Republican committeeman of the Nineteenth (now Twenty-fifth) Ward until shot to death on March 21, 1928.

Since Carrozzo's growing labor empire was part of the Torrio-Capone combine, Mike Carrozzo's circle of friendships grew.

From Loop and First Ward, his power now extended throughout the city. Every Italian and Sicilian family in town with a ne'er-do-well son too lazy to report for work daily turned to Capone or Merlo or Esposito for help in finding a job. These big leaders simply phoned Mike Carrozzo and put the member of the family on a city payroll. Carrozzo's unions were important to gangsters as well as politicians.

Keeping all his original unions, Carrozzo constantly reached out for more. He picked up the asphalt workers, the concrete and paving inspectors, the brick and granite and other laborers—all of which had their separate unions, with elected officers and paid functionaries who saw to it that dues and assessments were regularly collected. He picked up the asphalt resurfacing workers (differing from the asphalt workers), the paving workers, the cement workers, the sewer cleaners, the house drain inspectors, and the roadbuilding workers.

Carrozzo ruled a total of twenty-three unions and with them

controlled all public paving projects in Chicago. He controlled the city's streets, from the original survey to the eventual maintenance.

Much of the paving work in the city was done by workers in city departments, but this was all maintenance work. New streets were built by private paving contractors who submitted bids. Mike Carrozzo passed the word among paving contractors that they had to add 5 percent for graft to any bids made if they wanted to get any city or county contract.

This in no way altered the competitive nature of the bidding, for all private paving contractors were treated equally. They simply had to pay the extra 5 percent to Mike Carrozzo if they wanted union labor to work on any project. And the politicians were thoroughly knowledgeable about Carrozzo's needs.

They saw to it that no street project could be started or completed without Carrozzo's labor unions.

The practice did not begin with Carrozzo nor end with him.

Mike Carrozzo faced one major problem in his bid for total dominance of all street workers in the city and county. That problem was the single black local 1002 of the Street Maintenance Employees. This local was ruled by a brawny black named William Baker, who called himself its business agent. Ordinarily Baker cooperated with Mike Carrozzo, but he never let it be forgotten that he was agreeing rather than taking orders. Local 1002 never had really been in Carrozzo's portfolio.

There had been no blacks in street work until World War I. That was when so much of the white labor force was inducted into the armed services that the city—together with private industrialists, merchants, and contractors—began advertising high pay for in-migrants from other areas of the country. Most of these in-migrants came from south of Mason and Dixon's line. Most of them were black. Many went to work in the stockyards and steel mills. Others worked on the streets.

Bill Baker, the man who organized and owned the black street workers' union, was a two-fisted slugger in his own right. He was happy to have worked his way up from the laboring ranks. He knew that his continued life of luxury depended on his careful investigation of all complaints made by his dues-paying members. Baker was a one-man grievance committee who could and would pull his workers off any job if his grievances were not sympathetically heard.

Baker spent much of his time riding around in his big black car, shiny as a new dime. When he reached any construction job on which his men were employed, he stepped out of his car to blow a shrill whistle he always carried.

The workingmen of his local all knew Bill Baker's whistle. When they heard it they knocked off work and gathered around his car. Some wanted to present grievances and others simply wanted to shake the hand of "the Man."

Baker was nearly always accompanied by a long-legged, coffee-skinned girl of the type of dusky beauty he favored; a different such girl every few days. When he whistled and his flock gathered around his car, Baker would expand visibly and turn to the dusky wench to inquire, "Is that control, or is that control?"

He enjoyed his job and his life.

Baker's men generally worked on private paving jobs, handled by private contractors, as distinct from the public paving jobs on which most of Carrozzo's street laborers worked. Mike Carrozzo's absolute power was limited pretty much to the city streets of Chicago. He knew that to extend his control into Cook County and the other seven counties surrounding Chicago he had to take over Bill Baker's black union.

Mike Carrozzo knew how to wait until the time was ripe.

Before Carrozzo took over the street sweepers' union the work was more or less seasonal. In the spring every householder in town would bring out a spanking team and carriage, and extra street sweepers were needed.

In the fall every householder and his yardman burned leaves on the streets in front of his home, and extra sweepers were needed. In the winter, when a heavy snowfall blocked arterial and side streets for days, hundreds of extra street sweepers were required. These needs were all determined by the ward superintendents, who were appointees of the various ward committeemen and aldermen. Carrozzo changed all that.

Early in his career as ruler of the street sweepers' union, Carrozzo pulled 4,000 of his workers off the job for a week. He told the mayor and the City Council he demanded steady employment, with a guaranteed annual wage, for all union members. When extra help was required, he would issue temporary union credentials to the men using brooms and shovels. This meant he could charge initiation fees, dues, and special assessments to all the extra men the ward superintendents hired.

Carrozzo further demanded wage increases. The street sweepers were to get an extra 50 cents a day. The street repairmen were to get an extra dollar a day. The pay of refuse dump foremen was to be increased from $165 to $200 a month.

These were high wages at the time. All Carrozzo's demands were met. He promptly increased the dues and assessments from all members of all of his unions. He promptly increased Dago Mike Carrozzo's salary.

Carrozzo told all union members how important it was that each register and vote.

He insisted that all members of their families be registered as well. He discussed at every union meeting the importance of electing the right men to public office, "Because if you don't, goddamnit, you ain't going to have no job tomorrow."

Every ballot in Illinois was numbered and when the voter applied to the election clerk for his blank ballot the number was written next to his name. Every precinct captain in Chicago made a point, after every election, of going around to check numbered ballots against names. The precinct captain, "secret" ballot or no, could not do his job properly if he did not know how his constituents voted. Mike Carrozzo kept accurate track. Those who did not vote right promptly lost their jobs. Or at least so they were told, and so they believed.

By the right men, of course, Mike Carrozzo always meant that faction of the party—Democratic or Republican—in which the Torrio-Capone combine was interested. So long as Mike Merlo lived, the Unione Siciliane had generally the same interests as the Torrio-Capone combine.

Then Merlo died in 1924, Torrio was nearly killed and left the city in 1925, and Diamond Joe Esposito was shot to death on March 21, 1928. The Capone political machine—not a one-man operation as it is generally presented, but a complex machine made up of many factors and compromises—stepped into vacuums as they opened.

With Esposito's passing, somebody was going to take over his Hod Carriers International Union and with it his seat on the executive board of the American Federation of Labor.

Mike Carrozzo was the ideal man for the job. Now he was no longer simply a local union leader, but a labor statesman to be consulted by the elected representatives in Congress and the President of the United States.

Any organization as powerful as the Capone Syndicate has to keep its fingers on every change in the power complex of the city and state. The president of the Chicago Building Trades Council, Patrick F. Sullivan, announced his candidacy for public office and seemed certain to be elected. Al Capone wanted his own man to succeed Sullivan as president of the Building Trades Council. Mike Carrozzo was selected to run for the office.

In this case the Syndicate found itself up against a group of professional union bosses who had no intention of giving up their claim to the monthly dues of so many members. They all knew the Capone method of union control. At the time of any union election fifty Capone gunmen entered the union hall, stationed along its walls and in the doorways, openly loading and unloading revolvers. The various union owners had no such armies at their disposal.

The old-line labor union owners maintained their own control over the dues of members—aside from an occasional swipe with a blackjack or a pair of brass knuckles—by their power to grant or withhold jobs. They could not match Capone's display of force. So they used wiles and strategy. After publicly advertising the date of the Building Trades Council election, they quietly advanced its date by two weeks. They fooled the Capone machine and put their own candidate in as president.

The man they elected to this key job was Martin J. Durkin, assistant president of the Steam Fitters Union. Durkin was to turn up on the national stage twenty-three years later when in 1953 he was named by President Dwight Eisenhower as Secretary of Labor of the United States of America.

When Mike Carrozzo's ambition to head the Chicago Building Trades Council was temporarily thwarted, he turned to the black street workers' union ruled by Bill Baker. There were a thousand blacks in Baker's union, mostly unskilled workers in the asphalt and concrete paving field, and they were good for $5 a month apiece in the way of dues. In addition, each was good for a special assessment of $10, about four times a year, whenever the union's boss needed an extra wing on his home or a new automobile. Carrozzo went after the blacks.

Carrozzo saw control of Bill Baker's local as necessary to monopoly in the street-paving field, not only for Chicago but in the hundred or so incorporated communities in its eight-county orbit. With dominance of the black local, Carrozzo could make his own terms to paving contractors.

The European roadways built by the Roman legions 2,000 years ago are made of granite paving blocks laid on deep beds of gravel. They have been traveled and buffeted by the hoofs of Attila's ponies and the feet of Hannibal's elephants, the caissons of Napoleon and the traffic of cars, trucks, and buses.

Those highways are just as good today as they ever were. No American politician in his right mind would want anything as sturdy as those Roman roadways in his own bailiwick. The money from contractors' kickbacks lies in visible and frequent repairs.

So, at the end of every Midwestern winter, the streets and highways of Chicago and its environs, including all its satellite communities, were buckled and pitted. The people were made uncomfortable by the cracks and potholes in the streets. Nobody objected every spring, when winter was definitely behind, to tax money being spent to repair all the street and roadway surfacing in sight. This was one of the continuing legitimate grafts for which every politician sought office.

For in Chicago and its environs, it's been alleged that some public works contracts carried with them 20 percent in the form of kickbacks to the politicians who approved the bids and made it all possible.

The city of Chicago really has only three seasons a year, a hot summer, a beautiful autumn, and a snowy and windy winter. With the exception of unseasonably warm days followed by sub-freezing temperatures, the Chicago winter lasts right up until June 1. That is when the street resurfacing annually began.

Mike Carrozzo made his bid for the take-over of Bill Baker's union local on June 6, 1930. Carrozzo's plans had been carefully laid. He had been cooperating for years with Dan Tagnotti, who was then running the truckdrivers' local owned by Marcus (Studdy) Looney. And he had cooperated for years with William E. Maloney, who ruled Local 150 of the Operating Engineers Union.

Tagnotti's men ran the trucks and Maloney's men ran the big steamrollers used in the laying and repairing of street paving.

When Carrozzo was ready to move, Tagnotti pulled his drivers off the trucks hauling materials for work on the streets by private paving contractors. Then the men running the scrapers and steamrollers for street surfacing were pulled off the jobs. The contractors on such jobs throughout the city expressed themselves mystified. They said they did not even know the workers had a grievance. The mystery was dispelled when Dan Tagnotti told them, "We are folding up Bill Baker's Local 1002. The work will be done by Mike Carrozzo's Local 1001. Any of Baker's men who want to join Carrozzo's local can go to Carrozzo's office at 100 North La Salle Street and pay their initiation fees. Then they will be eligible to go to work on these paving projects."

The contractors quickly met and decided on a policy of neutrality. They closed down the jobs and laid off all the blacks in Bill Baker's local. The blacks, like any other men whose loyalty is necessarily to the source of the weekly paycheck, flocked to Carrozzo's office. In humble spirit they came, and they came not in vain. Carrozzo walked among his black brethren, shaking hands and slapping backs. He made everybody welcome—$50 a head.

Each of the more than a thousand black men was told he would have to pay the $50 initiation fee to join Carrozzo's Local 1001. But Carrozzo was reasonable.

If any did not happen to have $50 in cash at the moment, he could sign up and $5 a week would be taken out of his pay until the initiation fee had been taken care of. What's more, Carrozzo would not demand any interest on the money, although he said he was advancing it out of his own pocket.

Carrozzo asked, "Could anything be fairer?"

The black men looked at one another. They did not know much about economics and did not realize that the Great Depression had already started. They did not know much about finance and not one had lost a dollar in the stock market crash of the autumn of 1929. But they all knew what a job was. They all knew that jobs were increasingly hard to find that spring, and that all their friends were out of work. They signed up with Carrozzo.

The paving strike was over and the contractors lost only a couple of days before going on with the same workers. The only difference was that Bill Baker once again had to join a work crew, and Mike Carrozzo at a single stroke had made $50,000.

Carrozzo saw to it that none of his new union members was laid off until he had paid in full the $50 initiation fee. He tried to keep them on payrolls as long as possible so they could swell the union coffers with their $5-a-month payment of dues. But there is a limit to what even a man of goodwill such as Mike Carrozzo could do for unskilled labor. As the Depression grew worse, most of the men lost their paving jobs and had to turn to other fields.

Until that brief strike in the spring of 1930, Carrozzo's jurisdiction had been effectively limited to paving jobs handled by city workers within the city limits. From now on he had charge of the labor for all paving projects throughout the metropolitan area. His alliance with Dan Tagnotti and Bill Maloney was cemented and held together for the future. And now for the first time Mike Carrozzo was cut in on a large scale on the per-ton graft which then and now is paid by all purveyors of asphalt, cement, sand, gravel, and reinforcing steel rods used in street surfacing in the Chicago area.

Everyone benefits by cooperation. By the time World War II came along, Bill Maloney was president of the International Union of Operating Engineers, with 150,000 dues-paying members in the United States and Canada. He, too, was a member of the executive board of the AFL-CIO. Like Carrozzo, he was consulted by wrinkle-browed Senators and Congressmen, and deferred to by the President of the United States.

7   The passing of the Dingbat

With Dago Mike Carrozzo on the executive board of the American Federation of Labor, Al Capone felt that he was getting a foot in the door of organized labor nationally. But he smarted over the loss of the Chicago Building Trades Council to Marty Durkin. He thought he might do the next best thing and take over the Chicago Teamsters Joint Council.

Capone's labor experts were Murray Humphreys and George (Red) Barker. The first was a lifelong thief. Barker was a man of good family who had been an honest bookkeeper and accountant before going into business for himself as an owner of labor unions. He was literate but he could handle a gun with the best of them.

Red Barker figured out a strategy to get himself elected to the Teamsters Joint Council. He talked it over with Humphreys, with Three-Finger Jack White, and with Ralph Capone. None could see any flaw in it. Ralph Capone took the plan up with his brother, Al. They got Al Capone's okay. Barker set out to put it into execution.

James (Lefty) Lynch, who ruled Coal Teamsters Local 704, was a member of the Teamsters Joint Council. Red Barker approached Lynch openly and honestly. He told him quite simply that Capone expected Lynch to give up partial control of Local 704 and his seat on the joint council. Barker said, "You can keep fifty percent of the dues and assessments from your local. We will double your membership so your income won't suffer. By signing up as many coal-truck drivers as you already have in the local, we will remove from competition that many potential strikebreakers. So the local actually will be stronger. What do you say?"

Lynch expressed himself as outraged at Barker's effrontery.

Barker had made his pitch and been turned down. He shrugged and turned away, washing his hands of the consequences of Lynch's refusal.

Lynch heard nothing more about it until he was at his summer home near Brown's Lake, outside Burlington, Wisconsin. He and his family were just preparing an outdoor barbecue at the close of a warm day in early autumn when a car drove up and parked. Danny Stanton and

Klondike O'Donnell stepped out. In the presence of Lynch's family, O'Donnell told him, "The Big Fellow sends you a message. You just retired from Local 704. From now on you stay away from the union office. You stay away from the joint council. Understand? Now, just so you don't forget. . . ."

Stanton and O'Donnell both drew revolvers. They took careful aim and shot Lefty Lynch through both legs. He fell and his family stood paralyzed with fear.

Stanton and O'Donnell looked down at Lynch, shook their heads as though in astonishment at his stupidity or reluctant admiration for his courage. Then they got in their car. Before they drove away, Stanton said to the Lynch family, "Get him to a doctor. He'll be all right. This time. . . ."

Lynch did not appear at the next meeting of the Chicago Teamsters Joint Council. Every man present knew what had happened to the missing brother.

Just as this meeting was called to order, Red Barker opened the door and entered the room. He asked, "Which was Lefty Lynch's chair?"

Somebody pointed to it. Barker drew it up to the table and relaxed in it.

Then Barker looked around at his fellow members of the joint council. This was the old dues-collecting outfit put together by Con Shea, taken over by Studdy Looney and Jack Sheridan and Mike Galvin. Now it was being taken over by a comparative upstart in the labor movement: Al Capone.

Barker knew that he was seated in the presence of as tough an aggregation of old-fashioned union muscle as could be found in the land. Every one of these men had slugged and clawed and terrorized his way to the top of his individual union. Barker knew that the rest of them permitted his presence only because he was a surrogate of Al Capone.

The men around Barker had risen to the top, as does scum in any boiling pot, because they had been ruthless in eliminating competition within union ranks. They recognized in Capone someone still more ruthless. None wanted to tangle with Capone's army of 600 trigger-happy outlaws. So the meeting was called to order, open for business.

Barker collected the dues and assessments from members of Local 704 of the Coal Teamsters, Chauffeurs, and Helpers Union. He kept the office staff on the payroll. Everything went along with the union office just as though Lefty Lynch had still been in control. The union treasury was turned over to the Capone Syndicate by simply withdrawing by check all but $1,000 from the bank and depositing the check to Capone's account.

Barker's Local 704 delivered fuel to the Loop and downtown district. Every skyscraper, bank, office building, hotel, theater, department store, and shop in the downtown area depended for its deliveries on members of this local. Barker waited for the first cold spell of winter. Then he threatened a strike against coal dealers.

Barker told the dealers that unless they granted his members an immediate pay raise there would not be one lump of coal delivered to the Loop or the downtown district. The dealers had no choice. They granted the drivers the raise demanded by Barker, adding its cost to the price of coal. The real estate owners who paid the higher price passed it along in the form of higher rents to their business tenants.

Barker gave all his drivers higher wages and trebled their dues and assessments. Presumably, everybody was happy.

Al Capone said that every labor union in the land, with its treasury, dues, assessments, and pension funds, is the sole property of the man who can take it and hold it. Capone laughed at the idea of democracy in the control of any union. He said, "The members will always vote for the loudest talker, the guy who promises them the most in the way of more pork chops. You give it to them with one hand and you take it away with the other. As long as their take-home pay is higher this year than it was last year they don't care how much you take from them in the way of dues.

"The union members look at dues the same way they do at taxes: just something you got to pay the thieves who run things."

Capone told Jim Doherty of the Chicago *Tribune* that if any union leader retained his post of leadership more than two years in succession the outsiders could accept as a fact of life that the leader was silencing opposition. Capone commented, "There's always some wiseacre who stands in the wings and criticizes. You've got two choices. You either buy these wiseacres off by giving them jobs on the union payroll at good salaries, or you scare them off. If they don't scare, you take them in the alley. When they get out of the hospital if they still want to squawk you get rid of them."

Since Capone felt that every union was an illegal business—monopolies meant to restrain by force members who wanted to be free agents in selling their services at their own price—he set out to take over the unions. While the chain of command in Capone's labor relations went from Ralph Capone down through Murray Humphreys to Red Barker, it was Barker who usually suggested the unions to be taken over.

Barker was a scholar. He subscribed to every union newspaper and magazine published locally or nationally. He read them avidly. He kept abreast of gossip in the world of trade unions.

Occasionally some union would want to build a new headquarters or in some other way invest surplus funds. The union's management might file a financial statement with a bank in order to get a loan. Barker usually managed to get hold of such financial statements. He kept his eye out for unions with substantial treasuries.

Barker performed the same function for Al Capone in the field of union labor that post-World War II "raiders" performed in the field of upperworld industry. The latter looked for those industries or businesses whose assets far exceeded in value their outstanding stock. Then they bought up enough stock to win control and liquidate the business at a profit. They lined up their sights, as did Barker, by studying balance sheets.

Humphreys was the nominal owner at the time of the sixty-one labor unions in the Capone empire. This was exclusive of the twenty or thirty unions owned by Mike Carrozzo. Ranking almost equally with Red Barker, under Ralph Capone and Humphreys, was Jack White, a veteran of the newspaper circulation wars.

White had been a safecracker. He fancied himself a dynamite expert even after one of his blasts was detonated prematurely and cost him all but the thumb and two fingers of his right hand. Ever after he was known as "Three-Finger Jack."

Barker and White had as their two principal aides in the matter of muscle Danny Stanton and Klondike O'Donnell. Stanton was a survivor of Ragen's Colts, the South Side Irish ethnic gang. O'Donnell was of the West Side family, as distinct from Spike O'Donnell and his brothers of the South Side.

For reasons which will be gone into a little later, Capone wanted to control unions in the entertainment field. The first of these brought into the fold was the union of theater treasurers controlled by William Frain.

This union was an excellent source of income. The treasurers were usually on a year-round payroll, whether the legitimate theater had a play on the boards or not.

Motion picture houses, unlike legitimate theaters, ran all day every day, winter and summer. Most of them had a chief usher, an assistant chief usher, a treasurer, a manager, and an assistant manager. This was all in addition to the two shifts of box office cashiers, and the checkroom attendants. Even the little neighborhood family movie houses often hired a man called a treasurer to check box office receipts.

In the burlesque houses, a big source of entertainment in the twenties, before television, the treasurer employed candy butchers or let this concession out on lease.

Bill Frain had made a good thing of his union of theater treasurers, and had done even better in a group which was part of this union—the ushers. He not only had ushers in every theater, but maintained a large staff of free-lance ushers available on a lease basis for sporting events, political conventions, and outdoor entertainment. He hired high school or college youths, put them in uniform, trained them in "crowd control." And they kicked back part of their wages as union dues.

Bill Frain, owning this gold mine, lived high off the hog. He came to the attention of John (Dingbat) Oberta. That was a mistake for Bill Frain.

Oberta was Polish, a sidekick of Polack Joe Saltis, but when he spoke before an Irish crowd he put an apostrophe in his name and talked with a brogue.

The micks in the crowd thought him fresh from the Emerald Isle.

Oberta had been a partner in the ownership of breweries with Saltis and with the McErlane brothers, Vincent and Frankie. But after Big Tim Murphy was shot to death, Oberta met the love of his life. While saying a rosary for Big Tim at the latter's grave, he caught the eye of the blond widow, Florence Diggs Murphy.

Florence Diggs was not one to mince words. She measured Dingbat Oberta with her shrewd blue eyes and told him across the grave of her late husband that she found him "a fine figure of a man." The Dingbat accompanied her home from the cemetery and did what he could to make the beautiful widow forget her sorrow. They were wed shortly after.

Florence Diggs liked a man given to oratory. There was not a better public speaker in Chicago, despite his lack of formal education, than Big Tim Murphy. Dingbat Oberta had much the same talent. When he was on the platform he had his listeners nodding in all the right places. When he wound up an hour's oration the applause was deafening.

The politicians used his services not only to slug the voters into line on election day but, in advance of elections, to sway the voters as an orator. One South Side Irish politician said of the Dingbat, "Half the time I can't follow his line of reasoning, but the boy certainly can drive the common herd through the garden gate."

Oberta, by the end of the twenties, had a few hundred thousand dollars in the bank. This was par for the course in Chicago bootlegging. But when he married the widow Murphy he thought he ought to go into something more respectable than bootlegging, something at least semirespectable such as owning a few unions or serving in the Illinois State Senate.

Oberta talked for himself at the next election, rather than for whatever politician paid the best for oratory. On election day he and his gang got out the vote for Oberta, instead of some other political hack. Oberta got himself elected Republican committeeman of the Thirteenth Ward and then ran for the state legislature.

The Dingbat had been indicted with Joe Saltis in 1926 for the murder of Mitters John Foley, who had been selling beer in their territory. This fact put no crimp either in Oberta's ambition or success. He was successively elected to the post of alderman in the City Council, and then Senator in the Illinois legislature.

Now Oberta wanted the semirespectability of union ownership.

By applying terror on the theater and special events ushers, as well as on their foremen, Oberta was able to separate this group from the theater treasurers. He took the ushers away from Bill Frain and began collecting their dues. Each gang of ushers was controlled by a foreman, frequently called the chief usher, and it was a simple matter to break a few heads among this group and have the rest collect dues for Oberta. But Oberta still wanted the theater treasurers.

Bill Frain, whose family still owns the ushering concessions at most public events throughout the nation, flatly refused to give up the treasurers' union. Since the American Federation of Labor union charter had been issued to the treasurers rather than the ushers, Oberta had the dues but he never could establish legal ownership of the ushers.

Oberta phoned Bill Frain and gave him an ultimatum.

Frain was to deliver that union charter to Oberta within twenty-four hours, "Or else. . . ." Frain never had to worry about what that "or else" meant. Before the twenty-four-hour deadline had passed, Dingbat Oberta was shot to death on March 5, 1930, and his body thrown in a ditch.

So there will be no mystery at this point, Bill Frain was never thought to have killed Oberta. The killing was just a lucky break for him. As will be told later, the Oberta killing was laid at the door of wild Frankie McErlane.

The widow Oberta, who only two years earlier had been the widow Murphy, was brave as well as beautiful in her double mourning. She laid the Dingbat to rest beside his predecessor, who also had been a state legislator. Oberta had been popular in his South Side territory. At his wake, mourners filed past the bier at the rate of 2,000 an hour for three days and three nights.

Before going on with the story of the theater ushers' union, a few more words ought to be said about Dingbat Oberta's funeral. They concern Father Pat Molloy, who will be remembered as having prayed at the grave of Dion O'Banion back in the fall of 1924.

And they concern Father Pat's boss, the archbishop.

George Cardinal Mundelein, keeper of the keys as archbishop of the Roman Catholic Church in the greater Chicago archdiocese, had no use whatever for hoodlums and gangsters. When drinking his nightly beer in the North Avenue saloon of Alderman Mathias (Paddy) Bauler, Mundelein occasionally expressed himself on the subject of "pimps, panderers, and prostitute-mongers."

Bauler said then and has never missed a chance to say since that while he always had gambling running wide open in his Forty-third Ward, he never took a penny from a girl.

Mundelein's feeling about hoodlums was strong. Early in the twenties he passed the word that they were to be denied extreme unction unless they had visibly reformed and called for a priest before death. He told his auxiliary bishops and all the monsignors that he would make no exceptions.

So far as is known every priest in the archdiocese took him seriously—except one. The Reverend Patrick J. Molloy had gone to the same backlot sandball games as had Dion O'Banion. They had been friends from boyhood. When O'Banion was shot dead, Molloy obeyed the episcopal injunction against a requiem mass and against extreme unction. But he conducted a quiet little service at the funeral home. And then he went to the graveside and publicly led a few prayers for the repose of O'Banion's soul.

Mundelein never by word or gesture indicated that he knew about this, although it was reported in the daily newspapers at the time. That was in 1924.

Now, less than six years later, Dingbat Oberta was dead. And the Dingbat was another of Father Molloy's friends. They had known each other on the South Side for years and had hoisted many a stein together. There was no requiem mass for Dingbat Oberta. But as with Dion O'Banion, the good priest turned up to conduct prayers at the wake and then again to lead the mourners in prayer at the graveside.

This was duly reportd in the daily press.

Cardinal-Archbishop Mundelein, seated at the desk in his great red-brick palazzo across the street from Lincoln Park, read the news stories and said something stronger than "darn." A few days later Father Patrick Molloy was on the train bound east for a ship sailing from New York Harbor. He was being exiled, right out of his native land, as punishment for his behavior and as an example to every other priest in the archdiocese. More of that a little later.

Oberta's demise left Bill Frain in sole ownership of the ushers and theater treasurers. A few days after Oberta's death, Bill Frain got a phone call summoning him to conference in the Capone suite at the

Metropole Hotel. The call told him to be there at 5 o'clock in the morning, and during a Chicago winter that means two or three hours before dawn. The last words Frain heard on the phone were ". . . and be goddamn sure you bring that union charter."

As far as Bill Frain was concerned, the fight was over. Oberta might be successfully defied, but Al Capone was the court of last resort.

Frain later told the story in a few sentences. "When you get that kind of a call, you go. I told them at the hotel desk who I was and who I was there to see. They called somebody and I was escorted upstairs in the elevator. Red Barker met me at the door of the suite.

"He said Ralph Capone was just counting up the night's receipts out at the Cotton Club in Cicero and then would be right in."

Frain said that when Ralph Capone arrived, he asked for the union charter. He read it carefully, to make sure of what he was getting. Then he handed it to Red Barker. Frain went on, "Nobody even said thanks. They never said good-bye. I waited a couple of minutes, then turned around and walked out of the suite. The atmosphere was so cold in that room that when I got out on Michigan Avenue and was hit by that piercing March wind it actually felt warm."

The full potential of the ushers' union had never been exploited until Red Barker took it over. He demanded that every theater, movie house, and auditorium in the city use his ushers. He decreed that all political and sporting events, indoor or outdoor, pay for what he called the "crowd control" that only his trainees could provide.

The motion picture houses successfully resisted the Barker demands by paying him a monthly sum in lieu of the union dues he might otherwise collect from their ushers. They were then employing youths of high school age at 25 cents an hour. They knew that if Barker gave the ushers "union protection" their salaries would be multiplied by five. The young ushers were not even aware that for every 25 cents the theater paid them, another 25 cents was paid Red Barker for their use by the show houses.

The political and sporting impresarios tried to fight Barker but were less successful than the operators of the movie houses in city and suburbs.

Barker paid his older and more responsible ushers $2 for each event at which they worked. They were to be found at the big-league ballgames, the prizefights, the afternoon and evening performances of burlesque and legitimate theaters, the ballet and opera and symphony. Out of this $2 a performance, the ushers paid union dues. These older and more responsible ushers were the family men, the ones who had something to lose. They formed the backbone of Barker's union.

Most of the ushers who worked for them at these events were unpaid.

They were youngsters happy to work free for the privilege of seeing—and being permitted to bring a girl to see—the play, the ballet, the opera, the boxing or wrestling match, the football or baseball game. They paid no union dues and probably had no idea a union even existed.

The impresario responsible for the production of the event had to pay the usher service a straight $5 per man for each "crowd-control expert" supplied by Barker. Once or twice some impresario briefly thought he had no use for Barker's usher service. Barker then had to change the man's mind.

One fight impresario of those days was named Walter George. He put on a boxng show at the huge Coliseum on South Wabash Avenue. He lined up his own group of youngsters, willing to work free of charge for the privilege of bringing their girls to see the fights.

Barker went to George and tried to negotiate the matter but George brushed him off. Barker got a full complement of ushers ready anyway, just in case Walter George at the last minute might change his mind and decide he needed them. Then Barker made his series of phone calls to City Hall, arranging a good deal of trouble for the impresario.

Just before the fights were to get under way, when the house had been sold out and the patrons were in their seats awaiting the first of the preliminary bouts, a fleet of taxicabs pulled up in front and disgorged a dozen official inspectors.

The building inspectors found the place overcrowded and the spectators' weight too much for the balcony structures. The fire inspectors found everybody in the place holding a lighted cigar or cigarette and declared it the worst firetrap in the city's history. The health inspectors found the hot dogs and popcorn were being sold under most unsanitary conditions and that the whole shebang might have to be put under quarantine.

Walter George did not even wait for the reports from the electrical inspectors, the plumbing inspectors, and the sanitary inspectors, who were about to seal shut the toilets and water fountains. George had seen that Red Barker arrived with the inspectors and listened carefully as they announced their findings. The fight announcer had been told to stall until the inspectors finished their work. He was perspiring, but talking gamely to an audience growing ever more impatient. Impresario Walter George now walked over to Red Barker and asked, "How much?"

Barker said, "The price has gone up. For tonight, twenty bucks a head for every usher I brought with me. And twenty bucks a head for these inspectors who had to leave their dinners to get over here."

George looked around and saw dozens of Barker's ushers, in their neat blue uniforms and white cotton gloves, ready upon signal to go into their routine of crowd control. He knew he might not profit a penny from the night's sellout crowd but he probably felt he was lucky to be getting away with his life. He told his cashier to count out to Barker the sum demanded. The inspectors were paid off, tore up their report sheets, and went about their business.

George said later that some of them even stayed to see the fights, which began just forty minutes late.

Red Barker, as noted, got his start in life as a bookkeeper. He studied and analyzed financial reports for pleasure as well as business. From this no one would be justified in drawing the conclusion that Barker was a bookish sort given to wearing thick-lensed eyeglasses and trembling in the presence of firearms. It was Red Barker who took over Local 704 of the Coal Teamsters after the shooting of James (Lefty) Lynch, its business agent.

There were variations, but the pattern of union takeover by the Capone forces generally followed certain lines. The leader of the union would be invited to Capone's office for a talk. Some came without coercion. At that time Capone was a more powerful man in northern Illinois and northern Indiana than any mayor or governor. An invitation was a command.

The union leader would be given an appointment at a specific hour. Capone would make the union leader as comfortable as possible, with drinks and cigars. Then Capone would discuss amicably with the union man the role which Capone envisioned for that particular union in his growing empire. He would offer to come in as the union leader's partner.

Capone would explain that he intended with his available muscle to double the union's membership and thus its dues collections. He assured the union leader that his income need not suffer at all. Capone specified in particular that he did not want to run the leader out of the union. Capone always had a shortage of manpower. He preferred that the current leader remain with the union and simply give Capone half the take.

This meant a fifty-fifty split on dues and assessments, and Capone was to have full control of the union treasury.

Some union managers, recognizing reality, agreed to this proposition. Capone put his own bookkeepers into the union office to make sure he got a square shake. Beyond that, so far as is known, he kept his word. The union leader continued with an excellent income, shaking down his members for whatever he could get, and Capone ruled the union.

Those who played fair with Capone lived out their years in peace. Capone's thugs kept the union members in line, saw to it that employers kept the members at work so they could be milked of dues, kept up their payoffs to police and politicians so such unions were not bothered.

Those who did not play fair with Capone did not live long. When one of them died, Capone or one of his aides would explain to police or newspapermen that the union leader tried "to get cute."

This meant he had sought to doctor the union books so he could hold out on Capone some of the dues and assessment money he was collecting.

Some union leaders did not take Capone in as a partner. Some frankly told him they had been so long in power that they wanted no further trouble. They had made their fortunes in the labor movement and were content to retire with their families to raise oranges in Florida or California. In such cases, Capone put one of his own men in charge.

Some flatly refused to give up the unions they ruled. They had lied and cheated, fought and clawed, slugged it out with employers and with rival union leaders to get and hold their places of power. They heard Capone's proposition and told him, "Stick it!"

These men would shortly thereafter get the heat. Phone calls would come every thirty minutes, day and night, each with a threatening voice. The union leader would be told what might happen to his wife, his children, his grandchildren. Maybe a car would even stop by the school attended by his grandchildren and they would be given a little note to carry home to Grandpa. The threat to the child was implicit.

Usually these tactics worked. When they did not, after a few weeks, a dynamite bomb would be touched off under the union owner's front porch. The time of such a bombing was important. At 2 o'clock in the morning, after everyone in the house had retired, there was little danger anyone would be hurt.

But when the front porch was demolished by a single stick of dynamite, the union leader got the message.

When all else failed, the union leader, who usually called himself the president or the business agent or the walking delegate, would be taken out of the game.

As early as the mid-twenties, Capone and his aides began to turn from total dependence on such illegal enterprises as bootlegging, bookmaking, and prostitution to the ownership of labor unions. The gangsters realized that union leaders were considered at least semirespectable by people in the upperworld. They felt that sooner or later Prohibition would be repealed and they would need other sources of income than those to be found in illegal alcohol and beer.

Capone sponsored diplomatic moves to end the gang wars in Chicago. Those gang wars had begun at the end of 1924, with the death of Mike

Merlo, and by the summer of 1926, Capone had sponsored the first all-Chicago gang peace conference. Less than three years later he sponsored the first nationwide all-America gang peace conference in Atlantic City.

Both these conferences accentuated the positive. Capone did not so much urge his underworld colleagues to lay down their arms and live at peace with their neighbors. Rather he asked them to agree on equitable divisions of territories, on the manufacture and import of products, on sales pricing and distribution, on regulation of the industry.

Since their industry was illegal, the government could not be called upon to regulate it. Capone told his colleagues they would have to police it themselves.

They would not be pacifists. They would kill any who made an agreement and then broke it. But they would try to reach agreement by peaceful means, rather than by killing each other in the streets.

None of the men who had risen to the top of the various ethnic gangs in Chicago, or of the various city crime syndicates in America, was stupid. All could see the wisdom of Capone's proposals. These were first steps toward the conglomerate of organized crime to be found in the United States today. They were the first steps toward Syndicate corruption reaching into the highest echelons of federal government.

In those years of the late twenties, Capone proved himself much more than the simple strong-arm thug Torrio had brought out from Brooklyn. Wealth and power changed him. He grew with it. Like any of the titans of nineteenth-century America, Capone the uneducated showed himself able to rule his new empire with imagination and resource. He planned for the future.

Capone gave interviews to such newspapermen as sought him out. Jim Doherty of the *Tribune*, Harry Read of the *American*, Clem Lane of the *Daily News* interviewed Capone at length. He discussed his plans with as much clarity as did Adolf Hitler writing at exactly the same time in his book *Mein Kampf*.

Capone said that when repeal came the underworld barons were going to be in a position to become upperworld barons in the same fields: the manufacture, distribution, importation, and sale of beer, wine, and alcoholic beverages. He said he wanted control of certain unions which would be important in his scheme for the future.

These plans were not secret. They were published. The police leaders in Chicago who were charged with keeping track of organized crime—the honest policemen, not those on the Syndicate payroll—were conversant with Capone's plans. They knew who was responsible and why, when some union leader was killed. They were usually helpless to prove, in a court of law, what they knew through their own intelligence.

Capone felt that when Prohibition ended the men who wanted to control all liquor traffic would have to control the teamsters. These truckdrivers moved the stuff from one place to another. They would have to control the bartenders. These were the men who could influence drinkers as to the brands they would call for. They had to control all the unions in places where liquor was sold.

The principal places where liquor would be sold after repeal were hotels, saloons, and cabarets. This meant that the men who controlled the liquor traffic would want to form or control unions of waiters and waitresses, cooks and bakers, the musicians and performers in nightclubs. Capone consciously aimed to take over unions in the entertainment fields.

Capone recommended the legalization of prostitution. Until the advent of Mayor Dever in 1923, with his program of reform, the city had a red-light district. Capone told reporters in interviews, "Reform did not end prostitution. All it did was decentralize it. Now the girls no longer are inspected once a week by health department doctors. Now they are not concentrated down on the Levee. Instead, they are living in the swank apartment houses, associating with the wives and daughters of the best people in town. They simply went underground."

Parenthetically, the coming of A Century of Progress proved Capone right. For two years the city had an influx of millions of tourists each week in summer. The city fathers did not want to legalize prostitution, but neither did they want epidemics of venereal disease. So they compelled every prostitute to register as a "masseuse" and to be examined weekly for "skin disease." Neon lights advertised MASSAGE PARLOR all over town.

In this period Capone met in their offices such men as Colonel Robert R. McCormick, editor and publisher of the Tribune; and Merrill C. (Babe) Meigs, publisher of the Hearst papers. A decade earlier it would have been inconceivable for either of these men of the upperworld to have shaken hands with the chief pimp of the Four Deuces.

Through this period Capone's every move was under the surveillance of Chicago police and of agents of the federal alcohol tax unit. These were underlings. Their bosses may have been paid off, but they still did their jobs and turned in their reports. Those reports are on file today. They tell who Capone saw in his daily business.

The Chicago gangsters most frequently in his company, besides those earlier named in this chapter, were Paul Ricca, Tony Accardo, Joseph C. Fusco, Edward (Dutch) Vogel, Frank Nitti, Frankie Rio, and the Fischetti brothers.

The politicians who visited him daily, apparently to get his orders every morning, included Daniel A. Serritella, Albert J. Prignano, and William V. Pacelli. These were at the time the majority floor leaders respectively in the Illinois State Senate, the Illinois House of Representatives, and the City Council of Chicago.

Apparently Capone was in daily telephone contact with most of his representatives on the East Coast, the Gulf Coast, and along the Canadian border. He is known to have been in constant contact by phone with the leaders of other underworld syndicates in New England, New York City, and down the Atlantic Coast to Florida.

The men from west of Chicago who were his most frequent visitors in these days were two from Kansas City, Joe Di Giovanni and Tony Gizzo, and two from Los Angeles, Jack Dragna and John Roselli.

Capone had a local and state legislative program to equal that of any entrepreneur of the upperworld. He dominated the Chicago City Council and the Illinois State Legislature and kept track of the progress of all federal laws in which he was interested. His interests were so wide that almost any prospective legislation could have some effect on some of his business somewhere.

Capone had an economic program quite aside from the takeover of unions. He wanted a monopoly on the soda water and ginger ale used in mixed drinks. His brother, Ralph Capone, to this day is known to his friends as "Bottles," because of the soft drink bottling plants he owned. Capone wanted a monopoly on the linens, soaps, detergents, and deodorants used in cabarets, hotels, and bars.

Sometimes he bought his way into companies handling such products, sometimes he muscled his way in, sometimes he set up his own companies and froze the older companies out of business. That could be done with terror, compelling users to buy only Capone products.

Capone wanted a monopoly on the uniform business. He knew that every chef, every waiter and waitress, every bartender and usher, every doorman and headwaiter wears some kind of uniform or apron to work. He wanted to control the sale of such garments. Failing that, he wanted control of the laundries and dry-cleaning plants which kept such uniforms clean and serviceable.

Frank Nitti was once to say on the witness stand that Al Capone hoped to see the day when "We would make a profit on every olive in every martini served in America." Meanwhile, Capone pushed his own brand name liquors and beers to the exclusion of all others on sale in Chicago and its environs. His beer was called Manhattan, and all hard liquor was sold under the brand name, Fort Dearborn Products.

Now it is time to talk about Father Pat among the headhunters.

8   A priest gets too friendly

Just as Robin Hood and his merry men of Nottinghamshire had their jovial Friar Tuck, so Al Capone and Dion O'Banion and Dingbat Oberta of Chicago had their happy companion in the person of the man universally called Father Pat. By the time of his death in 1970, he was honored by his church with the title of Monsignor, but it was as Father Pat that the Reverend Patrick J. Molloy was known to two generations of Chicagoans.

Born on St. Patrick's Day on Emerald Avenue in the community within Chicago known as Bridgeport, Pat Molloy was a boyhood neighbor and friend of Richard J. Daley, later to become Chicago's mayor. They grew up together. They played ball together with the Hamburg Social and Athletic Club. They remained lifelong friends, one going into the priesthood and the other into the secular political arena.

So far as anybody ever reported, Father Molloy never did a mean thing in his life. He was a happy and healthy Irish boy at the turn of the century, beloved by all. If he had a fault, said his neighbors, it was that he was a bit studious for their taste. But when he remained an acolyte through his high school days at Nativity parish, the friends of his childhood saw that he was headed for a life in the Church. In such a case, they said, being studious ought to be a fine thing.

Pat Molloy sailed through his early schooling, then attended Sacred Heart College and St. Bernard's Seminary in Rochester, New York. He accepted Holy Orders in 1917 at the hands of Archbishop Mundelein in Chicago's Holy Name Cathedral. All of his old neighbors and friends came to congratulate him on the occasion of his first mass.

Father Pat called each by name and had a good word for everyone, reminiscing about some childhood mischief in which he had indulged. His eye had the same old twinkle. His voice had the same Irish lilt.

Neighbors looked at each other and smiled in a pleased and proud way as Father Pat compared his rich new parish at Lawrence and Kenmore avenues—St. Thomas of Canterbury—with the old corner at Thirty-seventh Street and Emerald Avenue. As his friends started homeward that day in June, with America freshly gone to war, they told each other that Father Pat, fine man and handsome priest that he was, still had a lot of the Old Nick.

Molloy's first post was as curate at St. Thomas. He stayed there until 1926. It was from St. Thomas that he went to say a few prayers for the soul of Dion O'Banion. Molloy's faith had taught him that only God knows what repentance a sinner might feel in that final momentary flash when death has come. The archbishop might like it or not, but Pat Molloy was not one to pretend friendship for a man in life and desert him when his soul most needs a friend. Not Father Pat.

For Father Pat Molloy was Dion O'Banion's friend. He was the friend of every man with whom he brushed shoulders, and he never went to a big-league game or a big-time prizefight without seeing every gangster in town. Gangsters, like politicians, never missed a sporting event at which they might see and be seen.

Those were not the only places Molloy saw the gangsters.

He liked a glass of beer as well as the next man, and while he never took a drink in public, he was not averse to a cocktail and a steak at some such place as Barney's Market restaurant on Randolph at Halsted Street.

Through the earliest years of Prohibition there was probably no man in the city, policeman or politician or priest, who had a better idea of what was going on in the underworld than did Pat Molloy. Men knew that he never violated a confidence, whether given in the confessional or in a casual meeting on the street. They brought him their troubles. He was called "Friend of the Friendless." The hoodlums, outlaws, safecrackers, and killers tipped their hats when they saw him and addressed him with respect. He never turned his back on one of them. When they parted company, Father Pat always said, "When was the last time you came to Sunday mass? Tonight I'm going to say a little prayer for you and I hope I'll see you in church next Sunday. Think about it, boy."

There was nothing wishy-washy about him. Pat Molloy had an Irish temper never far from the surface and there are stories of the times he felt it necessary to castigate or speak a word of reproof to someone who got out of line. Occasionally it was a policeman.

But usually Father Pat handled things in a light-humored way.

Some official high in the police department, knowing how Father Pat walked fearlessly through all neighborhoods of the city at any hour of the day or night when he felt needed, once gave him a revolver. He urged the priest to carry it on his missions of mercy.

Molloy may or may not have ever carried the revolver again, but he had it in his pocket that night when he came home to the parish house.

The hour was close to 3 A.M., and Father Pat, hurrying along the deserted street, saw a man at work on the newly sodded lawn before the church property. The priest halted to see what was going on. A brawny black man, with a dumptruck parked at the curb, was bent over stacking squares of fresh green sod to be hauled away. Molloy drew the revolver from his pocket, held it against the black man's neck, and said, "Now let's put it all back in place, just as it was."

The man looked around, saw the pistol and the priest who had seemingly appeared from out of nowhere, and fainted dead away. Father Pat got a garden hose and turned a stream on the fallen man to revive him. The thief started up and saw the revolver still pointed right between his eyes. Father Pat sat on the concrete siding until dawn, watching the man put the sod back in place and tamp it down with a sprinkling. Then Father Pat gave the man his blessing and watched him drive away.

From St. Thomas, in that fine rich neighborhood, Father Pat was posted to St. James church, down at Twenty-ninth Street and Wabash Avenue. This was not long after O'Banion's burial and Father Pat might have guessed at his superiors' displeasure. St. James was in the Black Belt.

Two years there and his superiors may have felt Father Pat had learned his lesson.

They sent him for two years to St. Brendan's, out at Sixty-seventh Street and Racine Avenue and then just as the year 1930 began, Father Pat was given his first pastorate.

Hitherto he had been a curate or an assistant. Now, less than thirteen years after ordination, he was put in charge of his own shop. He was given Annunciation parish, 1650 North Paulina Street, in a good, solid, homeowning neighborhood where most of the residents were Polish. Molloy was felt to be mature. He was being given a chance to show what he could do.

All these years, Molloy had been active in civic affairs. The friends of his childhood were succeeding in politics, as he was succeeding in the priesthood, and he was chaplain of every important public endeavor in sight. He had been chaplain immediately after World War I of the 202d Coast Artillery of the Illinois National Guard. A priest is also a politician, and advancement in his chosen profession is not hurt by public exposure in good causes. He is seldom hurt by having his name in the papers connected with affairs that reflect favorably upon his faith and Church.

But that coin has two sides. Father Pat Molloy had only been pastor of Annunciation parish for a couple of months when Dingbat Oberta got himself shot to death on March 5, 1930. And Father Pat blew his career.

He had been Oberta's friend in life and he showed up at the funeral home and graveside ceremony to do whatever a priest might do to help Oberta's immortal soul on its way. As far as Archbishop Mundelein was concerned, Father Pat Molloy was finished.

The priest was told he had a few days to put his affairs in order.

Then, on April 17, 1930, Father Molloy was escorted by some of his fellow clerics and put aboard the Commodore, a crack train bound for New York. There was a brief tearful and embarrassed scene as good-byes were said. Father Pat was handed a ticket for the Argentine aboard the SS *Pan America* of the Munson Line. He was given the name of the archbishop to whom he was to report in Buenos Aires and was told, "You can do whatever you want but don't ever come back to Chicago." The good priest was sent into exile.

An announcement out of the Chancery office on Cass Avenue (now North Wabash Avenue) was brief:

> For a long time Father Molloy had been under doctors' care but he declined to lay down his duties. The duration of his absence is still indefinite, but Father Molloy expressed the hope that he will return to Chicago in time to arrange the annual football game at Soldier Field, through which funds are raised for the Sisters of Mercy.

The announcement did not indicate what year, when it spoke of the annual football game. Father Pat's friends, who knew him to be healthy as a horse, were shocked by the announcement. Gradually the word got around among the knowing politicians and the underworld. Other priests in Chicago suddenly straightened up and marched in close-order drill. None had hitherto doubted the authority of Archbishop Mundelein. From now on, when the cardinal raised an eyebrow every priest in sight began to tremble.

For Father Pat had been the most popular priest in the city. His attendance at every sporting event of the day was always cause for an announcement from the ring or the press box. His sponsorship of dances, picnics, and boat trips for young people of whatever parish he happened to be working in always got good notices. Every reporter in town, every radio announcer went out of his way to help any project being pushed by Father Pat.

When he left St. Thomas, up in the Edgewater neighborhood more than 800 of the most prominent men and women in Chicago's Roman Catholic community turned out for a testimonial and farewell banquet in his honor at the Edgewater Beach Hotel.

The speakers included Patrick J. (Paddy) Carr, the Cook County treasurer and at the time one of the most powerful men in the

Democratic Party in Illinois; Robert M. Schweitzer, the county clerk who later refused to turn over to his successor a "vest-pocket fund" of several million dollars; and Judges Bernard P. Barasa, Joseph McCarthy, and Herbert Immenhausen. Those names do not mean much to today's readers, but in their time—in the mid-twenties—they were as well known to the people of the Middle West as was Al Smith to the people of New York City.

Molloy, tall, slender, and handsome, rose from the banquet table at midnight and halted the festivities. It was apparent that every man in the great dining hall wanted a chance to express his regard publicly for the thirty-four- year-old priest. That testimonial was held on April 26, 1926.

Now only four years later, Molloy was on the high seas bound for oblivion. Father Pat's friends rallied to his defense. He had friends in the highest places in the land, as well as in the underworld. The men who undertook to plead his case were of the stature that constantly met and talked with Cardinal Mundelein, prince of the Church and archbishop of the wealthiest archdiocese in the world.

But Father Pat's friends found, whenever they brought up Molloy's name, that the sterner side of the genial archbishop came to the fore. He turned into a man of stone. Father Pat's friends learned not to press Mundelein.

So far as the outside world was concerned, Father Pat was still pastor of Annunciation parish. His work was being carried on during his "temporary" absence by an acting pastor with half a dozen assistants.

Father Pat reported to his archbishop in Argentina. He was told that he had no special duties, his salary as a priest would continue, he could do just about as he wanted with his time and energy. Except for one thing: He could not go back to the United States.

He was to report occasionally to the Argentine chancellory, draw his salary checks, and write the monthly reports as required of every priest. Those were his sole secular duties. He still had his personal duties as a priest, that of saying mass daily and other such obligations, and was not prohibited from giving the sacraments of the Church. He simply was given no responsibilities. He had no job. He was not wanted.

A lesser man than Father Pat might have gone mad in such a situation. He survived and lived to tell of his adventures and travels to some of the most inaccessible spots on earth.

Molloy explored the Upper Amazon, journeyed among the headhunters, learned to make the poison of curare with which darts are tipped to be dispatched from a blowgun. In the far reaches of Mato Grosso in Brazil, an area in which few priests had ever been known to travel, he found a painting of the Crucifixion by Velasquez. The work had been an heirloom in the family of an old resident. The heirs had no idea of its value. Father Pat bought it, and when he returned to Chicago it hung in his bedroom.

Molloy crossed the Equator twelve times during his exile. He had trophies from the hunt and from fishing to attest his prowess in every sport. He brought back a hammered copper urn which had been given him by German Busch, later president of Bolivia.

He loved to walk, and collected walking sticks—thirty or more of them—and every one had a tale. One he had found on Robinson Crusoe Island, 500 miles off the coast of Chile, at which a ship stops only once a year. Another was an ebony cane from French Indochina, with a grinning face of Mephisto inlaid in ivory. There was another cane of ebony inlaid with ivory, topped off with the carved head of an elephant. This one Father Pat had brought from Colombo, Ceylon.

He had bamboo canes from Madagascar and the East Indies, a teakwood cane from Zanzibar, a bamboo cane which was the gift of a Zulu plantation owner and which was loaded with lead to a six-pound weight. This one had a head of iron, to be used on unruly slaves in the back country.

Molloy attended the Eucharistic Congress in Buenos Aires in 1934, as he had attended this international Roman Catholic convention in Chicago in 1926. He remained the friendly Irishman, attracting all who met him, willing to work twice as hard as anyone else in any cause that interested him.

The various American consuls with whom he came in contact brought him to the attention of the Department of State. Molloy was used by the department in what was then called social work—now called intelligence—up and down the South American continent.

Back home his friends never quit trying. The most influential of them was Bishop William David O'Brien, for whom Dion O'Banion had served as altar boy at Holy Name Cathedral. O'Brien, ordained in 1903, served as an auxiliary bishop to Cardinal Mundelein. O'Brien interceded with Mundelein before Molloy's exile, when Mundelein wanted to punish the priest even more severely.

Years later, when O'Brien felt that Mundelein had cooled off sufficiently, he interceded for Molloy. Molloy was permitted to return to Chicago.

The errant priest, after his six years of exile, was graying and bent, but had as much energy as ever. He plunged into the work of remodeling and redecorating, at a cost of $80,000, the entire church plant at Paulina Street and Wabansia Avenue.

Six years after his return, on June 2, 1942, Father Pat was given another testimonial dinner at the Edgewater Beach. This was on the occasion of the twenty-fifth anniversary of his ordination.

John F. Cuneo, leader of the Italian Catholic community in Chicago, was general chairman of the event. Others on the committee sounded like a who's who of politics in the Middle West: State Senator Charles Bidwill and George Kiefer, Judges Matthew Hartigan and John Sbarbara (of Sbarbara funeral home fame), Police Captain John Prendergast.

Cuneo is possibly the most powerful lay member of the Roman Catholic Church in the United States, not excluding the Kennedy clan. When Pope Paul VI meets anyone from Chicago, he recalls with delight his stay at Cuneo's palatial estate in Libertyville, a northern suburb of Chicago.

When Father Pat had completed the work at Annunciation—and after Cardinal-Archbishop Mundelein had died in 1939—Molloy was sent as pastor to St. Leo's parish on the South Side. This parish, at 7747 South Emerald Avenue, was said to be one of the largest in the country.

Molloy had been sent there by Cardinal-Archbishop Samuel Stritch. He immediately started a building program, which was a test of his ability to raise money. On a strict pay-as-you-go basis, never saddling a penny of debt on the 5,000 Catholic families in the parish, Molloy added $3,000,000 worth of improvements to the church plant.

The school was modernized, the high school got a new faculty building, the high school chapel was renovated, a rectory and a convent were built, ground was acquired with which to add play lots for the 1,500 schoolchildren and parking facilities for churchgoers.

Cuneo and Father Pat's other Italian friends have always had a direct line to the Vatican, outside the usual Church channels of the Chancery office. Molloy had proved himself. On August 12, 1957, he was named a monsignor by Pope Pius XII. This is not a clerical but a secular title, which made Molloy a knight of the papal court. The title is given in the United States, say the gossips, either for unusual piety or for unusual talent in the raising of money.

Molloy had made a great comeback for a man six years in exile.

Nearly a decade later, Father Pat retired. His Christmas greeting mailed in 1966 had enclosed with it a business card which bore the legend: "Monsignor Patrick J. Molloy. No phone. No business. No address. No worries."

Every Thursday until the time of his death, Father Pat came to the Loop in the morning, spent a few minutes in the City Hall office of Mayor Daley, and then joined the mayor and a few friends at lunch in the dining room at the Bismarck Hotel. In June 1967, Father Pat celebrated his fiftieth year in the priesthood. This time Mayor Daley was chairman of the banquet in the Conrad Hilton Hotel. Co-chairmen were Matthew J. Danaher, Cook County clerk; and Monsignor Lawrence Lynch, who had succeeded Molloy as pastor at St. Leo's.

Father Pat had seen a good deal of life in his seventy-eight years.

One of the men he sought to befriend in the twenties, a man who died a natural death of pneumonia during Father Pat's years of exile, was a laughing Irishman of the Dion O'Banion type named Frankie McErlane. Frankie, for all his laughing, was too rough even for Father Pat.

Sometime past midnight on Saturday, December 1, 1923, Morrie Keane was driving a truckload of beer from Joliet to the South Side of Chicago. On the seat in the cab beside him was William Egan. And behind them, with another truckload of beer, came Martin Brandl. In those days the best of highways were much like back-country roads today and the huge beer trucks by agreement with the state police usually kept off the traveled highways and took to the dirt roads.

The night was wet and cold, a miserable night for this sort of driving, but the men were to get $3.00 a barrel just for driving the trucks. There were seventy-five barrels on the two trucks, adding up to $225. They figured this to be a soft touch.

Shortly after they had passed Lemont, on the Sag Road, two open touring cars came abreast of the two-truck caravan and curbed the lead truckdriver with a burst from a shotgun "across the bow." Both trucks halted. Keane and Egan were dragged from their truck, tied hand and foot, and shoved into the tonneau of one of the touring cars. Brandl was never heard of again.

Two of the men from the touring cars got into the beer trucks to continue driving them to Chicago, but to a destination differing from that toward which they had started. Beer at the time was worth $50 a barrel on the wholesale market, so the haul was valued by the hijackers at something better than $3,500.

Egan was frightened but alert, and he remembered all that happened. His story of his adventures became part of the police record and a cause for wonderment among all who heard it.

Two of the hijackers got into the front seat of the car in which Egan and Keane had been dumped. The car moved down the road to halt near the other truck and touring car. The two stickup men stepped out. Neither Egan nor Keane could see what was happening, but they heard a burst of gunfire. Then the two men returned to their car, climbed into the front seat in a leisurely manner, and drove toward Chicago.

The $3,500 hijacking haul obviously would be split among fewer thieves than the number who had started out after the beer trucks. Egan and Keane could whisper to one another and now their fright took on a new dimension. They were in the hands of killers and they had been witnesses—or at least auditors—to murder. Egan told the story.

"Pretty soon the driver asks the guy with the shotgun, 'When are you going to get rid of these guys?' The fat fellow laughs and says, 'I'll take care of that in a minute.'

"He was monkeying with his shotgun all this time. Pretty soon he turns around and points the gun at Keane. He didn't say a word. He just let go, straight at him. Keane got it square in the left side. It kind of turned him over. Then the fat fellow give him the other barrel in the other side.

"The guy breaks the gun open, ejects the shells out of the car, loads up and gives it to Keane again. Then he turns toward me and says, 'I guess you might as well get yours, too,' With that, he shoots me in the side.

"It hurts like hell so when I seen him loading up again I twist around so it won't hit me twice in the same place.

"This time he got me in the leg. Then he gives me the other barrel, right in the puss.

"I slide off the seat. But I guess the fat guy wasn't sure we was through. He let Morrie have it twice more, and then he let me have it again in the other side."

Egan retained consciousness throughout this shooting. He said his face was numb and his eyes were closed but his hearing and other perceptions unimpaired. The fat man scrambled across the back of the front seat while the car was still in motion and took hold of the fallen Keane. Egan's story goes on: "He opens the door and kicks Morrie out into the road. We was doing about fifty miles an hour by the sound. I figure I'm next, so when he drags me over to the door I set myself to jump. He shoves and I light in the ditch by the road."

Billy Egan became one of the world's few survivors of the one-way ride.

And that was Billy Egan's first acquaintance with Frankie McErlane, the laughing Irishman who could train a shotgun point-blank on a man bound and helpless and without saying a word, "let go, straight at him."

Egan later had a chance to identify Frankie McErlane as "the fat guy." He refused to do so. Nor would he identify Willie Channell as the driver of the death car. But Channell was identified by a garage attendant. He worked on McErlane's car after Channell, a paroled killer, brought it in at dawn full of bullet pocks and bloodstains.

The garage attendant identified Frankie McErlane as the man who sat beside Channell when the latter brought the car into the garage.

After being locked up for weeks as a material witness, the garageman gradually realized that in Chicago the witnesses are held while the killers go free on bail. With that realization, the garageman got smart. He developed amnesia, could remember nothing of events on that early December day, and was let out of jail so he could be in the bosom of his family in time for Christmas. Nothing was ever done about Frankie McErlane or Willie Channell in this case.

Egan lived on, despite the shotgun slugs that tore away the right side of his face and the others that had lodged in his body and leg. He considered himself lucky by comparison with his companions of that fatal night.

Frankie McErlane, as promising a killer as ever graduated from the ranks of circulation slugger for Chicago newspapers, lived with his mother at 6941 Anthony Avenue on the city's Far South Side. Occasionally he would shack up with some waitress or other, but mostly he stayed at mother's side. Mother saw to it that on most Sundays, he got up for mass, no matter how hung over he might be. He always carried a rosary. Possibly that was why Father Pat Molloy thought there might be hope for him.

When sober, Frankie McErlane could be as charming as any rogue. When he drank, his light blue eyes were said to turn glassy. And when McErlane's blue eyes took on that certain glaze, those who knew him best left their drinks half-finished and got out of the bar in a hurry.

That glaze, said McErlane's drinking companions, meant certain death for somebody.

His police record shows that by 1911 Frankie McErlane was an auto thief who twice had bought his way out of the Bridewell, and who had served a term for armed robbery in Pontiac Reformatory. Then he had occasion to kill a policeman in the presence of a seventeen-year-old girl, who became the state's chief witness. McErlane got out on bail, the girl was slugged and left for dead in the street and McErlane got drunk. But the girl recovered and lived to testify against him.

Frankie McErlane was sent to Joliet State Prison and participated in a sensational break with Earl Dear, Lloyd Bopp, and Big Joe Moran. McErlane was captured out West and returned to prison.

Then came the do-gooders, the social workers and psychologists. They talked to Frankie McErlane, watched him fingering his rosary, were charmed by his really delightful smile, felt sure that he had seen the light and been rehabilitated.

The do-gooders won for McErlane a parole from Joliet prison in October, 1921. The laughing Irishman emerged to a world where Prohibition was the order of the day and a slugger could find a ready market for his talents.

McErlane allied himself at once with three other veterans of the newspaper circulation wars, Ralph Sheldon, Walter Stevens, and Polack Joe Saltis. In a smaller way, they shared Johnny Torrio's vision of the opportunities opened with Prohibition. But this quartet did not want to own breweries when it was so easy to hijack somebody else's trucks loaded with beer.

By the time Billy Egan survived his one-way ride, Frankie McErlane was an expert at the art of hijacking.

A few months after Billy Egan was shot, McErlane and some of his boys got a little drunk in a roadhouse outside of Crown Point, Indiana, with the predictable result. Thad Fancher, a lawyer in the town, was shot dead. The Chicago boys staggered to their car and had driven across the state line into Chicago by the time they were caught.

Frank Cochrane, a native of Crown Point, was a willing witness.

McErlane fought extradition from Illinois to Indiana. At one of his extradition hearings he was brought from jail in a state of roaring drunkenness, and his county jail guard was just as drunk. The judge was not on the McErlane payroll and he ordered an investigation. The inquiry developed the fact that McErlane had been drunk most of the time during his stay in the Cook County jail. On one of his sprees, he clubbed a fellow prisoner so badly that the man was sent to the jail hospital.

McErlane got out on bail. Frank Cochrane was killed in Crown Point—clubbed to death—and the word was passed to all who had been in that Indiana roadhouse on the night Thad Fancher was fatally shot. Then McErlane turned up in Chicago again and said he would quit fighting extradition.

The authorities brought Frankie McErlane to trial in Crown Point, but it was a farce. All the witnesses were either dead or too frightened to talk. They were put under oath but could scarcely remember their names.

Frankie McErlane's infectious booming laughter was heard right there in the courtroom. The jury found him not guilty.

That Frankie McErlane. A great sense of humor.

Wherever he went in the next few years he left a trail of broken heads and stiffening corpses. Then, in 1929, love came to Frankie McErlane. He began to play house with a shoplifter named Elfreda Rigus, who liked to be known as Marion Miller. Since Frankie was a man of violence, their love play was something less than tender. In one of their amorous games the following January, Frankie was shot in the right leg and taken to German Deaconess Hospital.

McErlane had left in his wake an enemy or two for every corpse. Word of his incapacitation in the hospital got around and somebody decided to take advantage of the fact. On the night of February 25, 1930, as Frankie McErlane lay in the hospital bed with his wounded leg in traction hoisted high above his head, the door to his room opened to admit visitors. McErlane turned his head in time to see two men in the doorway drawing weapons.

McErlane reached under the pillow to get his own revolver and the hospital quiet was broken with the roaring of guns. The visitors fled, one of them dropping an automatic pistol in his haste. Frankie McErlane had been wounded in chest, groin, and left wrist. He told police, "I won't identify nobody for you. McErlane takes care of himself. Remember that, next time you find some rat in a ditch."

A few weeks later the inquest was held over the bodies of Sam Malega and John (Dingbat) Oberta, whose bodies, torn by bullets, had been found in a ditch. A hardware dealer called as a witness identified the pistol dropped in McErlane's hospital room as one that had been sold to Malega.

Then the horror that walked in McErlane's shadow began to tread on his heels. On the night of June 6, 1931, police were called to South Shore Drive, where Frankie McErlane stood on a corner blazing away with a shotgun. A second shotgun lay at his feet. The street was empty and there was no indication that anyone else had been present. "They tried to get me," muttered Frankie McErlane.

Four months later McErlane's sedan was found parked in front of 8129 Phillips Avenue, on the Far South Side. In its back seat lay the body of his amorous friend Elfreda Rigus. She had been hit by four bullets. At her feet, the trademark of the crazed killer, lay the bodies of her two dogs. Both had been shot to death. In the car as well were bags packed with Elfreda's and Frankie's clothing, as though they had been planning a trip.

A few blocks away, in the McErlane bungalow at 7753 Bennett Avenue, police found all the signs of a drunken party. A neighbor said that Frankie and Elfreda had been in the best of cheery spirits the previous evening when they announced they were going on a honeymoon jaunt.

But Frankie McErlane could not be found.

McErlane had to scurry a bit to raise enough money to put in the fix on this case. Ten weeks later, when certain everything had been taken care of, he surrendered. He was all innocence and had only just learned he was being sought. On December 30, 1931, Frankie McErlane walked out of court a free man. The state had chosen not to prosecute for want of sufficient evidence. McErlane laughed.

And on October 8, 1932, a year to the day after the fatal shooting of Elfreda Rigus and her two dogs, Frankie McErlane died of pneumonia in a hospital downstate in Beardstown, Illinois. His death was anything but peaceful. It required four strong men to hold his threshing body as, in his final delirium, Frankie McErlane sought to fight the phantoms which stalked his straying mind.

The do-gooders had their way. Frankie McErlane was finally free.

9 Caesar deals with the ambitious

The Plantation was a Prohibition era gambling casino housed in a white frame and red brick structure that might have served as the model for Tara in Margaret Mitchell's *Gone with the Wind.* Slender fluted columns rose two stories to support the roof above a shallow veranda running around the front and two sides of the house. This veranda, during evening business hours, was bathed in the soft glow of many spotlights set about the landscaped estate.

Two huge black doormen were on duty during business hours. They were dressed as masters of the hunt, with black silk toppers, bright red frock coats, white doeskin breeches and gloves, and jet kneelength boots. They greeted all guests. None could remember a time when both men were not smiling broadly, exuding goodwill like old family retainers, respectfully addressing by name the regulars among the Plantation's monied clientele.

The atmosphere of the Deep South created by the appearance of the place, and by these happy symbols of warm hospitality, was enhanced by the aroma of night-blooming jasmine and the pastoral late-spring sounds of innumerable crickets and croaking frogs in ponds scattered about the grounds. The Plantation was a northern Indiana showplace.

In a soundproofed room at the rear of the lovely old house the host rose from the table at which he had entertained a dozen close friends and business associates. The host was Al Capone, a man so powerfully built that at a distance he appeared shorter than his nearly six feet.

Capone had the assurance of a man who knew himself to be one of the wealthiest merchants in the world, with businesses grossing upward of $300,000,000 a year and a personal fortune estimated at $60,000,000. Now he waited a moment for the last bits of conversation to cease. Soon every man at the long table had turned to face the standing host. Capone smiled and spoke quietly: "Boys, I wanted you all to see the Plantation. I think we got a great place here. I hope you like it and I hope you enjoyed the dinner. We ate well, we talked a lot, we had a few drinks in pleasant company. Now I got a surprise for you."

Capone paused dramatically. Then, moving with the driving energy that characterized all his actions, he went to the cloakroom, picked up two packages, and returned to the table. Each package was the size and shape of a magnum of champagne. Each was gift-wrapped in tissue paper.

Once again standing behind his chair, Capone held one of these packages in each hand. He gripped them as one might the necks of bottles, holding them extended from the length of his arms. With all eyes upon him, he turned his magnetic smile first toward the man at his right and then toward the man at his left. Nodding to each in turn, Capone said, "For Johnny. And for Joe."

Even as he spoke, Capone's smile disappeared. His swarthy face suddenly showed intense emotion, a blazing anger which turned the great scar on his left cheek into a double slash of angry red tissue.

Capone swung rapidly with either arm, knocking his astonished neighbors from their chairs with the heavy Indian clubs.

Neither victim had a chance to dodge. Each still looked pleased as he was struck. Their reflexes might have been slowed by the wine, or they might even have been slightly drugged. Or their host's movements might simply have been totally unexpected and unbelievably rapid. In any case, each was hit solidly by one of the blows. Each was stunned.

Capone again swung the heavy clubs, giving John Scalise and Joseph Guinta no chance to recover. Blow followed blow, Capone's eyes never rising from his fallen victims. Capone was a man driven by his passion.

The others at the table stood as though momentarily paralyzed. One man recovered more quickly than the others, and his right hand reached inside his dinner jacket toward the .45 caliber automatic pistol slung there in its underarm holster. As Albert Anselmi's hand touched the pistol butt, another pistol muzzle was suddenly pressed against his ear. His neighbor said, "Hold it, Bert."

Anselmi remained immobile a moment, then withdrew his hand.

Other eyes flickered from the drama at the head of the table to this byplay. The pistol at Anselmi's head was held by Vincenzo de Mora, alias Machine Gun Jack McGurn, standing balanced like the prizefighter he was.

A tense stillness succeeded Capone's sudden murderous violence. Capone straightened from the two fallen men, who lay half hidden by the chairs and table. Capone's eyes turned from this pair to Anselmi, rigid at the point of McGurn's pistol. Capone said, "Come here, Bert. Come and look at them."

McGurn's pistol was shifted smoothly from his right hand to his left. His right hand slipped inside Anselmi's double-breasted jacket and came out holding Anselmi's weapon. With both pistols, McGurn nudged the white-faced gunman.

Anselmi's eyes were fixed on those of Capone. He seemed in a trance, held under the leader's spell. Once his body began to move he almost stumbled. His shuffling feet brought him near the two who lay unconscious on the floor. Anselmi halted. Capone told him, "Take a good look, Bert. You guys thought you could set me up for a pigeon. You offered fifty thousand to the man who got me. Neither of them had the guts to try it. You haven't got the guts. You guys make me sick."

Capone, still holding one of the Indian clubs, used it to poke Anselmi gently in the chest. Anselmi looked down, then up again. His face, already drained of color, looked dead. Capone poked him in the chest again and said, "Tell the boys, Bert. Tell them how you and Johnny hired Ralph Sheldon to get me. Tell them how Jack shot Sheldon four days ago."

Capone's final words snapped. Anselmi tried once to talk, but no words came. Capone waited as the others watched.

Anselmi finally said, "Not me, Al. Honest to God. Johnnie. It was his idea. His and Joe's. Believe me, Al, I wouldn't—"

Anselmi halted in mid-sentence. Something he saw in Capone's eyes caused him to cringe. He said, "No, Al. Please—" as the first blow was struck.

The Indian club broke Anselmi's upraised arm and still had force enough to send him crumpling to the floor. He screamed as Capone, once again caught up in his passion, swung several times.

Finally, Capone threw the club at the man, who now lay still.

Capone appeared not to take his eyes off the three men lying at his feet as he reached his right hand across the table toward McGurn. No word was spoken. As though the action had been rehearsed, McGurn laid Anselmi's automatic—cocked and off-safety—in Capone's hand. Capone did not seem to aim. He fired once, twice, three times. Each of the fallen men jerked as he was struck by a bullet. Capone snarled. "Double-crossers. Yellow bastards. What did you want, anyway?"

Those who witnessed it said later that the killings seemed to be done in sorrow, as though Capone's anger had burned itself out. Two of the fallen men for years had been Capone's most trusted companions, his chauffeurs and valets, his bodyguards. The third had been his personal choice to head the powerful Unione Siciliane.

Capone now handed the pistol back to McGurn. The latter carefully and professionally, using two hands, let down the hammer of the heavy automatic until it rested on a shell in the chamber. He flicked the safety lever on. Then he picked up a napkin and rubbed every exposed surface of the pistol before bending to replace it in the holster on Anselmi's body.

All watched this operation silently. After a moment Capone looked about the table, his eyes resting briefly on each of the men present.

Each had been at his side for years. Each had risen in his shadow to wealth. Capone glanced down at the men on the floor and said, "This is the kind of thing we got to get away from. Tonight I go to Atlantic City to meet with a lot of hotheads from all over. I got to make them understand that we can't go on with this kind of thing. What the hell, we're not punks anymore. We got families. We got to settle down."

Capone looked at Frank Nitti, Charlie Fischetti, Paul Ricca, Frankie Rio, Jake Guzik, Tough Tony Capezio, and the others. Then he glanced again without emotion at the three bodies. He made no attempt to move away from them. He continued: "Before I went East, I had to straighten things out with the Unione. Joe Guinta just resigned as president."

With these words, Capone's heavy face showed the first hint of a grin. The others at the table, immediately responsive to his altered mood, tried tentative smiles. One of the men repeated, "Joe just resigned," and chuckled. In a moment there was general smiling and movement. The crisis appeared over.

When Capone reached for his glass, an Asti Spumanti from which the sparkle had gone, the others lifted glasses. They drained what was left of their drinks. Capone made a last reference to the bodies on the floor: "These three were asking for it. They got it. Anybody got any questions now is the time to ask them."

One after the other, each of the men about the table shook his head slowly and gravely. Capone looked from one to the other as they did so. His eyes came to rest on Frank Nitti. "I'll be away for a week, maybe longer, Frank. Look after things. Any questions, ask my brother Ralph. I'll catch the midnight train out of Gary. Frankie Rio will come with me."

Turning to McGurn: "Clean this up, Jack. Get rid of them. They'll be giving the Plantation a bad name."

Everyone chuckled at Capone's humor.

Capone once again entered the cloakroom, this time to emerge with his summer-weight Borsalino. He pulled the hat on carefully, its brim snapped down partially to cover the unsightly scar from ear to mouth at the left side of his broad face. Before leaving, Capone turned once again to Nitti. The handshake between these two emotional men of the Mediterranean became a manly embrace. Nitti muttered, *"Buon' notte. Cum Deus."*

Turning to Guzik, Capone smiled. "Don't take any wooden nickels, Jake."

Capone took a final look around the room and said pointedly, "Everybody stick around awhile. Let's go, Frank."

Rio lifted the heavy bar which supplemented locks on the room's single heavy door. He glanced up at the roaring fan, set high in the one windowless wall, and judged that its racket effectually covered every sound from within, short of a dynamite blast.

Rio walked the length of the short hallway, opened a second door as heavy as the first, then stepped into the night air to make sure no enemy gunman waited in the shadows.

Capone followed Rio into the cool of the May evening.

Fireflies lent their phosphorescence to the landscaped lawn. The perfume of magnolias in early blossom scented the balmy air. From the great dining room at the front of the building Capone heard the moan of a saxophone and the beat of drums as a famous orchestra played a popular tune for dancing couples. From the open windows of the casino above the restaurant Capone fancied he heard the clicking of roulette wheels in motion and the faint hum of elegant conversation punctuated by laughter.

Harry Hitchcock, manager of the establishment, stepped out from under one of the big sycamore trees where he obviously had been standing sentry duty. He asked, "Everything all right, Al?"

"Everything's fine, Harry. You got a good chef. The boys send their compliments on the scallopine. What kind of house we got tonight?"

"Big dinner crowd. Good spenders. About two-thirds in their own cars and the rest using the limousine service from the Loop. Ought to be a lot of action at the tables."

Rio brought a black car to a purring halt in the driveway. Capone stepped in as Hitchcock spoke his farewells. The car moved, under Rio's effortless driving, to the wide curving lane which led to the highway. At a word from Capone, Rio halted the car. The two doormen quickly approached. Capone reached out a window to hand each a crisp new banknote.

Their loud and repeated thanks followed the black car as it bore Capone off toward the highway and his rendezvous with the hotheads in the East.

Streaks of dawn were brightening the sky May 8, 1929, when Patrolmen Louis Tebedo and Charles Plant of the Hammond police found the three bodies. They had been dead "four or five hours," said the medical examiner, but rigor mortis had not yet set in because of the unseasonably warm weather. The policemen's attention had been drawn to a new car apparently deserted on a tree-bordered road far from houses, a few miles inside Indiana across the state line from Chicago.

The car, which proved to have been stolen, was nosed partially into a ditch.

In the space behind the front seat a blanket was thrown over two dead men. They were identified as Scalise and Guinta. Forty feet away, lying in a ditch where it apparently had been thrown from another car, lay a third body, identified as that of Anselmi. The policemen saw at once that the victims had been beaten as well as shot. Bruises and broken bones were evident. A coroner's inquest later established the full extent of this mayhem.

Scalise had been shot through the center of the forehead, in the right ear, in the right wrist, in the left knee, in the left hand. The left hand's little finger had been shot off. Scalise's eyes had been blackened, his jaw broken by a blow. A flesh wound on his chin appeared to have been inflicted with a bludgeon.

Guinta had been shot twice through the head, once through the heart, once in the right breast, once in the right arm.

The medical examiner said he had been "beaten on the head repeatedly."

Anselmi had been shot once through the chest from the front, once in the right side, three times in the right shoulder. The bone in his left arm near the shoulder had been broken by a heavy blow.

Homicide detectives experienced in the ways of the underworld testified before the Lake County coroner's jury that, "In many such cases all of the men present fire pistols at the victims so that all potential witnesses become equally guilty and none can later testify against the others without incriminating himself."

The jury reported officially, "Three known members of the Capone gang came to their deaths by gunfire at the hands of persons unknown."

Capone, who like all gangsters and politicians generally made a point of attending the wakes of acquaintances, was conspicuously absent when Scalise, Anselmi, and Guinta were laid out. The underworld buzzed with rumors of what might have been a scandal until a few who were in positions to know passed the word: "They were rats. The Big Fellow took care of them."

This triple shooting was one of only four in which Capone was known to have figured personally during the decade in which he contributed so much to Chicago's colorful history. He was held responsible for dozens of deaths, many of which he was said to have decreed directly, but so far as is known there were only four times at which he handled a smoking pistol in the presence of witnesses.

In August, 1922, about three years after his arrival from Brooklyn, Capone's name appeared for the first time on a Chicago police blotter.

He was identified as "Antonio Caponi" and he gave as his address the notorious Four Deuces brothel. On this occasion, Capone had drawn a pistol during the midnight hours at the corner of Randolph Street and Wabash Avenue in the Loop to threaten Fred Krause, a taxicab driver of 741 Drake Avenue. Since Krause later changed his testimony there was some doubt as to whether he actually had been scratched by a bullet in the arm.

Two years later, on April 1, 1924, Al Capone was with his brother, Frank, engaging in a pistol battle with Cicero police in front of an election polling place near the Hawthorne works of the Western Electric Company. The Capone cousin, Charlie Fischetti, was with them. They had contracted to deliver the vote for insurgent politicians. In the battle, Frank Capone was shot dead. Al and Charlie Fischetti fled.

This was the time hitherto noted when the Torrio-Capone outfit by the same democratic processes used by all politicians put their own slate in control of Cicero, the sixth-largest city in the state. Torrio was still boss of the gang, but Capone was its operating director. Cicero at that time was a West Side suburb of Chicago. Today, like Hamtramck in Detroit, the town of Cicero is completely surrounded by the expanding city of Chicago.

Cicero is a city of homeowners. Their taxes are the lowest of any metropolitan community in the state, because most of the tax bills for municipal services are picked up by the places of business along honkytonk row on Twenty-second Street west of Cicero Avenue. The tax money thus raised pays for their school system, with one of the highest educational standards in the state.

The honkytonks—gambling joints, brothels, and striptease burlesque bars—do not bother the homeowning dwellers in the city. Honkytonk strip might as well be in another world, catering as it does to Chicago tourists brought out by taxicab from the Loop. The police virtually limit their activity to keeping drunken tourists from driving out of the honkytonk area into the rest of the clean and spacious city.

No thief of any sort is permitted to prey on the Cicero population or on its thriving industries. This is guaranteed not by police and politicians, but by the underworld leaders who want to keep a base of operations.

The residents of Cicero like it this way.

But to get back to Al Capone as a publicity-shy gunman.

A month after burying his brother as a result of the street battles which delivered Cicero into the keeping of the Torrio outfit, Capone had occasion to do something which won him fealty of all within his ken.

He killed a man publicly—the killing might more truly be called an execution—for no other reason than that the man had roughed up one of Capone's employees.

This story, seldom mentioned publicly, is told and retold by the gossiping gangsters wherever they congregate. As far as they are concerned, it marks Capone's emergence as the single leader worthy of their loyalty. Because of this, even in death they give him and his memory their allegiance.

On May 8, 1924, a dozen or more habitués of Heinie Jacobs' street-corner speakeasy at 2300 South Wabash Avenue saw Al Capone enter the place in his shirtsleeves. He was red-faced and out of breath, obviously from running to the scene. He looked around the bar and everyone noticed him, half the patrons of the place being unaware at the time who the excited man was.

Then Capone's eyes, fresh from the outside sunlight, grew accustomed to the dim interior of Jacobs' place. He saw Joe Howard, a tough thief who a few hours earlier had roughed up the roly-poly little Jake Guzik, chief bookkeeper for the Torrio-Capone combine. Guzik was unarmed and defenseless in the presence of physical violence. Joe Howard, a neighborhood bully, had been boasting of how he "made the little Jew whine."

Now Al Capone walked over to confront Howard at the bar. "Are you Joe Howard?" The man nodded. Capone drew a revolver, held it toward the shriveling Joe Howard, and said, "Whine, you fucking fink." Capone waited for several seconds, then emptied the revolver into Howard's body.

Joe Howard was a gunman in his own right. He was known to have killed three men. He had been a safecracker and burglar before he got into the big money during Prohibition. He tried to rob the Old Rose Distillery warehouse at 447 North Clark Street and as he was helping lift the last of ten barrels aboard a truck in the alley he was surprised at the work by Police Sergeant Irwin Holberg of the East Chicago Avenue station. The case dragged along for months until Howard could put in the fix with the prosecutor and judge, when it was finally dismissed.

Howard made a living hijacking trucks loaded with whiskey or beer when he could get a tipoff in advance. But whenever he drank any of the stuff he stole he could not help looking around for the smallest man in sight and showing how hard he could hit. Howard was a good slugger. When he hit Jake Guzik, he started out slapping his face backward and forward, watching his head bob from side to side, before he swung one heavy fist.

Guzik and his three brothers were pimps and thieves and gamblers but never had gone in for the rougher work associated with so many in their neighborhood. Guzik was happy to scurry out of sight of Joe Howard and the humiliation of the latter's fists.

When he appeared in Capone's office upstairs over the Four Deuces, Jake's jowls were flaming red and his eye already swollen and turning black. The hour was near 6 o'clock of the warm May afternoon. Capone took one look and said, "Who did it?"

The full story of that public execution came out before the inquest into Howard's death, continued and continued again until Capone could get to all the witnesses and make sure their stories were not incriminating.

The story was simple. Heinie Jacobs, proprietor of the little neighborhood saloon, was drowsing behind the cigar case. George Bilton and David Runelsbeck, one an auto mechanic and the other an aging carpenter, had stopped by for a friendly drink on their way home to their furnished rooms in the area. Joe Howard was down at the other end of the bar, sounding off to whoever would listen. Few of those gathered in the homely little spa had ever heard of Jake Guzik.

Immediately after Howard's killing, Chief of Detectives Michael Hughes questioned the witnesses. Runelsbeck said that Joe Howard appeared to know Al Capone and had reached out as though to shake hands when greeting him with the words, "Hello, Al." Runelsbeck said Capone held a revolver against Howard's cheek when he shot him the first time. After that he fired five more shots into the fallen man's body.

The inquest opened next day, May 9. Overnight the witnesses had changed their stories. Heinie Jacobs remembered that he had been called to a rear room to answer the telephone just before he heard the shots. Runelsbeck, visibly frightened, was certain he could not identify the man who had done the shooting. Bilton was missing. So was Capone.

Jacobs and Runelsbeck were charged with being accessories after the fact, a technical charge meant to keep them in police jurisdiction so long as their testimony might be required. The inquest was continued until May 22. When Capone did not show up for the inquest on that date, it was continued indefinitely.

Finally, on June 11, Capone walked into the Cottage Grove police station and gave himself up. When questioned about the killing of Howard he said, "I am not a gangster. I do not know Johnny Torrio. I run a respectable used furniture business at 2222 South Wabash Avenue. I have nothing to do with whatever brothel may be operated at that address under the name of the Four Deuces. I had heard of Howard, but I was out of town the day of his death."

The inquest reopened on July 22. Police Captain James McMahon presented the case against Capone, a slender case based on hearsay evidence with no testimony whatever to back it up. The verdict of the coroner's jury in the case of Joe Howard reads in part:

> . . . came to his death from hemorrhage and shock due to bullet wounds in the head, face and neck; said bullets being fired from a revolver or revolvers in the hand or hands of one or more unknown white male persons. We recommend that the unknown persons be apprehended and held to the grand jury upon a charge of murder.

The unknown persons were never apprehended. Al Capone was never again bothered in this case.

A few words about Jake Guzik are in order, since he will appear again in these chronicles. He was one of a family of twelve, one of five brothers who earned their first nickels running errands for the prostitutes of the Levee district on the Near South Side. Their name on police blotters of the early years of the century was spelled however it happened to sound to the Irish cop making the collar. Thus it appears as Guzik, Guzak, Cusack, Cusick, and in several other variations.

They all apply to the five brothers. Harry and Jake became best-known of the family.

Harry and his wife, Alma Guzik, were convicted on a white slavery charge. All the Guzik boys had been pimps before they entered their teens, since that was the accepted way of earning money in their home neighborhood. But after that first conviction, Harry Guzik learned an important lesson. From then on he kept every policeman and politician in sight on his payroll.

The First Ward committeeman said, "Harry's fingers are always greasy from the money he counts out for protection." His greasy thumb was mentioned. From then on, he was called Greasy Thumb.

Somehow, as Jake Guzik came into wider prominence through his early connection with the Torrio-Capone combine, the name of Greasy Thumb came to be identified with him instead of his brother. Jake gradually rose through the Capone ranks until he was the organization's treasurer. He never betrayed the Capone trust.

Not until five years after the Howard killing, on May 7, 1929—when Scalise, Anselmi, and Guinta were eliminated—was Capone again known personally to kill.

A lot of beer had gone over the road in those five years.

In those years Johnny Torrio had retired, selling out his interest in the business for $5,000,000 to Capone. Torrio's retirement was speeded by bullets.

The remnants of the old Dion O'Banion gang had determined to their own satisfaction that it was Torrio who had decreed the Irishman's death on November 10, 1924. Less than three months later, in front of his South Shore apartment at 7011 South Clyde Avenue, they caught up with Torrio.

The gang leader had just returned with his wife, Anna, from a Loop shopping trip. Mrs. Torrio had left their car and entered the apartment house lobby. Torrio started to follow with an armload of packages.

Just at that moment a blue Cadillac drew abreast of the parked Lincoln in which Torrio had been riding. Hymie Weiss stepped out with a sawed-off shotgun blazing as he hit the street. Torrio fell. Then Bugs Moran followed Weiss, bringing an Army model .45 automatic pistol into position for firing. Schemer Drucci stayed in the car's front seat, keeping the motor running.

Moran squeezed off a couple of shots. Then he went to Torrio's side for the coup de grace, a single shot point-blank through the head. But at that moment a laundry truck approached. Drucci tooted the Cadillac's horn to signal Moran. The latter fled without firing.

Torrio spent sixteen days in Jackson Park Hospital. Then he went to the Lake County jail in Waukegan, to serve out a nine-month sentence for bootlegging. While still in jail he sold out all his interests to Capone. When he left jail, Torrio headed back for Brooklyn.

Capone showed forbearance after the shooting of his mentor. Everyone in Chicago who knew anything about the underworld knew that Hymie Weiss, Bugs Moran, and Schemer Drucci had shot Torrio. But Capone did nothing. Not just then.

Nearly two years later, on October 11, 1926, Weiss was shot to death in front of the Holy Name Cathedral. Drucci's death, on April 5, 1927, has already been recounted. Moran died of lung cancer thirty years later while serving a ten-year sentence for bank robbery in Leavenworth Federal Penitentiary. The manner of his dying was such as to give him ample time to seek the last rites of the Catholic Church.

The fact that Moran outlived Al Capone was no fault of the Big Fellow. He had planned to get Moran, with the rest of his gang, on the morning of February 14, 1929. Moran overslept and was late in arriving. Seven of his associates died of machine-gun bullets in the garage at 2122 North Clark Street in what came to be known as the St. Valentine's Day Massacre. Capone arranged to be out of town at the time.

Possibly the greatest change in the five years between the death at Capone's personal hands of Joe Howard in 1924—and Anselmi, Guinta, and Scalise in 1929—took place within Al Capone himself. When the mantle of empire fell to his shoulders from those of Johnny Torrio, maturity was thrust upon the twenty-six-year-old Capone. The responsibility sobered him.

He had been a swaggering roughneck whose idea of fashionable dress ran to striped silk shirts and bright tan shoes.

He had been a hard-fisted saloon fighter whose boast was that he stomped his own snakes in his own way. Now he found himself the sole head of a great business with a weekly payroll of over $300,000 to more than 1,000 persons. This was his own estimate.

Besides the 600 gunmen on his payroll, Capone had more than sixty in the capacity of what might be called foremen or sergeants, and a dozen or more who were his lieutenants. Each of these last-named was a field-grade officer in his own right and acted more or less independently within his own area. Someone once defined an executive as a man who can make minor decisions without being called on the carpet. By this definition Capone kept a fairly large executive staff.

His brother, Ralph, was near the top, most trusted because of blood. Other blood relatives were the Fischetti brothers and Frankie Rio. Joe Fusco and Lou Greenberg were bosses in their own right. So were Murray Humphreys and Red Barker and Three-Finger Jack White. Paul Ricca and Frank Nitti were emerging as men able to think for themselves. Tony Accardo was still a simple machine gunner and Joey Aiuppa a rising star, but still thought of as little more than a fast boy in the boxing ring.

Al Capone was the man who had to walk with kings. He was accepted publicly as an equal—and privately as "the boss"—by mayors, governors, United States Senators and Congressmen, and judges at all levels up to and including the highest benches in the land. This stature was accorded Capone not merely in Illinois but throughout the nation east of the Mississippi.

Capone adapted to his new friends and new surroundings. He grew more quickly than anyone would have deemed possible. He began to dress conservatively, to erase the four-letter words from his vocabulary, to speak softly, smile almost continuously when in public, meet newspaper reporters with modesty, and speak intelligently of industry problems.

Capone came to the office of Hearst publisher Merrill C. Meigs in 1929 to question the newspaper's fairness in constantly referring to him as "Scarface." He agreed with Meigs that his manner of life made news of whatever he did, but, "Does your newspaper consider it fair play to refer to a physical disfigurement every time it mentions my name?"

Meigs, tall and dignified, and a former football hero at the University of Chicago, admitted he never before had considered the matter. He said he wanted to think it over and discuss it with his editors. Capone took his leave with courtesy and phoned next day to know what Meigs' decision had been. Meigs said, "You are right. The word 'Scarface' will not again be used except in direct quote from some police official or similar authority."

Meigs said he arrived at his decision with no feeling of compulsion. He said simply, "The man was right. I just had not thought of it before."

Capone was brought by Max Annenberg to the Tribune Tower offices of Colonel Robert R. McCormick, editor and publisher of the great morning daily. Annenberg thought Capone might be able to counsel the publisher—an American emperor in his own right—in the conduct of negotiations with a striking union.

McCormick later admitted his astonishment in finding Capone clean, courteous—almost courtly, in fact—and with an amazing grasp of facts, figures and nuances. Annenberg later said Capone's summation of the situation helped the publisher solve a problem.

Al Capone's inner growth during these years was phenomenal.

But if the gangster chieftain seldom drew a revolver and sought to leave behind his reputation as a barroom brawler, he still did not feel he could back away from a fight when challenged. His quick temper remained barely held in check. His rocklike fists sometimes came into play.

After the Torrio-Capone combine had put their slate of politicians into office in Cicero on April 1, 1924, their mayor, Joseph Z. Klenha, began to take himself seriously. He told the newspapers that while he had accepted Torrio-Capone aid in winning office, he intended to govern Cicero independently and to enforce the laws of municipality, county, state, and nation. He added, "And in this I refer particularly to those gangsters. They can get out and stay out of Cicero."

Capone drove up to the City Hall of Cicero. He had an aide call Klenha outside, and the mayor came accompanied by two policemen. Capone ignored the presence of the policemen, and on the City Hall steps, in full view of any passing citizens, Capone slapped the new mayor into a state of unconsciousness. Klenha had been bought and paid for. He never again sought to welsh on his debt to the Capone forces. Capone never again publicly treated Klenha with anything but deference.

A little later some of the members of Cicero's City Council began discussing a proposal to restrict power of the Torrio-Capone combine.

Capone entered the council chambers during the deliberations. He slugged one of the aldermen. He grabbed another by the neck of his jacket and held him in the air with his left hand while he cocked his right

fist as though preparing to release a Sunday punch. A motion to table
the ordinance was immediately voiced, seconded, and unanimously
adopted.

Arthur St. John, editor of a newspaper in Berwyn, the suburban
village lying adjacent to the south border of Cicero, said editorially that
he thought Capone should be restrained. He was taken from his office
and beaten by unknown assailants. His brother, Robert St. John, edited a
paper in Cicero. He commented publicly and disparagingly about
gangsters who hire sluggers because they are afraid to "come out in the
open like men and do their own dirty work." Al Capone personally
called on Robert St. John and beat him senseless.

Jim Doherty, the Chicago *Tribune* reporter who has been mentioned
earlier in these pages, asked Capone if he thought tactics such as these
were going to help in the establishment of the era of peace in the
underworld of which Capone so often talked. Capone replied, "Now you
know damned well, Jim, that those things can't be let pass. Somebody
else in my shoes might have killed those guys. If I waited and let them
get away with this they might try more and more until finally they had to
be killed. This way they learn their lesson and nobody really gets hurt."

But these and similar frays were not daily occurrences in the new life
of Al Capone, burgeoning manufacturer and importer, merchant and
lobbyist in legislative halls.

Possibly, like many a man before him, Al Capone regretted the
passing of the years when life had been so simple. All too young he had
had to learn to become an administrator, to delegate authority and hope
it was used wisely, to run an empire half a continent in size.

Capone knew the loneliness of command. He alone was responsible
for the smooth functioning of what would today be called a
conglomerate. He had branches of his smuggling operation in seaports
at each coast and on the Gulf of Mexico. He had offices in Canada, in
Mexico and other lands south of the border, in the islands of the
Caribbean. He frequently commented to newspapermen, "That
slugging and shooting—cowboy stuff. It's for the kids. Why kill a man
when you can buy him so cheap? You learn his price—and you pay it."

That formula apparently was graven on Capone's soul. Every time he
said it his listeners would remember the difference between Torrio and
O'Banion, Torrio offering to buy off two policemen for $300 and
O'Banion saying he could have them killed for less. Capone had learned
from Torrio. He used the formula with police, prosecutors, jurists—with
politicians at every level. He used it with businessmen and bankers. He
told newspaper interviewers, "I got nothing against the honest cop on

the beat. Most of them you can't buy. So you just have them transferred someplace where they can't do you any harm. But don't ever talk to me about the honor of police captains or judges. If they couldn't be bought, they wouldn't have the jobs."

Capone knew that a man's price was not always to be counted in currency of the realm. Some men would bend for a friend, some out of fear for their families, some for a public greeting from a world champion or a film star. Capone could usually arrange whatever it took. He had the great gift of empathy. He could put himself in another man's place and avoid the gaffe that might alienate a man who would otherwise cooperate.

He knew that the politician's basic drive is toward power and that money is only a tool to attain it, but that the businessman's basic drive is toward money. At the same time Capone recognized every man's capacity to delude himself and to cloak his most materialistic actions in robes of shining idealism.

Capone said that some men who would not pocket a crooked penny were unable to resist the tug of obligation if a pet charity were substantially helped. Some responded to the chance to strut public platforms and mouth platitudes for quotation in newspapers. Some would sell their souls for four tickets on the fifty-yard line when Illinois played Notre Dame, so they could take a business associate to watch Red Grange dump the Fighting Irish. Some who could be reached by none of these gambits could not say no to an occasional bottle of Very Special Old Pale imported cognac.

Capone could be as obvious as a bull or as subtle as a snake. He was to need every shade of persuasion he could bring to bear at the Atlantic City conference of his peers in the traffic of booze, broads, and bookies. Capone left the scene of the Anselmi-Guinta-Scalise triple murder in high spirits as he headed eastward.

10 The first underworld peace conference

Hymie Weiss might not have been killed on October 11, 1926, had he not proved completely intransigent about any proposal to bury the hatchet in the Chicago gang wars. Presumably Al Capone could have had him killed at any time after Weiss shot Johnny Torrio on January 24, 1925. Capone ordinarily was not the man to hold back. But at first it was Torrio who ordered no retaliation. After he retired, Capone had other things on his mind. One of those things was underworld peace.

Capone had not liked the eruption of the gang wars after O'Banion's death on November 10, 1924. Capone's profits, like those of his colleagues in the purveying of booze, broads, and bookies, depended on the tourist trade. And if Chicago got such a reputation as to keep tourists away, everybody would suffer.

So Capone sought peace in the underworld. Like any other emperor, he sought to consolidate in diplomacy what had been won in war. He sent to all surviving gang leaders in the Chicago area an invitation to a peace conference on October 21, 1926, in the Hotel Morrison.

Hymie Weiss not only sent the invitation back with a rude message, but vowed that if any such peace conference ever were held he would personally attend with shotguns blazing and hand grenades exploding. That message was his death warrant. Capone considered Hymie Weiss "a madman." He later told a police captain, "When a dog's got rabies, nobody's safe. The dumb thing's just got to be killed."

Hymie Weiss was killed ten days before the peace conference opened.

The conference opened with Jake Guzik in the chair. Capone did not attend, said Guzik, because he felt that his presence might act as a red flag to many who felt they had grievances. Capone had stipulated in his invitations that those attending come unarmed and leave their bodyguards at home. Even so, said Guzik, Capone felt that more might be accomplished if nothing further were done to stir up old rivalries. Those present could see the wisdom in Capone absenting himself.

Guzik was more than chief accountant for the entire Capone empire. He was generally recognized throughout the underworld as a shrewd diplomat. Guzik had never carried a gun and on more than one occasion said the fact that he had been unarmed had saved his life. Now, on Capone's behalf, he told the assembled gang leaders he would offer a program which he felt might appeal to all men of good sense. Besides Guzik, the assembly included Antonio Lombardo, then president of the Unione Siciliane; Eddie (Dutch) Vogel of Cicero; George (Bugs) Moran of the O'Banion gang; and Maxie Eisen with his proxies for what was left of ethnic gangs.

Eisen controlled several unions among the Jewish fish sellers and chicken merchants. He collected tribute from every pushcart peddler in the Maxwell Street district and every rag picker who roamed the alleys in search of unbroken bottles and scrap metal. As soon as the conference got under way, after the opening remarks, Guzik turned the gavel over to Maxie Eisen. He was considered neutral.

Edward (Spike) O'Donnell and his three brothers of the South Side were represented at the meeting; as was the West Side gang of Myles and Klondike O'Donnell. The Saltis-Oberta beer combine on the Southwest Side was represented, as was the Roger Touhy group from the northwest suburbs. Johnny Patton, the boy mayor of Burnham, a southwest suburb in the Cicero-Berwyn-Stickney area, was present.

So far as anyone knew, the only armed men in the room were two of the highest-ranking men in the police department, there to keep order.

Guzik asked for the floor and traced the rise and fall of a score of gangs which had seen the coming of Prohibition as a bonanza. He gave the box score of the killings which had relegated most of the gangs to history: 215 gangsters had killed one another and 160 were killed by police.

He said of 1926, "Since January first of this year, forty-two have been killed by us within the city limits of Chicago and ten outside the city, but still within Cook County. This is in addition to the sixty of us killed this year by cops. I don't have to name them. You all know their names."

Then Guzik got to Capone's proposal. This was that the city be divided up into territories, with each gang responsible for keeping the peace in its own neighborhood.

Each gang would be free to manufacture or import its own beer and liquor or to buy it from whatever source it desired. There would be no force or compulsion to distribute alcohol products at the wholesale level.

Within its own territory, each gang could set its own retail price levels.

Prices would be kept low by competition, since the customer could go wherever he wanted to do his drinking. But on phone orders, no bootlegger would enter another gang's territory. If a bootlegger got a phone order to cater a wedding or banquet in another gang's territory, he would turn it over to the other gang.

Virtually the same rules would apply to prostitution and to gambling. No gang would operate handbooks or wirerooms in another man's territory. No gang would permit any of its member pimps to hustle prostitutes in another man's territory or to put his own girls to work in a hotel or rooming house outside his own territory.

Each gang would be responsible for its own local protection, the payoffs of police and ward politicians at the local level. And each gang would pay a proportionate share into a slush fund to be used downtown for City Hall payoffs, downstate for legislative payoffs, and in the courts for bondsmen and lawyers. This would save everybody money. There would no longer be duplications of graft and political contributions. Bondsmen and lawyers could be put on annual retainers to represent all.

Guzik said that inasmuch as the question of who got what territory was likely to occasion considerable discussion, he asked agreement in principle on this basic proposal before opening an area-wide map.

All of those present were millionaire businessmen. They were the ones who had survived, and they had survived because they usually exercised sound common sense. After some discussion they tentatively agreed to accept the Capone proposal in principle.

Now came the touchy part. The city was at that time dominated by two main gangs. The Capone combine held the Loop and downtown districts through Chinatown, south of Twenty-second Street, and west along that entire belt clear into the western suburbs. Even though the Jack Zuta group was getting a strong foothold on Madison Street, they were not yet threatening Capone. The other gang, remnants of the old Dion O'Banion group, held everything north of the Chicago River. This was a tremendous stretch, from the Loop to Evanston and beyond.

So when Jake Guzik outlined Capone's proposal for territories, everyone present was surprised. Far from seeking to extend his territory, Capone was offering to give up great chunks of it and guarantee their sanctity to the ethnic gangs which kept to their own neighborhoods.

Thus, Capone proposed that he limit his own territory to the Far West Side and the western suburbs. This was an astonishing concession.

Capone proposed that the South Side be divided between Ralph Sheldon and Joe Saltis, from the Chicago River to the Indiana line, and from Lake Michigan on the east to the city limits on the west. Inasmuch as both Saltis and his chief lieutenant, Vincent McErlane, were in prison at the time, their territory would be held in trust for them until they emerged. (Vincent McErlane was a brother of Frankie, earlier discussed.)

Ralph Sheldon was a known Capone partisan, so his position was strengthened by Capone support. The support ended in his sudden death in 1929 when, as related in the Anselmi-Guinta-Scalise story, he set out to earn the $50,000 bounty on Capone's head.

Bugs Moran and Schemer Drucci, leaders of the old O'Banion gang, were to have the North Side from the Loop to Belmont Avenue, from the lake west to the north branch of the Chicago River. One of the conditions of their being guaranteed its sanctity was that they undertake to secure approval of the entire territory division from the imprisoned Saltis and McErlane.

Roger Touhy and his brother, Ed, with their partner, Matt Kolb, got the northwest suburbs from the city line west to Elgin and from North Avenue to the Lake County line in Illinois.

The rest of the North Side within the city was to be kept by the ethnic gangs who operated along Milwaukee Avenue and bought most of their products from the big manufacturers.

The area for nearly a mile in each direction from Halsted Street and Roosevelt Road was to be left in the hands of Terry Druggan and Frankie Lake.

Each gang leader was to permit lesser gangs to operate within his territory "as mutually agreed." Capone's source of bootleg alcohol, the Genna family organization of hundreds of little kitchen stills, would thus continue operating within the Druggan-Lake area. And Druggan-Lake operations would be conducted within what was essentially the Saltis-Sheldon area.

This was the division of territories ultimately agreed. The agreement was preceded by some intelligent discussion and a good deal of bombast. Gangsters are like businessmen in that they want to be heard whether or not they have anything to say.

In any case, the city and suburbs, an area embracing eight counties, was partitioned into what international statesmen would call spheres of influence.

Some of the men present had obviously been sampling their own wares before the meeting. Roger Touhy wanted to tell everyone how much better beer he made than that provided by anyone else in Illinois. He told the group, "The secret is in the water. We get ours from an artesian well near Roselle. I went to the American Brewmasters' Institute and hired the best man they could recommend. We have ten fermenting plants, each a little brewery in itself, so we won't be put out of business if some smart young Prohibition agent wants to break one up with axes.

"Beer sales are really a six-month proposition, with most drinkers turning to hard liquor during cold weather. But it costs us four-fifty a barrel to produce and I sell it at fifty-five dollars a barrel to two hundred roadhouses, nightclubs, and saloons. At the top of the season we sell a thousand barrels a week. I still have time to keep up with my fishing."

Touhy said that his other big source of income in the suburbs was slot machines. He said he paid off police and politicians so the machines could be openly played in drugstores, gas stations, and groceries as well as saloons and roadhouses. But Touhy said there was no prostitution in his territory. "The suburbanites and farmers won't hold still for bawdy houses. Beer and slots are okay, but not girls."

At that time there were more than forty old-time breweries operating in the city and suburbs.

They were supplying beer to more than 20,000 speakeasy and roadhouse outlets. Not all the suburban areas were as free of prostitution as the Northwest Side where Touhy operated. Half of them had prostitutes working on the premises as did all the hotels in cities and suburban towns. Besides the slot machines and brothels, every gang leader in the suburbs had taxi-dance halls and punchboards for the youthful trade.

There were nearly 3,000 bookmakers accepting horserace wagers in the territories under discussion.

After any amount of conversation and some jockeying back and forth, Maxie Eisen won agreement on most of the territories. The leaders agreed on written rules for keeping the peace. One point in that written agreement reads: "Leaders of factions are to be held responsible for any infractions of the pact, and unfriendly activities of the rank and file are to be reported to the delegates for disciplining by the respective leaders."

Then the famous peace conference of 1926 gave a standing ovation to Maxie Eisen and Jake Guzik. Everybody went home filled with a spirit of goodwill and comradeship.

The peace pact actually succeeded for a while. For two months not a gangster was killed in Chicago streets.

Al Capone's prestige was enhanced nationally, in the upperworld as well as in the underworld, by his leadership in the cause of peace.

When the fighting again erupted it was not so much over sales of beer and whiskey as over control of the Unione Siciliane di Mutuo Soccorso negli Stati Uniti.

This was a fraternal benefit insurance society which had been chartered in Illinois on September 17, 1895. Even then it had thirty-two branches across the nation. While its name, on February 8, 1926, had been officially changed to the Italo-American National Union, it was still spoken of as "the Unione."

Mike Merlo's death in 1924 had left a vacuum in leadership of the Unione. A series of presidents had briefly succeeded Merlo, each in turn being removed from office by sudden death. None had brought to the job the personal prestige radiated by Merlo.

Everyone wanted control of the Unione, which sold death benefit insurance to virtually all the immigrants from Italy and Sicily. Whoever owned the society had a treasury as great as any to be found among labor unions. With every Italian family in the country paying weekly premiums, the society's owner had a better source of income than any union's dues and assessments.

Most of the families in the Unione, to be sure, were those of simple workingmen who swung picks and shovels. But in every city where the Unione operated there were plenty of old "Mustache Petes" who had come from Europe filled with a nostalgia for the Camorra of Naples and the Mafia of Sicily. Many of these old-timers had got their start as youthful Black Hand extortionists and then had gone on to the operation of import businesses dealing in olive oil, cheeses, and other products used in every Italian home.

These were the hustlers, as distinct from ordinary people, who are always the hustled.

Each knew the value of the Unione if he could get control of it, or even share control with some such powerful robber baron as Al Capone in Chicago or Frankie Yale in Brooklyn.

The Unione had its own publications through which every Italian and Sicilian family in the land could be reached. Inasmuch as most of these immigrants had not yet learned English, this represented influence in elections beyond the reach of the wealthiest of politicians. Every man of any nationality who hoped for a political future courted the Unione. The man who owned the Unione controlled the Italian vote.

When the war for Unione control waxed hot around its national headquarters in Chicago, Al Capone jockeyed for power along with all the other factions in Little Italy. Then Frankie Yale entered the picture. Not content with his power as East Coast sachem of the organization, he sought to take over national headquarters by proxy. This put him on a collision course with Capone.

At this time Capone had his own import representatives at the Gulf ports and in Florida, dealing with the smugglers of liquor from the Bahamas and Cuba. But Frankie Yale acted as Capone's representative in the New York area. Yale's men met the smugglers at the coves along Long Island, transferred the cases of liquor to trucks, and started it on its way west. Yale's men met Capone's trucks coming up the coast from Florida and gave them safe escort through the hijack-ridden New York area until the liquor was on its way west. Yale was well paid for all this service and Capone was pleased with the arrangement.

Suddenly Capone's trucks from the East Coast came under attack.

Hijackers were hitting every third load, sometimes killing the drivers, taking all the imported liquor for which Capone had laid out hard cash.

Nobody had to spell things out for Al Capone. He saw immediately that Frankie Yale, trying to muscle in on the Unione in Chicago, was intent on financing his move with Capone's own money. Capone recognized the ironical arrangement known in literature as "the fine Sicilian hand." Knowing Frankie Yale, Capone did not even negotiate.

On July 1, 1928, Frankie Yale was driving along Forty-fourth Street in the Homewood section of Brooklyn when his car was overtaken by a green sedan and curbed. For the first time in the history of New York gang wars, the sound of Thompson submachine guns was heard. Frankie Yale was killed and everyone in the underworld recognized Capone's work. The submachine gun had become known as "a Chicago chopper." The Chicago trademark on the Yale killing was a warning to the ambitious everywhere that the Unione's national headquarters were going to remain in the Midwest.

Naturally the daily papers on the East Coast had a field day. This was the most sensational killing they had seen. They played it up and mistakenly said that the murderous Chicago gang wars had moved their battlefields eastward. And so on. The reading public got stirred up, wondering if the East Coast streets would be safe for their playing children. Even the national political leaders in Washington, as will be seen a little later in these pages, were dismayed by the killing.

Then only four months later New York's peace was shattered by another killing of even greater import to the general public: that of Arnold Rothstein. He was shot November 4, 1928, in the Park Central Hotel.

There was no direct connection between the two killings. Nobody at any time thought Capone had anything to do with Rothstein's death. But both Yale and Rothstein were notorious and both their deaths received the widest possible publicity.

Yale had started out as a pimp, was a lifelong thief, and through his control of the East Coast branches of the Unione had become to regional politicians their most important source of Italian votes.

But Rothstein had been ever so much greater in his power and influence, since he was the entire East Coast underworld's principal political fixer and payoff man. Every politician in the region might court

Frankie Yale every two years when an election was coming up. But every politician in the region sent his bagman around to Rothstein once a week to collect an amount equal to his salary on the public payroll.

Rothstein was more than a payoff man. He was the underworld's financier. Such drugs as opium, morphine, and cocaine had been outlawed since the United States Supreme Court upheld the Harrison Narcotics Act in 1921. Seven years later the illegal dope was still needed to supply the habits in Chinatown and Harlem.

Rothstein imported and distributed the stuff himself, and financed its importation by others.

When an underworld chieftain saw a chance to import a quantity of narcotics and needed a quick $100,000 to make a buy, he turned to Rothstein. Similarly, when the captain of a smuggling ship had a quantity of liquor he wanted to get rid of in a hurry, any underworld leader could turn to Rothstein and borrow the money.

In addition to this, Rothstein owned dozens of labor unions. He was established and trusted, powerful and wealthy. His death was a shock.

The shock waves over Rothstein's death were not limited to New York's City Hall. They were felt in Albany, Hartford, Trenton, and even in Washington—wherever there was a legislator, a High Court jurist, or a strategically placed bureaucrat who wanted to supplement his income.

Federal officials, state police, and county authorities dogged the steps of New York homicide detectives investigating the Rothstein shooting. Everyone feared that Rothstein's account books might fall into the hands of some reporter who would make them public.

That was the reaction of the upperworld. The underworld leaders scurried in every direction to make sure the police and politicians who had accepted Rothstein's payoffs did not interfere now that he was dead. They felt that Rothstein's death had jeopardized a liquor import business from the Caribbean which was grossing $125,000,000 annually. Weeks went by before their businesses once again could run full blast.

Eventually Frank Costello (born Frank Saveria) emerged as the East Coast payoff man to whom police and politicians went for their weekly pay from the underworld.

The peace conference which Capone had sponsored in Chicago had its repercussions in every big city in the country where underworld gang leaders felt their incomes were imperiled by the publicity given street wars. All had begun moving toward the solution pointed in Chicago. Now the sudden deaths of Frankie Yale and Arnold Rothstein had once again started the ink flowing on the front pages and every radio news commentator sought to hold his audience by hinting at further killings.

A nationwide peace conference among underworld leaders of the various regions and cities seemed called for. Nobody today remembers who first conceived such a conference. All agreed to it.

Max (Boo Boo) Hoff was the underworld boss in Pennsylvania. From his headquarters in Philadelphia he invited underworld leaders from all over the nation to meet in Atlantic City and attempt to agree on territories as the Illinois gang leaders had agreed in Chicago. Hoff told those invited that he had discussed the proposal with Johnny Torrio in Brooklyn, respected by all as an elder statesman of crime.

The great peace conference was to open May 9, 1929, and the delegates were to remain in session at the President Hotel on the boardwalk in Atlantic City until they had agreed on all problems facing the industry.

The underworld is prestige conscious. Al Capone at the time was the most publicized gangster in America.

The peace treaty by which he had brought a pause in Chicago gang killings had been given national publicity. The others invited to Hoff's conference were told they would have the benefit of Capone's counsel in their own area problems.

Besides Max Hoff, Johnny Torrio, and Al Capone, the meeting brought together Frank Costello, Charles (Lucky Luciano) Lucania, and Arthur (Dutch Schultz) Flegenheimer from New York; Enoch J. (Nucky) Joynson of Atlantic City, who was the delegates' host; Abe Bernstein of Detroit's Purple Gang; and representatives from St. Louis, New Orleans, and Miami.

There were others whose names were never disclosed or never recorded. Bugs Moran should have been there from Chicago, but he had been hiding since Schemer Drucci was shot, a year earlier, still thanking Heaven he had survived the massacre on St. Valentine's Day.

The meeting lasted three days and when it was over Capone announced, "We fought out our disagreements with words instead of bullets. When we agreed on everything we signed on the dotted line."

This was the conference for which Capone was heading when he and Frankie Rio left the Plantation after the deaths of Anselmi, Guinta, and Scalise.

In Atlantic City, Capone had spent a lot of time with Torrio. They had discussed the killing of Joey Guinta, president of the Unione, and the fact that a good many hotheads would be after Capone's scalp until Guinta was forgotten and replaced. They had discussed Bugs Moran's constant stream of threats and defiances, issued since the previous February to any reporter who would give them space in a newspaper.

A few years earlier, Johnny Torrio had spent ninety days in the Waukegan jail after recovering from his wounds. Now he told Capone that jail was the best vacation he had ever had. With his wealth and notoriety, he had been treated as an honored guest. Wardens and guards are like anyone else, happy to oblige the man whose money they can spend and whose favor they can curry in event of possible future need. Torrio suggested that Capone was hot and would be well advised to get out of circulation for a while. Torrio said, "The safest place in the world is inside a jail. Let's ask Boo Boo."

Max Hoff ran the state of Pennsylvania as Costello ran New York, Willie Morretti ran New Jersey, and the Prendergast-Binaggio combine ran the state of Missouri. All these men were like Capone in Illinois in that they could pick up a telephone and call by his first name a governor or a United States Senator. Each was depended on by judges in his home community for substantial campaign contributions and to deliver the vote on election day. Hoff undertook to arrange a term in jail for Capone.

Hoff arranged for the arrest of Capone and Frankie Rio shortly before midnight on May 16, 1929, in a Philadelphia movie theater. Capone, who had not carried a pistol in years, put one in his pocket on this occasion so there would be a specific charge on which he could be held.

When they were picked up, the night court set bond at $35,000 and, although Capone was carrying $50,000 in his pocket at the time, he elected to enter a cell. Fifty thousand dollars buys just as much comfort and luxury in Philadelphia as it does anywhere else on earth. Capone and Frankie Rio got the softest beds in the house and spent most of the night playing gin rummy with various police officials who came in to make their acquaintance.

Hoff had taken care of everything. Mayor Henry A. Mackey of Philadelphia spoke pontifically to the press: "From what we hear, Capone is running away from a gang that wants to kill him."

The next morning Judge John E. Walsh in Philadelphia's municipal court heard Capone and Rio enter pleas of guilty. He sentenced them to terms of one year each, with good behavior to be counted toward time off. Capone was given No. 90725 in the Holmesburg County jail until he could be moved to the Eastern Penitentiary with No. 5527-C. The understanding was that if prison proved onerous, Hoff could arrange for Capone's parole at any time.

The stay in prison proved anything but onerous. From the moment he reported to the warden's office, Capone was welcomed as though it were the governor himself making a visit.

Capone's private cell rivaled the warden's living quarters in the amenities with which it was equipped. A French screen hid the private toilet, the floor was covered with thickly padded rugs, and the chest of drawers matched the cabinet radio.

A phone was put in so that Capone could make limitless long-distance phone calls at state expense. But even Capone was astonished in May, 1929, when the warden asked if he wanted a stock ticker installed so he could follow the market.

Capone told the warden, "No, thanks. I never gamble."

Capone could receive his wife in the privacy of his cell whenever he wanted and Mae came to visit him every week at first and later every month during his stay. When she left their Chicago home, their school-age boy was left with his grandmother, Mrs. Theresa Capone.

Throughout his stay, Capone received Max Hoff and the gang leaders from Chicago in his cell. For some reason never explained he elected to meet his lawyers only in the warden's office. Capone was represented during this Pennsylvania hiatus by Bernard Lemisch and Benjamin M. Golder, the latter a Congressman from Philadelphia.

The gang leaders who conferred regularly with him in his cell included his brother Ralph, Jake Guzik, and Frank Nitti. This was the same Nitti who twenty years earlier had been Lou Greenberg's barber and who had fenced the stolen jewelry which Greenberg and Dion O'Banion filched from fallen drunks. Nitti was rising in the Capone organization.

Capone immediately embarked on a public relations program inside and outside the penitentiary. His first act inside was to buy $1000 worth of the artsy-craftsy work of other inmates. He bought virtually all the ship models, inlaid cigarette boxes, and other trinkets the men had made during incarceration. He had the stuff gift-wrapped and mailed to friends.

A Philadelphia newspaper carried a story about an orphanage in the city which was short of funds. Capone promptly sent the $1,200 needed to pay off the mortgage.

All who had contact with him in the prison remarked Capone's winning ways and genial disposition. Dr. Herbert M. Goddard of the Pennsylvania board of prison inspectors removed Capone's tonsils and operated on his nose. After some months of observation of this model prisoner, Dr. Goddard told newspapermen, "I cannot believe all they say of him. I have never seen a prisoner so kind, cheery, and accommodating. He does his work—that of file clerk—with a high degree of intelligence. I see him many times a week, often with his wife, his eleven-year-old son, and his mother. He is an ideal prisoner. You cannot tell me he is all bad."

The regular visits of his Irish wife probably had much to do with keeping the thirty-year-old prisoner tractable. Mae Coughlin was a couple of years older than Capone and had mothered him since they were married twelve years earlier. Capone was a healthy young man, full of beans where girls were concerned, and had always had female companionship readily available. There was never a hint that he sent outside the prison for call girls, as many of the wealthier prisoners frequently did.

Capone thrived on the prison regimen. He gained eleven pounds on the wholesome food, supplemented by what delicacies he or his friends happened to think of. He kept regular hours, putting in some time daily at his prison library job of filing papers and books.

He cultivated friendships among the other inmates who were proud to be associated with an outlaw of his reputation and were hopeful of being employed in his organization after he left the prison.

He later said that the principal thing the prison gave him was leisure to think. For years he had been on top of every smallest detail of his business. Now for the first time he could sit back and see it in perspective. He could see losses as well as gains and could plan for the repeal of Prohibition, which had been predicted by every underworld leader gathered at the Atlantic City conference.

At this point Capone began to formalize the Chicago organization.

A board of directors was set up so that details of the business no longer would be carried in the head of just one man. Johnny Torrio of Brooklyn was brought in on an annual retainer as senior counselor to this board. Others serving on it were Ralph Capone, Paul Ricca, Murray Humphreys, Anthony (Mops) Volpe, Jake Guzik, and Frank Nitti.

In Al Capone's absence, Frank Nitti was to serve as executive officer.

Nitti was in charge of operations; Jake Guzik, in charge of administration.

Nitti's lieutenants in various fields included Rocco de Grazio, alcohol; Joe Fusco, beer; Dennis (Duke) Cooney, prostitution; Bert Delaney, in charge of warehousing facilities; Anthony (Joe Batters) Accardo, enforcement; and Frankie Rio, street-gang liaison.

Nitti's right-hand men were Phil d'Andrea, managing promotion and sales; and Louis (Little New York) Campagna, dispatcher and traffic manager.

Guzik was office manager in charge of personnel and accounting. He put Hymie (Loud Mouth) Levin in charge of collections. For years Guzik had used William R. (Billy) Skidmore as a political fixer to collect weekly tribute from bookmakers, casino operators, and whorehouse operators; and to make the weekly payoffs to the City Hall, the state legislature, the judges on the bench, and the prosecutors in the state's attorney's office as well as the state police.

Skidmore, by mid-1929, was confining his operations principally to gambling. He was operating his own casinos, in partnership with William (Big Bill) Johnson, and was cooperating with the anti-Capone forces of Jack Zuta and Barney Bertsche. So Jake Guzik decided to handle his own collections and payoffs.

After that, Guzik sat two nights a week in St. Hubert's Old English Chop House and Grill at 316 South Federal Street, eating a leisurely dinner and sipping at a glass of wine. One of the evenings was devoted to collections and the other to payoffs. The restaurant was frequented by city and state politicians, jurists and prosecutors, and police officers of the highest rank. Guzik could pass to each his weekly envelope with the graft enclosed.

Accardo's enforcement crew at the time included Machine Gun Jack McGurn (born Vincenzo de Mora), Tough Tony Capezio, Claude (Screwy John Moore) Maddox, Sam (Golf Bag) Hunt, Jimmy (King of the Bombers) Belcastro, and James (Red) Forsyth, alias Jimmy Fawcett.

Murray Humphreys' labor activities and some of his aides have been introduced.

Frankie Rio, when he got out of prison, was to continue sales promotion work and ironing out grievances among the ethnic gangs which saw to it that the Capone products were used in their home neighborhoods. These included Jews, Greeks, Irish, Poles, Italians, and blacks. They still kept their old names, such as Ragen's Colts, the Circus Gang, the 42 Gang. The price they paid for the Capone organization's products at wholesale included the cost of centralized protection, together with bondsmen and lawyers. Rio always told them, "You guys got a bargain."

No industry or business in America was better set up to weather an economic depression as the 1929 stock market grew more and more erratic and moved toward the crash soon to come.

11 Public relations in Sicilian dialect

Capone said he enjoyed prison life for a few months but then he began to miss the excitement of the outside world. In the prison library he read avidly the daily newspapers and the more popular magazines. He followed news of the stock market crash and its aftermath as he once had followed sports results. The news of closing banks and factories, and of widespread unemployment, dominated the radio in his cell. He wanted constant financial reports from his business enterprises. He was restless and wanted to get out.

Max Hoff urged him to stay in the prison during the winter of 1929–30 but with the first hint of spring, Capone insisted on freedom. Arrangements were made for him to leave the prison on March 17, 1930.

Back in Chicago, Capone put into effect a gigantic public relations program he had planned. He seemed suddenly to feel an overwhelming urge to go legit. He wanted to be ready when Prohibition was repealed to carry on those of his businesses which were publicly acceptable. These included the handling of liquor, the operations of handbooks, and the race-news wire industry. But he wanted to get out of prostitution and the other areas frowned upon by the people he had formerly called "the goodie-goodies." He was not looking for the ascetic life, but appeared to want respectability.

The public relations program was worthy of a Madison Avenue agency. Clerks in the county bureau of vital statistics were paid to keep the Capone headquarters informed of births, marriages, and deaths of people with Italian-sounding names.

Capone had his aides send, in his name, appropriate messages or small gifts to the living, and wreaths to the dead. Even graduating classes of the city's high schools were studied so messages of congratulations might be sent Italian or Sicilian young people, anyone whose name ended in a vowel.

Anyone mentioned in the news with a name that sounded Italian might be surprised to find in his mailbox a few days later a little note of comment or congratulations signed "Al Capone." Any Italian or Sicilian reported by Capone's sources to be in any hospital in the city or suburbs received cut flowers or a blooming plant accompanied by one of Capone's engraved cards and a handwritten signature.

Capone's business enterprises were being efficiently run by the staffs he had trained, so he spent more time in a social life. This was not limited to appearances at prizefights and ballgames. He attended wakes and christenings. He spent his Sunday mornings in the Italian communities dispensing largesse and getting acquainted with people to whom earlier he had been but a name.

The teeming Italian and Sicilian colonies at the time were near Oak and Orleans streets, and in the Maxwell Street area near Taylor and Halsted. Capone frequented them. He was often in the growing Italian suburban community in Melrose Park.

Capone took time to talk in his Neapolitan dialect to older men and women in the streets, passing out a little currency where need was apparent. And in that summer of 1930, the illiterate and unskilled were already feeling the pinch of need.

Capone appeared to understand. He obviously enjoyed the feeling of munificence as he scattered a handful of silver coins among a crowd of youngsters who followed him down the street. Thousands of middle-aged and elderly Italians and Sicilians today recall that their unruly mops of hair were once mussed by a laughing Al Capone.

The project at first was designed to placate the Mustache Petes, who resented Capone's interference in affairs of the Unione. They had been grumbling at the lack of stability in the organization since Mike Merlo's death and had been attributing this fact to Capone and the others who lived outside the law. Actually, the mortality rate among Merlo's successors as president of the organization read much like the "begats" in the Bible. Merlo died November 9, 1924.

Angelo Genna had been the first to take office after Merlo. He was shot to death May 26, 1925. Samoots Amatuna, who had courted one of Mike Merlo's daughters, stepped into the office and was shot to death November 13, 1925. Antonio Lombardo changed the organization's name when he took office but he was shot to death September 7, 1928. His successor, Giuseppe Guinta, was shot to death by Al Capone on May 7, 1929. Joe Aiello, one of Capone's rivals, succeeded Guinta and was shot to death on October 23, 1930.

The organization's original charter was issued to six men whose family names still appear in news stories dealing with organized crime. The six were Calogero Fusco, Carmelo Priolo, Giuseppe Mirabella, Dominic

Miraldi, Andrea Russo, and Francesco Piazza. The six claimed 4,000 members and branches in thirty-two communities in 1895.

That was in the era when fraternal benefit insurance societies were springing up like wild flowers in a pasture.

The Capone heirs won their first firm and enduring hold on the organization when they put Frank Nitti in as president after Joe Aiello. Then Phil D'Andrea stepped into the presidency and he surrounded himself with such other officers as Tony Accardo, Paul Ricca, and Ricca's lawyer, Joseph I. Bulger (born Imburgio). Imburgio, man of mystery, lived a double life and disappeared December 2, 1966, when he apparently crashed his private plane near Spring City, Tennessee. Two things were missing from the site of the crash: Imburgio and millions of dollars he carried in a suitcase.

But to get back to the period when the United States sank into the economic depression from which it was to emerge only ten years later with the onslaught of production for World War II.

Capone's trifling gifts of currency were good public relations on a word-of-mouth basis but were given little or no mention in the daily press. Their principal value lay in the fact that they brought to Capone's personal attention the need among Italian and Sicilian families of Chicago and the suburbs. Thousands were jobless. Married children were moving in with their elders. Many were hungry.

Every ward politician had always made a practice of sending baskets of groceries and bags of coal to the needy on winter holidays. Capone asked his aides to send such baskets on a weekly basis to the growing number of families who turned to him for help. Before that first summer of depression had passed, he got another idea: He would open a soup kitchen in or near the Loop.

This project started in a small way as a pilot operation. Even in his charity work, Capone exercised hardheaded judgment. At first, only coffee and sweet rolls were served to the unemployed in an old storefront on the west side of State Street near Congress Street. A half-dozen missions in the area were serving coffee with hymns. But unlike any other soup kitchen in the city, the Capone operation was spotlessly clean. Instead of using homeless drunks as cooks and waiters, he paid good salaries and hired stable and competent help.

The various coffee roasters and blenders in the city were shown the wisdom of contributing their product "for the benefit of the unemployed." The various bakeries of the city were tapped for day-old sweet rolls, doughnuts, and coffee cakes.

Before the winter of 1930–31 set in, Al Capone's soup kitchen was serving hearty beef stew, chili con carne, and thick rye bread as well as coffee and thin hot chocolate. The place was open daily including Sundays and holidays from 6 o'clock in the morning until 10 o'clock at night.

The unemployed were encouraged to come in, get warm, and eat as frequently as they wanted to go through the lines for refills on tin plates. The food was solid stuff, tastily prepared. Bouncers kept order and gently pushed people out to make room for others after they had hung around long enough to get warm. The soup kitchen filled a genuine need for the city.

Like any philanthropist in the upperworld, Capone financed this goodwill venture in a businesslike way. Packinghouses and South Water Market commission merchants were the contributors of meat, potatoes, carrots, onions, and beans.

Each was assessed a certain amount each week. Some objected. Capone's men told them, "The Big Fellow doesn't want to see your trucks wrecked. He doesn't want to see your tires slashed. Do your bit without complaint."

Two weeks before Christmas, 1930, the price of beer to Loop speakeasies went up from $55 to $60 a barrel. The beer cost Capone $4 to manufacture. The Loop speakeasy proprietors, told of this increased price by Capone's salesmen, were also told, "The Big Fellow says we've all got to tighten our belts a little to help those poor guys who haven't got any jobs."

Capone, during this public relations era, kept himself in the public eye by attending prizefights, dog races, horseraces, and baseball games. He talked freely to newspapermen on any subject, whenever he was approached, and sometimes did not wait to be approached.

Merrill C. (Babe) Meigs, after whom Meigs Airport in Chicago is named, was publisher of the Chicago *Evening American* when a startling bit of intelligence came his way: Al Capone was said to be using the newspaper's circulation delivery trucks for transportation of illegal alcohol at night. Meigs ordered his circulation manager to investigate the rumor. The report turned out to be accurate. Meigs ordered the practice halted and the dismissal of drivers known to be guilty.

A day or so later, Meigs got a call from a man who identified himself as Al Brown and who asked an appointment. When the man was shown into his office, Meigs recognized Capone. The visitor came right to the point: "Mr. Meigs, you laid off some of my boys because they were doing a little emergency work for me. Maybe I handled it wrong. Maybe I should have paid you for the use of the trucks. Anyhow, I want to square things with you, pay whatever you think is right, and have my boys get their jobs back. They got families, you know."

Meigs said there was no chance of the fired drivers being rehired. He said that in using the Hearst circulation trucks for the delivery of illegal bootleg liquor, the drivers had forfeited any hope of future trust by their employer.

After some further discussion, all on a friendly basis, Capone left. A few weeks later "Al Brown" phoned again. Meigs recognized the voice and set up an appointment. This time Capone complained about use of the name "Scarface," as earlier noted in these pages.

After he had won his point on this issue, Capone kept after Meigs. The publisher said he found Capone to be an excellent bargainer. Capone asked that in the newspaper columns no further reference be made to the fact that he had started life as a pimp and once managed the Four Deuces for Johnny Torrio. Meigs quoted Capone: "I've got a mother who never misses mass unless she's too sick to get out of bed. I've a wife who loves me as dearly as any woman could love a man. They have feelings. They are hurt by what the newspapers say about me. And I can't tell you what it does to my twelve-year-old son when the other schoolchildren, cruel as they are, keep showing him newspaper stories that call me a killer or worse."

Meigs said Capone had tears in his eyes when he spoke of the cruelty practiced on his son in the schoolyard.

Capone went on to say that he felt he was supplying a need to the citizens of Chicago and that he was only the head of a widespread organization engaged in making and distributing beer and alcohol. He argued that the community benefited by his purchases of malt, hops, sugar, and grain from which the products were manufactured. He argued that if the Capone organization were not handling the beer and alcohol, supplying the city's needs, someone else might come in who would be a great deal more lawless.

Capone argued that nobody ever was killed except outlaws and that the community was better off without them.

Meigs shook his head as this impassioned plea drew to a close. He told Capone, "So long as you are engaged in this criminal enterprise, your activities are newsworthy and will be reported. So if your son and your wife and your mother are hurt by it, you have only yourself to blame. If you retire from the rackets, your activities no longer will be newsworthy. Your name will appear less and less frequently in the newspapers. Eventually you will be forgotten. The choice is yours, not mine."

When Capone was ready to leave the office after this visit, he asked if

Meigs would shake hands with him. Meigs would and did. As they parted, Capone said, "I like to talk to you, Mr. Meigs. You never give me any bullshit."

Meigs, a gentleman in every inch of his six-foot-six frame, was left speechless by this accolade.

A few days after this visit by Capone to Meigs' office, on June 9, 1930, another killing in downtown Chicago nullified much of the public relations campaign to clean up the Capone image.

The victim this time was Alfred (Jake) Lingle, a veteran reporter for the Chicago *Tribune*, who was shot to death shortly after noon in the pedestrian subway under Michigan Avenue, which he had entered from the public library steps on the Randolph Street side. The killing was in what Chicago calls "gang-style."

All the Chicago newspapers spoke out editorially against the increasing boldness of gang killers in the city. The fact that Lingle turned out to be a crooked newspaperman, while widely publicized, never got the public's attention as did the original story of his shooting.

In the aftermath of this killing, each of the Chicago daily papers began looking into the activities of their rivals' reporters. The *American* used its columns day after day to expose Lingle's underworld connections. So the *Tribune*, on a tip, sent investigative reporters to Florida to see what they could find out about writers for the *American*.

The *Tribune* was able to print pages of pictures showing Harry C. Read, city editor of the *American*, relaxing with Al Capone on the latter's Palm Island estate in Biscayne Bay off Miami Beach. Read, who had always acknowledged Capone's friendship, said he cultivated the gang leader only as a news source.

Suddenly, Babe Meigs realized that Capone probably had been briefed as to Meigs' sympathetic nature before coming to call on the publisher. Meigs felt he had been had. He promptly fired Harry Read.

Lingle's death brought a flare-up of underworld trouble. The gambling combine of Jack Zuta, Barney Bertsche, and Billy Skidmore had been seeking to expand the territory agreed at the 1926 conference. Zuta's string of brothels was run independently of his partners in gambling. He decided to branch out as a muscleman. With a crew of sluggers and torpedoes, he began cruising the area just west of the Loop looking for tribute. The crew shook down whores on the streets. They went into gambling joints, brothels, and speakeasies and demanded weekly payments.

Naturally, the proprietors of these places complained to Capone, whom they were already paying for protection. Capone phoned Zuta, warning him to call off his dogs, and punctuated the warning by having

Jimmy Belcastro touch off a dynamite bomb in Zuta's branch headquarters at 623 West Adams Street. The building was wrecked.

Zuta got the message and attended to his own business for a while. Then he thought he would try again in the wake of Jake Lingle's shooting, sure that Capone would not want any public trouble just at this time. Zuta was wrong. He was shot to death publicly, called off a dance floor for the execution, on August 1, 1930.

Capone's activities in the summer of 1930 were not confined to his public relations work among the members of the Italian community. He wanted to consolidate his position on every front. Instead of simply paying incumbent politicians to do his bidding, he wanted to put into office his own men.

His young lawyer, William J. (Billy) Parrillo, had been wangled an appointment to the federal prosecutor's office. He was now an Assistant United States District Attorney. His First Ward fixer, Dan Serritella, had served his apprenticeship in the City Hall and was now on his way to the legislature.

Capone permitted himself to be photographed with Roland V. Libonati, of the Illinois legislature. Libonati soon went to Congress. All recognized him as Capone's man.

At this time Capone's initials on an application were sufficient to win any man appointment to the police force in Chicago, in any of the suburban communities, in any of the counties in the area, or on the state highway patrol working out of Springfield.

But Capone was building his political organization solidly, from the bottom up. He cultivated the ward committeemen and the precinct captains who rang doorbells and fixed traffic tickets. He made these men his own, knowing that from among their ranks would emerge the political leaders of the future. They would be Capone men all their lives, long after Capone himself was buried.

Gangsters do not live in a world populated solely by outlaws and politicians. The wide publicity given the 1926 underworld peace conference had repercussions not foreseen by its signatories. The men and women of the Establishment, the ones who subsidize opera and the symphony and run the banks and major industries, began for the first time to consider Capone in some light other than as a nine-day-wonder to fill news columns in the penny-dreadful press.

These people began in 1927 to consider what the Capone image might be doing to the city's economy. They thought about it again after the Frankie Yale killing in the East. Gangsters became the subject of luncheon talk at the Attic Club and the Chicago Club. They became the subject of dinner talk on Lake Shore Drive and in suburban Lake Forest.

A consensus began to take shape: It was time to stop brazen outlawry.

General Charles Gates Dawes of Evanston, one of the nation's leading bankers, who at that time was Vice President of the United States, was very much a member of the Chicago Establishment. He and his brother, Rufus, who headed the family bank in the Loop, told friends that the frequency and savagery of gang warfare in the Chicago streets was leading some of the men of Wall Street to wonder if their money was safely invested in Chicago.

Two decisions emerged from these discussions, both traceable directly to the peace conference of 1926. First, the business leaders revived the idea of a world's fair, which had been talked about even before Philadelphia scheduled its 1926 exposition. Second, they decided that special prosecutors would have to be sent in from Washington to find some federal charge on which the city's gangsters could be prosecuted.

They felt that an exposition larger than anything ever seen before in the Middle West might restore Chicago's image before the world. They believed that if they could bring millions of visitors from every nation to see the city's progress they could do more than in any other way to convince the world that most people in Chicago never actually saw a gangster.

They decided they needed ten years to plan and build the sort of exposition they had in mind. Since Chicago had been incorporated in 1837, they decided to put on the exposition in 1937 and to call it "A Century of Progress."

Long before that exposition was ready to open its doors, they hoped to have Al Capone and his minions behind bars and the city restored to the relative law and order of pre-Prohibition days.

The Dawes brothers were important to both plans. Rufus Dawes became president of the World's Fair Corporation. Charles G. Dawes recommended as its chief executive, to start planning immediately, a bright young army engineer of Washington, Major Lenox R. Lohr.

No one then foresaw the stock market crash of 1929. When it came, with financial panic and deflation, the Chicago leaders decided against canceling the exposition. Instead, they would move its opening date up four years. They would open immediately after the next Presidential inauguration, in the spring of 1933. Someone asked how they could keep the name, "A Century of Progress." He was answered, "Hell, old Fort Dearborn must at least have achieved village status by 1833. If it did not, who is to know the difference?"

Vice President Dawes continued to pull strings in Washington. Three months after Capone's peace conference, in mid-January, 1927, a new United States Attorney was appointed for the Northern District of

Illinois. He was George E. Q. Johnson. One of the conditions of his appointment was that he was not to interfere with the work of a special prosecutor who would be sent out from Washington.

The special prosecutor, sent to Chicago three weeks after Johnson's appointment, was a thirty-year-old lawyer who in only eighteen months had made a reputation in the Washington headquarters of the Internal Revenue Service, or the Bureau of Internal Revenue as it then was called. The young lawyer, Dwight H. Green, had a background interesting principally because it was so unspectacular.

Green had been a newspaper reporter in Chicago while attending law school. When he received his degree, he worked as a law clerk for the legal firm which represented the Hearst newspapers in Chicago. After he had a little experience, he filled out an application for federal employment and was offered a minor job in the income tax office. On the strength of that job, he married.

For his first nine months in Washington, Green was in the interpretative division of the bureau's legal department. For nine months he simply wrote opinions on questions involving interpretations of the revenue laws. Then he was transferred to the Board of Tax Appeals Division. For the next several months he got plenty of practice trying cases before the board.

So far as Dawes or any of his Chicago friends were aware, Green was completely without political connections or friends at court. They felt that if anybody might be able to withstand the pressures and inducements which Al Capone would certainly offer, this young man could do so. Green was specifically instructed that while he would be attached administratively to the office of the district attorney in Chicago, he would be operationally responsible only to his superiors in Washington. Green was told, "Your job is to send the Chicago gangsters to prison. You can call on revenue agents, special agents, or agents of the Special Intelligence Division of the Treasury Department. You can have the staff you need as quickly as you can show the need for it. Go to it."

In Chicago, Green found many of the revenue agents keeping scrapbooks and files about doings of leading gangsters. If a columnist had reported some gangster dropped a bundle of currency on a prizefight or a horserace, the story had been clipped and filed under that gangster's name. Such items as the story about the $30,000 armored car said to be used by Capone went into the file, as did that of the 200 silk shirts said to have been owned by Samoots Amatuna.

Green reasoned that either a grand jury or a trial jury would accept the fact that before a man could spend cash he had to receive it.

The idea seems obvious today, but at the time Green took charge of the Capone investigation the federal income tax law had been on the books only fourteen years. Green's staff worked quietly and successfully. They took three years preparing their first case.

In the spring of 1930, just after Al Capone left Eastern Penitentiary in Pennsylvania, the government accountants had their case against Frank Nitti. They presented to a federal grand jury in Chicago evidence indicating that Nitti had spent $624,888 during the years 1925, 1926, and 1927. The government said that to have spent the money, Nitti must have had income at least in that amount. And that Nitti should have paid $227,940 in taxes on such an income.

Capone sought to put in a fix on Nitti's case. The first step was to approach Billy Parrillo, his personal lawyer for whom he had bought an appointment as assistant United States attorney in the federal district of Northern Illinois. Parrillo nosed around and came back to report Dwight Green's entire staff was on such a tight rein out of Washington that no fix was possible in Chicago.

Then Capone, through the members of Congress who were on his payroll, sought to straighten things out in Washington. They worked on the Treasury Department, which controlled the Bureau of Internal Revenue, and on the Attorney General's office, under whose command the Chicago prosecutors worked. They came up against stone walls. Capone's men told him, "The Cabinet members are nothing. Anybody can fix them. The staff in the White House can be fixed if a little money is spread around. But there is a second echelon of anonymous men who simply cannot be touched personally and won't permit a fix by their bosses."

Capone at first thought this anonymous second echelon consisted of ordinary bureaucrats, federal employees who depended on their salaries, lived in hope of their pensions, and resented the riches they saw in the hands of gangsters. Capone sent emissaries to Washington with virtual carte blanche in the spending of money. But they never could seem to reach the right people. One lawyer told him, "I spent forty thousand dollars in just one office, spreading it around. I left a thirty-thousand-dollar bundle in a deserted office at night and waited across the hall in the men's room so I could peek and see who got it. A United States Senator sneaked in, picked up the newspaper-wrapped bundle, and sneaked out again. Later I learned that we had not bought a goddamn thing."

Capone had come up against the oligarchy, the real rulers of America, the men who could not be fixed. They were neither elected representatives at any level, nor jurists on any bench, nor bureaucrats dependent on their government payrolls and pensions.

These were the men of Wall Street, partners in investment banking firms or corporate law offices, high-ranking employees of shipping firms and giant industrial combines. They move in and out of Washington, serve a few years for whatever administration happens to be in power, and then return to their own firms.

Usually they marry into the areas of power if they are not born into them. They attend the right schools, court only the right debutantes, join only the right clubs, and accept the tutelage of their mentors in what Ferdinand Lundberg was even then speaking of as "America's Sixty Families."

These were the men in the Cabinet departments, usually bearing the title of undersecretary or special deputy or special counsel, who were behind the Dawes brothers in Chicago's preparation for its world's fair. These were the men who carried the orders of the corporate owners of the nation, and who saw to it that politicians from the President down carried out the orders.

And this was the group that could not be bribed. The powers behind the scenes had decreed that the gang leaders be sent to prison. Al Capone had always been dimly and instinctively aware that such a power existed. But never before in his career had he come up against it.

Frank Nitti's case was called in a federal court in Chicago that November. He pleaded guilty. He was fined $10,000 and sentenced to serve eighteen months in Leavenworth penitentiary. He served most of his term, winning a few months off for good behavior.

For the first time the people of Chicago and of the nation had seen the Capone combine come up against a power that could not be bought.

Ralph Capone was next on Dwight Green's list. He was charged with failure to pay all the tax due on his income from 1922 through 1928. He was indicted and brought to trial. He was found guilty, sentenced to pay a fine of $10,000, and ordered to serve three years in Leavenworth.

He entered prison November 7, 1931, to emerge thirty months later with time off for good behavior.

Even before Ralph entered prison, Al Capone had been indicted and brought to trial on October 6, 1931, charged with income tax evasion. He anticipated, as did everyone else connected with the case, a fine and a "normal" sentence of two or three years. But Federal Judge James H. Wilkerson had his orders. Whatever his personal feelings in the matter might have been, he had no choice but to bang his gavel and say: "Eleven years."

Capone was through. He knew it and everyone else knew it. His unprecedented power in the city and the state had rested on the implied boast that he was invincible. Once that balloon had been pricked, any cop on the beat with enough physical courage could roust Al Capone like a common thief. Capone personally was through, after spending a fortune on lawyers and in fruitless efforts to buy off everyone from the White House down. Now it remained only to make arrangements to keep his business enterprises together and operating until he could return to resume control.

Capone instructed his lawyers to use every tactic to delay his entry into prison for at least six months. He wanted to wait until Frank Nitti was free and able to run things in Capone's absence.

Al Capone entered the federal prison at Atlanta on May 4, 1932.

By that time, Nitti was back and had the reins in his hands.

The next of the gang to go was Jake Guzik, the pimp who had been an accountant until he displayed the management genius which took him to the top. Guzik was charged, indicted, tried, and found guilty of income tax evasion. He was ordered to pay a fine of $17,000 and to serve five years in prison. He entered Lewisburg penitentiary on April 8, 1932, a month before Al Capone surrendered to begin his term.

Guzik served less than four years, leaving prison on December 16, 1935, to come back to his old post in the Capone enterprises.

Al Capone never publicly returned to Chicago, although he was known to participate in the direction of his business from Ralph's farm home at Mercer, Wisconsin. The Syndicate, something that in the upperworld would later be called a conglomerate, had been put together by Capone but its direction fell to Frank Nitti, the one-time barber.

12 The tricks of the diplomats

The cleaning and dyeing industry in Chicago had been a monopoly long before Al Capone. The great cleaning and dyeing plants of the city were organized into a price-fixing outfit called the Master Cleaners and Dyers Association. This employers' union in turn owned the two labor unions in the field, the inside clerks and the outside delivery men. A tidy little operation and profitable for its owners.

But within the cleaning and dyeing association there was a great number of small shopkeepers who legitimately could not call themselves either master cleaners and dyers, nor prospects for membership in any labor union. They were the little one-man tailor shops in every neighborhood. They were shopowners, free-enterprise entrepreneurs, and they paid their association dues just as though they had a voice in their own destiny.

These were not tailoring establishments in the European sense of the word. None of these tailors could cut, make, and sew. They could produce nothing from scratch. But they could run a steam pressing machine, or hire someone else to do it for them, and sew on buttons, repair tears and rips, shorten sleeves, or let out seams. Mostly they served as drops for people who wanted laundry work, or cleaning and dyeing work.

The tailor would accept the work, then send it out to be done.

The men who owned the association got too greedy. They kept boosting prices higher and higher. Finally the general public ceased having clothing cleaned commercially in the city. Many householders did their own cleaning with a bucket and a can of naphtha from the nearest hardware store.

Others took their soiled suits and overcoats to the suburbs where they could get the services of independent cleaners.

The independents had small, modern, inexpensive cleaning machines. They were out of the high-rent district. Mostly they did not have to pay out a percentage of their gross in the form of dues and assessments to an association. So they could work much cheaper.

The immediate sufferers were the little tailor shops in every neighborhood. Even when the quantity of work fell off, they still had to pay the black who ran the pressing machine. They still had to pay the boy on a bicycle or the helper on a delivery truck who picked up and delivered work in the neighborhood.

They still had to pay their dues and assessments to the Master Cleaners and Dyers Association even when they realized no benefits.

Some of them complained that conditions in the industry were unbearable. They decided to do something about it. A hundred of such little tailor-shop owners on the North and Northwest sides of the city withdrew from the monopoly association. They organized a cooperative cleaning plant, calling it the Central Cleaning Company, installing Ben Kornick as its president. Naturally the whole idea had been Kornick's.

No monopoly can work if there is any competition in the field. Competition would force prices down to the market level, to the level of supply and demand. The Master Cleaners and Dyers Association had no choice.

If it were to live and its owners were to continue occupying fine country estates this new independent cooperative had to go.

So the association hired strong-arm men from the underworld, who told the shopkeepers they could have their cleaning done wherever they wanted, so long as they kept on paying dues and assessments to the association's owners.

Further, the strong-arm boys told the little tailors, they had to keep the black pressing-machine operator on the weekly payroll and he had to keep paying dues to the inside workers' union. Also, the tailors had to continue hiring just as many delivery helpers as ever, paying just as much in weekly wages, and the delivery helpers had to pay union dues.

In other words, anybody sewing buttons commercially in Chicago was running a closed shop whether he wanted it or not. He was not going to hire any nonunion labor, nor lay off any of his union help.

Even as the racketeers were getting this message across to the little tailors and their inside help, the strong-arm boys were making the message clear to the drivers and helpers on the pickup trucks used by the tailors. Drivers were pulled from their trucks, shown a pair of brass knucks, and reminded of their union obligations and responsibilities.

These were the tactics applied to the little tailors, to their inside help, and to their outside help, as soon as they signed up with Ben Kornick and his Central Cleaning Company. The racket bosses had something else in mind for Kornick's premises, his trucks, and his employees.

At first the trucks entering or leaving the premises of the Central Cleaning Company plant were simply turned over on their sides. When the independent operation continued, strong-arm boys emptied the trucks and strewed the clean garments about the streets so that they were smeared with dust and oil. When even this tactic did not halt the independent operation, garments in Kornick trucks were sprinkled with acid.

That was the time every tailor began adding a nickel a garment to the price of cleaning and calling it "insurance." The practice continues to this day. No government, upperworld or underworld, ever abolishes a tax once it has been imposed.

Ben Kornick and his backers felt they could not fight the tactics of the Master Cleaners and Dyers Association. But they knew someone who could. They met with George (Bugs) Moran, who with Vincent (Schemer) Drucci ran the remnants of Dion O'Banion's old gang. Kornick contracted to pay Moran and Drucci $1,800 a week if their gunmen would ride shotgun on Kornick's trucks and see that they got through the blockades with their cargoes of clean garments. That took care of the North Side.

A similar situation arose on the South Side. Morris Becker owned and operated an independent chain of retail cleaning shops. Becker's were not little tailoring shops, but simply drops for garments to be cleaned. The pressing was not done on the premises, but at the central plant.

Morris Becker operated his own cleaning plant.

The Master Cleaners and Dyers Association had let Becker run, thinking their hands were full elsewhere and that he could always be knocked out of the game.

Now they sent their messengers around to see him. When they threatened Becker, he did just what any law-abiding citizen is supposed to do: He turned to the law for protection.

In Chicago?

Morris Becker made his complaint to the state's attorney's office. A prosecutor took him before the county grand jury, where he repeated his story. Nobody could say it was not a clear complaint, naming names and citing instances. Becker told the grand jury under oath: "I was introduced to Mr. Sam Rubin by my foreman. I was told Mr. Rubin worked for the Master Cleaners Association. I said, 'Oh, you're that Mr. Rubin I hear so much about.' He said, 'Yes, and you will hear a great deal more. I'll tell you something, Becker. You have to raise prices.'

"I replied, 'The Constitution guarantees me the right to life, liberty, the pursuit of happiness—and to set my own prices.'

"Rubin said, 'The hell with the Constitution. As far as you are concerned, I am a damned sight bigger than the Constitution.'"

Becker said he later was visited by Arthur Berg, secretary of the

Master Cleaners Association. Berg told him he would have to contribute $5,000 to a fund to be used in maintaining monopoly cleaning prices. Becker quoted Berg: "I am getting all of them to put up five thousand dollars apiece."

Morris Becker's testimony was supported by the testimony of his son, Theodore Becker. On the strength of this testimony and other evidence the grand jury indicted fifteen members of the Master Cleaners and Dyers Association.

They hired Clarence Darrow as their lawyer. By the time the case came to trial the fix was in, from top to bottom. The jury heard the Beckers. They heard a prosecutor present a half-hearted case. They got instructions from the judge. And the jury only took fifteen minutes to bring in the verdict: not guilty.

Morris Becker nodded his head. The verdict was just what he had expected. He had no intention of appealing or going through any of the other legal motions. He had tried to be a good citizen, tried to use the law the way it was written. But he knew what the alternative would be.

As he left the courtroom, Morris Becker went to the nearest public telephone booth and called the Metropole Hotel. He asked for Mr. Al Brown and was told to identify himself and state his business. In a few minutes he was told to go to his office and await a call. A conference would be set up, probably in the next day or two.

Next day, Morris Becker was called downtown to a conference with Al Capone, Jake Guzik, and Louis Cowan. Cowan was Al Capone's principal bail bondsman, kept on a retainer for day or night service. As the conference opened, the others were joined by Abraham Teitelbaum, Capone's personal lawyer. They talked in general terms and then specifically.

As a result, Morris Becker's old company went out of business and he organized a new corporation, the Sanitary Cleaning Shops, Inc. Al Capone explained that he needed such a corporate setup for his own protection, so that if Becker failed it would not imperil his other enterprises.

The limited nature of corporate liability was perfectly plain to Becker. He was delighted with the arrangement.

The articles of incorporation, studied by Walter G. Walker, attorney for the Employers Association of Chicago, showed that $25,000 had been given to Capone, Guzik, and Cowan.

Becker waited a few days until the corporate documents had been recorded in Springfield and then he called a press conference. He told newspapermen the history of his dealings with the Master Cleaners Association. He said he now was "paying Al Capone twenty-five thousand dollars a year for the use of his name." Becker went on: "I have no need of the police, of the courts, of the law. I have no need of the Employers Association of Chicago. With Al Capone as my partner, I have the best protection in the world."

Things turned out just the way Morris Becker hoped they would. He never again had any trouble with the Master Cleaners Association. No pirate in his right mind in Chicago in the twenties would attack a ship flying the house flag of Al Capone. A score of years later a reporter looked up Morris Becker and asked him about this partnership with Capone. Becker said, "Al Capone was scrupulous in living up to his bargain. I was equally scrupulous. I never had anything to complain about with him, and I tried to give him nothing to complain about with me. We never became close friends but our relations were always correct. If I had it to do over again I would never ask a more honest partner in any business."

That statement was made at a time when Al Capone was out of circulation and the Capone Syndicate apparently posed no threat to Becker or his family. Becker presumably felt under no compulsion.

His words were thoughtful and seemed to come from the heart. A different view of Capone from that usually voiced.

An employers' association is almost always put together by some jackleg lawyer who makes a career of Cassandra-like predictions. He keeps his sponsors thinking their livelihoods are threatened. Because of this, they are happy to pay monthly membership dues into the association that supposedly stands between their businesses and the threatened calamity.

Nobody had to explain the technique to Al Capone.

In the twenties the Midwest Garage Owners Association was the property of David (Cockeyed Mulligan) Albin.

In due course it came to the attention of the Capone group and Murray Humphreys was told to scout the outfit. Humphreys and Red Barker called on Albin. They told him not to attend future meetings of the association. Then, as had been done in the case of Lefty Lynch at Burlington, Wisconsin, they sent Danny Stanton around to put a bullet through Albin's foot to make sure he got the message.

Albin never showed up at another meeting of the Midwest Garage Owners Association. The way that Humphreys and Barker handled things left the garage owners little cause for complaint. Humphreys and Barker went into the Maxwell street area to talk to members of the 42 Gang. This was a rowdy bunch of youngsters who patterned themselves after Ali Baba and the Forty Thieves. Except that at their first roll call there were forty-two members present. So they called themselves, for want of a better name, the 42 Gang. The survivors of that old bunch, among others, included Salvatore (Sam Mooney) Giancana, and Sam (Teats) Battaglia.

Humphreys and Barker got a dozen members of the 42 Gang to roam the streets methodically at night, puncturing with ice picks the tires of automobiles parked at the curbs. The Garage Owners' Association placed newspaper ads and radio spot announcements urging automobile owners to protect their cars from such vandalism by parking them in garages overnight.

The campaign was successful. The incomes of the garage owners doubled within a month. Humphreys and Barker collected from the garage owners, in addition to their monthly dues, a stated amount for each car stored in their facilities overnight.

Ten percent of this revenue was distributed among membership of the 42 Gang.

This was the underworld equivalent of Junior Achievement, teaching youngsters the profits to be earned in free enterprise.

Humphreys and Barker observed, as they personally led the gangs of young hoodlums on these nightly forays against cars parked along the city's curbs, that there was an astonishing number of cars not in daily use. Some of these parked cars would have their tires punctured and continue to sit at the same curb, day after day, with the owner apparently unwilling to have the tires repaired.

This gave Humphreys an idea. What the city needed was to have a towing service to keep the curbs clear of cars which constantly occupied space on the streets. Humphreys felt they interfered with traffic.

Humphreys and Barker decided on which of the members of the Midwest Garage Owners Association would have the monopoly on this towing service for each neighborhood of the city. Through their political connections downtown, they got special permits issued to such garage owners. Then the politicians issued orders to the police to ticket the cars which appeared abandoned and if the tickets remained on the cars, to call for tow trucks and have them impounded in private garages.

Similarly, when a car was involved in an accident on the street or highway, the policeman was instructed to call for a tow truck. The calls were routed to the favored garages. The policeman who made the call got a stated kickback, at first $2 and later $5 for each such call.

Capone always believed in sharing the wealth, all along the line.

Barker got an idea for a little side money on the garage towing racket. As long as there have been lawyers, there have been ambulance chasers. Now Barker arranged for the policeman's call, reporting an auto accident, to be routed to a favored lawyer. The lawyers made their kickbacks, if and when they got the cases, to the Capone organization.

As soon as the publicity about Al Capone being taken in as a partner by Morris Becker had died down, Humphreys turned his attention to the Master Cleaners and Dyers Association. Humphreys and Barker had been present when Morris and Theodore Becker told Capone all they knew about the association. Humphreys needed only to approach Sam Rubin and Arthur Berg with his proposition.

Capone had been particularly impressed with the intelligence that John G. Clay, in seventeen years as secretary-treasurer of the Laundry and Dye House Chauffeurs Union, had built a $300,000 treasury. He said to Humphreys, "Nobody ought to keep a sum like that in a bank, just drawing interest. Let's put it to work in the American way."

Humphreys went after the owners' association first, knowing that as soon as he had it under control he could move quickly on its unions.

The terror began with midnight telephone calls to Rubin and Berg and the others who ran the association. Their hands were far from clean, since they had been hiring thugs to frighten every little tailor in town. They were told, in these midnight phone calls, that if they did not voluntarily ask Humphreys to take charge of their association, their wives would be dipped in acid.

They reported the calls to police. The racket squad picked up Humphreys for questioning. He said, "For heaven's sake, fellows, would I be nutty enough to use my own name if I was making the calls?" Humphreys was freed.

The association man who had informed to the police was held up next night by two thugs who broke one of his arms. Dynamite blew the porches off the homes of some association leaders. Humphreys was called in to halt the terror.

Immediately, Humphreys reached out to grab the $300,000 treasury.

Humphreys had once run a cleaning and dyeing shop. He knew the business. He took over the Master Cleaners and Dyers Association, then took over the two unions: inside and outside.

Control of the unions and of the employer associations took on a new urgency for Capone during the two years between the time he left Eastern Penitentiary in Pennsylvania and the time he entered Atlanta Penitentiary in Georgia. The newspapers in Chicago were filled with news of A Century of Progress, due to open in 1933. Emissaries of the upperworld were visiting foreign lands arranging for national displays.

But Capone did not wait for the world's fair actually to open. Land had to be cleared on Northerly Island, off the lakeshore at Twenty-third, and a gigantic building program had to be undertaken. Through his unions, Capone controlled the trucking and much of the construction work.

He had failed in his bid to take over the Chicago Building Trades Council, but he was in a position to make trouble unless he collected regular tribute from everybody.

The private contractor who wanted to do any building within a large American city first figured the actual cost of the job according to specifications laid down by the engineers. Then he added 10 percent for overhead and 10 percent for profit. This was the basic cost of the job. The contractor may have felt that he could shave it a bit if he had a particularly efficient operation, an uncommonly cheap source of materials, or a connection with the engineers which assured they would approve shortcuts and shoddy workmanship.

Having done all this in Chicago in the Twenties, the private contractor added 20 percent to his final figure "to take care of the boys downtown."

This was just as true on construction jobs ordered by private enterprise as on city, state, or governmental work. Except that in contracting with private enterprise, the contractor added a full 20 percent only if the work was to be done in the Loop or downtown areas. In outlying areas he might be able to get by with paying 10 percent or 15 percent graft for the privilege of working.

This was true not simply of new construction but of repairs and maintenance. The formula applied in tuck-pointing or window washing or building cleaning and sandblasting. If the 20 percent was not paid at the time of application for a building permit there would be a delay. One delay after another attended every step of the work until all profits were eaten up and performance bonds had to be paid.

Capone's men went around to all the contractors who were accepting construction jobs on Northerly Island and told them they had better figure an additional 10 percent on everything. They intended to collect this 10 percent "off the top." No contractor could refuse. The Capone demand did not change the competitive nature of bids, since it was assessed against all contractors in the field.

The promoters of A Century of Progress were seeking to earn all they could from businesses on the fairgrounds. They had all kinds of concessions they were prepared to offer for a price: the popcorn concession, the hot dog concession, the hamburger concession, the soft drink concession, the bus concession, the hat check concession, the rickshaw concession.

Several of the Capone men invested their personal money in such concessions, Murray Humphreys keeping the popcorn concession for himself. He hired a manager, who in turn hired help and rented booths. Humphreys ran the whole thing as a businessman, stopping by each night to count the receipts. Each week, during the two years of the fair's operation, he was able to bank a few thousand dollars from popcorn sales.

Space for cabarets and restaurants on the fairgrounds was being leased. Several of the Capone aides invested their personal money to buy stock in such enterprises. In addition, the Capone group leased its own such operation, to be called the San Carlo Italian Village.

The enterprise prospered so long as the fair was open. Capone was in prison at the time but one or several of the officers of his organization was present nightly to see that the Italian Village was run with dignity.

While seeking to put his affairs in order before going off to prison, Capone felt he had one major dream as yet unrealized. From the time he had opened his soup kitchen in the spring of 1930 and learned a little about the fresh milk industry, Capone had been fascinated by it. Time and again he told his aides, with wonder in his voice: "Do you guys know there's a bigger markup in fresh milk than there is in alcohol? Honest to God, we've been in the wrong racket right along."

Capone expected to be locked up for a maximum of two years. During that time he expected the repeal of Prohibition. When he emerged, he hoped to be the owner of an established retail dairy business competing for the sale of milk to every family in the Chicago area. He talked of his dream: "You gotta have a product that everybody needs every day. We don't have it in booze. Except for the lushes, most people only buy a couple of fifths of gin or scotch when they're having a party. The workingman laps up half a dozen bottles of beer on Saturday night and that's it for the week. But with milk! Every family every day wants it on the table. The people on Lake Shore Drive want thick cream in their coffee. The big families out back of the yards have to buy a couple of gallons of fresh milk every day for the kids."

So Capone concentrated on getting his dairy business in operation.

Steve Sumner, business agent for Teamsters Local 753 of the Milk Wagon Drivers Union, testified under oath as to the planning and conversations which preceded the chartering of Meadowmoor Dairies, Inc. Sumner said that in the late spring of 1931, just after Capone was indicted, two of Capone's representatives came to call on him. He identified them as Murray Humphreys and Frankie Diamond, alias Frank Maritote, whose brother, John Maritote, had married Capone's sister, Mafalda Capone.

Sumner said Humphreys and Diamond asked his help in starting Meadowmoor Dairies, Inc. He quoted Humphreys as saying, "Since

1926, Capone has been trying to diversify his investments in legitimate business even while consolidating his brewing and distilling empire. He is opening a retail dairy business."

Sumner said under oath that Humphreys and Diamond not only wanted to make sure he would give them no union trouble when Capone launched his dairy. They also wanted Sumner to buy into the enterprise. Sumner refused. Humphreys then gave him an alternative. Sumner quoted Humphreys as saying, "Your union has a million dollars in the treasury. I will hand you a hundred thousand dollars cash today. All you have to do is walk away. Leave town. I'll take over from here."

Sumner, who was still a walking delegate at the age of eighty-one, said, "Out of the question."

As soon as he left Humphreys and Diamond that day, said Sumner, he ordered sheet metal contractors to make the union headquarters bulletproof. The place was turned into a fort. Sumner ordered bulletproof glass installed in his car.

He armed his chauffeur and he hired bodyguards for his office and his home.

But as it turned out, Sumner was not bothered by Humphreys.

The president of Sumner's Local 753, Robert G. (Old Doc) Ritchie, was kidnapped by Humphreys in December, 1931. Sumner testified under oath that Humphreys and Red Barker demanded $50,000 for Ritchie's release. Sumner paid it and Ritchie was freed.

Sumner gave this testimony on October 19, 1933, before a master in chancery who had been appointed by Federal District Judge John P. Barnes. The master in chancery, as it happened, was the same George E. Q. Johnson who had lost his post as district attorney with the election of President Franklin D. Roosevelt. All Republicans were replaced by Democrats.

On that occasion, Steve Sumner told Master Johnson, "I handed Murray Humphreys fifty thousand dollars' cash in December. Two months later, on February 23, 1932, Meadowmoor Dairies, Inc., was chartered with capital of fifty thousand dollars."

Meadowmoor Dairies, at 1334 South Peoria Street, was chartered almost three months before Capone entered Atlanta prison on May 4, 1932. The company was represented by Billy Parrillo's law firm, Parrillo, Roach, and Schaub.

Murray Humphreys was later accused by the Internal Revenue Service of failing to pay income tax on the $50,000 ransom that Steve Sumner had laid out for the release of Bob Ritchie. Humphreys pleaded guilty to the charge, paying the tax plus penalty and interest.

The case in which Judge Barnes had appointed Master Johnson to take testimony was a suit brought on behalf of Meadowmoor Dairies by Billy Parrillo's law firm. The brief asked that receivers be appointed for the four largest retail distributors of fresh milk in Chicago: Bowman Dairy Company, Borden Milk Company, Wieland Dairy Company, and Wanzer Dairy Company. The suit asked that these four and fifty-one other defendants be enjoined from "interfering with independent dairies."

Meadowmoor then operated under what is called the vendors' system to avoid hiring union milk drivers and paying union wages. This is the system used by the daily newspapers to get around the child labor laws by calling their newsboys "little merchants." Meadowmoor sold fresh milk to drivers at 5 cents a quart and the drivers resold it, primarily to stores, so that the milk brought an average retail price of 7 cents a quart.

But the men who were establishing Meadowmoor were not accustomed to being denied. When the smoke settled, Meadowmoor was permanently established on the Chicago scene. The company has prospered ever since.

Having taken testimony in the case, Master Johnson reported to the federal court of Judge Barnes on January 19, 1934, that "persons of ill repute and criminals undertook to act for the Meadowmoor Dairy Company."

At the time Meadowmoor filed its lawsuit with the federal court, Walter R. Schaub, of Billy Parrillo's law firm, was vice-president of the corporation. In Meadowmoor's annual report filed June 8, 1934, Schaub was listed as corporate treasurer as well as director. At that time C. W. Schaub was listed as president, secretary, and director of the corporation. In Meadowmoor's annual report filed June 2, 1941, Walter R. Schaub was still listed as treasurer and C. W. Schaub was still listed as president.

But in that 1941 report, the corporate secretary of record was J. Parrillo of 3322 Polk street. Billy Parrillo's parents, who lived at that address, were Pasquale Parrillo, who had died in 1938, and Mrs. Josephine Parrillo.

In 1961, Meadowmoor Dairies, Inc. amended its articles of incorporation to become officially the Richard Martin Milk Company. Under the new articles, the company no longer was required to file an annual report listing officers and directors. The name Meadowmoor still appears on the milk products which are the equal in quality of any sold in the Chicago market. The Meadowmoor products have captured a good share of the Chicago market.

Meadowmoor's entry into the fresh milk field was said by Capone to be one of the best things that ever happened for the health of the people of the Chicago area. The new competition, in the depths of the Depression, caused the old established dairies to bring their fresh milk prices down so their products were within reach of families whose incomes had been reduced.

Until Meadowmoor's advent, the city of Chicago never had had a legal definition of Grade A milk. The Capone adherents in the city council—and the Capone organization at the time was credited with control of the strongest bloc—fought for a definition of Grade A. They insisted that no fresh milk of lesser quality be offered for sale in the Chicago market area.

The Capone bloc in the council fought for a dated-milk ordinance, under which fluid milk could not be offered for sale as fresh milk more than seventy-two hours after it left the cow.

The date by which the milk was to be sold was clearly stamped on the container, where the consumer could read and understand it.

The old established dairies fought every change proposed. They expressed themselves through their lawyers as unalterably opposed to the dated-milk ordinance. They called it unnecessary and probably unconstitutional.

Every newspaper reporter covering the day by day story of that floor fight in the Chicago city council saw the anomaly. Usually the forces of the upperworld, bankers and merchants and commercial giants, were portrayed as the protectors of the people; and the forces of the underworld, pimps and thieves and racketeers, could be portrayed as the underminers of popular health.

But this story had to be delicately handled so that the daily newspaper reader would have no hint of the antagonist and protagonist in this battle for the health of Chicago's babies.

The Capone forces won. Children had the protection of a dated-milk ordinance in Chicago.

A generation later and after Heaven knows what political pressure and expenditure of money, the major dairies of Chicago were able to get that dated-milk ordinance changed. They hired witnesses to swear that with the invention and perfection of modern refrigeration such a practice of dating milk was no longer necessary. The Chicago health department agreed to the change.

The date was to appear on the milk carton, but in code. Health inspectors could tell how old the "fresh" milk was, but mothers buying it from the grocer's refrigerator would not be able to read the code. No "fresh" milk consumer in future, with homogenization so that souring could not be detected, would know how long since the milk left the cow.

The reporters who had covered the original battle for the dated-milk ordinance and been unable to report it truthfully in the columns of their daily papers could do nothing but shake their heads at the new battle. Even the lawyers for the biggest dairies in the land shook their heads right along with the reporters in the press room.

No Ralph Nader appeared to help the consumers fight the nation's entrenched dairy interests. The big dairies by this time had become much bigger than they had been two generations earlier when Al Capone was on the scene.

Now they were listed on the big stock exchanges. They bought advertisements in the daily papers which reported the facts but carefully avoided giving their readers the story behind the story.

This too was part of the legacy of Al Capone.

13 The lord mayor shot to death in duel

America is a land of overwhelming dimensions where some men grow bigger than life-size whether in the worlds of respectability, politics, or the underworld. In no other land could the mayor of a great city and the chief of its gangster population fight a battle which left one dead and the other seriously wounded. But before Frank Nitti could feel secure as successor to Al Capone he and Mayor Cermak had to have their shoot-out.

Nitti did not seek it. Cermak would have it no other way.

Politicians in Chicago were not happy with the way Dwight Green had come to town and put the leading lights of the underworld on ice. Every criminal in town grumbled and wondered what he had been paying protection for all these years if the politicians could not guarantee him immunity from the law. Cermak, president of the Cook County Board and Democratic political boss of Illinois, needed some of the stardust glamour beginning to surround Dwight Green. Defeated in his bid for the United States Senate in 1927, Cermak decided to be mayor of Chicago in 1931.

Judge John H. Lyle, in his book *The Dry and Lawless Years*, quotes Cermak as saying, "I am against this Mafia business. As soon as I am elected mayor I am going to call in their leaders—and I know who they are—and tell them to fold their tents. If necessary, I will assign some tough coppers. . . ."

Within four years those words could have been engraved on Tony Cermak's tombstone.

A little background is required to know the late Mayor Cermak.

He was born near Prague in 1875, brought to the United States as a child, and worked with his father in the Braidwood coal mines south of Joliet. What schooling he had came from attendance about three months each year in a country classroom conducted by George Brennan, a teacher with an interest in politics.

Cermak came to Chicago at sixteen, worked as a brakeman on a railroad, and—remembering the lessons of George Brennan—became a precinct worker for the Democratic Party in the Lawndale neighborhood where he lived. The district then was populated by immigrant Bohemians who soon were to be replaced by Jews and still later to be followed by blacks.

But when Tony Cermak got to Lawndale he was completely at home among people of Eastern European stock. His heavy shoulders and brawny fists won him a place among the district's young men. Had he been stupid as well as strong, he might have ended up a slugger. But Cermak had brains and the way to the top had been pointed by George Brennan. Cermak set out to organize the non-English-speaking voters of his neighborhood and to use the organization as an escalator. Before he was old enough to vote, Tony Cermak was a practical politician.

Cermak became a joiner. He got into every club and society among his own people and some outside. He even joined the Freemasons, frowned on by many peasant Catholics from Bohemia.

The political organization which Tony Cermak started and owned was called the United Societies. Every brewer and liquor distributor in Chicago and its environs was a member.

Every saloonkeeper and dancehall proprietor was a member. Every gambler and gunman, every tart and every tough along Twenty-second Street, all of whom knew Tony Cermak as a good fellow, had signed up as a member.

Cermak went to Roger Sullivan, Democratic boss of the state, and said he could deliver the vote in Lawndale. Sullivan, who made it his business to keep abreast of such things, took the measure of this tough young Bohemian and said, "What do you want?" Cermak did not hesitate. "A seat in the legislature." Sullivan said, "You've got it."

Just like that, in 1902, at the age of twenty-seven, Tony Cermak became a statesman.

From the day he arrived in Springfield, he made friends and traded influence. In his committee memberships at first, and chairmanships later, and still later as Speaker of the House, Cermak kept his eye on the main chance. He was frequently in a position to speed or delay legislation sought by the most powerful men in Illinois, the bankers and industrialists and State Street merchants of Chicago.

Cermak never blocked such legislation but he managed to hold it up long enough to let the men of power know there was in Springfield a chap named Tony Cermak.

The boy from Braidwood broadened his acquaintanceship among the men who own and operate legislatures.

Cermak never gave up the United Societies. Every whore and pimp in town knew that if the cops gave them less than a square shake for the money they paid they could turn for redress to Tony Cermak.

Just in passing it ought to be noted that after Tony Cermak's demise, the city paid him a touching tribute. Twenty-second Street, from Lake Michigan to the city limits and beyond, for generations had been known as the Street of Whores. Chicago renamed it Cermak Road.

With all Tony Cermak's other activities, he never forgot the Bohemian peasant virtues of thrift. He turned a dollar where he could. He was a realist. He knew that the politician at whatever level is a second-rate man, dangling like a puppet on strings pulled by the men of money. Cermak constantly sought to improve his financial position so he could deal on more equal terms with the men who wield the money power.

Cermak had launched his own real estate and insurance business the day he entered the legislature. He seldom accepted direct payoffs, but figured ways that men who wanted favors could buy insurance through the Cermak agency. There are no laws against insurance agents accepting cash premium payments.

Cermak was in a position to know in advance where the state contemplated building highways or other projects which would improve land values. His real estate firm always took options on the farmland which would be thus improved, later selling the options at tremendous profits.

Nobody ever criticized him for this. The common citizen is so naïve even today that he thinks a real estate operator accepts an unpaid appointment to a school board simply as a matter of public service.

When the politicians saw a chance to make fortunes overnight by buying up land surrounding Chicago and selling it to the county to be held in perpetuity as forest preserves and playgrounds for the people, Cermak got in on the ground floor. He bought what options he could afford and cleared others through his office at standard commissions.

After three terms in the legislature, Cermak was worth a million dollars. Before he became mayor of Chicago at the age of fifty-six, he was worth seven million. This does not mean Cermak was greedy. Far from it. He split the take with other politicians up and down the line so that none was envious of his success. To this day the professional politicians of Chicago, as distinct from the dilettantes, will tell you, "Tony Cermak was the greatest mayor the city ever had."

When Roger Sullivan died on April 14, 1920, his place as head of the Democratic Party in Illinois was taken by George E. Brennan, the man who once had been Cermak's teacher. Cermak was slated for the presidency of the Cook county board and, when elected to that post, left the legislature.

Always loyal to the old politicians, he set Billy Skidmore up in the junk business by giving him the $100,000-a-year contract to handle scrap iron from county institutions. When Brennan died on August 8, 1928, the party mantle fell to Cermak's shoulders.

Now Cermak was in a position to deal directly, rather than through middlemen, with the Establishment. In every large city there is a gathering place for the men who own and operate the legislatures and the city councils, and who choose governors and Senators and Presidents. In New York it is the Economic Club, in San Francisco the Commonwealth Club, in Chicago the Chicago Club. Cermak was invited to a series of tête-à-tête meetings at which the men who run things could size up this ambitious Bohemian from Lawndale.

Cermak's peasant table manners caused eyebrows to raise, but he talked straight and to the point.

His hosts saw that he was not Presidential timber, but then not having been born an American citizen he was not eligible for the Presidency. Cermak appeared the man who could get the job done if elected mayor of Chicago.

Cermak wanted and needed the support of these men, both to retain his tenuous grip on the Democratic Party throughout the state and to win in his bid for the post of mayor. Since Cermak wanted something they could grant or withhold, the men of power did some horse trading. They asked Cermak's support of a little project which for some time had been under discussion behind closed doors, a scheme to become known as the Kelly Plan.

The name grew out of the fact that one of the men who had hatched the scheme was Dennis F. Kelly, papal knight and president of The Fair store, then one of the great State Street department stores. The Kelly Plan had to do with tax assessments.

Under state legislation, Cook County had a board of tax assessors and a board of tax review. D. F. Kelly, as chairman of a citizens' committee on public expenditures—a group representing bankers, industrialists, merchants, and great real estate holdings—wanted to abolish these two boards temporarily. As an emergency measure, he asked that in place of these two boards:

1. The president of the Cook County Board and the governor of Illinois agree on one man who would serve as tax assessor.

2. The president of the county board and the governor each appoint one man as a two-man panel of tax review.

If Tony Cermak got the nod of the men of the Chicago Club, he would be Democratic boss of the state and in a position to name the next governor. Cermak was already president of the county board.

This would mean that Cermak would name the man chosen by the

Chicago Club as tax assessor and would also name the two they selected as the tax review panel. The voters of Cook County would simply lose their franchise as far as these important offices were concerned. The men even had the timetable worked out.

After his election as mayor of Chicago, Cermak was to request the governor to call a special session of the legislature to consider a law embodying this tax proposal. Such a call was to be made during Christmas week, a time when the voting public has its mind on things other than tax assessments.

Even for Chicago, which has seen everything, the Kelly Plan was something special in the way of proposed legislation. But Cermak wanted to be mayor and the gentlemen of the Establishment told him, "Take it or leave it." Tony Cermak took it.

Nobody ought to get the idea from this that the industrialists and bankers and merchants of Chicago were seeking to corrupt a tax assessor's office which previously had been honestly administered. Such was not the case. The tax office in Cook County had been administered on the basis of greasing palms.

But the men behind the Kelly Plan felt that tax assessment was being inefficiently administered. With an elected board of tax assessors, and an elected board of tax reviewers, too many palms had to be greased. Even after a businessman got to the end of the line, having paid every politician who seemed to have anything to do with it, he never knew if some joker in the middle might not double-cross him.

With one appointed assessor and two appointed reviewers—all responsible to Tony Cermak—the businessmen felt they could pay their bribes and depend on results in the way of lowered tax assessments.

The businessmen gave Cermak an out in that they did not demand the Kelly Plan be instituted as a permanent thing. They knew that a smart fox does not have to remain very long in a henhouse. They asked only that their own accountants be put into the tax-assessment offices long enough to fix up the books so they would not have to worry for a generation or so about their real estate taxes being high. On this basis, Cermak accepted the scheme.

The men promised him that by 1934 the jobs would once again be elective and that every politician would once again have a chance at the big plum from which he and his friends could retire in decent dignity.

Everything went according to schedule on the Kelly Plan. Cermak announced it on December 28, 1931, eight months after his election to the office of mayor on April 7. The new governor, Louis L. Emmerson, dutifully called a special session of the legislature. Emmerson was a

Republican from downstate Jefferson County, but he too had had his tête-à-tête sessions in the Chicago Club.

D. F. Kelly, Knight of Malta, knight commander in the Order of St. Gregory, principal financial adviser among the laity to the late Cardinal George Mundelein, led the procession of merchants, bankers, and industrialists who testified before legislative committees.

Cermak played the part of shrinking violet, deferring to the wisdom of men of business and finance, "who know so much more about this subject than a Bohemian boy from the coal mines of Braidwood." Cermak, questioned by newspaper reporters, said, "The city is almost bankrupt. Credit is exhausted. Schoolteachers have worked without pay but if we do not have money for coal the schools will have to close. In this crisis there is no place for politics. As county chairman of the party I am conscious of the patronage jobs that go with the board of assessors and the board of review. Under the Kelly Plan we will lose those patronage jobs. But in this crisis we are willing to declare a moratorium on politics."

A selfless statement such as that is the Chicago politician at his best. Naturally Cermak's statement was printed without comment by the daily newspapers of Chicago, whose publishers were participants in the scheme to take the tax burden off business and place it on the small homeowner.

This was the Tony Cermak, tough and practical, who had gone on record before he took office as saying, "As soon as I am elected mayor I am going to call in the [gangster] leaders. If necessary, I will assign some tough coppers. And I will get rid of them [the gangsters]."

But Cermak's hands were full in the first months after he took office. The man who took over as mayor on April 7, 1931, found the city in the worst financial doldrums of its history. Mayor William Hale Thompson had just completed a third term, seldom drawing a sober breath in his suite at the old Stevens Hotel and just as seldom seeing the inside of his City Hall office. In his absence the town was run by his corporation counsel, Sam Ettelson.

It was a wide-open town, for political thieves at every level as well as for the underworld. The treasuries had all been looted. By the device of tax anticipation warrants, the city's income had been spent for years to come before it ever was collected. Policemen, firemen, and schoolteachers were unpaid. Tony Cermak had his work cut out for him.

That winter of 1931–32 came the Kelly Plan, without which Cermak would have had no support from the bankers in trying to get the city's finances back on an even keel. After that, Cermak was up to his hips in national politics, with the Democratic convention coming in summer.

Cermak was aware when Frank Nitti took over the underworld empire after Al Capone entered prison in May, but Cermak was too busy just at that time to worry about it. In the primaries, that spring of 1932, Cermak brought out the votes for his whole personal slate. He chose Henry Horner to be governor and Thomas J. Courtney to be state's attorney of Cook County. He slated them and he nominated them, with the smoothly operating political machine he had put together.

Next came the national convention to nominate the men who would head the November ticket. Cermak was busy before this convention lining up delegates who would vote for Franklin Delano Roosevelt as their party's standard-bearer. Cermak was busy during the convention with his politicking, and busy in the months after the convention helping see to it that the Democratic party swept the country in a landslide election.

The Illinois machine, headed by Tony Cermak, was one of the party's bulwarks. Until Roosevelt and Horner and Courtney were safely elected that November, Tony Cermak had no time to make good on his promise to get rid of the city's top gangsters. But once the election was out of the way, Cermak had to face up to this unfinished business. A Century of Progress was due to open in six months, on May 27, 1933, and Cermak wanted the city safely under control of the half-world of politics rather than the underworld before that world's fair opened its doors to millions of visitors.

Cermak had threatened that if the gang leaders did not get out of town he would "assign some tough coppers." He did. On December 19, 1932, Cermak sent two of "the tough coppers" to pick up Frank Nitti. The two later testified under oath that Cermak had given them the office number at which they would find Nitti. The policemen were Harry Lang and Harry Miller. The latter was the one of the four Millers brothers, two of whom Dion O'Banion had shot back in 1924.

Harry Lang and Harry Miller both held the rank of detective sergeant in the police department. They had been made Cermak's "front-office men," his bagmen for the collection of underworld tribute, immediately after he took office as mayor. Both were from Lawndale. Both owed their jobs to Cermak's political sponsorship.

In plain clothes, at 1 P.M. on that winter day a week before Christmas, Lang and Miller drove to 221 North La Salle Street, two blocks north of City Hall. As they parked, they hailed a passing police squad car. They asked Detective Sergeant Chris Callahan to join them, saying they "might need some help inside."

The policemen took the elevator to the fifth floor, walked to Room

554, entered, and saw Frank Nitti with five other men. The office was a handbook and wireroom. Sergeant Callahan later testified, "We took the six men from the little anteroom into a larger office. We searched them. Nitti had no gun. While I held Nitti by the wrists, Detective Sergeant Lang walked up to Nitti from behind and shot him three times."

Police Sergeant Callahan said Nitti staggered to a chair and collapsed.

Then he turned to look at Lang and asked, in what Callahan described as a tone of surprise, "What's this for?"

Lang walked alone into the little anteroom and those remaining in the larger office heard a single shot. Lang came back among them, bleeding from a minor flesh wound in his left hand. Newspapermen arrived a few minutes later. Lang told them—and nobody at first denied his story—that he and Nitti had fought a gun duel. Lang said Nitti had a hideout gun on his person and got off one shot before Lang shot the little gang leader several times.

Everyone in the office assumed at that point that Nitti, who had slipped to the floor and lost consciousness, was either dead or dying. A police physician who arrived to treat the superficial wound in Lang's hand said that Nitti had been hit at least three times, twice in the back and once in the neck. Nitti was taken to Jefferson Park Hospital, where his father-in-law, Dr. Gaetano Ronga, was a staff physician. Nitti recovered consciousness long enough to tell police, "I didn't shoot Lang. I didn't have any gun."

Immediately after this shooting, Lang and Miller were hailed as fearless policemen. The police department granted them extra compensation for meritorious service. The city council voted them the city's thanks as heroes. Mayor Cermak paid stirring tribute to their courage in "going up against gangland guns" and killing the man who had succeeded Al Capone.

But Frank Nitti did not die. Under his father-in-law's personal care, and with an astonishing constitution, Nitti almost at once began to recover.

As word of his recovery spread from his hospital room there was consternation and fear in the mayor's office. Lang and Miller wanted to get out of town. Cermak was too nervous to work.

Forty-eight hours after the shooting, with Nitti still refusing to die, Tony Cermak decided to get away from the more than 600 gunmen assumed to be ready to avenge their fallen leader. Cermak left for Florida on December 21, 1932, with a public statement in a voice which he tried to make firm. Cermak told the police, "Wage bitter war on the gangsters until they are driven from our city."

Lang and Miller fled with Cermak.

Two weeks after being taken to the hospital, Nitti was able to listen to the intelligence his men had been able to round up. He learned that Detective Sergeant Harry Lang, only five minutes before starting out for Nitti's office that day, had been offered $15,000 by Teddy Newberry if Nitti was killed.

Newberry was a bootlegger and gunman who had been affiliated over the years with first one faction and then another. He had been a member of Bugs Moran's gang until Al Capone had wiped it out in the St. Valentine's Day massacre of 1929. Then Newberry had joined Capone's forces.

Nitti dispatched men to take care of Teddy Newberry, who then was running a gambling casino called the 225 Club at 225 East Superior Street. Newberry was still wearing the diamond belt buckle given him by Al Capone when his body was found January 7, 1933, in a ditch on a lonely road near Gary, off the Dunes highway in Indiana.

Now Nitti dispatched a man to take care of Tony Cermak. The mayor was taking his ease in the Florida sunshine, recovering a bit of his courage in the belief that he was half a continent removed from a dangerous killer who had a score to settle.

On February 15, 1933, just five weeks after Teddy Newberry had been taken care of, Mayor Cermak was with President-elect Roosevelt, in the latter's open car, just after FDR had made a late afternoon speech to 4,000 Miami residents and tourists.

That was when Giuseppe Zangara, who had won prizes for pistol shooting in the Italian army, shot Tony Cermak. Cermak died three weeks later, on March 6.

Carrying out an assassination in the vicinity of the President-elect of the United States was different from shooting Teddy Newberry and tossing his body into an Indiana ditch. The Secret Service men were all over Bayfront Park that day. They had tackled Zangara before he even squeezed off the sixth bullet from his pistol. Zangara was later electrocuted in Florida's Raiford prison.

The late Judge Lyle, who had known Tony Cermak, and who knew as much about such things as any non-Mafia man of the era, said flatly, "Zangara was a Mafia killer, sent from Sicily to do a job and sworn to silence."

When Frank Nitti had sufficiently recovered, he was charged with shooting Detective Sergeant Harry Lang. Nitti was brought to trial.

Lang, who had sworn under oath before a grand jury that Nitti shot him, had second thoughts about the matter. He refused to repeat this testimony when facing Nitti in court. The meritorious service awards to Lang and Miller were revoked.

Nitti went to Florida to complete his recovery in the same sun which had been sought by Tony Cermak.

Then, Assistant State's Attorney Charles Dougherty, later a circuit court judge in Cook County, felt that he had been made to appear foolish in his prosecution of Nitti when Lang reneged on his testimony. So Dougherty charged Lang with attempted murder in the Nitti shooting.

He further charged Lang with perjury for the testimony he had given under oath before a grand jury. Lang was defended by Abraham Lincoln Marovitz, now a district judge on the federal bench in Chicago.

Nitti was not interested in prosecuting Lang, who had done the shooting. As far as he was concerned, Lang was just a hired torpedo. Nitti had wiped the slate clean by accounting for the man who put the gun in Lang's hand, so Nitti had no further interest in the case. But Nitti was subpoenaed to testify in the state's case against Lang. Nitti took the witness stand on September 26, 1933.

The little gangster appeared at ease in the witness chair. He was neatly attired in a blue serge suit. He did not look at all as prosperous as the government had proved he was in his income tax evasion trial. Nitti on the witness stand answered questions in a low voice, contending at all times that his only business was "legitimate."

He said his real name was Frank Nitto, but he was known as Nitti. He said the office in the La Salle-Wacker building which he frequented was not his own, but that of Joe Palumbo. Nitti was then questioned further by Abe Marovitz.

Q—How many times had you been to that office before December?
A—Several times.
Q—You say this was Palumbo's office. What was his business?
A—Oh, he took bets on horses.
Q—What business have you ever had?
A—I was in the restaurant business at 901 South Halsted Street.
Q—When was the last time you were in a legitimate business?
A—I am in a legitimate business right now, in the restaurant business at 5829 Madison Street.

Marovitz was assisted in Lang's defense by Attorney William A. Rittenhouse. The latter told the jury, "Lang shot Nitti in pursuit of his duty as a member of Mayor Cermak's special squad, organized to war on the Capone ring."

Although the charge against Lang was assault with intent to kill, the jury found him guilty only of simple assault. The first charge would have carried a minimum sentence of one year. The second carried a minimum of one day in jail.

Marovitz promptly moved for a new trial and the petition was granted. After eighteen continuances the case against Lang finally was thrown out of court on May 31, 1934. The prosecutor, Charles Dougherty, said, "All efforts to find Frank Nitti have been unavailing."

The outcome had been predictable from the time of Cermak's death. Lang was a frightened man at that time when told he might be indicted for the Nitti shooting. He told newspaper reporters, "If they indict me, by God, I'll blow the lid off Democratic politics." That kind of talk gets a man somewhere. But when he surrendered April 13, 1933, after he had been indicted, Lang told reporters, "Any statements attributed to me, to the effect that I would 'blow the lid off Democratic politics' if indicted, were not authorized by me."

Lang was talking to the same reporters both times, but still kept a straight face. He had made his point. The politicians had seen the light. When Marovitz brought Lang into court the bond was set at $15,000.

So much money poured in from unidentified sources, from men who asked that their names not be disclosed, that the court had $45,000 in cash from which to make the bond. Lang chuckled publicly as he saw how many politicians had laid out heavy cash to prevent his spending even one night behind bars, where he might be tempted to talk to newspaper reporters.

Two postscripts to this story ought to be added. Lang and Miller, of course, were first suspended and later dismissed from the police force when they were exposed as simply a pair of hired gunmen.

Lang waited a couple of years before suing in circuit court on November 16, 1936, for a judicial review of the Civil Service Commission ruling by which he had been discharged from the police force. Lang's writ of certiorari said the commission proceedings were improper and the reasons for his dismissal had been insufficient. He asked that he be reinstated as a detective sergeant in the Chicago police department with full pay for all the time he had missed.

The second little postscript has to do with Lang's source of income while waiting for the heat to die down so he could sue for his old job with back pay. On April 24, 1934, a year after his indictment in the Frank Nitti shooting, Lang became business agent and owner of the Hebrew Butchers Association at 3420 Roosevelt Road. This was the racketeering outfit that had been organized by Maxie Eisen, czar of the fish peddlers, who served as chairman of Al Capone's first peace conference back in 1926.

14 "How would your old lady look in black?"

When running for the mayor's job in late 1930 and early 1931, Cermak had told everyone that he was running the gangsters out of town. The small businessmen saw what they interpreted as evidence that Cermak was delivering on his promises. In quick succession they saw prison doors close on Frank Nitti, Ralph Capone, and Jake Guzik. They thought the millennium at hand and quit their weekly payments to Capone collectors who had sold them protection.

This tribute of course was simple extortion.

As soon as Nitti began recovering from his wounds he sent out enforcers to once again get the flow of tribute money started. The usual tool was the bomb. In the first seventy-five days of Nitti's drive, beginning February 1, 1933, bombs were exploded in forty offices and warehouses.

None was meant to destroy anything. The total damage from all of them was less than $100,000. They were intended to impress businessmen with the fact that the Capone organization's demands were not lightly to be brushed aside. Virtually all the bombings were handled by James Belcastro, Capone's "king of the bombers" and his understudies.

Belcastro's citizenship had been revoked in 1931, but deportation does not automatically follow such action.

Belcastro needed money for legal appeals and he took any contract job given him by Nitti in the Syndicate's drive just before the world's fair opening.

Franklin Delano Roosevelt was inaugurated President on March 4, 1933. The history books tell of his dynamic leadership in the first 100 days in office.

Out in Chicago, Frank Nitti did not do too badly in the matter of dynamic leadership in his own 100 days preceding the world's fair.

One of Roosevelt's first acts had been to legalize the manufacture and sale of beer with an alcoholic content of 3.2 percent. Every brewery operated by or under lease to the Capone organization was turning out

3.2 beer for sale up and down the fair grounds midway on Northerly Island, from Twelfth Street to Twenty-third Street. The trucks were rolling night and day to stock the saloons along West Madison Street, North Clark Street, South State Street, out in Cicero, and the nightclub belt along Rush Street, wherever the Capone organization was strongly entrenched.

But the concentration was on the fair. Murray Humphreys had the popcorn concession and his young agents hawked their product on every corner. Other Syndicate leaders had the hatcheck concessions, the parking concessions, the towel and soap and disinfectant concessions.

The San Carlo Italian Village, daily gathering place for the clan, was run by Ricca, Greenberg, and Fusco, with Joe Bulger as a front. Everybody in the organization had a piece of something, whether the union of college-boy rickshaw pullers or the uniformed private police force which patrolled the fairgrounds.

Ralph Capone's bottled waters, carbonated and noncarbonated, plain and flavored, were virtually the only soft drinks except Coca-Cola available on the grounds. Syndicate purveyors sold the hot dogs and hamburger meat which gave sustenance to millions of visitors daily.

Charlie Fischetti was quoted, "If a wheel turns on the fairgrounds, we get a cut of the grease on the axle. We got the whole place sewed up."

Millions of visitors to the world's fair in 1933 and again in 1934 were steered from the grounds to brothels and casinos running wide open. Every neighborhood had its massage parlor, at none of which could anyone get a massage. All the girls shared their earnings with the Capone gang.

A limousine service from the gates of the world's fair offered tourists free transportation to hotels full of call girls, striptease shows, floating crap games, and all-night drinking spots. Every Capone operation in Cicero ran wide open, virtually twenty-four hours a day, to keep up with world's fair business.

Nitti felt he had done his job as ramrod for the outfit when the world's fair officially opened. He had not yet recovered fully. He stayed in Chicago just long enough to appear as a defendant charged with shooting Detective Sergeant Harry Lang. When that charge was dismissed, Nitti took off for Florida with Charlie Fischetti.

They headed for Fischetti's home on Biscayne Bay at Miami, a showplace later owned by Chicago Alderman Mathias (Paddy) Bauler. It was summertime and the season was long over in Florida. But the men who had met with Al Capone in Atlantic City in 1929 now came to Miami to meet with Frank Nitti.

When the Kefauver Senate Committee held hearings twenty years later, the record included documents from this meeting.

Frank Erickson was there from New York. Meyer and Jake Lansky came from New Jersey. Jack Dragna came from Los Angeles. Others present included Nig Giovanni of Kansas City. All accompanied Frank Nitti north to visit the world's fair and compliment Nitti on his organization.

At this meeting the men agreed that nationally they should:

1. Get control by investment of the nation's legal liquor trade.

2. Push their own brands of beer and legal liquor through control of bartender and restaurant unions and employer associations.

3. Expand bookmaking operations and seek to take over the race wire news services as well as scratch sheets.

4. Invest in the food business, in hotel and restaurant operations, in cocktail lounges and saloons, in retail liquor stores.

5. Seek to influence or control or take over such unions in the entertainment field as embraced musicians and nightclub acts.

This program had already been agreed to by Nitti and the rest of the Chicago group. Now the Chicago group was able to compare notes with leaders from other cities and adopt some refinements when they proved feasible.

The various gangs agreed, as they had with Al Capone, that they were not to invade one another's territories for purposes of business competition. They were to commit no violent acts in one another's territories. They were each to give the others every possible cooperation.

The men in the Capone organization in the summer of 1933 were too busy to do anything except rake in the money from the millions of fair visitors. Light beer was legal and the Nineteenth Amendment to the Constitution soon was to legalize the manufacture, importation, and sale of whiskey. In early fall, Nitti met with his board of directors on the third floor of the Capri Restaurant at 123 North Clark Street, across the street from the City Hall and County Building.

Every one of the Capone Syndicate's top men, with the exception of Jake Guzik, who was then in prison, attended the fall meeting. Among those present were Charlie Fischetti, Paul Ricca, Louis Campagna, Sam (Golf Bag) Hunt, and Murray Humphreys.

Nitti, an articulate and forceful speaker, was quoted later: "We've got the world by the tail with a downhill start.

"The bartenders' union is our biggest lever. After we get national control we will have every bartender in the country pushing our brands of beer and liquor.

"They will have to handle our soft drinks. They will get their pretzels from us and their potato chips. That goes for every hotel, restaurant, cocktail lounge, and private club in forty-eight states.

"As Al used to tell us, we'll see the day we make a profit off of every olive in every martini served in America."

But A Century of Progress, which stayed open for five months that summer, had proved so successful in 1933 that Chicago's leaders decided to reopen again the next year. The Capone Syndicate board of directors was kept busy that winter tending to business which had necessarily been neglected during the world's fair summer.

In 1934, they all followed the same routine of virtually day and night work during the second year of A Century of Progress. Everyone in the group was spread thin, trying to supervise activities on the fairgrounds from 10 o'clock in the morning until midnight and then keep up with gambling operations in the county after midnight.

Ralph Capone, in addition to his soft-drink interests, was still running the Cotton Club in Cicero at 5342 Twenty-second Street. The gang was running the Yacht Club at 100 East Superior Street, with Nick Circella, alias Nicky Dean, as manager. The Owl Club was the big casino in Calumet City, as Ralph's Place and the Fort were big casinos near Glenview. All were Syndicate operations.

The day-to-day operations of all the Outfit's businesses were such that it was the spring of 1935 before Nitti and the rest got around to the matter of the bartenders' union. This union was the property of George B. McLane, a professional union thug who had been a bartender before he became a labor statesman.

McLane in 1910 became business agent of Local 278, the Chicago Bartenders and Beverage Dispensers Union (AFL). When the Eighteenth Amendment went into effect in 1920, McLane put the union charter in his trunk and opened a speakeasy. With repeal, he dusted off the old charter and announced he was back in business.

McLane testified under oath as to the steps by which the Capone Syndicate took over his union. This was after he charged that Nitti and the others in five years had split up "more than a million dollars" paid in dues by the 5,300 members of Local 278.

McLane had gone to court to ask that Nitti and the others be enjoined from further "looting of the treasury." Judge Robert Jerome Dunne of the circuit court ordered testimony be taken by Master in Chancery Isadore Brown. On October 17, 1940, McLane answered questions of his attorney, A.C. Lewis.

Q—Will you tell us what happened in the spring of 1935?

A—I received a telephone call in union headquarters from Danny

Stanton. He wanted five hundred dollars to go to the Kentucky Derby. He said he would send over two men for it. I told him I had no right to give out union funds.

McLane said he knew Danny Stanton as a labor slugger, one of the musclemen for Red Barker and Murray Humphreys of the Capone organization. McLane said that half an hour after the phone call from Stanton, two men came to his office. McLane refused to give them the $500 they demanded. One of the men phoned Stanton from McLane's office, then handed McLane the phone. McLane quoted Stanton: "You son of a bitch. We'll get the money and take the union over."

Attorney Lewis continued the questioning.

Q—What was your next contact with the [Capone] gang?

A—Two or three days later I received an emissary from Frank Nitti. He said Nitti wanted to see me at the La Salle Hotel. When I got there, I told Nitti about Stanton. Nitti told me, "The only way to avoid incidents like that is to put one of our men in as a union officer." I told Nitti that would be impossible. He said "We've taken over other unions. You'll put our man in or you will get shot in the head."

McLane said he next was summoned into Nitti's presence in the third-floor private dining room of the Capri Restaurant. He said this dining room was so private that, "You couldn't get there unless the elevator operator recognized you." The questioning continued.

Q—Whom did you see in the private dining room?

A—Frank Nitti, Little New York Campagna, and Paul Ricca.

Q—Any others?

A—Joe Fusco and Charlie Fischetti.

McLane said that on this occasion Nitti completed a conversation before turning and inviting McLane to his table. Nitti once again demanded that "one of our men" be installed as a union officer.

McLane told Nitti the union's executive board would not accept the installation of a representative of the Capone Syndicate. Nitti said: "Give me the names of any board members who oppose. We'll take care of them. We want no more playing around. If you don't do like I say, you'll get shot in the head. How would your old lady look in black?"

McLane thought of his wife and replied, "Christine never wears black."

Nitti smiled and said, "You put my guy on the union payroll or she will be in black."

McLane said he was next summoned to appear before Nitti in the Capri Restaurant in July, 1935. This time, besides Nitti, there were present Ricca, Campagna, Fusco, Sam Hunt, Harry Guzik—one of Jake's brothers—and Fred Evans, who worked as auditor and partner for Murray Humphreys in several of the latter's enterprises. McLane said that in addition to these men, "There were several others I didn't know." McLane, testifying under oath, said: "Nitti done the talking. He said, 'Why haven't you put our man in as an officer of the union? What are you stalling for? I'll give you a man without a police record. The bartenders in all the places that the syndicate owns will join the union.'"

Nitti asked McLane how many union members were current on the books and how much dues they paid. Told that there were 5,000 members who paid $4 a month apiece, Nitti commented, "Twenty grand a month! We'll do a lot better than that!"

McLane told Nitti of a union executive board meeting which had been held the previous week. He said the board members refused to accept a gangster as an officer. Nitti demanded the names of the men who had opposed the suggestion. McLane told Master in Chancery Brown, "I refused to give them the names."

McLane said he was told; "We'll take care of that. This is your last chance. This is the only way we'll stand for anything. Put in our man or wind up in an alley."

Attorney Lewis asked a question.

Q—Were you terrified?

A—Yes, I went back to the union board and told them about the threats to me and to them—what it meant. They had no alternative. They agreed, in the latter part of July, 1935, to putting a man on.

McLane was summoned to the Capri Restaurant a week or so later, early in August. Nitti, Ricca, and Campagna were present. Nitti rose from the table to visit another table and return with Louis Romano, a man McLane never had seen before. Romano had been one of Al Capone's bodyguards in the twenties. Nitti said: "Here's your man. He has no police record. He'll go along with you as an organizer and as assistant. His salary will be seventy-five dollars a week out of the union treasury. You'll have to make provision to raise it later. Romano will see that all the Syndicate places join the union."

So Louis Romano became business agent of Bartenders Local 278. Romano was a product of the 42 Gang, and had snatched purses from boyhood with such thieves as Sam Battaglia and John D'Arco.

McLane was next summoned to Nitti's presence in the Auditorium Hotel. Lou Greenberg invited McLane and accompanied him to Nitti's suite. In Greenberg's presence, Nitti told McLane that all the city's bartenders were to push certain brands of beer and liquor. Nitti named the brands: "Manhattan and Great Lakes draft beer, Badger and Cream Top bottled beer, all the products of Gold Seal Liquors, Inc., Fort

Dearborn whiskey, and all the products of the Capitol Wine and Liquor Company."

Greenberg owned Manhattan Brewery. Joe Fusco owned both Gold Seal and Capitol. Fort Dearborn was the Syndicate's own brand.

A few weeks after this meeting, McLane was taken by Louis Romano to see Nitti in his Bismarck Hotel suite. Attorney Lewis questioned McLane.

Q—How did you find Nitti?

A—Romano took me to his room. Johnny Patton [the boy mayor of suburban Burnham] was there. He was connected with Sportsman's Park racetrack. We talked about wine and beer at the racetrack. Patton said the bartenders were not pushing the right stuff.

McLane explained to Nitti and Patton that the bartender cannot always compel the customer to buy the brand favored by the bartender or even by the owner of the saloon.

When the general public had the choice of such nationally known brands of beer as Budweiser, Miller's High Life, and Schlitz, they simply refused to accept the Capone Syndicate beers. Nitti told him, "Tell those bartenders that if they don't push our stuff they will get their legs broken."

McLane had almost limitless power over the work of union bartenders. He could assign them to work or forbid them to work. He could get them temporary jobs or permanent jobs. The favored bartender could be sent to the hotel or club bars where drinkers were known to tip liberally.

The shrewd bartender could be assigned to bars at sporting events where it was possible to steal as much as $50 a night by using a bar cloth to wipe change off the counter into a sink full of soapy water.

The bartender who incurred McLane's disfavor could be kept unemployed for months, while his dues had to be paid.

McLane still later was summoned to Nitti's presence at the Seneca Hotel, owned by Greenberg. Both Greenberg of Manhattan Brewery and Joe Fusco of Gold Seal Liquors were present.

Then, late in 1938, the president of McLane's Local 278, Robert Santchi, died in Michigan. By this time Murray Humphreys was out of prison and once again directing union labor affairs for the Capone Syndicate. Humphreys told McLane that he wanted Louis Romano installed as union president. McLane said that Humphreys and Romano on that occasion drew pistols and threatened him in the presence of Attorney Harold Levy.

The lawyer, Harold Levy, was present during McLane's testimony.

At this point he sprang to his feet and called McLane "a dirty liar." Afterward, Levy denied to reporters that he had ever been present in McLane's office during gunplay. Levy had been McLane's lawyer in the summer of 1934, when McLane was accused of attempted extortion in connection with a strike.

That strike was at the French Casino, Lawrence Avenue and Clark Street, which later was operated by Mike Todd, the film impresario. The 1934 strike was called by McLane, representing the bartenders; by Max Caldwell, representing the waiters; and by William Brooks, representing the stationary engineers.

McLane and Caldwell were accused by the French Casino's owners of offering to call off the strike for a payment of $10,000. When tried on this charge, June 10, 1935, McLane and Caldwell were represented by Levy and by Attorney Abe Marovitz.

In testifying as to the pistol threat by Humphreys and Romano, McLane said, "Louis Romano and Harold Levy came to my office. While we were talking, Murray Humphreys and Fred Evans walked in. As they sat down, Romano told me, 'I'm taking over.' My desk drawer was open a few inches and they noticed it. Humphreys and Romano pulled pistols and ordered me away from the desk."

McLane said that after he moved to a chair in the corner of his own office, Romano slipped the pistol back into his shoulder holster and went on with what he had been saying. "We're taking over. You will receive your pay.

McLane said he turned to Harold Levy for counsel.

"I asked Harold Levy, as attorney for the Outfit, where he fitted into this picture. Levy said, 'Turn it over to them.'"

So Romano became president of Bartenders Local 278.

Shortly afterward, McLane testified, "They slipped me a bullet and told me to get out of town for my health." McLane explained that one of the Syndicate's ways of warning a man was to have a bullet dropped into his pocket. Anyone who had dealings with the Syndicate was expected to recognize the bullet's meaning. McLane left town for a few months. When he returned, Louis Romano had organized and become president of a food and beverage joint council, similar to the joint councils of the teamsters' unions and of the building trades' unions.

The Romano joint council embraced fifteen local unions, most of them affiliated with the bartenders. The joint council was supposed to adjust jurisdictional disputes among the locals. Membership in the joint council, and payment of per capita dues by the local unions, was mandatory. Attorney Lewis questioned McLane as to the locals and the Capone Syndicate representatives who headed them.

Alphonse Capone, sensitive about the two deep knife-slash scars on his left cheek, wanted all photographs taken from the right.

STATE OF ILLINOIS,

Department of **State.**

WILLIAM H. HINRICHSEN, Secretary of State.

To all to Whom these Presents Shall Come--Greeting:

WHEREAS, a **CERTIFICATE,** *duly signed and acknowledged, having been filed in the office of the*

Secretary of State, on the _____17th_____ *day of* _____September_____ A. D. 189___1_, *for*

the organization of the _____

Unione Siciliana di Mutuo

Soccorso negli Stato United

America. –

under and in accordance with the provisions of "AN ACT CONCERNING CORPORATIONS,"

approved April 18, 1872, and in force July 1, 1872, a copy of which certificate is hereto attached,

Now, Therefore, *I, WILLIAM H. HINRICHSEN, Secretary of State of the State of Illinois,*

by virtue of the powers and duties vested in me by law, do hereby certify that the said _____

Unione Siciliana di Mutuo

Soccorso negli Stato United America

is a legally organized Corporation under the laws of this State.

In Testimony Whereof, *I hereto set my hand, and cause to be*

affixed the Great Seal of State.

Done at the city of Springfield, this _17th_

day of _September_ _____ *in the year of our*

*Lord one thousand eight hundred and ninety*_1_

and of the Independence of the United States the one hun-

dred and __In th__.

W.H. Hinrichsen

Secretary of State.

Certificate of Incorporation of the Unione Sicilana.

State of Illinois,
Cook _____ COUNTY.

To WILLIAM H. HINRICHSEN, Secretary of State:

We the Undersigned, *Carmelo Triolo, Giuseppe Mirabella, Andrea Russo, Domenico M. Minaldi, Francesco Piazza Palotta & Calogero Fusco di Giacomo.* Citizens of the United States, propose to form a ~~Corporation~~ *Society* under an act of the General Assembly of the State of Illinois, entitled, "*An Act concerning Corporations,*" approved April 18th, 1872, and all acts amendatory thereof, and that for the purposes of such organization we hereby state as follows, to-wit:

1. The name of such ~~Corporation~~ *Society* is the *Unione Siciliana di Mutuo Soccorso negli Stati Uniti d'America*

2. The object for which it is formed is *The voluntary and charitable benevolence and assistance of a member towards the other in case of sickness.*

3. The management of the aforesaid *Society* *Annually* shall be vested in a Board of ~~eight~~ *5* Directors, who are to be elected ~~one on the first~~

4. The following persons are hereby selected as the Directors to control and manage said Corporation for the first year of its corporate existence, viz: *G. C. Triolo Pres., G. Mirabella V. Pres., Dom. M. Minaldi Sec., Franc. Piazza Palotta Fin. Sec., A. Russo Treas., + three Trustees to serve for the remaining* ~~term of 1895 (December)~~

5. The location is in *Chicago Ill* in the County of *Cook* State of Illinois.

Signed:

Carmelo Triolo
Gius. Mirabella
D. M. Minaldi
Andrea Russo
Fusco Calogero di Giacomo
Francesco Piazza Palotta

Frankie Lake (together with Terry Druggan) ran the Valley Gang in Little Italy on Chicago's Near West Side. He was known as a bootlegger and killer.

"Big Jim" Colosimo started as a simple Black Hand extortion expert and grew to be chief pimp of Chicago's First Ward. He and his wife, Victoria Moresco, owned a string of whorehouses and recruited Midwestern farmgirls to work in Chicago for a few years and then see the world (the whorehouses of South America and East Africa). When he was killed in 1920, the most powerful Chicago politicians—judges, state senators, and legislators, aldermen and high police officials, and Michael Igo, who later sat on the federal district bench for decades—asked to be listed as honorary pallbearers.

"Diamond Joe" Esposito also started as a Black Hand extortion man, then got into labor slugging and made a fortune. A ward committeeman, he ran the Bella Napoli Café, owned the Hod Carriers' Union, and was an executive committeeman of the AFL—sought by anyone who wanted to be a mayor, governor, senator, or police official. He was also sought as a councillor by the President of the United States. He was killed in 1928.

The 1928 wake for Diamond Joe Esposito brought mourners by the hundreds to his home. They filed in the front door and out the back, hour after hour, for three days and nights.

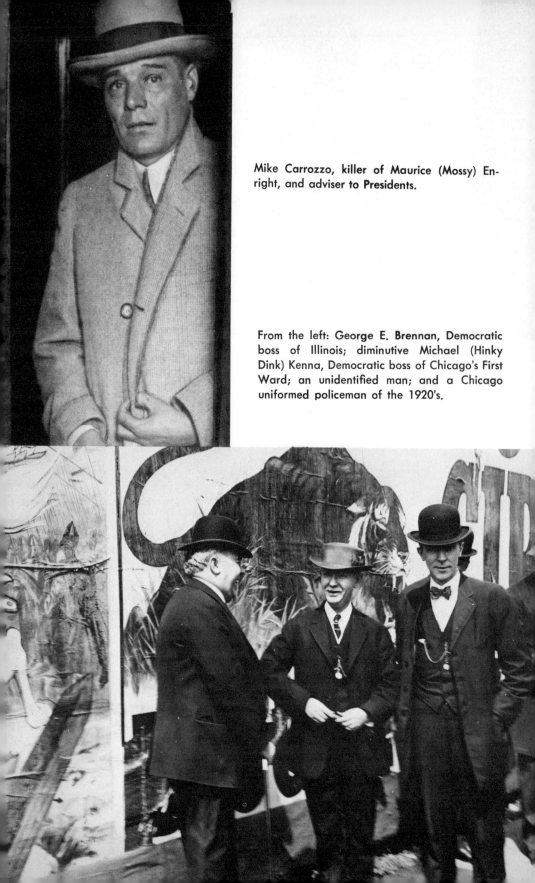

Mike Carrozzo, killer of Maurice (Mossy) Enright, and adviser to Presidents.

From the left: George E. Brennan, Democratic boss of Illinois; diminutive Michael (Hinky Dink) Kenna, Democratic boss of Chicago's First Ward; an unidentified man; and a Chicago uniformed policeman of the 1920's.

Two-Gun Louie Alterie was a member of the Dion O'Banion Gang. A Westerner and lover of the real Western-style shoot-out, he had many during the Prohibition Era.

Two-Gun Louie feigned insanity to beat a murder rap. He lay in a hospital bed, fitting jigsaw puzzles together. Here he winks for the photographer. When all the witnesses against him were killed, Alterie dropped his insanity plea. He simply said to the court, "What murder?"

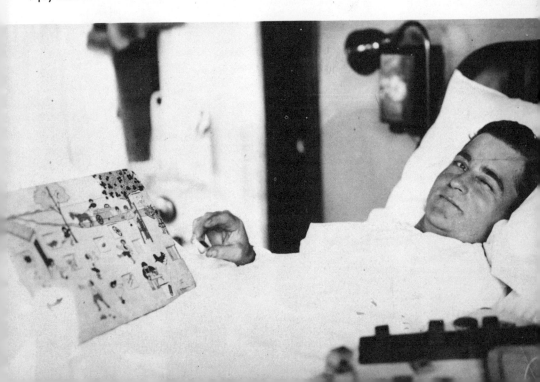

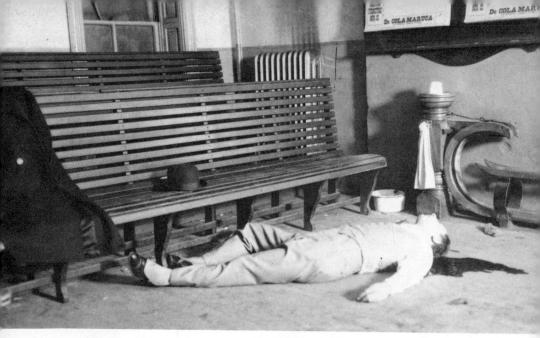

"Machine Gun" Jack McGurn (born Vincent Gebardi) was shot to death in a bowling alley one wintry midnight. The killers dropped a comic valentine on his face to indicate it was nothing personal, "just business."

Machine gunners waited for days in this second-story room on the west side of State Street. When Hymie Weiss appeared, they shot him to death, their bullets chipping the cornerstone of the Holy Name Cathedral. Weiss had spread word that Al Capone could hold the 1926 underworld peace conference "only over my dead body." Capone took him at his word.

Edward (Spike) O'Donnell operated this speakeasy at 1148 West 79th Street.

Spike O'Donnell (wearing hat) stepping onstage for a police showup. One of several brothers who ran a South Side bootleg gang in the 1920's, Spike was also an extortionist, a labor statesman who owned the laundry workers' union, and a killer to match Capone in everything but the craft for long-range planning.

Frankie McErlane, veteran of the newspaper circulation wars. He was hired as a slugger first by Max Annenberg for the *Tribune* and later by Moe Annenberg for the *Herald and Examiner*. McErlane went on to become the most vicious killer of his time. Moe Annenberg went on to become father of the ambassador to the Court of St. James's.

On South Phillips Avenue, then one of the prairies surrounding Chicago, a crowd is peering into Frankie McErlane's car at his mistress and her two puppies. Something the girl had said upset McErlane, and he killed all three.

View from the North Clark Street garage on February 15, 1929, the day after the St. Valentine's Day massacre took place.

A group of happy jurors did not take long—nor need the horseshoe for luck—to decide that Albert Anselmi and John W. Scalise (a pair of Al Capone's machine gunners) had nothing to do with wiping out the Bugs Moran gang in the massacre. So Anselmi and Scalise went free. But four months later they incurred Capone's wrath and the Big Fellow personally beat and shot them to death.

Detective Sergeant Harry Miller, sent by Mayor Cermak to shoot Frank Nitti in the back. Nitti lived.

Giuseppe Zangara, sent by Frank Nitti to shoot Mayor Cermak. With Roosevelt standing at Cermak's side, Zangara hit Cermak.

Sam Battaglia, one of four brothers who successively headed the 42 Gang, the underworld equivalent of Junior Achievement.

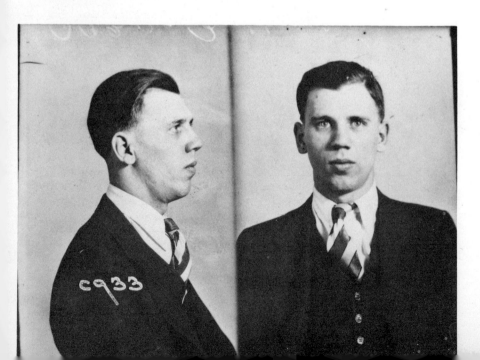

"Greasy Thumb" Jake Guzik, treasurer of the Al Capone enterprises, whose right thumb was always greasy from the ink on money with which he paid off police and politicians.

Louis Romano, inserted as president of the bartenders' union by Frank Nitti, over George McLane's objections. In this picture Romano, a boyhood chum of John D'Arco and Sam Battaglia, was testifying before the Senate.

Attorney Harold Levy and George McLane, owner of the Chicago bartenders' union. McLane testified at length on how Frank Nitti and the other heirs to the Capone empire took over the union to push their own brands of liquor.

(Left) Eddie (Dutch) Vogel, old Capone stalwart, last survivor of the famed 1926 underworld peace conference.

(Right) John D'Arco, Chicago's First Ward insurance tycoon.

Barney Balaban, Chicago movie theater tycoon, with Ann Marsters, a *Herald and Examiner* reporter. One of seven entertainment tycoon brothers, he submitted to extortion and paid bribes of $150 a week to Tommy Maloy of the motion picture operators' union and to George E. Browne of the stage hands' union. Those trifling bribes touched off the $1,000,000 film industry extortion.

Willie Bioff in court with his lawyer, Abe Marovitz (on crutches). Bioff was a notorious pimp who became a leader in Hollywood society until Westbrook Pegler exposed him. Bioff returned to Chicago in the midst of the $1,000,000 extortion to serve a six-month sentence for beating old whores who weren't giving him his cut. Abe Marovitz is now a federal district court judge in Chicago.

Attorney Charles Lounsbury, left, with George E. Browne, head of the stage hands' union. Browne still lives in fear of being blown to kingdom come by Capone heirs.

Ralph O'Hara, union slugger, left, with Tommy Maloy, owner of the motion picture operators' union.

"Bathhouse" John Coughlin, First Ward alderman, liked to keep cool on a hot day with a palm frond fan and a quart of ice cream. Originally a rubber in a North Clark Street bathhouse, Coughlin loved tailor-made lavender suits. He wrote poems to the beauty of Chicago in moonlight and sunlight.

Q—Besides Local 278 of the bartenders, what other unions belonged to the joint council? The waiters?

A—That's right.

Q—Who is the head of the waiters' local?

A—Guy Swinehart.

Q—Is Swinehart affiliated with anybody?

A—Danny Stanton.

McLane named the men representing the Capone Syndicate in the management of Local 25 of the waiters, Local 38 of the hotel clerks and auditors, Local 88 of the cooks, Local 29 of the institutional employees, Local 356 of the black waiters, Local 376 of the South Chicago bartenders, Local 484 of the waitresses, Local 594 of the miscellaneous workers, Local 602 of the checkroom employees, and Local 629 of the soda fountain and luncheonette employees.

Another union affiliated with the Romano joint council was the Chicago Waiters Alliance. George Sanders had been business agent of this union until April 5, 1939, when he disappeared. The rumor was that he had been shot to death and his body buried in quicklime. McLane testified, "Sanders' wife, Margaret, was told George had gone away on a drunk. She was put on the payroll of the waiters' union for a few months by Danny Stanton. Then she was dumped to shift for herself."

Attorney Lewis continued questioning McLane about Capone Syndicate control of the various unions in the Chicago area affiliated with the AFL International Bartenders, Waiters, and Hotel Employees.

Q—How about the miscellaneous hotel employees?

A—That is headed by Jim Blakely and John Lardino.

Q—Who is Blakely affiliated with?

A—Danny Stanton.

Q—Stanton operates these unions from behind the scenes, is that right?

A—That is right.

Q—Who heads the bartenders' local in South Chicago?

A—A fellow named Frank Trengalli. They brought him in from the West Coast. He was affiliated in Los Angeles with Willie Bioff, who runs the film industry unions for Frank Nitti. Trengalli has charge of Local 376 and Local 394 of the bartenders.

Q—What about Local 450 of the bartenders, out in Cicero?

A—Henry Mack is the front man. The local is controlled by Johnny Moore and Patrick O'Brien.

Q—Johnny Moore? Is he the one they call Screwy Claude Maddox?

A—That is right.

Q—He is an old associate of Al Capone?

A—That is right.

Q—What about the cooks' union?

A—Topenero is the Outfit's man.

Q—What about the checkroom attendants?

A—Red Campbell is the head of that and it belongs to the Outfit.

In his testimony, McLane used the term "the Outfit" interchangeably with "the Syndicate." He said the Romano joint council collected a per capita tax of 10 cents a month from each of 30,000 members of the fifteen local unions. He said this entire $3,000 a month was taken by Romano "out to Cicero." Under questioning, McLane said that by "out to Cicero" he meant to the payroll headquarters of the Nitti organization.

Attorney Lewis continued questioning.

Q—What are the expenses of this joint council Romano set up?

A—None, except for stamps and printing letterheads.

Q—Do they hire anyone?

A—No, they pay a secretary five dollars a meeting.

Q—Did Romano ever tell you who got the money?

A—Yes, he told me the Outfit.

The Romano joint council earned $25,000 a year besides the $36,000 a year collected in dues, by publishing a Christmas Yearbook. Advertising salesmen got on the telephone and "clouted" all the cabarets, nightclubs, cocktail lounges, taverns, liquor companies, breweries, and soft-drink distributors for ads. Space in the yearbook was expensive. Every politician in Cook County was expected to buy a space in which he could extend "Yuletide Greetings" to the union owners.

After the yearbook's editor and advertising manager were paid, and all the printing and engraving bills had been paid, said McLane, the book still netted $25,000 a year and up. This was Organization money, just like the dues collections, and went directly into the coffers of the Syndicate.

McLane said that Frank Nitti, who controlled all bartenders, waiters, cooks, and checkroom attendants in the Chicago area through the Romano joint council, wanted to extend his control to the AFL international union.

Nitti made no secret of his plans. He told McLane he wanted through McLane to get control of the Chicago Federation of Labor. Then Nitti proposed to elect McLane to the presidency of the international union and a seat on the executive board of the American Federation of Labor. McLane testified, "Nitti said he did not just want control of the union but of the vast retail market nationally for beer, liquor, and mineral waters."

In addition to the union of bartenders and cocktail-lounge waitresses, McLane said, Nitti wanted an employers' association. So a corporate charter was taken out at Springfield, Illinois, for the Chicago Tavern and Café Owners Association. McLane said that in 1937 he was told to meet Danny Stanton in a saloon at Sixty-eighth and Halsted streets to get this association started. McLane testified, "I met Stanton at Nitti's orders. Stanton had the problem of organizing the tavern owners and liquor dealers. He wanted to take from my union, Local 278, six or seven hundred bartenders who owned their own taverns. This would be the nucleus for his association."

When the Capone organization was ready to try for national control of the bartenders' union in June, 1938, McLane was summoned to Nitti's suite in the Bismarck Hotel. Besides Nitti at this meeting, McLane testified, there were George Browne, president of the AFL International Alliance of Stage and Theatrical Employees; Willie Bioff, walking delegate for his stagehands' union, whose headquarters were in Hollywood with the motion picture industry; and Nick Circella, alias Nicky Dean, the Capone group's watchdog charged with keeping Browne and Bioff honest.

McLane did not know at the time of his testimony that through Browne and Bioff the Nitti organization was extorting nearly $2,000,000 from the nation's film industry. McLane said; "They told me they wanted to run me for president of the AFL International Bartenders, Waiters, and Hotel Employees Union.

"They said they only needed me in that job for two years. Nitti said the Syndicate would make enough in two years to give the union back to us." Nitti told McLane on this occasion that the Capone group had put its own men in as presidents of several other AFL international unions and there would be no problem about having McLane voted into the top job. Lewis questioned McLane.

Q—Did they mention any names?

A—Yes, Joe Esposito and Mike Carrozzo of the hod carriers, George Browne and Willie Bioff of the stagehands, George Scalise of the building service employees. (Bioff had served jail terms as a pimp. Scalise had gone to prison as a white slaver.)

Q—At this meeting with Nitti, what was said and by whom?

A—Bioff talked first. He said he could deliver the West Coast votes. He said he would contact various organizations in Seattle including the teamsters, of which Dave Beck was then international president, and see that the people voted for me for president of the bartenders' international.

Q—Did you say anything about not being a candidate?

A—I tried to explain to them that they were going into an organization twenty-eight years old and it was pretty near impossible to beat.

McLane explained that the AFL bartenders' international dated back to 1910. He went on: "I said the others in the organization would know I was being used strictly as a yes-man, as a Syndicate front man. I said I would either wind up in the penitentiary or out in the alley. I told Nitti I did not favor to run.

Q—Did Nitti make any threats?

A—Yes, he gave me to understand that I would run or I would be found dead.

McLane said that at this point the others in the meeting began to talk about what they would do with the bartenders' international once they had taken it over and how they would split up its treasury. Nitti called them back to business. Nitti wanted to hear the exact mechanics of how they proposed to take control rather than what they would do after they got it. McLane said, "They parceled out the country. Bioff was to line up necessary votes on the West Coast. Browne was to take care of the East, Boston and around there. Dean had some other place. I was to run whether I wished it or not."

McLane said the bartenders' local union in Miami was owned by Danny Coughlin, brother-in-law of Al Capone.

After he left that meeting with Nitti in the Bismarck Hotel, said McLane, he got on the long-distance phone and called his labor friends all over the country. He told them that under no circumstances did he want to be elected general president of the AFL bartenders' international. He said he did this secretly, knowing he might be killed if Nitti ever found out about it.

In the weeks before the biennial convention of the bartenders' international union, McLane said, Louis Romano was at his side almost day and night.

His campaign was personally masterminded by Frank Nitti, who approved all the letters and literature sent out. But when the convention was finally held, McLane was defeated for the presidency by Ed Flore of Buffalo. Louis Romano insisted that McLane throw his hat in the ring for vice-president and he was elected fifth vice-president of the international.

When they returned to Chicago, McLane was summoned to Nitti's suite in the Congress Hotel. Louis Romano accompanied him. McLane said, "Nitti raised hell about my drinking. He said he wouldn't stand for me publicly criticizing the Capone Outfit. He told me he wanted me to get on the wagon and quit drinking. There is an unwritten law in the Outfit, which applies to anybody in contact with the Outfit. They are not allowed to drink because they might shoot their mouth off. If they shoot their mouth off they will be found in an alley.

"Nitti said he didn't want to lose a man of my standing, because he wanted me to be their means of taking control of the Chicago Federation of Labor. Nitti said they wanted me to do that. So I agreed to get on the water wagon."

A few days later Murray Humphreys visited George McLane in his office and told him, "Why don't you get some sense? You have been in the labor game all your life. Here you haven't got a quarter and your home even has a mortgage on it."

McLane replied, "I can go to sleep at night. I ain't going to push nobody around for you or anybody else."

Humphreys said, "That's the trouble. We call it business and you call it pushing people around."

McLane's testimony was corroborated at several important points under oath by his brother, Michael J. McLane, and by another bartenders' union official, William Salvatore.

State's Attorney Thomas J. Courtney said, on June 5, 1940, that the grand jury was investigating disbursements of more than $1,000,000 from the treasury of the bartenders' union in and around Chicago. Courtney's assistant, Wilbert F. Crowley, took McLane before the grand jury where he said substantially what he told Master in Chancery Brown.

Up to this point, Frank Nitti and Paul Ricca had been content to caution George McLane to "quit drinking and sounding off." Now McLane was told, "Shut up or else." McLane's brother said George McLane understood the "or else" to mean that after one more word he might be killed out of hand.

Indictments were returned against Murray Humphreys, Frank Nitti, Paul Ricca, and Louis Campagna. They were charged with conspiracy to defraud members of the bartenders' union. Ricca and Campagna disappeared, but Humphreys and Nitti were brought to trial November 29, 1940, in the criminal court of Judge John M. Bolton.

Neither Judge Bolton nor Assistant State's Attorney William B. Crawford was aware that George McLane had finally decided to take seriously the warnings given him by Nitti and the others. McLane was told that if he so much as opened his mouth in court his wife, Christine, would be abducted and kept alive as her husband was daily sent one of her hands, then her feet, then her arms.

After Prosecutor Crawford made his opening statement to the jury, George McLane was called to the stand as the state's first witness. Crawford questioned McLane.

Q—Do you know the defendant, Murray Humphreys?

A—I must refuse to answer on grounds that to do so might tend to incriminate me.

Q—Do you know the defendant Frank Nitti?

A—I must refuse. . . .

With McLane unwilling to testify in open court, the charges against all the defendants were dismissed for want of prosecution. McLane's testimony before the grand jury was entered in the trial record.

Just as Al Capone had failed in his plan to take over the Chicago Building Trades Council, so had Frank Nitti failed in his bid to take over the bartenders' international union. But Nitti had absolute control, through Romano's joint council, of every union in the area which was in a position to push the Organization's products.

This included virtually all bartenders in the Chicago area.

15 A hoodlum quotes the bishop

The difference between the old-fashioned professional union slugger such as George B. McLane and the emerging labor statesmen of the Capone empire had never been better summed up than in Murray Humphreys' words to McLane: "You call it pushing people around. We call it business."

McLane expressed himself as frightened by the callousness of these Capone men with whom he had to deal. McLane could scarcely be called a man who walked in childlike innocence. In thirty years behind the mahogany he had learned other uses for a bung starter besides tapping a barrel of brew. He did not achieve or retain the privilege of collecting $4 a month from each of 5,000 barkeeps without knowing which end of a gun gets hot.

But McLane confessed himself scared by Nitti and the others.

What frightened him was that they did not drink, they did not chase broads during business hours, they could not be swayed by the most piteous appeal. They were as single-minded as saints in their devotion to profits for the Organization. No action was ever considered from the viewpoint of morality. Each action was judged from the pragmatic view of whether it might speed or slow the objective.

There are people in this world so naïve and uninformed that they doubt the existence of conspiracies formed to attain and continue power and profits, whether in the upperworld or in the underworld. George McLane became a believer. He was to say before his death that the great underworld complex spawned in the days of Big Jim Colosimo and Johnny Torrio had hewed to the line of its objective without deviation for two generations.

In the roaring twenties of the Prohibition era the smoking pistol had been the gangster's open sesame. Those gangsters grouped under the Capone aegis who survived the transition from Prohibition to Repeal attained their results with the bribery of officialdom. For the most part they could lay aside personal animosities and problems. They refused to feud, as had gangsters in the twenties. Murder and mayhem were still

195

weapons in their arsenal but only after other means failed. From force they had turned to diplomacy. That was in the thirties.

With the forties came World War II with its tremendous opportunities. Rationing and scarcity were turned to account. The organized underworld could print ration stamps on the same presses and with the same plates used by the government. No one without a microscope could tell one "official" sheet of ration stamps from another which was counterfeit.

In the war years the underworld bought up and warehoused the items in short supply: cigarettes and liquor, tires and gasoline, automobiles and trucks and tractors.

They found this the simplest thing on earth to accomplish. Paul Ricca echoed Capone's old philosophy when he said, "You find the Washington office in charge of stockpiling the stuff. You spread a little money around and that office arranges for you to get twenty percent of the government's stockpile. Those guys in Washington are smart. They know that if they don't build their bank accounts before the war is over they will never get another chance."

At state level, during the forties, the Capone Syndicate found millions of dollars could be turned as profit by filling the freezers of butcher shops with horse meat instead of beef. They found a way to counterfeit the cigarette tax stamps and avoid paying excise taxes.

When the fifties came along the shortages were in Europe and Asia. But the stocks needed to supply the shortages were in the United States. The politicians at the top tipped off the Capone Syndicate men as to the items in short supply. The Syndicate simply stockpiled them and sold them when the time was ripe at profits that were astronomical.

During the war American leaders who were directing Allied military operations in Sicily had approached exiled leaders of the Chicago and New York underworld to ask aid. Benito Mussolini's policy for a generation had been anti-Mafia. The naïveté of American military leaders reversed that policy overnight. The international underworld put its own people into positions of power in Sicily and Italy. They exacted tribute to build their coffers.

After the war, the leaders of the Capone Syndicate in Chicago found they no longer were persona non grata in the offices, clubs, and country estates of the upperworld businessmen and bankers. The Syndicate leaders had children who had grown up, attended the best schools, and intermarried with young people they met at those schools. Social and moral standards became blurred.

Now people in the underworld, like their counterparts in the upperworld, simply called their undertakings business. There was a time when men of the stature of Colonel Robert R. McCormick or Merrill C. (Babe) Meigs would have refused to shake the hand of an Al Capone who started life as a towel boy for whores. But the time came when such towers of the upperworld were happy to claim acquaintance with Capone and his successors.

This is part of the legacy of Al Capone.

Several men mentioned in these chronicles deserve to be discussed in greater detail. One is Joseph C. Fusco, bearing the same family name as one of the six men who chartered the Unione Siciliane back in 1895. Fusco was important in Nitti's scheme to control liquor sales in Chicago through ownership of breweries and distributorships.

Because the name Fusco appears on the Unione charter, the name carries weight among immigrant Italian and Sicilian families comparable to that of a signer of the Declaration of Independence to a native-born American.

Fusco was twenty years old on May 29, 1922, when first convicted and fined $50 on a bootlegging charge. He had been caught two years earlier driving a truckload of beer from suburban Lemont into Chicago. Since Lemont had no brewery, the beer's source was probably Joliet.

Fusco was in a truck registered to the Rural Motor Service Company. He was a sturdy youngster of eighteen when arrested, stood five feet seven, and weighed 200 pounds.

Fusco was mugged, fingerprinted, and fined. According to the records.

Years later Fusco was to deny he ever had appeared in court, ever had been tried on any charge, ever had paid a fine. Realizing the importance of the name Fusco to politicians of Chicago, he probably is telling the truth despite the evidence of the court records.

A common practice then for the defendant with clout was for the judge, after accepting a payoff, to make a notation on the daily court sheet to the effect that the trial was held. The notation would be an entry of a plea of guilty and in the column which recorded disposition of the case was written "fined fifty dollars and costs."

Often the judge did not handle the matter personally. Every judge had a personal bailiff, who served as a middleman between briber and bribee. The payoff went to the personal bailiff. The bailiff turned the money over to the judge. If there was even a suspicion that the bailiff had held out on a judge, the bailiff would be out of a job in a matter of minutes.

Fusco testified under oath on September 9, 1952, that he was simply a driver for bootleg beer trucks until 1923 or 1924. Fusco said he got his start as a beer salesman after a visit to Al Capone in the Lexington Hotel.

Fusco said he sold beer from 1923 or 1924 until Prohibition was repealed in 1933. Then he became a salesman for the Drexel Beverage Distributing Company, an outfit owned by Ralph Capone.

Later, said Fusco, he became a salesman for Gold Seal Liquors, Inc., at 701 Harrison Street, and bought into the company in 1941.

Fusco was indicted October 3, 1924, by a federal grand jury for a violation of the Volstead Act involving 1,446 quarts—125 cases—of whiskey. He later said Prohibition agents raided the truck firm for which he worked. He and the other defendants on the conspiracy charge were found guilty, said Fusco, "But the judge set aside the verdict," and they all went free.

Fusco said he had been arrested "half a dozen times" during the Prohibition years. He shrugged off testimony about those arrests with the words, "You know how police officers want to get promoted. They take you to the station, push you around for an hour or two, then throw you out."

None of Joe Fusco's criminal record can be found in the files of the Chicago police department. Al Capone early in the game showed his men how to bribe a policeman or prosecutor with access to the files to destroy fingerprint cards, front- and side-view mug shots, and typewritten records of offenses.

Not until the Kefauver Senate crime investigating committee of 1950 did the federal agents dig out Fusco's criminal record—or at least part of it. They did it by the slow process of going through the files of the Cook County criminal courts for the years from 1920 to 1930.

The first conviction they were able to find for Fusco was that of May 29, 1922. This was three months before Al Capone first came to police attention as a loudmouth gunslinger in August, 1922.

Fusco and Capone struck it off as friends from the day they met. Both were fearless sluggers, both convivial companions. They remained firm friends until Capone's death in 1947.

When Fusco testified in Chicago before the Kefauver committee on October 17, 1950, he gave his address as 7342 Prairie Avenue. Actually Fusco then lived at 8011 Loomis Street with his wife and four children. He maintained a suite at the Conrad Hilton Hotel. The address he gave the Senators was that of Al Capone's mother, Mrs. Theresa Annunzio Capone.

Kefauver explained that Fusco gave the Capone home address "as a mark of respect for his late friend, Al Capone, and as a sign of defiance to the Senate investigators." Kefauver was correct. The two most important words in the vocabularies of the old associates of Al Capone are loyalty and respect.

During Prohibition years, Fusco served briefly as a Capone bodyguard before being set up by the latter as a beer distributor. Fusco was indicted with Capone in 1931 on an income tax evasion charge in connection with bootleg liquor sales. A decade later the defendants settled the tax liability in a civil case and the criminal charges were never pressed. Fusco told the Kefauver group, "Until the repeal of Prohibition I was a bootlegger of beer. Al Capone recommended several persons where I could get beer, including Jack Nolan and Joe Saltis and Bert Delaney."

Even before repeal, Fusco owned a piece of the San Carlo Italian Village at A Century of Progress.

His partners in the enterprise included Paul Ricca, Lou Greenberg, and Joseph I. Bulger, the last-mentioned being the ostensible owner of the place.

Kefauver said that after repeal, Fusco muscled into the Gold Seal Liquors, Inc., a whiskey distributorship, but Fusco claimed he bought his way into the company with $30,000 he had saved. He said he was able to buy a piece not only of Gold Seal but of its subsidiaries, Rembrandt Distributing at 8608 Commercial Avenue, Cornell Distributing at 5926 South Kedzie Avenue, the Bohemian Brewery, and the Bohemian Wine and Liquor Company, both in Joliet.

Kefauver asked Fusco how, with his reputation of arrests and convictions, he ever had been issued federal and state licenses to enter the wholesale and retail liquor business after repeal. Fusco was unusually frank in his reply.

The government bureau gave him a little trouble, Fusco said, so he ascertained the two men in the bureau who had responsibility for processing licenses. Then, "I put those two men on my payroll and got the license."

Twenty years after he got the original licenses, a question arose as to whether they ought to be taken away from Fusco. But apparently the grease had been applied in all the right places. One after the other, the various responsible officials told why Fusco could not be touched.

Henry G. Morthorst, who headed the federal alcohol tax unit in Chicago, said there had been hearings concerning Fusco's federal license. But testimony and evidence did not appear to warrant revocation of the basic liquor permit granted Fusco in 1933.

Max Loeb, who headed the Chicago office of the Illinois Liquor Control Commission, acknowledged that the statute said anyone licensed to sell liquor to the public ought to be of "good character and reputation." But Loeb said the provision did not apply to Fusco because, "The state of Illinois does not question a man's character or reputation if he has a basic permit from the federal government."

A city license might have involved an inquiry into Joe Fusco's character and reputation. But William Prendergast, who as city collector was in charge of such licensing, said Fusco required no city license because "his business is strictly wholesale."

Fusco told Kefauver that he held the exclusive distributorship in the Chicago area for many brands of whiskey. He handled the Schenley and the Seagram lines. He handled the Whitely line, which included King's Ransom scotch. Kefauver noted for the record that Whitely was owned by Frank Costello, then head of the New York City crime syndicate.

Cash income from all his businesses in 1950, said Fusco before the Senate committee, exceeded $20,000,000 gross per year.

The Senators debated among themselves whether to pressure authorities of Chicago, the state of Illinois, and the United States to strip Joe Fusco of his liquor distributorship. Just a little publicity about the bribery which Fusco admitted might result in his losing the distributorship, the breweries, and the chain of liquor stores. But the Senators decided against "precipitate action." They had in mind a Kansas City murder which had resulted from similar action.

In Kansas City a distributorship similar to that of Joe Fusco had been held until 1944 by Joe Di Giovanni, who so frequently accompanied Tony Rizzo when calling on Al Capone at the Metropole Hotel. Joe Di Giovanni was earning $80,000 a year in profits from the distributorship.

Then the Missouri State Liquor Control Commission got a sudden attack of morality and legality. They decided to strip Joe Di Giovanni of his liquor license because in applying for it he had failed to mention his various arrests in murder and kidnap inquiries.

In February, 1944, a gambler named Wolf Riman moved in on part of Joe Di Giovanni's liquor territory, taking over part of the distributorship. A week later Wolf Riman was shot down in the street.

When the Kefauver committee got to Kansas City, the Senators subpoenaed Joe Di Giovanni to ask if he had killed Wolf Riman. Di Giovanni all but laughed aloud as he replied, "Who, me?" Kefauver asked if Di Giovanni had any idea who might have killed Riman. Di Giovanni thought a minute and then replied, "No, Senator, I'm afraid I don't." Then Di Giovanni added, with a smile, "I'm legit, now."

The Senators were fresh from this experience in Kansas City when they questioned Joe Fusco in Chicago about his liquor holdings. They found Fusco modest about the part he had played in the sale of beer through the Chicago area during the Prohibition period. No one would have known from Fusco's quiet demeanor that just as Al Capone had been Public Enemy No. 1 on the first such list ever published, so a year later was Joe Fusco listed as Public Enemy No. 1 on the second.

The Chicago Crime Commission in 1931 had disclosed that Joe Fusco was "the beer boss of the Capone Syndicate."

With Fusco on that second list of public enemies was a notorious company which included Charlie Fischetti, Capone's cousin; Sam (Golf Bag) Hunt, then one of Capone's top blazers, as assassins were called; Claude Maddox, alias Screwy John Moore; Louis (Little New York) Campagna; and Tony Accardo, alias Joe Batters, who was just then emerging as an understudy to Machine Gun Jack McGurn.

A few weeks before this second public-enemy list was published, Joe Fusco got into an altercation at Chicago police headquarters, 1121 South State Street. On the night of July 13, 1931, Police Sergeant John T. Coughlin, who had just been transferred downtown, seized a truckload of Capone beer.

Capone was current in his regular weekly payoffs to the police from top to bottom. There was no heat being brought on the police by clergymen, newspapers, or do-gooders. As far as Joe Fusco could see, there was no excuse whatever for Sergeant Coughlin to have seized that truckload of illegal beer and parked it under police guard in the alley behind police headquarters.

So even though at the time there was a federal court order out for his arrest on a beer sales indictment, Joe Fusco came storming into police headquarters. He was sure of his rights and he was a man not to be denied. He vehemently demanded return of his truckload of beer, telling Coughlin, "And I mean right now, not tomorrow."

The federal agents had been notified of the beer truck seizure even before Fusco arrived at police headquarters.

The newspaper reporters who covered the night police-beat already had called for photographers to get pictures of the beer truck. Fusco's appearance caused embarrassment all around.

The police, who had been on Fusco's payroll for years, tried to quiet him down and get him into a back room where they could talk to him. When they did so, they tried to talk him out of his demand for this particular truckload of beer. One of the policemen asked Fusco, in the presence of reporters, "How would it look if we let you walk out of here and drive away with that truckload of beer?" Fusco said, "You should have thought of that before you drove it into the alley."

The police and Fusco finally agreed that they would abide by the mediation offered by Dennis (Duke) Cooney, the Capone vice chief for the First Ward. Cooney was called from his Club Royale Frolics.

Cooney threatened aloud to make every cop in the district live on his salary for a month if they did not release the beer to Joe Fusco. Both Cooney and Fusco made some choice remarks about bureaucratic interference with free enterprise.

A compromise was reached. Fusco would be publicly refused return of the truckload of beer and would leave the police station. Later in the night, after the excitement had died down, the truck would be mysteriously "stolen" from its parking place behind police headquarters and delivered to Fusco's garage.

The compromise proved pleasing to everyone. Fusco and Cooney went away smiling. The federal agents went away glum.

The newspaper reporters on the midnight trick returned to the press room in police headquarters to go on with their permanent card game. The district commander took Sergeant Coughlin into the back room for a serious lecture on the facts of Chicago life.

In the excitement, nobody thought to tell Joe Fusco he was supposed to be arrested on sight for the federal beer indictment.

Those who see Joseph C. Fusco today, a genial millionaire of peaceful mien and manifold charities, find it hard to recognize in him the Fusco of the era of wonderful nonsense.

Fusco got off to a flying start in the sale of beer after repeal because he was willing to grant credit to saloonkeepers on his own unusual terms. In those years of 1933 and 1934, money was tight. The Depression was not yet over. The man who decided to go into the saloon business had such limited funds that he could not pay for his whiskey and beer.

Fusco would deliver beer to anybody with a license to operate a saloon. If the owner did not pay for the beer on the date the payment was due, two of Fusco's collectors came around to "clout the damper." This was the turn-of-the-century expression for a thief who emptied the cash register.

Eventually the credit account would be current. Fusco's approach was pragmatic.

Within fifteen years after repeal—by 1948—the Capone Syndicate was the acknowledged owner of 17 percent of the Chicago area's retail liquor outlets. This included street-corner saloons in home neighborhoods, slick cocktail lounges at busy city intersections, and retail package liquor stores in every section of the area.

Even the liquor stores that were independent had to buy a certain percentage of their stock from Syndicate distributors. They had to stock Syndicate brands of beer and liquor.

Jack Bichl, the Chicago sales manager for National Distillers, said he knew nothing of Syndicate activities in the trade. By coincidence, even as a reporter was getting this reply from Bichl the interview was interrupted by Bichl's secretary. She announced that Milton Friedman was on the wire. Friedman was president of Gold Seal Distributors and other Fusco enterprises.

A few days earlier a story in *The Union Server,* the liquor-trade paper, told of Bichl addressing a Stevens Hotel dinner meeting of the sales forces of the Joe Fusco companies.

Fusco's holdings expanded. He took over the Joliet Citizens Brewing Company, installed two new boilers, added a railroad siding, rewired and otherwise renovated the plant, bought new trucks and trailers.

By interlocking directorships, he controlled Steel City Liquors in South Chicago and Midwest Liquors in East Chicago.

Friedman, who was president of Gold Seal Distributors, was also president of the Illinois Wholesale Liquor Dealers Association. In that capacity he dealt with Joseph O'Neill, who was president of AFL Local 62, of the Liquor and Wine Salesmen's Union.

When asked why Fusco's companies were apparently exempt from salary demands made in other areas of the industry, O'Neill said Fusco had produced evidence that he could not afford to pay such wages as those of the Hiram Walker Distilleries in Peoria.

When Timothy J. O'Connor was made chief of detectives in Chicago, he served notice on the underworld by ordering the arrest of Joe Fusco. On November 16, 1948, Police Sergeant Frank Pape of the robbery detail picked up Fusco near Gold Seal Liquors, Inc., at 701 West Harrison Street, and brought him downtown for fingerprinting. Front and side photos were made of Fusco and he was put through a showup. He was not identified by any crime victims. Then he was freed on a $10 bond, to guarantee his appearance in court next day.

Judge Harold P. O'Connell was obviously embarrassed next day when the case of the State vs. Joe Fusco, charged with disorderly conduct, was called. Fusco did not appear, but was represented by Attorney Benjamin Nelson. The lawyer said his client was out of town. The judge dismissed the case.

Joe Fusco was called "the Crime Syndicate liquor representative" in Lake County, Indiana, on May 11, 1949, by Metro Holovachka, deputy prosecutor. In a speech before the Women's Citizens Committee in Gary, Holovachka said that Fusco's representative was Abe Kaplan. Just as Fusco ran the Capone Syndicate liquor interests, said Holovachka, so the horserace wire services were run by Jake Guzik, represented by Harry Hymes, and gambling was run by Guzik through William J. (Sonny) Sheetz. Holovachka said, "Sheetz runs the Big House in Indiana Harbor, the country's biggest gambling casino north of the Mason-Dixon line. The casino has one hundred sixty employees, who earn twenty-five to forty-five dollars a day, and the payroll is said to exceed two million three hundred thousand a year. The average daily take at the Big House is upwards of twenty-five thousand, so the place annually grosses more than nine million one hundred twenty-five thousand, of which fifty percent is profit."

Fusco told the Senators that in addition to case-lot gifts of liquor to "people in public life," which he considered necessary to the smooth operation of his business, policemen "haunt" his places of business at Christmastime hoping for tokens of good cheer from the former Public Enemy No. 1.

Fusco said he was a cousin of the De Stefano brothers, Rocco, Frank, and Vito. He said he and Rocco De Stefano had been colleagues as bootleggers during the heyday of Al Capone, and had been partners in legal liquor businesses after Prohibition.

Nearly three years after the Kefauver Senate hearings, the Illinois Liquor Control Commission on January 21, 1953, voted 2 to 1 to issue wholesale liquor licenses to three of Fusco's firms: Bohemian Brewing Company at 1216 South Sangamon Street; Bohemian Wine and Liquor Company at 100 Collins Street in Joliet; and the Joliet Citizens Brewing Company at the same address.

All three members of the commission were appointees of Governor Adlai E. Stevenson. The chairman, Chalmer C. Taylor, and Sol A. Hoffman voted approval of Fusco. W. Willard Wirtz voted disapproval. Wirtz issued a strongly worded dissent, criticizing Fusco's reputation.

Six witnesses, including Police Commissioner Timothy O'Connor, testified that Fusco never ceased being an associate of hoodlums. But Fusco had twenty-five witnesses, including a Catholic priest and a bishop, on hand to testify to his sterling character.

Among those who swore that Fusco was a man of good repute were the Reverend James A. Walsh, pastor of St. Felicita church at 1526 East Eighty-fourth Street; and Bishop Bernard J. Sheil of the Roman Catholic archdiocese. Others who testified that Fusco was honest, upright, charitable, and a credit to the community included Thomas J. Callaghan, former chief agent in Chicago for the United States Secret Service; and Walter R. Schaub, president of Meadowmoor Dairies, Inc., former law partner of Al Capone's old legal eagle, Billy Parrillo.

Fusco himself told Kefauver and the other Senators that Bishop Sheil considered him a great fellow. Fusco said that Sheil named Fusco a fund-drive chairman for the Catholic Youth Organization.

Fusco was testifying under oath as to a conversation with the bishop: "I said to him, 'Won't I embarrass you?'"

"The bishop said, 'Let me worry about that, Joe. I know who and what you are. You are all right with me, Joe.'"

After Lou Greenberg, millionaire chairman of the board of Canadian Ace Brewing Company, was shot to death December 8, 1955, Joe Fusco was questioned about his holdings. Fusco said then, "I own the Merit Liquor Company at 372 West Ontario Street; the Van Merritt Brewing Company in Joliet; and sixty-four percent of the Bohemian Brewing Company in Joliet."

In the sixties, as happens from time to time, the Capone Syndicate began bombing various businesses to stimulate sales of Syndicate products. A special Cook County grand jury began, on September 11, 1964, looking into the matter of more than a hundred such bombings of bars, taverns, cocktail lounges, and restaurants in the previous thirty-three months.

An official of the state's attorney's office said, "A majority of thirty-one restaurants bombed or set afire in the last thirty-three months were buying beer, wine, and whiskey from Joe Fusco firms."

Joe Fusco today is known as a multimillionaire, a go-getter as a businessman, a graying grandfather full of years and wisdom, generous to church and charity, spending his days in sunny Florida.

16 The genius outsmarts himself

Fred Evans was the only Capone slugger who legitimately could claim a college education. He studied accounting, architecture, and engineering, and earned his degree at the age of nineteen. He amassed a fortune and when shot to death on August 22, 1959, at the age of sixty, he reckoned his personal wealth at more than $11,000,000.

Evans and Murray Humphreys in the mid-twenties were partners in the Artistic Cleaners and Dyers at 741 South Cicero Avenue. Evans was a veteran of the cleaning and dyeing wars earlier discussed. Long after Frank Nitti no longer was at the helm, Evans was selected as the man to bring the laundry and linen supply business of the city into the hands of the Outfit.

Born in St. Louis, Evans was brought to Chicago as a boy and was graduated from high school. He studied accounting at the University of Chicago. Then he turned to architecture and engineering, earning his degree at the Champaign-Urbana campus of the University of Illinois in 1918. He sold jewelry for a while and in the financial depression of 1922 began buying up distressed merchandise.

Evans attended every sale held by the post office, the Railway Express Agency, and the insurance companies which sought to recoup on losses in railroad accidents. Evans rented a drafty old garage at Halsted and Van Buren streets to store the stuff. He met Murray Humphreys, then a short-order cook in Messinger's Restaurant at Halsted and Adams streets.

The two were of an age, both about twenty-three, and Humphreys pointed out to Evans that stolen merchandise could be sold right along with the distressed stuff from his warehouse.

Louis Romano at the time was a youngster just learning to snatch purses and steal cars with the Battaglia brothers. The stolen stuff was .brought to Fred Evans when Murray Humphreys would vouch for the thieves. Evans' garage became a gathering place for the toughs of Halsted Street.

In this way Fred Evans became a college-educated fence for stolen merchandise. When some of the boys wanted to use his garage as a beauty parlor for stolen cars, he set a price on the action. One would clout a fairly new car early in the evening and bring it in for treatment. Others would swarm over it, filing numbers off motor and body, giving the whole thing a quick-dry paint job, and getting the car out of the garage before daylight for sale in a used-car lot.

From stolen cars to stolen beer and whiskey was an easy step. The toughs were hijacking truckloads of illegal liquor in the streets of Chicago and on the highways leading into the city. They brought the trucks directly to Evans' garage to be unloaded. Then the trucks were driven to the other end of the city to be abandoned.

This was in the period before Al Capone called the 1926 peace conference to eliminate such anarchism. In those early hijacking days, gangsters had no sense of humor about losing a load of hootch. Often they caught the hijackers and many a morning some gutters in Chicago ran red with blood.

Evans always had a bankroll from one source or another. When the boys were broke he would advance them $5 any day of the week with the understanding they were to repay $6 the next Monday.

So Evans got into the loan-shark business. The training was not wasted. Eventually Evans, tall, slender, and distinguished-looking, became part-owner of the Security Discount Corporation at 100 North La Salle Street. Then, as a Loop banker, he was in the big time of the loan-shark racket.

Evans was one of those completely coordinated men who can put everything he learns to use. In this way he and Murray Humphreys had much in common. Evans' early days in the jewelry business stood him in good stead when appraising stolen gems later. The 42 Gang in the twenties and the Capone Syndicate in later years turned to Fred Evans when hot ice had to be appraised before being offered for sale.

One of Evans' close friends in this period was George Scalise, the pimp who became president of the AFL International Building Service Employees. Frank Nitti put Scalise into the big job. Scalise was indicted in Chicago for pocketing $118,000 of the union's funds. Then he was convicted in New York on a similar charge. He had earlier been convicted of operating a stable of whores.

Fred Evans was caught with a garage full of illegal alcohol in May, 1924. At first he pleaded not guilty. Then he changed the plea to guilty in what was obviously a deal. He paid a fine of $250.

If the American universities had the system used by European universities, Evans might have been stripped of his degree upon conviction of a felony. But it would not have mattered. In the circles in which Evans by then was traveling, a college degree might have been considered a hindrance rather than a help. Evans never traded on his higher education.

The time was to come when he felt that his education did not really start until he left the ivy-covered halls of conventional learning.

Evans worked with Humphreys on a few holdups but he once said, "I never went for the heavy stuff." Evans preferred not to carry a pistol or be put in a position where he might be compelled to use one. Sensibly enough, he felt that his trained mind ought to be the equivalent of a hot pistol in the hands of a brute.

Evans became what Al Capone and Frank Nitti called an all-around hustler, or a man who could have figured a dishonest angle on the account books kept by Saint Peter. Evans was so busy that he neglected his first wife and lost her. She was Donna Levinson, sister of Louis (Sleep-Out) Levinson, who then was gambling czar of the Newport-Covington area in Kentucky and later transferred his operations to Las Vegas. Donna Levinson Evans divorced Fred Evans on a charge of cruelty in 1924.

Evans' loan-sharking operations gave him much in common with Lou Greenberg, who besides operating Capone's Manhattan Brewery (later Canadian Ace) ran the Roosevelt Finance Company at 3159 Roosevelt Road. Evans and Greenberg became close. So close that Evans' second wife, Mathilda, and one of Greenberg's wives, Esther, became the joint owners of record of a West Coast luxury hotel.

A Los Angeles police captain in 1951 testified before the Kefauver committee that a plot by Chicago and Minneapolis gangsters to have the Los Angeles mayor removed from office had been hatched in the Evans-Greenberg hotel.

Evans was a partner with Murray Humphreys in the popcorn concession at A Century of Progress, both in 1933 and 1934. Humphreys called Evans "a financial wizard."

Evans loaned Louis Campagna $20,000 in 1937, not at usurious interest rates, but at a straight 5 percent a year. Campagna repaid the principal in 1941. Evans came up with some of the money needed to pay Campagna's income tax deficiency when the latter was in prison with Paul Ricca and the others in the million-dollar movie shakedown in 1943.

Evans admitted he was one of those who dropped a bundle of money on the desk of Eugene Bernstein, lawyer and Twenty-fourth Ward politician, with the words, "This is for Louie."

But Evans' real contribution to the Syndicate was in his organization of the laundry and linen supply business.

As in every other field, the Capone forces simply took over the rackets already being operated by others in the cleaning and dyeing and in the laundry business. As far back as 1927, the laundry business had been organized by Simon J. Gorman, who got his start as a thug and slugger when business agent for the Cook County Horseshoers' Union.

Gorman ran the Laundry and Dye House Drivers and Chauffeurs Union, Local 712, of the International Brotherhood of Teamsters. Gorman thus negotiated for the workers. Gorman also owned the Allied Laundry Council, and in this capacity he negotiated for the owners.

The five outfits in Gorman's council were the Chicago Laundry Owners Association, the Chicago Wet and Dry Laundry Owners Association, the Chicago Linen Supply Association, the Chicago Hand Laundry Owners Association, and the Laundry Service Association of Chicago.

The names all sound pretty much alike but each embraced a different set of owners. Incidentally, the interests of each conflicted with the interests of the others.

The Chicago Hand Laundry Owners Association, for example, was composed of the owners of little shops who had virtually no capital invested. They ran drops where people could leave bundles of soiled laundry. The laundry was sent out to wet-wash laundries. When returned, the owners or their employees would iron it and return it to the customers when they called.

The Chicago Laundry Owners Association did finished work and usually had trucks to deliver it to the homes of customers. The members of this association had nothing but contempt for the little fellows who called their shops hand laundries. While the other associations all employed union labor, the Laundry Service Association of Chicago operated on an open-shop basis. The members employed drivers who had no union affiliation, or if they employed union drivers they had no working agreement with the union.

Simon Gorman had them all in the palm of his hand, union or antiunion, and earned a little profit wherever he turned. He called himself labor secretary of the Chicago Laundry Owners Association at a salary of $7,500 a year. In addition, he sought to collect $10,000 apiece from each of the member businesses in a scheme to get the Chicago City Council to pass a zoning ordinance which would restrict the building of laundries in any neighborhood except the industrial area.

The Chicago Linen Supply Association was composed of members who bought and owned linen, supplying it on a rental basis to barbershops, offices, restaurants, clubs, and the speakeasies then operating. This was the organization that Frank Nitti deemed important.

Simon Gorman was the liaison man between the linen-supply association's members and the saloons operated by the Capone Syndicate. Capone and Nitti began to see the possibilities in Gorman's operations. They felt that Gorman was a penny-ante dealer in the way he shook down the little hand laundries for 10 percent of their weekly wash bills. Gorman's biggest salary, from any of the outfits he controlled, was the $18,000 a year he was paid by the Chicago Wet and Dry Laundry Owners Association.

The take-over of the laundry rackets in Chicago was part of the Capone-Nitti grand plan but had to take a lesser priority than some of the most pressing problems such as the bartenders and the liquor distribution after the repeal of Prohibition. Through the period of World War II, Fred Evans and Murray Humphreys kept abreast of both the cleaning and dyeing rackets and the laundry and linen rackets, maintaining a modicum of control. They knew that Spike O'Donnell, of the old South Side bootleg gang, had a piece of the laundry action and they knew they could take it all whenever they wanted.

Frank Nitti had been dead seven years when Fred Evans' emergence as a laundry and cleaning entrepreneur became public knowledge. In 1950, Evans' pressure began to be felt.

Within a year he had muscled in on forty-seven of the biggest accounts held by the Roscoe Overall Service, Inc., according to George C. Bulk, the firm's president. Evans later told federal agents that Joey Glimco, boss of the taxicab drivers' union, AFL Teamsters Local 777, was his silent partner in this operation.

Glimco then owned a deodorizer manufactory. Every public toilet in the city and suburbs displayed a neat little decal indicating that its deodorizers were provided by Glimco's firm.

Evans' laundry business was important to the Syndicate in its operation of brothels. Every Syndicate-operated brothel in Chicago and the suburbs—all of those which called themselves "massage parlors" and "health clubs"—had to rent their towels from one of the concerns operated by Fred Evans.

The Evans pickup men on his trucks carefully counted the soiled towels picked up daily at each of the Syndicate brothels. The tally was kept on sheets. The brothel department of Syndicate operations thus knew the number of tricks turned by the whores and had a double-check on the figures turned in each morning by the house manager.

Evans was providing a towel and linen service to hotels, motels, bars, restaurants, nightclubs, hospitals, and brothels throughout the Chicago area. Glimco's own firm, a chemical company, supplied deodorizers, disinfectants, and detergents for the same places, as well as for all the gasoline service stations in the area.

One of Evans' places of business was the Industrial Garment Service, Inc., at 5409 West Lake Street. At the same address, he ran the Western Laundry Service.

Four other establishments were at 2621 Chicago Avenue. They were Linen-of-the-Week, Dust-Tex, the Infant Diaper Service, and the Crib Diaper Service. The Lake Street address was headquarters for Evans' commercial and industrial linen services, and the Chicago Avenue address for his home services.

Murray Humphreys by this time had become chief political fixer for the Capone Syndicate. His job was to grease palms in the right places so Syndicate enterprises could get lucrative contracts. Evans' industrial garment service got the contracts to supply aprons, overalls, and industrial rags to the city of Chicago, the Railroad Retirement Board, the United States Post Office in Oak Park, and the United States Coast Guard in the Chicago area, among other accounts.

Fred Evans figured in some way as yet undisclosed in the Bobby Greenlease kidnapping. The Kansas City boy was killed by his abductors and never returned home. But on October 4, 1953, the kidnappers collected $600,000 in ransom money. About 90 percent of this money was in bills of $20 denomination. The bills had been photographed before the ransom was paid. Not half of the money was ever recovered. Today there is a total of $303,720 in bills of either $10 or $20 denomination which has not come to light.

Part of the Bobby Greenlease ransom money turned up in Chicago on May 31, 1955. Some of the $20 bills made up a total of $686 paid for a cashier's check at the Sears Bank and Trust Company, 3401 West Arthington Street.

The cashier's check was requested by one of the bank's regular customers, F. Evans, and made payable to L. Patrick. Fred Evans and Lenny Patrick, one of the Syndicate's gambling bosses on the North Side of Chicago, were thus connected.

Lenny Patrick was the man said by Police Lieutenant William J. Drury to have participated in the assassination of James M. Ragen, czar of the racing news wire service, when the Capone Syndicate had to eliminate Ragen to take over his publishing empire.

Evans was a meticulous record keeper. For ten years before his death the agents of the Internal Revenue Service each year called him to their office and ordered him to bring in his books and records. Each year they checked his income tax returns down to the penny. They never conceded that Evans was honest but they said he was a master bookkeeper.

But nobody ever pushed him on the Greenlease ransom money. One explanation for this lapse may have been found in Murray Humphreys' magic with police, prosecutors, and politicians. Another explanation might have been that Evans himself had something going with the federal agents at the time.

That ransom money was the indirect cause of Fred Evans' death. When Dwight Green came to Chicago to send Al Capone to prison for income tax evasion, he found that the agents of the Internal Revenue Service had their own ways of handling gangsters rendered untouchable because of their political connections. Maybe the men at the top were told to lay off a certain gangster, but the agents at the bottom could harass the man just as honest policemen can harass crooks despite the payoffs in the chief's office.

When nothing was done to press Fred Evans for an explanation of the Greenlease ransom money, the agents of the Internal Revenue Service in Chicago began to leak information about Evans' bookkeeping practices. Gradually the word got around among newspapermen and police that Evans' annual income tax returns were so perfect that they listed the names of the gangsters to whom he paid money—and exactly how much—in connection with his business operations. As this rumor began to sweep through the Syndicate underworld not even Murray Humphreys could save Evans.

On August 1, 1959, Evans' office was broken into. This was only two months after the ransom money turned up. Seventy-one dollars in cash was taken. Detectives of the burglary detail said it was obvious from the way the desk and filing cabinets had been ransacked that the thieves were interested in records rather than money. Presumably the Syndicate wanted to ascertain if the rumors about Evans' bookkeeping were true, before a decision was made to eliminate a man who had time and again proved himself such an asset.

The rumors must have been true. Three weeks later, Evans was shot to death in what was clearly a contract kill.

Evans was killed just as he was moving into the launderette business in a big way. His first steps had been to gain control of a laundry machine company and of a mortgage bank. This was no trick for a financial manipulator of Evans' experience. With these two instruments, Evans would sell laundry equipment on credit. He advertised widely, urging people with a little money to invest to consider opening neighborhood shops equipped with a dozen or more automatic laundry machines and a few gas-heat dryers.

Anybody with half enough capital could buy the machines from Evans. He would lend them up to 50 percent of the cost of the machines, taking a chattel mortgage on them.

Evans made the proposition particularly attractive. He took prospective purchasers to see his industrial laundry plant and his home service laundry plant. He told the men who bought his automatic washers and dryers that until they got established he would throw them the overflow business both from his diaper and home linen services and from his industrial laundry services. Their machines would thus be kept busy all the time. The overflow business would tide them over until their launderettes began to pay a regular profit as they built up neighborhood goodwill.

Naturally, when the businessman was saddled with a heavy mortgage and had spent all his working capital in fixing up his launderette, Evans would suddenly withdraw the overflow accounts.

Then Evans simply foreclosed on the mortgage and took control of the launderette. The system worked with about 90 percent of the launderettes which Evans had equipped. The other 10 percent were able to raise enough extra capital to buy themselves out of the hole.

The governing body of the Syndicate sat in judgment on Fred Evans in a kangaroo court. The records snatched in that office burglary on August 1, 1959, were scrutinized by men who understood every accounting entry. Murray Humphreys, as Evans' sponsor, was asked if he wanted to advance any valid reason why the sentence of death on Fred Evans should not be carried out. Humphreys passed.

At high noon on Saturday, August 22, 1959, Evans was heading for his Cadillac in the parking lot next to his office at 5409 West Lake Street when the hired torpedoes caught up with him. This was one daylight killing for which there was the perfect eyewitness. Mrs. Alice Griesemer of 328 North St. Louis Avenue had seen the whole thing and was not reluctant to talk.

Mrs. Griesemer told police she had been watching a man—who turned out later to be a hired killer—seated on the steps of a building across the street. She had found him interesting because, with the August temperature in the high 90's, he was wearing a heavy jacket. Most places of business are closed on Saturday. The man sat there for nearly an hour during which Mrs. Griesemer watched, apparently doing nothing but waiting.

Then Fred Evans left his plant and started walking into the parking lot.

The man in the heavy jacket immediately rose and ran across the street to intercept Evans. Simultaneously, a second man emerged from the alley, holding a handkerchief across the lower part of his face, and he too ran to intercept Evans. Mrs. Griesemer said, "The two men grabbed Evans. They slammed him against the wall near his car. Both had pistols. One reached out and snatched an envelope from Evans' pocket. Both men shot Evans. As he fell, they walked away."

Evans was found lying half over an envelope in which was a $5,000 interest coupon from a United States Government bond. A note on his desk indicated that to the last few minutes of his life he had been figuring his profits. The note bore scribblings of various sums and the notation, "Total resources 11 million dollars."

Evans owned two luxury hotels in Los Angeles. One of his safe deposit boxes at the First National Bank of Chicago yielded $116,370 in currency. A box next to it yielded $339,165. A third box at the Uptown National Bank in Chicago yielded ten packets of currency totaling $36,300. The rest of his visible estate consisted of paid-up insurance policies, stocks and bonds and other securities, and more than $50,000 worth of diamonds mounted in three bracelets, two rings, and a brooch.

Evans' safe deposit box yielded the 1942 trust agreement covering his ownership of an apartment hotel at 5100 South Cornell Avenue, and a second trust agreement covering his 25 percent ownership in 1,628 shares issued on the apartment building at 1263 West Pratt Avenue.

Evans had learned from Al Capone, as had Joe Fusco and Murray Humphreys, not to be niggardly in paying police, prosecutors, and politicians. He always kept on his payroll a few bureaucrats who could help him in their various capacities.

One who presumably mourned Evans' passing, since it cost him $5,000 a year, was Clemens K. Shapiro, who was in charge of sales tax collections in the Chicago area for the state of Illinois.

Shapiro was earning $13,572 a year on the state payroll when Evans paid him an extra $5,000 each year, carrying his name on the payroll of Industrial Garment Services, Inc., as a salesman. Three months after Evans was shot to death on August 22, 1959, Shapiro was dropped from the company payroll. He remained on the state payroll.

Shapiro's career is not unusual for a man in Illinois state politics. He was always held over in his state job, regardless of which party happened to be in power. He had come to public attention for the first time in 1932 when indicted on charges of embezzlement, forgery, and conspiracy in the theft of $46,000 from the Division State Bank of which he was then vice-president. The bank closed its doors shortly after Shapiro was indicted by the May grand jury.

The charges against Shapiro were pending for three years. On May 3, 1935, the charges were dropped for want of prosecution.

In that same year of 1935, Shapiro was found guilty by a jury in the municipal court of Judge John J. Lupe on charges of misrepresenting $1,000 worth of bonds sold to a Chicago dentist. There was no sentence. Shapiro was merely ordered by the court to reimburse the dentist.

With these activities in his record, Shapiro was deemed the perfect man for a position of responsibility in the state revenue office. He soon became assistant to the director, exercising control over the machinery for the collection of state sales taxes from retail businesses.

Keeping track of these businessmen is as simple as noting their names and addresses on computer cards. If a single month passes when such a businessman does not report and turn in the taxes he has thus collected, an honest state revenue director can pick up a phone and find out why. Unless the revenuje director or his deputy is in business for himself.

In Illinois it was common for the businesses with the right connections to avoid turning in their sales tax collections.

Shapiro apparently proved his goodwill to the satisfaction of Fred Evans. Otherwise he would not have been on the laundry payroll.

17   Slumming at Duke Cooney's

Morris Llewellyn Humphreys (he adopted the middle name) may have been the highest-paid hit man in the Chicago underworld. The story is that he earned something more than $40,000 for killing Roger Touhy after the old northwest suburban beer runner got out of Stateville prison in Joliet.

Humphreys was said to have arranged or personally handled several such jobs before Touhy but certainly never before earned this kind of money for dropping anybody. Few men in the underworld, unless of the stature of Al Capone himself, ever have anything like a $50,000 price put on their heads.

More of that in a moment.

Humphreys died November 23, 1965, in his Marina Towers apartment at 300 North State Street. The medical examiner called it a heart attack, a coronary thrombosis. The examiner also found a small laceration just below his right ear. The assumption was that somebody armed with a hypodermic needle full of nothing but air could have caused the puncture and thus the blood clot to the heart.

Humphreys' body was found in his skyscraper apartment by his brother, who uses the name of Jack Wright. A few hours before his death Humphreys had been scuffling with agents of the FBI who arrested him on a warrant charging perjury. He was sixty-six.

Because of his name, Humphreys was sometimes called in underworld circles "the Hump." This in turn led to his being sometimes called "the Camel." He was one of Capone's favorite sluggers, principally because he had a gift of gab and would rather talk than shoot if given a choice.

The Syndicate used him in such delicate maneuvers as the kidnapping of Robert L. (Old Doc) Ritchie, who ruled the milk wagon drivers' union.

Humphreys' death was as mysterious as his origins.

Throughout his life he had been secretive about his beginnings. He said his father was William Bryan Humphreys, a native of Illinois, and his mother—depending on which records are consulted—was either

Betty Wrigley or Betty Lox. She was said to have come from North Wales, but that may have been one of the Hump's trifling deceits. His father's origin is mysterious, despite records, which can be altered.

Humphreys' known history begins when he attended the Haver elementary school at 1472 South Wabash Avenue in 1904–05–06. Those records indicate he was born April 20, 1899, one of ten children. Unless other members of his family some day talk, his history will always remain in the shadows.

The police records show that Humphreys was arrested February 13, 1915, charged with larceny. He was sent to the House of Correction for sixty days. The sentence indicates a previous history of lawlessness, as judges in 1915 did not—on a first offense—put sixteen-year-old boys in with hardened criminals.

By the following year Humphreys had learned to fix a case by getting a felony charge reduced to a misdemeanor charge—and then pleading guilty to the lesser offense. He was arrested for burglary on March 29, 1916, when living at 707 East Thirty-seventh Street and using the name of John Hall. He asked to see the city prosecutor and when they were alone Humphreys told him, "You try to get me indicted for burglary and I will weep in front of the grand jury. They probably won't indict because I am only sixteen. But even if you get me to court the do-gooders will say that because of my extreme youth I ought not be sent to prison.

"However, if you reduce this charge to one of petty larceny I will plead guilty. I will get a light sentence. You will get a conviction that looks good on your record. Everybody will be happy. What's more, you will receive a suitable gift before the case goes to court."

The prosecutor nodded his head. He recognized the wisdom in the youngster before him, a tall and skinny kid with a mop of curly black hair and a genuinely likable expression on his puppylike face. The prosecutor, having accepted the proposition, was astonished next day at the expensive quality of the gift he received. The diamond-studded wristwatch was wrapped and on his desk, left by an anonymous donor.

Even as a boy, Humphreys was generous with police, prosecutors, and jurists.

Humphreys talked well at sixteen. He not only knew the right words to use in the right places, but he knew which were the right ideas and how they could be presented in the most persuasive way. The upperworld people with whom he came in contact frequently thought of him as college-educated, and Humphreys did nothing to disabuse them.

In the burglary case when he was sixteen, he might have been sent to prison for a considerable term as a second or third offender. Instead, the prosecutor and judge let him go with six months in the House of Correction.

From that time on, Humphreys' problems were solved. He had learned to talk his way out of most charges, usually by a compromise accompanied by a substantial gift. He was never niggardly with politicians and they one and all appreciated his generosity. Although frequently arrested for carrying concealed weapons, for such disorderly conduct as shooting in the direction of a man to whom he was talking as a way of emphasizing a point, or for robbery at gunpoint, Humphreys seldom went to court.

The first place to put in the fix, he always said, was with the cop who makes the collar. Humphreys would offer $1,000 in cash to avoid an arrest which might cost a $10 fine. If the policeman could not be fixed, said Humphrey, the next man in line was the prosecutor. A smart prosecutor can always arrange a typographical error in the writing of a warrant or an indictment, so that a friendly judge could later declare the document invalid.

If neither the arresting officer nor the prosecutor was amenable to a bribe, Humphreys sought out the judge. He instructed his lawyers to seek out the members of the jury. Humphreys felt that judges and jurymen, like anyone else with whom he had contact, could be bought. Only when all attempts at bribery failed would Humphreys turn to the intimidation or elimination of witnesses.

Humphreys' reputation for paying generously made him one of the most trusted men in the underworld as far as jurists were concerned. Through the years of the Capone organization's greatest expansion, Jake Guzik was the payoff man for police and ward politicians but Murray Humphreys usually dealt with mayors, judges, governors, and members of Congress.

Humphreys was not nearly as open in his conversation with reporters as had been Al Capone. But when he talked, he could be equally philosophical. One of his statements is worth quoting: "The difference between guilt and innocence in any court is who gets to the judge first with the most."

Or: "Go out of your way to make a friend instead of an enemy."

Still another of Humphreys' aphorisms: "If you ever have to cock a gun in a man's face, kill him. If you walk away without killing him after doing that, he'll kill you the next day."

Or: "No good citizen will ever testify to anything if he is absolutely convinced that to do so will result in his quick and certain death."

Humphreys worked with Red Barker in the takeover of labor unions and their treasuries. Barker, the bookkeeper, would research the state of financial affairs in unions. Humphreys kept a list, based on Barker's studies. Humphreys' list of unions ripe for plucking showed amounts in their treasuries adding up to more than $10,000,000.

One of the top prizes was the union of milk wagon drivers, with a treasury of $1,300,000 and an income of $250,000 a year in dues. This was owned by Steve Sumner and Old Doc Ritchie.

Then there was the union of painters, ruled by Art Wallace; the circular distributors ruled by Johnny Rooney; the electricians, ruled by Umbrella Mike Boyle; the film projection machine operators, ruled by Tom Reynolds and Tommy Maloy; one of the teamster locals, ruled by Mike Norris; the Teamsters International, ruled by Patrick (Paddy) Burrell and Dave Beck.

The Teamsters International, later taken over by Jimmy Hoffa, was said to have $8,000,000 in strike funds in Indianapolis and Cincinnati.

Humphreys and Barker told Capone they could take over the teamster locals one by one in Chicago, putting the treasuries into Capone bank accounts, and then could take over the international with its strike funds. They had not then dreamed of pension plan funds and foundations.

Humphreys had been a loner in the underworld until, as earlier noted, he joined up with Fred Evans in the early twenties. Evans did not want to carry a gun but Humphreys had no such scruples. Evans had the big garage to which Humphreys could bring trucks of liquor he hijacked. This activity was what brought him to the attention of Al Capone. He hit one of Capone's trucks, sending the driver fleeing at gunpoint and driving off with the load.

Although Humphreys was unaware of the fact, the driver had seen him about and recognized him. He told Capone.

Al Capone could have had Humphreys killed. But before doing so, he ordered him brought in for questioning. Capone was then building his organization and Johnny Torrio was still in Chicago. When Capone talked to Humphreys he recognized talent in the man. As far as Capone was concerned, simple gunmen—cowboys, as he called them—were a dime a dozen. But a thief with Humphreys' gift of gab was rare.

Capone put Humphreys out on the street as a beer-truck driver, the lowest echelon in the hierarchy, telling him, "First, you got to learn the business." For a thief still in his young twenties, being hooked up with the Torrio-Capone combine was an honor not to be taken lightly.

Humphreys felt gratitude to Capone for not killing him after the hijacking. He set out to prove that Capone's confidence in him was not misplaced. Capone kept the youngster in mind—while they were both of an age, Capone always felt and acted as a father to his young troops—and gave Humphreys greater and greater responsibilities. Capone said, "Anybody can use a gun. The Hump uses his head. He can shoot if he has to, but he likes to negotiate with cash when he can. I like that in a man."

Humphreys had run his own cleaning and dyeing shop with Fred Evans and he was a natural when Capone went after the unions and employers' associations in this field. From then on his rise was rapid. Capone liked Humphreys' quick grasp of opportunities. Capone said of him, "Nobody hustles like the Hump." Humphreys kept his eye on the main chance and turned a dollar where opportunity offered.

On the night of January 10, 1929, he was drinking with the twenty-three-year-old Miss Marjorie Adair in the Royale Frolics cabaret at 426 South Wabash Avenue. This is now the site of one of Jimmy Wong's Cantonese restaurants but at the time it was headquarters for Dennis (Duke) Cooney, who ran First Ward vice for the Capone organization. Humphreys was not intending to work that night. He was simply out with a girl for a good time.

The Club Royale, as Cooney called it in his advertisements, had a chorus line which put on a floor show every couple of hours. Between shows the orchestra played for general dancing. Businessmen in town for conventions were steered to the place by bellhops in their hotels and cab drivers on the streets.

The chorus girls would sit at the tables with the tourists, ordering drinks and available for dancing. When the girls and the waiters together had decided that an unattached male had both a bankroll and a belly full of bootleg booze, the girl would get him out on the dance floor.

The girl would dance her partner around behind a pillar and signal a waiter with a blackjack. The waiter would watch the room's lighting, so arranged with spotlights as to flash different colors and brief moments of darkness. When the lights were right, the waiter would tap the dancing gentleman lightly and help the girl hold the body upright.

The waiter and the girl, in full view of other dancers, then would help the gentleman out the back door as though for a breath of fresh air. The man would be quickly stripped of wallet, wristwatch, cufflinks, and anything else of value on his person.

The waiter would blink a flashlight down the alley to a waiting police squad car and the unconscious victim would be delivered into police hands.

The man would wind up spending the night in the lockup ("You were found unconscious in an alley!") and the waiter and dancing girl would return to their work inside. The arresting police officers would be around later that night for their cut of the take.

Foolish people of the upperworld liked to take their guests slumming to Duke Cooney's joint, where they could drink gin and see gangsters.

On this particular occasion, Murray Humphreys and Miss Adair had just returned to their table after a round of dancing to the moaning saxophone when the Hump saw a party being seated at the next table. There were three couples in the party.

Humphreys' knowing eye appraised the jewels with which the ladies were festooned. Humphreys handed Miss Adair a $20 bill and told her, "Get lost. I'll phone you tomorrow." Miss Adair got her wrap and left.

Humphreys then went to Cooney's office and phoned Rocco Rotunna of 815 South Rockwell Street, boss of the Auto Wreckers Union. Rotunna, then thirty years of age, was free on $150,000 bond awaiting trial for a shooting at the Parody Club on North Clark Street. Rotunna was simply "playing gin rummy with a friend" when called. He said he and the friend would be right over. He was happy to pick up a little loot.

Humphreys did no more drinking that night.

He waited until the three couples of upperworld people were ready to leave, then followed them to the door and pointed them out to Rotunna and his friend at the curb.

The three couples later turned out to be Dr. and Mrs. Frank Pierce of 1235 Astor Street, a Gold Coast address; and their guests, Mr. and Mrs. Luther S. Hammond of 237 East Delaware Place, another Gold Coast address; and Mr. and Mrs. C. H. Murphy of Detroit.

For their slumming in Duke Cooney's saloon, Mrs. Pierce had chosen to wear a perfectly matched necklace of natural pearls valued at $40,000, three diamond bracelets, three diamond rings, and other less impressive jewels. She kept the lot warm on this night in early January under a full-length natural mink coat.

Mrs. Hammond wore several rings and a mink coat. Mrs. Murphy's string of emeralds, the envy of Detroit society, reflected the glow of the cabaret lights like so many delicate prisms.

The Pierce party emerged from Cooney's nightclub, walked across the street to catch a cab headed north, and told the driver—Roy Dellefield—to turn east at Van Buren Street. At Michigan Avenue their cab was halted by a traffic light.

The streets, icy at that time of year, were virtually deserted in the early hours of the morning. Rotunna's car drew abreast of the halted cab and Rotunna and his friend leveled pistols at Dellefield's head.

Rotunna and his friend left their car with Humphreys and slipped into the cab's front seat with Dellefield. He did not try to be a hero.

He moved over when ordered to do so and Rotunna's friend drove.

They went east to Lake Shore Drive and then south along Lake Michigan's shore.

Humphreys waited until they were a block ahead before following in Rotunna's car. He sought to avoid being seen by the Pierce party.

The Pierce party, having put away a quantity of Duke Cooney's liquor, viewed the adventure in a somewhat humorous light. The situation looked less humorous when they stopped at Thirty-first Street and the ladies lost their jewels and their furs. They were all permitted to shiver in Dellefield's cab while Rotunna and his friend carried the loot back to the car behind, driven by Murray Humphreys.

Detective Sergeant Pete Bernacchi, upon receiving the complaint, went around to every major fence in town. He explained the Gold Coast origin of the stolen furs and jewelry, saying the connections of the victims made their property too hot to handle. Bernacchi demanded to be tipped off when the thieves sought to sell the plunder.

A few days later Humphreys and Rotunna were on the South Side, shopping for buyers. They were asking bids on the stuff in the store of a widely known receiver of stolen goods when Bernacchi walked in. They were arrested and the stolen property returned to Dr. Pierce.

Pierce and his friends were invited to a police showup. Rotunna and his friend, with Humphreys and Miss Adair, stood under glaring lights. The entire Pierce party was positive in its identification. They recognized in Humphreys and Miss Adair the handsome couple who had been seated at the next table.

The holdup took place January 10. The positive identifications were made a few days later. The accused were taken to court for arraignment January 29. In less than two weeks the witnesses, under what threats was never disclosed, decided not to testify. The case was dropped for want of prosecution. Murray Humphreys later said, "No hustler in his right mind could have passed up that loot."

A year went by before Humphreys again came to police attention. Early in 1930, when he was sharing a room with Ralph Pierce, Police Detectives Louis Capparelli and Michael Casey knocked on the door in the Paxton Hotel at 1430 North La Salle Street. At that time the hotel was being managed by Paul (the Waiter) Ricca. Humphreys was not home but the door was opened by Pierce, a young Capone gunman who later was indicted in the film industry shakedown.

The two detectives pushed Pierce back into the room and entered. They found in the room two loaded .38 caliber revolvers. Just then the door opened to admit Humphreys. He was carrying a loaded .38 revolver in a shoulder holster. They disarmed him. He said, "You have no business being in this room without a search warrant. I live here and have a perfect right to carry a gun when in my own house. You cannot arrest me for vagrancy, because I am business agent for the Bill Posters Union."

The union at that time was owned for Capone by Machine Gun Jack McGurn.

Having made the point of his total innocence of any wrongdoing, Humphreys withdrew a wallet from his pocket, counted out ten $100 bills and asked, "Can't we settle this right here among friends?"

Capparelli and Casey took the two men to the station, but they might as well have freed them on the spot. Humphreys spent the $1,000 anyway. Both Humphreys and Pierce were admonished by a stern judge—and then found not guilty.

Next time the police got a search warrant. Municipal Judge John H. Lyle, who had no time for racketeers, on November 5, 1930, issued vagrancy warrants for the arrest of Humphreys and Pierce. The police knew the pair could be found in Frank Nitti's speakeasy at 901 South Halsted Street. They went there and made the pinch.

In addition to Humphreys and Pierce, the police picked up their companions: Paul Ricca, for whom Al Capone had stood up as best man at a January 3, 1927, wedding; Roland V. Libonati, who had just been elected to the Illinois legislature and was later to be elected to Congress; Anthony Prignano, former alderman who then was on the city payroll as inspector of paving in the Public Works Department; and Saul Tannenbaum, of 1257 Roosevelt Road, a city prosecutor in the office of the Corporation Council of the city of Chicago.

All were taken to the lockup and put in custody of Chief of Detectives John Norton.

Three minutes later Norton was visited by State Senator James B. Leonardo, Alderman William V. Pacelli of the Twentieth Ward, and City Sealer Daniel A. Serritella, who was soon to be in the Illinois legislature.

Norton recognized the limitations of a chief of detectives against that kind of pressure. He freed all but Humphreys and Pierce, who had been arrested on a warrant issued by a judge.

Humphreys' police record has already been noted. Ralph Pierce, although only twenty-five years old, had made a good start in the underworld. He was a suspect in the robbery of the private bank of Joseph Fekete & Son at 2321 West Chicago Avenue, and he was a known election slugger for Judge Morris B. Eller, who ran the Twentieth Ward.

Thirty minutes after the lockup doors clanged shut behind them, a court bailiff appeared with an order for Humphreys and Pierce to be produced forthwith in the municipal court of Judge Francis Borrelli. This was one of the judges who had walked respectfully, head bowed and hat in hand, as an honorary pallbearer on May 15, 1920, when Big Jim Colosimo of the First Ward was laid to rest. Borrelli had also paid his respects to the deceased Dion O'Banion.

Borrelli scarcely listened to the five minutes of discussion before his bench by lawyers after Humphreys and Pierce were brought in. Then he all but apologized to the two gunmen as he turned them loose.

On April 15, 1932, three weeks before Al Capone was taken away to prison, Murray Humphreys was caught working a protection racket on the securities brokers of La Salle Street.

These stock and bond salesmen, accustomed to advising others on the wisdom of investments, had no difficulty understanding the wisdom of investing $100 a week apiece in what Humphreys called the Investors Protective Association. Humphreys had assured them that membership in his association would guarantee that no stench bombs or dynamite would be thrown into their brokerage offices.

Humphreys in this enterprise was associated with Teddy Newberry, who was later to die after putting a price on Frank Nitti's head.

Even in that Depression spring of 1932, when stock and bond salesmen were starving in the streets, Humphreys had found a hundred or more brokerage offices happy to sign up with his outfit. After giving the Capone organization its usual 10 percent off the top, he was still cutting up $10,000 a week.

When A Century of Progress was about to open in the late spring of 1933, the police were given the green light to harass underlings in the Capone hierarchy. Humphreys and the others briefly took a pushing around.

Despite what has been said in these pages about crooked cops, it goes without saying that most policemen are decent family men and reasonably honest. They know which of their fellows are regularly collecting from the underworld. They do not snitch on their fellows, but they refuse the gangsters' largesse when it is offered to them.

To get on the department payroll in the first place the Chicago cop had to have political sponsorship in addition to passing civil service examinations and physical qualifying tests. A ward committeeman's signature had to appear on his application for the job. When he had completed his probation and was to be promoted to patrolman, a ward committeeman's approval was again needed.

The politician who thus sponsored—and took responsibility for—the policeman was known in Chicago as the policeman's "Chinaman."

When a policeman got into any kind of difficulty the first question asked by his superiors or by City Hall was: "Who's his Chinaman?"

The same system worked in the case of some prosecuting attorneys and judges, but that system is not under discussion just now. The point is that policemen were told they could harass hoodlums without getting into trouble downtown.

Even the crooked cop who fawns on his gangland paymaster secretly resents the latter's arrogance. Humphreys was high on this list. Many policemen at some time or other had felt envy at the roll of pocket money, always $20,000 or $30,000, which Humphreys carried.

They envied Humphreys his happy-go-lucky manner, his lean good looks, his college-boy attitudes, his tailor, and the definite flair with which he wore his clothes.

So the cops began to make life miserable for Murray Humphreys.

The Hump recognized it as one of the hazards of his profession. He bore with it until the fix could be put in the right quarters and the "harass hoodlums" order was lifted. In the interim he had to bear the harassment with equanimity. He would be stopped wherever he walked and compelled to stand facing buildings, with his weight resting on arms extended full length, like any common hoodlum. He kept his cool. And later, when it was over he saw to it that every cop who had treated him thus spent the rest of his life walking a beat out in the sticks.

Humphreys, whatever else is said, always had style.

When Tommy Maloy was killed in the Syndicate's takeover of the motion picture operators' union, the federal investigators learned that a theater chain had bought stock and carried it in Maloy's name. This was in 1928 and 1929, when the stock market was booming. The little union czar pocketed $25,000 in earnings from this stock.

The stock deals are a favorite ploy in the underworld.

Humphreys died in November, 1965, and nearly a year later, on September 15, 1966, he was the subject of a hearing in the United States Tax Court in Chicago. Humphreys was shown to have earned a quick $42,000 profit in a 1961 stock deal with Jake (the Barber) Factor.

Humphreys had reported this profit on his income tax return as a capital gains transaction, on which he would have had to pay only 25 percent tax. The Internal Revenue Service lawyers had gone into tax court to argue that the money was a payoff for services rendered and that therefore Humphreys' estate should be compelled to pay the straight income tax rate on the profit.

The records showed that on July 25, 1960, Factor sold Humphreys

400 shares of First National Life Insurance Company stock at $20 a share. Eight months later Factor bought this stock back for $125 a share. This was a 6-for-1 return. The transaction took place within eighteen months after Roger Touhy was shot to death in gangland fashion.

Touhy had been imprisoned twenty-six years on conviction of having kidnapped Factor, an international swindler and ex-convict. Touhy died proclaiming that Factor never had been kidnapped but faked the whole thing.

Federal Judge John P. Barnes received from Touhy during the latter's imprisonment a petition for habeas corpus. Barnes studied the entire record of the Factor "kidnapping" case. In a 60,000-word opinion, Barnes concluded: "The court finds that John Factor was not kidnapped for ransom or otherwise on the night of June 30th and July 1st, 1933. . . . Roger Touhy did not kidnap John Factor and, in fact, had no part in the alleged kidnapping of John Factor. . . ."

The same Judge Barnes in the same opinion wrote of Jake Factor:"He has learned all that a boy and man can learn as a bootblack, washroom attendant, newsboy, barber, high-pressure stock salesman, Florida land salesman, bucket-shop operator and confidence man—except to be honest. So far as the so-called business morals are concerned, he is completely amoral."

Factor, at the time of Roger Touhy's death, was engaged in a public relations campaign designed to improve his image before the world. Touhy was a threat to that image. So long as Touhy was alive he would holler from the rooftops that Factor was a fraud and a phony.

Somebody wanted Roger Touhy dead. He was killed by shotgun blasts on December 16, 1959.

18 Following the classic union formula

After his recovery from wounds suffered at the hands of the mayor's crew of assassins, Frank Nitti sought to consolidate gains made in the underworld empire by Al Capone. And he sought to extend the empire to prove himself Capone's worthy successor. For a couple of years of world's fair activity, expansion had almost come to a halt.

Capone still had a voice in affairs of the Chicago Syndicate. From Atlanta penitentiary he had been moved to Alcatraz, but his visitors brought out word regularly. Capone wanted Nitti to concentrate on the entertainment industry, which appeared so ripe for the plucking.

Nitti sat in daily conference with his council: Paul Ricca, Tony Accardo, Joe Fusco, and Joe Burger, the lawyer. All were avid movie fans. All saw every Hollywood film made after Capone's imprisonment launched the gangster cycle which included *Little Caesar, Scarface, Public Enemy,* and a dozen other celluloid epics more or less reflecting one facet of Chicago.

If the motion picture machine operators in theaters ever glanced up from their work to look at the films they showed they must have yawned in boredom. Members of the operators' union then as now were participants in a gang drama which has been unreeling since before World War I. Right now the union produces more thrills, for those who keep their eye on it, than *The Perils of Pauline.*

The principal figure in that drama in the early thirties was Thomas E. Maloy, a rough-as-a-cob Irishman born in Chicago in the 1893 year of the World's Columbian Exposition. Maloy had come into ownership of AFL Local 110 of the Motion Picture Operators Union. He was spectacularly laid to rest at the age of forty-two, early in 1935, after representatives of a business rival caught up with him on Lake Shore Drive at Twenty-fourth Street. One of the men had a sawed-off shotgun; the other a .45 automatic pistol.

The Capone Syndicate thus took over ownership of the union.

As with virtually every other business enterprise brought into the syndicate fold, the union had been a moneymaker for its owner long before it ever came to the attention of Frank Nitti and the rest of the council.

For the last fifteen years of Tommy Maloy's life he had run the union—and, to a great extent, the entire motion picture industry in Chicago—with brass knuckles and blackjacks, blazing pistols and blasting dynamite. Maloy had learned the union business as an understudy to Maurice (Mossy) Enright, whose 1920 death at the hands of Dago Mike Carrozzo and Big Tim Murphy has been earlier recounted.

The union's first owner was Elmer D. (Jack) Miller, who made his rounds on a bicycle. Under his guidance—a combination of persuasion and threat—Miller had brought most of the city's operators into a union which paid him a good wage.

Jack Miller was able to pocket enough from the dues paid by union members to open a theater of his own. He was delighted to leave the union business to become a theater owner. Just at this time, Tommy Maloy's talents were brought by Maloy's friends and publicity directors to the attention of the union members. As one of Maloy's friends told it at the time, "Some hoodlums were trying to muscle in on the union. Two of them were carrying guns and they climbed the steel ladder to Maloy's booth. He kicked them in the teeth, disarmed them, and chased them out of the theater."

The story of this heroism was sufficient, inasmuch as Jack Miller had already resigned his union job, to assure the post being offered Tommy Maloy. Actually the facts were somewhat different. At the time the incident occurred, Maloy was running a gambling layout over the theater's stage and he thought the two armed thugs were holdup men. He really did disarm and chase them. Then he turned the incident to account in his race for election as union business agent.

One man ran against Maloy in this election. Even his first name is lost to posterity and the records list him only as A. Williams. Maloy and a couple of friends threw him bodily into the street and Maloy's sole rival for the post was out of the race. In five minutes, Tommy Maloy was installed as the elected business agent of Local 110.

Maloy had learned from Mossy Enright to work with other union owners. He had been working with Michael (Umbrella Mike) Boyle of the electricians' union and seven others when indicted for conspiracy by a county grand jury in 1921. They were all charged with extorting money from the builders of the Stratford Theater to permit nonunion workers to install the seats. Tommy Maloy and Umbrella Mike Boyle and the others charged the contractors a flat rate of $2 a seat to permit the installation.

When the grand jury was gathering the evidence which led to these indictments, Umbrella Mike Boyle refused to testify and was cited for contempt. A judge promptly sentenced Boyle to jail.

Umbrella Mike Boyle for years had been paying off the politicians. Now he called a promissory note.

Governor Len Small of Illinois granted Boyle a pardon before the jailer could lock the cell door behind him.

The Republican party machinery of the state was then in the hands of Len Small as governor, Robert E. Crowe as state's attorney of Cook County, and William Hale Thompson as mayor of Chicago. They ran it the same way Tony Cermak and his successors later ran the Democratic party machinery. When Crowe would convict a wrongdoer the man could buy a pardon from Small. Then Small and Crowe would split the take and Crowe would go into court for more convictions. The voters returned this team to office year after year.

Small sold 8,000 pardons in the eight years of his incumbency as governor, between January 10, 1921, and January 13, 1929. Within two years after he entered the executive mansion for the first time, Small was brought to trial in Waukegan, charged with stealing hundreds of thousands of dollars during his years as state treasurer. He spread some of the money around and was acquitted.

Tommy Maloy followed the classic formula of trade union "ownership." He collected monthly dues from the members under the threat of depriving them of their jobs. Then he collected weekly payoffs from the owners of motion picture theaters under the threat of depriving them of union operators to show their films. Nobody in the trade union business has ever improved on the formula.

Al Capone was often quoted for his famous bit of philosophy, "Nobody argues with a gun." Tommy Maloy once said at a union meeting, "No politician ever turned his back on a bundle of currency."

Maloy's popularity among politicians was unquestioned.

The manufacturers of motion picture projection equipment were able to advertise in 1920 that their machines were so nearly automatic that "Any intelligent boy can learn to run one in half an hour." Maloy did not permit intelligent boys to join the union. He realized that only by keeping a small and selected membership roll could he boost wages for union members as high as $175 a week.

During the fifteen years from 1920 to 1935, when the motion picture entertainment industry was in its greatest era of expansion and new theaters were being opened almost every month in Chicago, Maloy's union admitted not a single new member.

If more operators were needed—and the need was constant at the time—Maloy issued temporary working permits to nonunion men. In time, more than half the operators in the city were "permit men." Every permit man drew the same weekly wage as the regular union members. Some of the permit men never missed a day's work in fifteen years.

There was one major difference between union men and permit men. The union men paid dues of $40 a quarter, little more than $3 a week. The permit men paid Maloy 10 percent of their weekly salaries which rose to $125, or as much as $12.50 a week.

The union rules said that at least two professional operators had to be in every theater projection booth on each shift. The union rules—which, of course, had been drawn up by Tommy Maloy—granted Maloy as business agent the power to waive the two-operator rule in the event of emergency.

One of the proprietors of the Balaban & Katz chain of motion picture theaters testified under oath that he paid Tommy Maloy $150 a week for years to keep the two-operator rule in a state of permanent waiver. The B & K houses only had to employ one projectionist per shift in each theater.

The B & K chain then set the pace in Chicago. Maloy assessed every other motion picture theater owner in the area at the same rates. None of this income ever appeared on the union books nor on Tommy Maloy's income tax returns.

Maloy had other sources of income.

In 1923 he maintained offices at Harrison Street and Wabash Avenue. His offices adjoined those of two other labor skates, Con Shea of the teamsters and Steve Kelliher of the theater janitors' union. Back of the union offices, where the members of all three unions were made welcome all day long, was a gambling parlor which Kelliher-Maloy-Shea ran as a three-way partnership. One way or another Maloy got back about half the money his union members earned.

Maloy and Kelliher had a falling out over the split of the take from the perpetual crap game and poker layout in the back of the union hall. Maloy was short, standing about five feet six, and smart, in that he never carried a pistol. He learned early in life that somebody else could always be hired to do the dirty work.

Maloy knew a labor slugger named Dapper Dan McCarthy, just then emerging as one of the top blazers in Dion O'Banion's North Side bootleg gang.

So when Maloy and Kelliher had their falling out, Maloy swallowed his anger, pretended to forgive and forget, but a few days later he invited Kelliher to join him and McCarthy for a drink in Al Tierney's resort.

Tierney ran the speakeasy at Calumet Avenue and Thirty-fifth Street, next door to the little movie house where Tommy Maloy got his start as a motion picture projection machine operator.

As soon as the three were seated at Tierney's bar an argument began. After only a few words, McCarthy drew and shot Kelliher between the eyes. Witnesses assured the police that Kelliher was armed. So when McCarthy pleaded self-defense the police said, "Forget it." Dapper Dan McCarthy had pulled the trigger but everybody in the trade recognized the work as Tommy Maloy's.

McCarthy profited by taking over Kelliher's union.

Big Tim Murphy, mentioned earlier, had for some time kept an eye on Maloy's setup. Murphy lived a full life as gambler, labor leader, state legislator, secretary to a Congressman in Washington, mail robber, prison inmate, and briefly husband to blond Florence Diggs. Murphy had already made his survey of Tommy Maloy's union and mapped the strategy by which he proposed to move in and take it over. When Kelliher died so suddenly, Murphy had second thoughts about the business and turned to other fields.

Like any other labor statesman, Tommy Maloy knew that his members were interested only in pork chops. His tenure as their leader would last only so long as he could stay out in front.

So each year he negotiated a new contract with representatives of the city's motion picture theater owners. In 1922 he got wages for operators raised from $66.65 to $80 a week for straight time and, with only one operator in the projection booth, he got time and a half for the members' overtime.

That year of 1922 was a depression year after World War I. The next year, Maloy got a $3-a-week increase for his members. In 1924 the rate went to $112 for journeymen and $55 for apprentices. The union members had to pay special assessments whenever Tommy Maloy wanted to buy a new car or take a Caribbean cruise with his family or current lady friend.

The constant wage increases kept the union members happy but put Tommy Maloy between two fires. His exactions made him more and more a problem to the theater owners. His fat pickings made him more and more the target of thugs such as Big Tim Murphy who wanted to take over. In 1927, Tommy Maloy drew fire from both sides.

Pete and Frank Gusenberg, a pair of thugs who were to die two years later in the St. Valentine's Day massacre of the old Bugs Moran gang, had a younger brother they wanted to place in a well-paying job. Tommy Maloy's spot seemed made to order for young Henry

Gusenberg. So his older brothers ran him for union business agent against Maloy.

The campaigning was spirited. No union meeting could be held without squads of police with drawn pistols standing on every corner. Maloy arranged a compromise before the election. Money changed hands and Henry Gusenberg was put on the payroll of a Loop theater as an operator at $175 a week.

This was for union wages plus overtime, even though Henry Gusenberg never had to appear at work. His name appeared on the payroll sheets. He was just one more "ghost" payroller.

Four operators had looked to Gusenberg's candidacy as a relief from Maloy's dictatorship. They had declared themselves. Ten days after the election their car was curbed in Lincoln Park.

The four realized what was happening and jumped from their car while it was still running. They heard the rattle of pistol fire behind them and one of the four, Arthur Devent, was dropped by a shot. Devent recovered but nobody in the union again questioned Tommy Maloy's rule for years.

Six months after Gusenberg withdrew as a candidate for business agent, the theater owners made an unsuccessful attempt to throw off Maloy's domination. On August 29, 1927, the owners locked out their union operators and shut down their theaters. Throughout the city only seventy-five small neighborhood movie houses showed films. The owners were led in their revolt by that same Jack Miller who had been Maloy's predecessor as union business agent. Miller, in less than a decade, had become owner of the employers' union, the Chicago Exhibitors Association.

Maloy's union operators were frightened when their paychecks were abruptly cut off. Maloy soothed them. He said, "Those owners are too greedy for their box office receipts to stick together. The greediest of them will open first and the rest will fall in line. Then we'll make them pay double time for every hour's work you guys have lost."

Maloy certainly understood the owners. A week after the lockout began came the Labor Day weekend. Youngsters soon to start the school year would be forming lines in front of every movie house, their money clutched in their hot hands waiting to be spent. The owners simply could not envision themselves turning away so much cash. The lockout was settled on September 4 so the theaters could reopen in time for the Labor Day holidays.

As in any such strike, the press and all the publicity was with the owners. Every movie house advertises every day in every newspaper. The operators' union never bought a line of advertising except in some racketeering clout sheet. So the theater owners were able to announce through the press that they had lost $1,350,000 in box office admissions during the few days of the lockout. They almost swooned two weeks later when Maloy compelled them to pay the union men for the time they did not work.

When the theaters reopened there was no change in the union contract.

In all his wage contracts, Maloy saw to it that working conditions and fringe benefits in some theaters were more desirable than in others. This was a conscious policy on Maloy's part. The better assignments were kept for the permit men who kicked back 10 percent of their wages to Maloy personally. No union man was ever permitted to find a job at a theater in his own neighborhood. The union made the work assignments. Maloy dealt with the owners and he personally assigned the men to work in each theater.

Maloy's lieutenant in the union's operation was Dr. Emmett C. Quinn, a dentist. Quinn carried a union card, the title of steward, and a pistol. Although he had never run a motion picture projection machine in his life, he was on the payroll of the Chicago Theater—largest in the Loop—as a "ghost" at $130 a week. Maloy's most trusted gunman, Ralph O'Hara, was similarly on a ghost payroll.

Maloy, as stated earlier, had a great many sources of income.

One of these sources came to light in 1929 when a lawsuit was filed by Erwin Wagner, owner of an electric sign company, naming as defendants Tommy Maloy and Ralph O'Hara; Thomas J. Flannery, who owned a competing electric sign company; and Michael J. Kennedy, city commissioner of gas and electricity.

Wagner's brief charged the defendants with conspiring to ruin his business. He said they were trying to transfer the electric sign business of every theater in the city to Flannery's company. Wagner said his own customers among theater owners were being threatened if they continued to use Wagner signs.

The brief said Ralph O'Hara called on owners using Wagner signs and told them to begin using Flannery service. If they did not, said the brief, O'Hara assured them that they would be compelled by union rule to put two operators in each projection booth on each shift. Further, O'Hara told them, they would find "electrical inspectors from Kennedy's office swarming over the premises as thick as cockroaches."

Naturally, Wagner's lawsuit never got a hearing.

Maloy was keeping up his payments at the City Hall and County Building.

On at least one occasion Maloy was actually defeated. That was in 1930 when he had a brush with George W. Krueger, who owned a motion picture theater in the west suburban community of Hinsdale.

Maloy demanded that Krueger put two operators per shift on the payroll of his little movie house, each at a salary of $108 a week. Krueger said the theater could not support a payroll of this magnitude. Maloy insisted. Krueger would not put the extra men on the payroll. Then the supply of films was cut off from Krueger's theater.

Krueger went to the Paramount Film Exchange at 1327 Wabash Avenue to protest. He should have known that the film distributors, like the exhibitors, have to get along with the unions. Krueger raised his voice in the film exchange and two sluggers beat him up, knocked out four of his teeth, and shot him in the leg.

This might have stopped anybody else. Not Krueger. Since he was a former operator, he threw Maloy's union men out of his theater and ran the projection machines himself. One night while four hundred patrons were seated in the theater the place was bombed. Krueger bought newspaper advertising space and aroused so much public indignation in the quiet suburb of Hinsdale that Maloy backed down.

Maloy was drawing an annual salary from the union of $25,000. This was supplemented by the kickbacks from permit men, a constant stream of gifts from theater owners such as the $150 a week paid him by the B & K chain, and a piece of the action whenever he could pull off some coup such as getting Flannery's signs to replace Wagner's.

And Maloy never gave up the back-room gambling parlor operated for the convenience of union members. But he had still other sources of income.

In 1930 he said he wanted to go to Europe as a delegate to an international labor conference. Doc Quinn suggested in open meeting that the union membership vote Tommy Maloy $5,000 from the treasury to defray expenses of the European trip. The members, knowing that Maloy could strip any one of them of his livelihood at a moment's notice, voted unanimously to give Maloy the money.

Then Doc Quinn, the union steward, suggested that a banquet in Tommy Maloy's honor be held in a Loop hotel. Every union member was given a block of tickets to the banquet and charged for them. They could sell them, use them, or throw them away. The banquet was held and 4,000 of Maloy's friends—or those who thought it wise to appear so—attended. The banquet earned a net profit of $17,000 which was turned over to Maloy to help defray expenses of his European jaunt. Even Congressmen don't do much better.

Maloy had been given $22,000 for a simple trip to Europe. Then as now, one could defray a great many expenses in Europe for $22,000.

The next year Doc Quinn suggested in open meeting that the union install a $4,000 bathroom in Tommy Maloy's house at 6806 South Chappell Avenue. Nobody voted against it. The year after that, Doc Quinn suggested the union install a $5,000 bar in Maloy's basement. Nobody voted against it.

Those years of 1930, 1931, and 1932 were years of financial depression. Maloy refused to recognize the fact. He demanded that the small movie theaters which paid no graft keep two operators on duty at all times.

The theater operators complained to the politicians. State's Attorney John A. Swanson of Cook County started an investigation of Maloy's union. Maloy packed a bag with cash and went to Springfield. Most of the legislators had been on his payroll for years. A bill was introduced requiring two operators in every booth at all times "for the safety of the public."

This was when Tommy Maloy invited the Capone outfit to come in.

The legislators who sponsored the bill were two of Al Capone's adherents, Daniel A. Serritella and James B. Leonardo. The man who accompanied Tommy Maloy to Springfield to see about getting such a measure introduced in the legislature was Murray Humphreys, the labor union representative on the Capone-Nitti board of directors.

A federal grand jury later was told that in addition to the cash that changed hands in Springfield, Tommy Maloy had to contribute $5,000 to Mayor Cermak to assure the support of Cook County Democrats for the measure. The money went from the union treasury directly into Cermak's bank account.

In this federal grand jury's inquiry into Tommy Maloy's legislative influences, witnesses were called to discuss the sudden death of Jacob D. Kaufman, a member of the union who had supported Henry Gusenberg's candidacy. Kaufman was shot to death June 20, 1931, in a garage at 9527 South Princeton Avenue.

The description of his killer, a dapper young man with curly black hair who wore white flannels that evening in early summer, exactly fit Murray Humphreys. The Hump would always handle a contract kill if the price was right.

Kaufman's death brought to light an affidavit he had made three years earlier. He swore that on July 10, 1928, gunmen posing as policemen took him to the office of Tommy Maloy. Kaufman said Maloy appeared convinced that Kaufman had hired assassins to kill Maloy. When Kaufman was freed, Maloy warned him he would be "taken for a ride" if he ever talked about the incident.

The federal grand jury turned up the fact that Tommy Maloy's brother, Joseph Maloy, had the City Hall job of licensing prospective motion picture machine operators. Those candidates sponsored by Tommy Maloy were quickly licensed by Joseph Maloy.

This licensing of union workmen is not limited to Chicago, but the politicians in that city take credit for thinking up the idea. They considered the licensing of motion picture projection machine operators in the twenties as a test to see if too many workingmen complained. None did, so just before the stock market crash of 1929 the city fathers began considering further licensing.

One alderman suggested that all bartenders be licensed. The excuse given was that each handled drinks for consumption by the public. The real reason was that with 5,000 bartenders working in the city, each susceptible to a $10-a-year license fee renewal, the city could have an extra $50,000 a year in income and each alderman would be able to control every bartender working in his ward.

The idea actually was referred to a committee for study before one of the city councilmen happened to mention that Prohibition was still the law of the land. Nobody was supposed to be a bartender because by law there were supposed to be no bars. Reluctantly, the aldermen dropped the idea.

But there have been recurrent thoughts of licensing since World War II. The aldermen from time to time have discussed licensing individual newspapermen, individual cooks and waiters and cocktail waitresses, individual radio and television announcers, even individual clerks in bookstores. The book salesmen licensing, like that of the operators of corner newsstands, was suggested because such salesmen can influence the reading matter bought by the general public.

So far none of these ideas has got off the ground in the Chicago City Council chambers. But the aldermen can always point to the motion picture projectionists as examples of public apathy toward such licensing.

Anyway, Tommy Maloy's brother issued individual licenses to any prospective projectionists whose applications came from Tommy.

This was true even when the candidates for such licenses proved unable to read or write. The illiterates were accompanied by experienced operators who would write their examination papers so that Joseph Maloy could license them.

The county grand jury on July 13, 1931, indicted Tommy Maloy and five others for conspiracy.

They were charged with restraint of trade, obtaining money under false pretenses, assault on the person of George Krueger of Hinsdale, violation of the city licensing ordinance, and destruction of property. The defendants besides Tommy Maloy included Joseph Maloy, Doc Emmett Quinn, Jack Miller of the exhibitors' association, and Thomas J. Reynolds, the stooge to whom Tommy Maloy had given the title of union president.

A grand jury can act, even if the judges and the prosecutors have all been paid off. The federal grand jury was investigating and the county grand jury had indicted. The newspaper editorial writers expressed the view that justice would triumph. Tommy Maloy waited until fall, after a few months had passed, and then called a promissory note. Assistant State's Attorney Charles E. Lounsbury went before Judge John Prystalski in criminal court to ask dismissal of the criminal indictment against Tommy Maloy and the others. Prystalski said from the bench that he could do nothing except comply with the request of the county prosecutor.

Eight rebel union members said they had gone to New York City to protest to officers of the AFL international union against Maloy's dictatorship. They particularly complained of the permit men, who apparently could never join the union.

The eight rebels sued for redress with an equity action filed in the federal district court in Chicago. The action was dismissed for want of jurisdiction.

Then the rebels carried their suit to the state courts. Maloy not only had the rebels fired from their jobs as projectionists, but had the union levy fines against them of $5,000 apiece. The courts upheld Maloy's right to fine the rebels.

One of the rebels, Fred F. Oser, went to Maloy's office on March 24, 1933, to see Maloy. Apparently Oser wanted a reconciliation, knowing that if he ever was to work again at the only job he knew he had to make his peace with Maloy. But Maloy was out and Ralph O'Hara simply shot Oser to death.

O'Hara was on Maloy's payroll as a "heavy," which means in union parlance a slugger who will not hesitate to kill. He would slug anybody at any time. O'Hara had been a dance-hall operator before World War I, then organized the piano tuners into a union, and in 1919 became business agent of the Chicago Federation of Musicians. In that job, O'Hara slugged the president of the federation. Out of work, he turned to Tommy Maloy.

As a matter of historical perspective, Ralph O'Hara shot and killed Fred Oser only three weeks after Tony Cermak—on March 6, 1933—died of the wounds inflicted by Frank Nitti's torpedo. Ralph

O'Hara pleaded self-defense in the Oser killing, when brought to trial in the criminal court of Judge James H. Fardy. A jury heard such evidence as there was. Fardy directed a verdict of acquittal.

Judge Fardy's reasoning was unimpeachable.

He told the jury that inasmuch as there was no surviving witness to the shooting except Ralph O'Hara, the jury would have to accept without question O'Hara's contention that he killed Fred Oser only when threatened.

On May 6, 1933, the newspapers learned that Tommy Maloy's financial affairs were under the scrutiny of Dwight Green and the Internal Revenue Service. Frank Nitti, Ralph Capone, Al Capone, and Jake Guzik had gone to prison for income tax evasion. The agents in Green's office hinted that Tommy Maloy might join the procession.

Maloy's trouble piled up. The State-Congress theater opened with rebel motion picture machine operators in the projection booth. Gasoline was sprinkled over the new seats in the refurbished theater at an hour when it was not open to the public and the resultant blaze closed the place permanently. The Cook County grand jury resumed its inquiry into Maloy's activities. Everyone on the grand jury knew Maloy had ordered the fire but no evidence or testimony was adduced to connect him with it. No prosecution was ever attempted.

The income tax investigators had difficulty tracing Maloy's income. Jack Miller of the exhibitors' association was taken before Federal District Judge John Barnes and held in contempt after he refused to answer the questions of a federal grand jury about Maloy's income.

Miller was asked about cash in the amount of $97,000 and checks totaling $22,491 which the B & K books credited to him. The federal investigators realized that Jack Miller, as head of the Chicago Exhibitors Association, probably turned the money over to Tommy Maloy. Miller contended that this money and similar sums from other theater owners had gone to a mysterious "Mister Nikolaus." The federal agents were sure Tommy Maloy had been the recipient but they could not prove it. A year later they were able to piece the story together and learn the reason for the payoffs.

When sound movies originally replaced silent pictures the sound was on phonograph records which had to be played in synchronization with the film as it ran through the machines. Tommy Maloy demanded that the theater owners hire extra union employees, known as faders, to regulate the sound and the synchronization.

Then the Hollywood moviemakers learned how to put the sound track right on the film. No longer did the phonograph records have to be synchronized. Maloy's faders no longer had anything to do. But no union ever dropped members simply because automation had done away with their jobs. Maloy told the theater owners that the faders would have to continue working in the projection booths unless and until the owners paid $1,100 for each fader dismissed.

This was obviously cheaper than keeping the faders on the payroll through eternity. The owners paid Maloy the sums demanded.

The income tax agents also learned that in 1928 and 1929, when the stock market was booming, a theater chain bought securities in Maloy's name. The little union chief pocketed $25,000 from the stock.

Early in 1935 the income tax sleuths had all their figures in hand. They had questioned Ralph O'Hara several times and found enough discrepancies in his answers that a federal grand jury indicted him for perjury.

The same federal grand jury on January 25, 1935, charged that Tommy Maloy had failed to report $350,000 of his income in the four years of 1929–30–31–32. The government said Maloy failed to pay $81,000 in income taxes due on this unreported income. Maloy on February 2, 1935, was arraigned in the federal district court and pleaded not guilty to the charges.

No one except Tommy Maloy and Dwight Green had been as interested in the progress of this income tax investigation as had Frank Nitti. He had watched every step of it.

Nitti had been working with Tommy Maloy for years. Maloy had sought Nitti's support in Maloy's race for first vice-president of the AFL International Alliance of Theatrical and Stage Employees at the 1934 convention held in Columbus, Ohio. At that time George E. Browne, business manager of Chicago Local 2 of the Theatrical Protective Union—the stagehands—was a candidate for president of the IATSE, as the parent union was called.

Before the 1934 convention the Chicago gang leaders had met both Maloy and Browne in Maloy's office several times to plan strategy. Sworn testimony later indicated that these meetings were attended by Nitti, by Charlie Fischetti, and by Louis (Lepke) Buchalter of New York City, there as a representative of Salvatore (Lucky Luciano) Lucania, the Syndicate boss in New York.

Only years later did the reading public learn that Syndicate leadership had passed a death penalty on Tommy Maloy on Christmas Eve of 1934. Nitti had arranged for George E. Browne to take over Maloy's union "in a caretaker capacity" with approval of the executive board of the international. So Maloy's arraignment on the income tax charges was academic. His fate had already been sealed by the underworld, rather than by the half-world politicians.

George Browne later testified that the fatal shooting of Maloy was done by "two torpedoes from New York for whom Frankie Rio had contracted."

Two days after his arraignment, on February 4, 1935, Tommy Maloy shortly after noon left the South Side hotel apartment where for three years he had been maintaining a beautiful nightclub entertainer. Maloy entered his car with Doc Quinn and they started toward the union office.

They were driving north on Lake Shore Drive, just in front of the deserted buildings of A Century of Progress, when a car drew up alongside. Two men were riding in it. A sawed-off shotgun was poked out of its window. The first blast shattered the window glass next to Maloy, who sat in the driver's seat. The second blast struck Maloy in the head.

The second gunman used a .45 caliber automatic pistol and shot Maloy several times.

The execution had been carried out with precision.

The killer car sped away. Doc Quinn brought Maloy's car under control.

Maloy had a fine funeral. His home and the union offices were filled with floral pieces. A thousand persons, presumed to be mourners, followed his coffin to the grave. One of the pallbearers was George Browne. He was appointed caretaker of Local 110 and went directly to the Maloy office as soon as the funeral was over.

One of Browne's first acts as interim union manager was to announce that all special permits issued by Tommy Maloy were rescinded and that anybody who was working as a projectionist in any movie theater in the Chicago area could continue to do so. This pulled the teeth of the rebels.

Only later were they to learn that George Browne was no better for the ordinary workingman than Tommy Maloy had been.

19 "Never saw a whore who wasn't hungry"

No single act of the Capone Syndicate was more dramatic than the extortion of $1,827,000 from the film industry of Hollywood. None was ever better documented. The two men who were the immediate instruments of this astonishing shakedown told their stories again and again in minute detail in the hope of winning clemency. Their stories stood up and corroborative evidence of every statement was presented in court.

The prime instrument of Frank Nitti and the Capone Syndicate in this almost surgical extraction of motion picture industry funds was labor statesman George E. Browne, president of the AFL International Alliance of Theatrical Stage Employees. Browne sat for six years on the select executive council of the American Federation of Labor. Among his peers were Diamond Joe Esposito, Dago Mike Carrozzo, George E. Scalise, and Dave Beck of the teamsters.

The life and times of George E. Browne and his partner in labor statesmanship, Willie Morris Bioff, could serve as the basis for a dozen rags-to-riches stories. Both started as poor lads. They became so successful that Browne achieved his ambition in that he could afford to "drink a hundred bottles of beer a day" and Bioff achieved his ambition to consort on terms of equality with members of the U.S. Senate.

Both accepted the support of the Capone Syndicate in their rise to affluence and power. Browne became, as a member of the AFL executive council, an adviser to the President of the United States.

When the going got tough, both Browne and Bioff showed their mettle by saving themselves from long prison terms. They testified against several men to whom they once had been willing to swear undying loyalty.

The million-dollar movie shakedown, as it came to be called, started almost two years before Tommy Maloy was shot to death. Maloy had been shaking down the Balaban & Katz movie theater chain in Chicago for $150 a week right up to that fatal day in 1935. The million-dollar shakedown started on a pleasant summer day in 1933, when George Browne discovered that Barney Balaban would stand still for a $20,000 bite.

Every grifter on the fringes of the underworld knows you can't cheat an honest man. So when one of the owners of the great B & K chain coughed up $20,000 in the middle of a depression, George Browne marked the business for bigger things in future.

Browne had not yet been elected international president of the IATSE, in the convention of 1934 at Columbus. But, since 1920, he had been business manager and rule · of the AFL Chicago Local 2, Theatrical Protective Union, into which 450 stagehands were paying dues. Browne took over the union at the age of twenty-six by the simple expedient of slugging the previous walking delegate several times with a length of lead pipe rolled in newspaper. After each tap, Browne asked the man, "You want to quit?" The first three times, the man replied, "No." The fourth time, Browne hit a little harder than he had intended.

This time the man lost consciousness. Browne momentarily panicked. Having no water at hand, he poured a bottle of cold beer in the man's face. Shocked by the icy brew, the man's eyelids fluttered, and before he was fully conscious he was saying, "Yes, yes, yes, yes, yes." When he had the strength to rise he staggered out of the union office and was never seen on the premises again.

That made Browne ruler of the union local, sole collector of the dues of 450 workingmen, sole arbiter of the men's right to jobs and a livelihood.

Browne rose from that lowly position of walking delegate in only fourteen years to become at the age of forty a vice-president of the American Federation of Labor. In this capacity he had an office in Washington, the ear of the President and of members of the Cabinet, and influence throughout the North American continent.

Browne was in demand as a patriotic speaker on Memorial Day, on the Fourth of July, and especially on Labor Day. He delivered onward-and-upward commencement addresses dealing with the homely virtues of frugality, thrift, and the American way of life.

But he had to give it all up when he was sent to prison.

Browne's life as a union labor leader had not been a bed of roses. After the stock market crash of 1929, the United States and the world knew financial depression. Few theatrical productions were being angeled and staged in New York City. Fewer still ever got as far west as Chicago. Half of Browne's stagehand dues-payers were out of work.

Browne accepted a pay cut for those of his union members who still were working. He made a speech to the union, telling the men "This is a time when all of us have to tighten our belts." He said he had been drawing $250 a week salary from the union but would accept a 25 percent cut in pay to $187.50 a week. In addition, said Browne, he would reduce his working days in the union's behalf from seven a week to five. He would cut his pay by another two-sevenths because, as Browne put it, "That's only fair."

Browne set his own Depression salary at $160 a week.

In those days, when nearly one-fourth of the men of working age in Chicago were unemployed and the rest thought $40 a week a pretty good income, George Browne would not starve on $160 a week.

From the date of Franklin D. Roosevelt's inauguration on March 4, 1933, there had been a nationwide upturn in business activity and optimism. When Chicago opened A Century of Progress on May 27, every newspaper in the city proclaimed that Depression was a thing of the past. The fact was that for a portion of the city's theaters, those showing motion pictures in the Loop, business was never better than during Depression years. Unemployed men and women were lined up every morning before the Loop theaters opened at 9 o'clock, waiting to pay their 25 cent admissions and escape for a few hours the realities of life outside.

The B & K movie theaters were presenting, in addition to feature films and comedy attractions, four shows a day of vaudeville. In 1933, Browne notified the B & K chain that they would be expected to restore the 25 percent pay cut which the stagehands took in 1930.

Despite or because of his daily ration of 100 bottles of beer, George Browne suffered from stomach ulcers. A few days after notifying the B & K chain that he would expect the pay-cut restoration, Browne entered a hospital for treatment. Barney Balaban, one of seven brothers in the motion picture dynasty, telephoned Browne in the hospital and asked to see him. Balaban said he wanted to discuss Browne's demand for money for the stagehands. Browne testified under oath that Barney Balaban offered him a substantial bribe if he would not press his demand for the wage increase.

Q—What did he offer you?

A—He said he was paying Tommy Maloy, business agent for the motion operators' union, $150 a week. He said he would like to take care of me like that.

Browne told Balaban he would think it over. He said they could discuss it at leisure after Browne got out of the hospital. Browne said he was at what labor statesmen call "the delicate stage" of any negotiations—trying to figure out the maximum that the traffic will bear before the other fellow digs in for a long and hard fight.

Browne consulted with his conscience and decided to ask for $20,000. This was not an arbitrary figure. Browne arrived at it by figuring out what he would have collected had Balaban been paying him $150 a week ever since the stagehands' pay cut went into effect in 1930. The sum came, in round figures, to $20,000.

When Browne left the hospital he phoned Barney Balaban and said he wanted that amount in a lump sum, in addition to $150 a week in future. Balaban thought the amount excessive.

Browne, without disclosing the formula by which he had arrived at the figure, said he would not accept less.

Balaban asked Browne to meet and negotiate with Leo Spitz, then attorney for the B & K chain, but later head of Columbia Pictures Corporation in New York and Hollywood. Spitz was a conciliator and compromiser. When they met, he told Browne, "Your asking price is too high. Balaban's offer is too low. Now let us see if we cannot arrive at a figure somewhere in between that will prove mutually satisfactory."

This standard lawyer's ploy fell on deaf ears. Browne, the lead-pipe man, lacked the legal education and diplomatic polish displayed by Leo Spitz. Browne replied, "Twenty thousand on the barrelhead or stink bombs at the busiest hours in every B & K house in town." Spitz recognized the inevitable. He went back to Balaban and said the chain would do well to pay the money gracefully. Balaban then asked Browne to join him for lunch at Gibby's Ogden Grill, a walk-up speakeasy then run by Gibby Kaplan at 192 North Clark Street. Balaban told Browne he would pay the $20,000 if they could figure out some gimmick to fool the stockholders in case they ever looked into the B & K books.

Browne suggested the payment be recorded as a charitable contribution. The check could be made out to the soup kitchen.

This soup kitchen had been opened by Browne and his partner, Willie Bioff, at Randolph and Franklin streets. It was a place offering free lunch to the unemployed stagehands of Browne's union.

Balaban went back to his office and wrote the check. Leo Spitz delivered it. Browne testified that Spitz kept $1,000 as a fee.

The Browne-Bioff soup kitchen served 3,700 meals a week. Nobody had to pay. The unemployed stagehands could come in and eat green pea soup or beef stew, with rye bread and coffee. They could sit all day and gossip with their fellows, smoking roll-your-own cigarettes the while. The 300 or so unemployed stagehands ate about 3,000 of the 3,700 meals a week, so the soup kitchen was important to them through those years before social security or unemployment compensation. Their food was that from the ordinary menu.

The deluxe menu accounted for more than a hundred meals a day. It consisted of roast chicken with chestnut dressing, roast duck glazed with orange juice basting, roast prime of beef, broiled double lamb chops or pork chops, tender porterhouse steaks. The deluxe menu occasionally had such delicacies as braised calf shank, oxtail stew, beef and kidney pie. It was created for men who knew and appreciated the better things of life. Once again, nobody paid at the Browne-Bioff soup kitchen.

The deluxe menu came into being because Willie Morris Bioff was a philosopher.

His philosophy on virtually every subject is quoted at length in transcripts of testimony taken by the government from him and from Browne. The particular bit of Bioff philosophy that applied to the soup kitchen was, "I never saw a whore who wasn't hungry and I never saw a politician who wasn't a whore. So we'll let the politicians eat for nix."

The soup kitchen was located just two blocks west of the City Hall and County Building. Every politician in town began eating lunch daily in the reserved-seat area of the Browne-Bioff soup kitchen.

The $20,000 check which Barney Balaban made out for George E. Browne was payable to "The Stage Hands Union Soup Kitchen." But after Leo Spitz got his $1,000, Browne and Bioff split the other $19,000. They needed no money to operate the soup kitchen, except for the minimal salaries financed out of union funds for chefs, waiters, and dishwashers. Browne and Bioff had found a way to serve 3,700 meals a week without buying food.

George E. Browne, born in 1894, had quit school when in fifth grade at the age of twelve and was apprenticed to the property department of a vaudeville theater. This job put him into the stagehands' union. He was a likely lad, not averse to doing a little slugging in a dark alley, and the union leaders of his time found use for his muscle. This paid him a bit extra. Testifying in court years later, Browne described these early union chores as "of an unstable nature."

Browne's first paying job with the union was as secretary pro tem of Local 2.

In 1920, as earlier recounted, he caused a vacancy to exist in the job of business agent. Browne first stepped into the job and then called a "democratic" union election to ratify his right to it.

Four years later, Browne was elected sixth vice-president of the stagehands' international union, the IATSE. In 1932, he was a candidate for the $25,000-a-year job as president of the international. Union politics is similar to national politics, in that a man will spend $100,000 or more—of union funds—to get himself elected to a $25,000 job from which he can collect graft of $500,000 a year.

Browne spent more than $100,000 for advertising, publicity,

entertaining, and general goodwill, but failed of election. With him on the slate in that year of 1932 was Tommy Maloy of the motion picture projectionists' union, who was seeking the post of vice-president.

Between the 1932 election and the next biennial election in 1934, Browne and Maloy got the support of the Capone Syndicate. This time the two contenders won handsomely. Browne was elected president of the IATSE and Maloy was elected vice-president. But that is getting ahead of the story.

In 1930, Browne was not yet aiming for the top job in his union. In the spring of that year, the legitimate theaters in Chicago turned off their lights because so few shows were being produced. That was when Browne accepted a 25 percent pay cut for stagehands and cut his own pay. There was much less work to do and George Browne had time on his hands. He looked around for a way to supplement his income.

Browne decided that the wholesale merchants of the Fulton Street Market needed to be organized. He felt he was the right man to do it. He spent $25 and had a lawyer draw up an application for a charter for a nonprofit organization to be called the Poultry Board of Trade. Browne and his wife were to own it, and their three children were to benefit. Browne sent this application to the Illinois capital at Springfield, together with check for $10, and in due course he got the charter which permitted him to set up in business.

Now Browne had some letterheads and business cards printed. He had some brightly colored decals printed, with mucilage on the obverse side. And he set out to convince food purveyors they needed organization. Browne went from store to store among the poultry dealers who sold fowl to the hotel and restaurant trade. He introduced himself, passed out literature, and told each merchant that the association stood ready to protect the place of business and its merchandise. Browne pointed to the facts of pilferage and vandalism with which merchants are always harassed. Browne told each merchant he could be protected against such hazards upon payment of $10 in initiation fees and $10 a week in dues.

Most merchants were busy as Browne told his story. Often they interrupted him in the middle with the equivalent of "Get lost." A few joined at the very first approach, paying Browne $20 and permitting him to paste the organization decal on their front windows. Browne wrote out receipts for the payments they made and continued on his rounds.

None of the merchants was too much impressed with George Browne.

A few days later, Browne made the rounds a second time. Now he told the merchants who had not signed up that their need for protection had increased. He said, "Some of the merchants who are members of the association don't like holdouts. They feel they are paying the freight for you fellows who are free riders. They think everyone ought to join and agree to fair trade practices.

"I have heard that some of them got so angry about it that they broke the windows of their neighbors who had not joined the association. Anything can happen. Truck tires can be slashed, places of business can be set on fire, kerosene can be poured over freshly plucked chickens and ducks and geese and turkeys."

At least one tough merchant, aided by his brawny son, actually threw George Browne out on the street when he heard these threats. But most merchants do not pretend to be tough. They just want to be let alone and permitted to operate their businesses in peace—and at a profit. They saw that paying Browne was like paying taxes, something nobody likes but something that everybody sooner or later would have to do. So a great many of the merchants now paid their ten-and-ten for membership.

That weekend Browne's foresight proved true. Those merchants who had not yet signed up with the Poultry Board of Trade had their windows broken, the tires on their trucks slashed, and a few of their dressed birds saturated with coal oil.

The tough merchant who had thrown Browne out on the street came to his place of business at 4:30 o'clock Monday morning to find that axes had been used to break up his cabinets, his freezer compartments, his cash register, and his walls. The refrigeration pipes had been chopped through.

Virtually all the merchants signed up with Browne that Monday.

After that, Browne went after the 10 percent who were determined they did not need his association. Instead of the tires of their trucks being slashed, the oil was drained from their truck motor crankcases and replaced with molasses. Instead of windows being broken, their shops were dismantled by ax-wielding vandals. Everything saleable in their places of business was piled in the middle of the floor, drenched with gasoline, and set aflame. The fire engines were kept busy in the Fulton Street Market.

All but a handful signed up with Browne. He was determined he would not permit even one holdout.

A few merchants reported Browne's activities to the police. But Browne, through the stagehands' union, had been paying police and politicians for years. There was no evidence to connect him with the vandalism of which he had warned merchants. The politicians who control the police passed along the word, "Lay off Browne." So the complaining merchants got nothing but a deaf ear for their stories.

Browne had the merchants signed up in his organization 100 percent, each paying $10 a week for the privilege of membership.

Now all the Gentile poultry dealers in the Fulton Street Market were protected against unfair business practices on the part of their neighbors and competitors. The entire operation had taken only a little more than a month of Browne's time and less than $100 of his bankroll. From now on his income from the association, of which he was sole officer, director, and employee, was more than $300 a week.

In the course of this interesting work, Browne had run into a man who was aiding the Jewish poultry dealers in exactly the same way that Browne was aiding those of Gentile persuasion. This man was Willie Morris Bioff. He called his organization the Chicago Kosher Butchers Association. Bioff sought Browne out to size up a possible rival. Browne told him at once, "You work your side of the street and I'll work mine." When Bioff saw what a reasonable fellow Browne was, he pitched in and helped organize the goyim.

Browne was no stranger to violence when Bioff joined him. Browne gave the appearance of being a timid businessman, but the appearance was deceptive. On January 26, 1925, for example, Browne was shot in the seat of the pants while dining and drinking in the restaurant of Ralph Amore, thirty-one, at 2100 Lake Street, Melrose Park. Amore was killed. Browne told police at the time, "I'll take care of it." Four weeks after Browne got out of the hospital, the man who fired the shots was found dead of bullet wounds.

Just in passing it might be pointed out that the man who picked Browne up in the snow that January night in suburban Melrose Park and took him to the hospital was his brother-in-law, Herbert C. Green, Sr. Green had waited in the car when Browne went into the restaurant and Browne had staggered almost to the car when he emerged after the shooting.

Half a dozen or so years later, after Browne and Bioff had become partners, Green sought to oust Browne as business agent of the stagehands' union. Green ran against his brother-in-law, Browne, in a union election. Bioff told Green to withdraw from the race. Green refused. Bioff smashed Green's skull with a blackjack.

Green did not die immediately of the attack. He lived on for seven years, but he was never right again. He was always befogged, his family said, and had to be cared for like a baby. But at the time of the attack Green was able to tell police, "Willie hit me over the head. He was mad because I refused to withdraw my name as a candidate against George."

Willie Bioff, like George Browne, never hesitated to use violence when he felt all else had failed.

Bioff was six years younger than Browne. Born in Odessa, Russia, he had been brought to Chicago by his parents at kindergarten age. The nice people born on the right side of the tracks always find it hard to believe such things, but by the time Willie Bioff was ten years of age he had learned how to earn money by working with little girls .

Willie would get a nickel's worth of candy and use it to entice a girl his age into the back room of a poolhall. The girl, sucking on a piece of candy, was amenable. Willie would tell older boys that for 10 or 15 cents they could enjoy the girl's favors on the top of an unused pool table.

The churchgoing public always asks, "How is this possible?" But the Willie Bioffs of every generation in every corner of the world always figure out a way.

Some of the older boys occasionally tried to enjoy the favors of one of Willie's girls without paying. Willie Bioff early learned to hit a boy from behind with a pool cue. Some of Willie's girls, as they grew past puberty and fancied themselves in love with some nice boy at school, occasionally wanted to quit the gang shags. Willie Bioff early learned to beat them up.

Willie developed a whole catalog of punishments for recalcitrant girls, such as twisting their nipples until they fainted from pain. He would tell the young girls, "Next time you talk this way, it's a dime's worth of acid in the face."

The do-gooders of the upperworld like to think that a boy who grows into a hoodlum, like the girl who grows into a whore, is the victim of environment. Nothing could be further from the truth. The boy or girl has weighed the possibilities and made a conscious choice. Willie Bioff and the little girls he grew up with understood each other.

Early in life, Willie Bioff slugged little girls and threatened them with acid. As time went on he wore silk shirts, had his nails manicured and brightly polished, and grew more refined in other ways.

One was in the way he treated the girls. He discovered, he once boasted, "If you slug a girl half silly and then tie her down, you can stuff her cunt with powdered ice. They tell me it's so cold in there it feels like fire. You got to gag the girl, she screams so loud, but you don't really hurt her permanent. But after ten minutes of that, she will get down on her knees to you any time you say the word 'ice.'"

Bioff had even less formal education than George Browne. Bioff left school in the third grade. By that time he was adept in the use of a leather blackjack or a razor-sharp knife. He knew more basic arithmetic than any teacher in the Chicago school system. After the third grade

Willie became a "steerer" on Halsted Street south of Madison, directing male passersby into Jack Zuta's brothels.

Little boy Willie would approach the walking male to ask, "Looking for a girl, mister? My sister is fourteen. Mom ain't home. You can stay with Sis for fifty cents. How about it, mister?"

If the man did not hurry away promptly, Willie would wheedle, "Please, mister. Sis promised me that if she got fifty cents she would take me to a movie. She never had a real man before. Just the two boys in her class at school."

Most men hurried away. One out of five hesitated, then followed Willie. The boy took the man to an adult brothel.

The woman he got was somewhat older than the fourteen-year-old promised. The man had to pay an extra dollar. But by the time the man left the house he was likely to bump into Willie Bioff, steering another client in the same fashion.

He had an ingratiating way about him. He would wink at the man he had misled if they happened later to see each other in the street.

Jack Zuta and Mike de Pike Heitler, partners in the operation of brothels in the area of Madison and Halsted, always paid their police protection. They always took care of the precinct captains, the ward committeemen, and the aldermen at election time. Everyone knew that no policeman would ever bother a steerer known to be working for their white or black brothels.

So when Willie Bioff was arrested, the knowing observers of the underworld assumed that the boy had tried to double-cross Heitler and Zuta and was being punished. That's the way brothel-keepers work.

A judge sent the youth, by this time grown husky, to jail. After thirty days Willie Bioff was paroled and brought before the court. The judge told him, "If we catch you pimping again we'll lock you up and throw the key away."

Bioff left the court and put his own string of girls to work that very afternoon. He needed money for the lawyers.

But he also needed some sort of legitimate job and he got it with Jerry Lahey, business agent for the Chicago Teamsters Union, who put Bioff on the payroll as a slugger at $35 a week. His job was to collect dues.

Bioff's system never varied and was uniformly successful. He waited until the teamster or trucker was busy loading merchandise, then would sneak up behind him with a blackjack and knock him senseless. Bioff would have a knife at the man's throat when he recovered consciousness. He would tell the man, "I could have killed you. Pay your dues. Next time you'll never wake up."

No better way of collecting money has yet been invented.

Bioff stayed with Lahey's union ten years. Then he took up the same kind of work with the Chicago Joint Teamsters Council No. 25, with its 20,000 members and its affiliation with the American Federation of Labor. Willie Bioff had business cards printed, identifying himself as "Labor Relations Counselor."

Naturally, he kept his brothels running full blast.

Bioff felt that his future was sufficiently assured that he could take a wife and found a family. He married Laurie Nelson and eventually fathered seven children.

In 1920, Willie Bioff was arrested again for pandering. He was caught selling the services of a string of prostitutes. One of them made a police complaint that Bioff had beaten her up.

Bioff was then twenty. He was sentenced to six months in the House of Correction but, under Jerry Lahey's protection at the time, he never entered a cell.

However, the court order remained on the books. A young Chicago reporter, who was later to become a syndicated national news columnist, saw how smoothly Bioff slipped out of court after being convicted. The young newspaperman never forgot the incident. Eighteen years later, when he saw Bioff living the life of a Hollywood millionaire, nails manicured and kerchief tucked in a jacket sleeve, the young newspaperman made it his business to look up the old records. He printed the story and brought so much heat on public officials that Bioff was finally compelled to cancel a Bahamas cruise and serve out his term in jail. The newspaperman was the late Westbrook Pegler.

But that is getting ahead of the story.

After the 1929 stock market crash, department store sales fell off. They had less need of delivery trucks. Teamsters were unemployed. The union laid off such sluggers as Willie Bioff. The pimp-turned-slugger, looking for a source of easy money, turned to the Fulton Street Market. Every grifter knows that a bourgeois merchant is the easiest touch on earth. Bioff organized the Chicago Kosher Butchers Association.

Bioff met George E. Browne and the two became friends. Browne later testified to Bioff's delight when he learned of Browne's connection with the stagehands' union. Browne quoted Bioff's philosophy: "No matter what anybody tells you, people do not have to eat. The only thing they really got to do is get laid or see a show whenever they can dig up the scratch."

Bioff's brothels filled the first need. He saw that Browne, in the stagehands' union, was connected with fulfillment for the second need. Bioff told Browne that the possibilities of the theatrical unions never had been fully explored. He offered to turn the power of his brains to an exploration of this subject in return for a share of the spoils. Browne and Bioff became partners.

Bioff's first idea had to do with a theater called the Star and Garter, a burlesque house at Madison and Halsted then operated by Nathaniel Jack Barger, the Minsky of the Chicago burlesque circuit.

The Star and Garter was one of three theaters at this corner, then Chicago's Skid Row. The others were the Academy and the Haymarket. Neither the Academy nor the Haymarket was doing much business. They simply showed movies continuously, all day and half the night, their customers being homeless men who boozed up on "derail" and other types of cheap liquor.

Derail was half water and half denatured alcohol, sometimes given an extra wallop for the jaded palate by the addition of 2 percent of Jamaica ginger. When supplemented by ginger it was called "jake." The boozers paid 15 cents and slept through the movies.

By contrast with the slow business in the Academy and the Haymarket theaters, the cash register at the Star and Garter never stopped ringing. Jack Barger had a pony line of near-naked girls whom he worked on starvation wages and a six-show-a-day grind. Every Skid Row bum who could get a quarter instead of 15 cents headed for the Star and Garter, where the live show could be seen in addition to films.

The Skid Row habitué, like any other male, enjoyed watching smiling girls as well as gangster films.

Jack Barger was doing so much business at the Star and Garter that he had his ushers go through the auditorium at each intermission and eject the sleeping men to make room for other paying guests. He wanted no such problem as confronted his competitors at the Academy and Haymarket, with sleeping patrons snoring away their lives.

Both Bioff and Browne knew Barger. They knew the kind of business he was doing, since Browne furnished the stagehands needed to move scenery for the dancing girls and baggy-pants comics. Bioff had known of Barger for years and knew the latter's love for money. More important, Bioff figured out a way to capitalize on Barger's profit sense. At Bioff's suggestion, Browne approached Barger and said, "Your competitors at the Academy and at the Haymarket see how well you are doing. They intend to put in pony lines and burlesque acts. They asked me to provide stagehands."

Jack Barger paled at the thought. He would lose the one advantage he had over his competition. After a little thought, Barger came up with the same answer to this problem as had occurred years before to Barney

Balaban when Tommy Maloy wanted to put two projectionists in every movie theater booth. Barger, in effect, asked Browne, "How much?"

Browne appeared to hesitate. Barger said the union leader ought to give a break to the theater owner who had been employing stagehands right along, rather than to two theater owners who never hired stagehands unless they found they could not do without them.

Barger, seeing that Browne was apparently weakening, offered other arguments. Barger said he recognized that if Browne kept half a dozen stagehands from working at each of the rival theaters, they would not be able to pay dues to the union. This could affect Browne economically. So Barger finally suggested that he put the name of George Browne on the theater payroll for $150 a week. Browne agreed.

Browne walked out of the Star and Garter with his first week's pay in his pocket. He met Bioff around the corner, reported how easy it had been, and peeled $75 of his bankroll for his partner. That set the pattern for the future.

Browne and Bioff worked the same pattern at the intersection of Sixty-third and Halsted, and at other places where one theater owner could be played off against another.

Bioff got the idea for the soup kitchen. Browne and Bioff still had their Fulton Street Market connections. They also had the political connections which Browne had made through his union payoffs, and Bioff made through his brothel payoffs. The soup kitchen was created with the idea of catering to downtown politicians.

Browne and Bioff went to the purveyors of the Fulton Street Market and, as had Al Capone a bit earlier, assessed them each a certain amount of produce each week. Space for the soup kitchen was rented. Daily deliveries of milk, meat, vegetables, and bread began to arrive. Large advertisements in *Variety* and other show-business papers proclaimed the opening of a soup kitchen where unemployed members of theatrical unions could meet and dine free of charge in the atmosphere of a gentlemen's club.

The politicians in City Hall, county buildings, and federal building were told they could eat without paying. They could donate something, but few did. Judges of municipal, county, circuit, and appellate courts were urged to lunch daily with unemployed stagehands. Few refused. Most of them, after tasting the fare prepared by the Browne-Bioff chefs, returned at least once or twice a week so long as the soup kitchen remained open.

The most publicized actors in the land were delighted to patronize the Browne-Bioff tables whenever they passed through Chicago. Harry

Richman, Helen Morgan, and Texas Guinan from the nightclub circuit were frequent guests. Al Jolson, Eddie Cantor, Ed Wynn, Ole Olson, Chic Johnson, and other stars of Broadway musical shows dropped in for lunch and were photographed with their hosts.

Newspapermen were accorded the same courtesy as politicians. Reporters and photographers, generally earning less than $50 a week, considered the Browne-Bioff menu dazzling in its epicurean qualities. Their editors were happy to rub shoulders with the celebrities of the theatrical world who could be found there almost daily.

The ordinary citizen has somehow become imbued with the idea that newspapers go around exposing evil wherever it gives off a stench. Such is seldom the case. If a tax assessor is exposed, chances are he raised newspaper taxes. If a judge is exposed, chances are he refused to fix a case in which a publisher's son was involved. The only evil regularly exposed by metropolitan daily newspapers is that emanating from persons completely without friends or influence, persons unable or unlikely to strike back. Browne and Bioff were not of this stripe.

The newspapers were always promoting benefit shows to which tickets were sold at high prices, the proceeds to benefit the pure-milk-and-ice fund, or the off-the-street boys' clubs, or some other such worthy cause. The newspaper promoting the show would take full credit for the money thus raised. But in order to put on such shows, the editors needed union fakers such as Browne and Bioff to blackjack the theatrical talent and compel actors, musicians, and stagehands to work without wages.

With the politicians and the newspapers thus kept friendly, Browne and Bioff had no fear of exposure. Their gold plating might have been thin but they were able to pass themselves off in the community as the 24-carat article and were praised everywhere as philanthropists.

Shortly after they opened the soup kitchen, the town began preparing for A Century of Progress. The whole city was cleaning up and painting up in preparation for the business which millions of tourists were expected to bring to the world's fair. Browne and Bioff were in on the ground floor. They knew that every kootch show on the carnival midway would need stagehands and they instituted a higher dues scale for the members of Local 2.

This was when Browne told Barney Balaban that the B & K chain would have to restore a 25 percent pay cut to its stagehands unless Browne got $20,000 in a lump and $150 a week for the future. Balaban's contribution to the soup kitchen followed.

Balaban thought he was alleviating pressure by paying. But his payment had quite the opposite effect.

Browne and Bioff realized that this richest theater chain in the area could be readily blackmailed.

Both of the blackmailers were later to testify as to their activities on the day that Leo Spitz brought them Balaban's check and insisted that he be permitted to keep $1,000 of the money. Browne said, "As soon as we were alone, Willie and me laughed and did a little fandango dance step in our office. Then we decided we ought to go somewhere and celebrate. Willie said we ought to go to the Club 100 to have a few drinks and talk to the girls. We both knew the guy who ran the club, Nicky Dean."

The Club 100, earlier called the Yacht Club, was at 100 East Superior Street and was ostensibly operated by Henry (Sonny) Goldstone, gambler and nightclub impresario. But its floor manager was Nick Circella, alias Nicky Dean. Circella, as it happened, was very close to Frankie Rio, a cousin of Al Capone and an enforcer for Frank Nitti.

Circella knew Frank Nitti's long-range plans for muscling in on unions having to do with the entertainment business. When Browne and Bioff went to the Club 100 that summer evening they were just like a couple of flies walking into the net of the most carnivorous spider in the world.

None of the principals then realized it, but the million-dollar film industry shakedown had already begun.

20 The President flatters union goons

Nick Circella was a smart operator, as knowing in his own field of cabaret management as were Browne and Bioff in the management of labor unions. Circella knew both the men, since he had been associated with his brother, August Circella, in the operation of burlesque houses on South State Street. He knew Browne and Bioff would be big spenders and he hastened to make them welcome.

Browne took the inevitable bottle of beer. Bioff took bourbon with water on the side. Circella said the first round was on the house. He told the boys, "You only live once," and he went away to send a couple of girls to their table.

Browne and Bioff drank and played the "26" dice game. They were led upstairs by the girls, where they drank and shot craps for a while. As they drank they boasted to the pretty girls. The most knowing of underworld whoremasters can be a chump when out on the town. Before Nicky Dean put them in a taxicab to send them home, he spent an hour in their company. He learned a good deal about their union work.

Circella could not wait next day to tell Frankie Rio about the stagehands' union which George Browne "owned." Both Circella and Rio had known Browne and Bioff—and their union connections—for years. But both Circella and Rio saw that right now the union might fit in with Frank Nitti's plans. Rio phoned to set up a meeting at the Capri Restaurant for lunch. Circella talked to Nitti and Paul Ricca.

Ricca, one of Capone's early associates, had managed the Dante movie theater in Chicago's Little Italy section and then the World Playhouse Corporation on Michigan Avenue, so he was considered a specialist in theatrical entertainment.

Ricca nodded knowingly as Circella told all he had learned from Browne and Bioff. Nitti made the decision and announced the plan of action.

A few days later, as they were to testify in court, Browne and Bioff were flattered by an invitation to a little social gathering in the west suburban community of Riverside. There was to be a party in the home of Harry Hochstein, political leader from what then was called "the Bloody Twentieth" Ward. Browne and Bioff recognized that the invitation was like one extended by royalty and virtually meant a command appearance.

Harry Hochstein had been deputy city sealer under Daniel A. Serritella, Al Capone's protege in the field of political statesmanship. When Capone entered prison and his cousin, Frankie Rio, took over Nitti's old job of enforcer for the Syndicate, Hochstein left his political post to work directly for Rio. Hochstein was chauffeur, bodyguard, and masseur.

Browne and Bioff had been told that the guest list was select and that those in Hochstein's home that evening were to include Charlie Fischetti, another of Al Capone's ubiquitous cousins, Frankie Rio, Frank Nitti, and Paul Ricca.

Upon their arrival they were introduced to Louis (Lepke) Buchalter, whose reputation already had reached Chicago from New York's garment district and who was said to be the most ruthless killer in the entourage of Lucky Luciano.

Browne and Bioff knew they were in fast company. They had expected some female guests but were disappointed. They soon were given to realize that this was a business meeting.

As at any house party, everybody had a few drinks and then was invited to fill plates from the hot chafing dishes on the buffet. The two or three servants who had originally been in evidence quietly vanished. Cups were filled from a steaming pot of Italian espresso coffee and everyone had a wedge of spumoni ice cream from a frozen bombe. Then Frank Nitti rapped a spoon against a glass and the room fell quiet. Nitti turned to George Browne: "The boys tell me that last year [in 1932] you ran for the president of the international union but didn't have enough votes to win."

"That's right."

"When is the next convention?"

"We hold them every two years. We meet again next June [1934] in Columbus, Ohio."

"You gonna run for president again?"

Browne told how much he had spent fruitlessly the previous year and concluded, "I'd sure like to run."

Nitti said, "Suppose this time we saw to it that you had enough votes to win. Hands down. No contest. Would you like that?"

"I'd love it."

This conversation came out in testimony under oath from Browne. Every word of it was verified by Bioff. Nitti's next words were, "In this world if I scratch your back I expect you to scratch mine. If you can win by yourself you don't need us. But if you want our help we'll expect you to cooperate. Is that fair enough?"

"That's fair enough."

Nitti's statement to Browne—an invitation to come in or stay out—is the type of invitation issued by the Outfit to anyone in politics, union labor, or the world of respectability. Despite all the talk of terror and torture, nobody enters the Syndicate except by choice.

When George Browne conceded the fairness of Nitti's words, Nitti looked around the room and apparently sought approval in the eyes of all present. Then he turned to Buchalter to ask, "Will you get in touch with Lucky and have him make sure that all the guys in Local 306 [the New York City stagehands' union] get behind Browne for president and Tommy Maloy for vice-president?"

Browne and Bioff testified that Buchalter replied, "When you're talking to me it's just like you were talking to Lucky himself. Harry Sherman is the president of Local 306. The election is in the bag."

Nitti corrected Buchalter at once. "No election is ever in the bag. We've got more than a year to organize the votes. We take nothing for granted. When we go in that union hall we want to know that we come out with Browne the president and Maloy the vice-president."

Buchalter pledged the support of every East Coast union local.

A few weeks later another meeting with "the boys from Cicero" was held in Tommy Maloy's downtown office. This time a new face appeared. Francis Maritote, alias Frankie Diamond, whose brother had married Al Capone's sister and who thus had become a brother-in-law of the Big Fellow, was present. Browne knew Diamond, who then was operating the experimental television attraction in the Garrick Theater on Randolph Street.

Tommy Maloy was enthusiastic at the support he was offered.

A few weeks went by and Browne and Bioff were asked to join the Syndicate brain trust for lunch at Guey Sam's, Al Capone's favorite Chinatown restaurant, at Twenty-second Street and Wentworth Avenue. Browne and Bioff testified that this was the first meeting at which they dealt with Ralph Pierce and Charles (Cherry Nose) Gioe. Pierce and Gioe after lunch got Browne away from Bioff. Pierce told Browne, "Frankie Rio wants to see you alone."

Pierce drove Browne to Lake Shore Drive and they turned south. After a few hundred yards another car, which had been following, drew up alongside. Both cars were parked. Rio and another man, never identified, got out of the second car and approached Browne. The latter's testimony before a jury reads: "Rio asked me if Willie Bioff was muscling me. I told him that Bioff and I got along fine. Rio told me, 'Okay, but if you have any trouble you let us know. We won't stand for anybody muscling any of our people.'"

This apparently was the Syndicate's way of telling Browne that he had passed the point of no return and was henceforth to consider himself part of the Syndicate.

The old burlesque impresario, Nathaniel (Jack) Barger, wanted to get into the path of the tourist dollars being attracted to the city by the world's fair. He gave up the Star and Garter and opened a Loop burlesque house, the Rialto, at the northwest corner of Van Buren and State. Barger had always kept George Browne on a phantom payroll at $150 a week. Barger later testified: "Bioff came to me one day and said he was my partner. This was only the second time I ever met the man. After that, every week he came and checked over my books. Whatever was my net profit for the week, Bioff claimed half of it."

Barger had the investment and the responsibility. Bioff, with none of the worries, took half the net. This could not last forever. Browne and Bioff by this time were regularly meeting with the Syndicate brain trust in Riverside, mostly at the home of Frank Nitti. One evening at one of these meetings, Bioff was told, "Put Frankie Diamond on the payroll at the Rialto for two hundred dollars a week. He can be the manager."

Browne and Bioff together conveyed the bad news to Barger. They were accompanied by Nick Circella. Barger told Bioff that from the amount his theater earned it would simply be impossible to pay Diamond $200 a week. Circella stared Barger down. Circella told Barger, "That's the story. That's the way it's going to be."

The Rialto had a new manager: Frankie Diamond.

After a few months, Diamond felt he had other fish to fry. He brought in his own replacement: Phil d'Andrea. Before Capone went to prison, D'Andrea had been one of his bodyguards. When Nitti's Syndicate duties required full time, he resigned the presidency of the Unione and D'Andrea stepped in as president.

D'Andrea drew the same Rialto salary as had Frankie Diamond, but cost Barger even more because D'Andrea put his sister on the theater payroll as a bookkeeper.

The Rialto could stand the extra costs through 1933 and 1934. With the world's fair on each summer, the city was overrun with tourists. Day and night, winter and summer, for eighteen months the cash registers in every tourist trap in the city and suburbs kept ringing.

The Rialto, nearest burlesque house to the world's fair, seldom had an empty seat at any performance. Of course the same could be said of every theater in town, every restaurant and saloon, every gambling casino such as Skidmore and Johnson's at Dearborn and Division streets.

When the IATSE convention opened in Columbus in 1934 there appeared to be more gunmen in the auditorium than voting delegates. Gunmen stood at each side of the stage, along both walls, along the rear of the auditorium. Some patrolled the aisles. The man in charge, on the floor constantly giving orders to the gunmen, was Lepke Buchalter, who eventually was to be executed in Sing Sing for the murder of a Brooklyn grocer.

Harry Sherman, president of the stagehands' New York Local 306, delivered en bloc the votes of his delegates. George Browne, business agent of Chicago Local 2, delivered the delegates' votes without a dissenting voice. City after city cast unanimous votes for the Capone Syndicate slate. Browne was elected president of this powerful AFL international union without opposition.

George Browne was called to the dais to accept the presidency conferred upon him in the republican way by the delegates assembled. Browne expressed himself astonished and humbled by this confidence in him shown by his colleagues and friends. He was so overcome with emotion that spontaneous tears prevented his giving the acceptance speech he had prepared. Through his tears, Browne could only repeat, "Thank you, boys. Thank you "

Browne later testified that the Syndicate billed the union for the traveling expenses and hotel rooms of all the gunmen sent to Columbus that week from distant parts of the nation. Browne approved the travel vouchers, hotel bills, and itemized statements of restaurant expenses prepared at his direction by secretaries in the union office.

All the formal niceties were observed.

As soon as the Chicago contingent returned home from the Columbus convention, Browne and Bioff were summoned to another social evening at the Riverside home of Frank Nitti. Browne's recollection of that meeting, in his own words, reads: "We agreed that the Syndicate had elected me president of the IATSE. We agreed that the Syndicate was to be partners—with me and Willie Bioff—in any proceeds that might accrue."

Browne said that at this party Willie Bioff got so excited he exclaimed, "We can make a million. Two millions!" But Frank Nitti, ever the conservative, cut Bioff short. Nitti told Bioff to pay attention to "strategy" and let the money take care of itself.

Browne drew a salary of $25,000 a year as IATSE president. He kept his salary of $250 a week, raised from the Depression low of $160, as business agent of Chicago Local 2 of the stagehands. He put Willie Morris Bioff on the IATSE payroll at $22,000 a year as his "personal representative."

Nitti and Rio said Bioff ought to go to New York City to look after affairs of the stagehands and other theatrical unions affiliated with the IATSE, such as the motion picture projectionists. Bioff was "to case the situation," as Browne later testified. A month later, when Bioff reported back, Browne began spending more time at the offices of the international union in New York.

Now, Browne began planning to move union headquarters to Washington.

The President of the United States, Franklin Delano Roosevelt, was trying to line up the labor vote to assure a Democratic majority in both House and Senate as a result of the 1934 elections coming in November. He talked to George Browne and asked him to move to the capital.

Browne was flattered, as were all other union leaders called in by Roosevelt for such little talks. Browne was assured by lesser administration officials that virtually every international union in the country was building headquarters structures in Washington. The administration could make money available on long-term and low-interest loans for such building purposes. The government architects and engineers were available to plan such structures.

The union leaders were to serve as an unofficial Cabinet to the President, counseling with him on domestic affairs. The unions needed such central locations to keep in touch with Congress, lobbying for legislation sought by labor.

Browne and Bioff looked around Washington and saw all the new construction under way by labor union leaders they had known for years.

They decided to move to Washington.

Nitti got wind of the proposed move.

The Capone Syndicate—and its affiliates such as that run by Lucky Luciano—had absolute control in such urban centers as Chicago and New York. But the syndicates had not yet taken over the government of the District of Columbia. Nitti called Browne long distance and ordered him to give up any moving plans. Browne could not understand Nitti's vehemence. Browne asked, "What's the matter? Are you afraid I'm trying to run out?"

Nitti replied, "You're goddamn right you'd run out."

For the first time, George Browne saw the naked iron fist.

Immediately after this telephone call, Nitti sent Nick Circella to New

York City. Nicky Dean was to be George Browne's constant shadow. Browne was to make no move affecting the international union without prior consultation with Frank Nitti. And Nicky Dean had been sent East "to keep Browne honest."

When Circella reported for duty, he told Browne that Nitti had ordered him put on the payroll at the same salary paid Willie Bioff—$22,000 a year. Browne phoned Nitti long distance to ask, "Where am I supposed to get the money?" Nitti said, "Pay Nick out of your own pocket if you have to. Don't be so stupid. Put it on your expense account."

The summer of 1934 passed rapidly for the top men in the Capone Syndicate. All were working virtually day and night, seven days a week, handling their enterprises both at the world's fair and throughout the rest of Chicago and its suburbs.

Millions of tourists each week meant hundreds of millions of dollars dropped on bars, paid to the cashiers at striptease shows, changing hands at crap tables in the Syndicate casinos. Hundreds of call girls in the Loop hotels, all working on franchises granted by the Syndicate, turned hundreds of thousands of tricks. Nobody in the Syndicate had time to relax.

When A Century of Progress closed its gates for the last time that October, the Syndicate leaders banked their deposits for the final time and went to Florida, Arizona, or California for their vacations. All but Murray Humphreys. He had to begin his prison term.

Browne one day turned to Bioff and said, "Barney Balaban pays Tommy Maloy one hundred and fifty dollars a week. We could handle Maloy's union." Bioff agreed.

Shortly before Christmas all the gang leaders returned to Chicago to spend the holidays with their families. Most of them make a good deal of Christmas, with giant fir trees festooned with colored lights on the front lawns of their suburban estates. A social evening was held once again at Harry Hochstein's home. Browne and Bioff mentioned the matter of Tommy Maloy's union to their hosts.

All the men at the party were accustomed to meet frequently in Tommy Maloy's office. All felt affection for the diminutive Irishman. But this was a business proposition. Friendship played no part in it. Browne testified that Frankie Rio turned to Frank Nitti to ask, "Will Maloy stand still for partners moving in on him?"

Nitti replied, "Not Maloy."

Rio asked, "Does he scare easy?"

"Not at all."

In their sworn testimony, Browne and Bioff agreed there was a pause at the party while all present considered this dialogue. Nitti broke the silence, saying, "We ought to have the projectionists."

Another pause ensued. Then Frankie Rio said, "I'll take care of it—after the first of the year."

In such a simple manner was the death sentence passed on Tommy Maloy. The little group in the room, with an agenda to equal that of any meeting of corporate executives, went on to the next order of business. The two torpedoes from New York, to whom Frankie Rio had let the death contract, caught up with Tommy Maloy on February 4, 1935. He was shot to death in his car at noon on Lake Shore Drive.

George E. Browne served as one of Maloy's pallbearers. Then, in his capacity as president of the parent international union, the IATSE, Browne named himself to take a "caretaker" role in the management of affairs of Maloy's union.

Three weeks later Frankie Rio died of a heart attack in his home. He was the first of the old Capone leaders to die a natural death. From that time on such deaths became commonplace in Capone ranks as the Syndicate grew to be so similar to the half-world of politics and the upperworld that death by violence of leaders became ever rarer.

Maloy was scarcely cold in his grave before, as Browne testified, somebody at one of the Frank Nitti business meetings suggested the need for "a little operating capital."

The group decided to shake down the owners of Chicago motion picture theaters for $150,000. There were half a dozen movie chains operating in Chicago and almost two years had passed since Barney Balaban had paid Browne a lump sum of $20,000. The shakedown started right after this business meeting.

Two weeks after Maloy's funeral, testified James E. Coston, zone manager for Warner Brothers in Chicago, George Browne and Willie Bioff came to the Warner office. Coston testified under oath: "Bioff told me 'the Bolsheviks' in the union were demanding that two operators be put in every projection booth in every movie house on every shift. Bioff said he could keep labor conditions just as they were if the major theater chains gave him one hundred thousand dollars in Chicago."

At that time the Hollywood film-producing companies also owned motion picture theaters which exhibited their products. Later, an antitrust action by the Department of Justice separated the functions of production, distribution, and exhibition, much as years earlier the Standard Oil Company was compelled to separate production from retail sale.

Coston testified that when Bioff told him $100,000 would have to be forthcoming, Bioff said Warner's share would be $30,000. Coston said he told Bioff the suggestion was "ridiculous." Coston quoted Bioff in reply: "You will be a damn fool. You're the big boss of Warner Brothers. Go over there to your desk and write a check. Because this is just a small amount of what it will cost you if they put extra men in the theaters."

Coston phoned his superiors in New York. He told Bioff he would have to fly East for a conference. Coston later testified that when he stepped out of his taxicab at Midway airport in Chicago, he found that he was to have flight companions. Browne, Bioff, and Nicky Dean had bought tickets on the same plane. In New York, the three shakedown artists accompanied Coston to the Warner Brothers office. While they waited in the outer office, Coston was authorized to pay the money. All flew back to Chicago together.

The next day, Bioff picked up the newspaper-wrapped bundle of currency in the office of a Chicago lawyer. Bioff telephoned Coston and reported, "I received the lettuce."

Coston testified, "From that time on, payments were always made in cash either to Willie Bioff at the Bismarck Hotel or to Nicky Dean at the Colony Club."

This $30,000 from Warners was the first of the "proceeds that might accrue" in which the Capone Syndicate shared with Browne and Bioff. The day the payment was made, Nitti and his group held a meeting in his Riverside home. Browne counted out $15,000 for Nitti. The latter thumbed through the sheaf of currency and then stacked it neatly on a table before going on with the meeting.

Nick Circella, with his salary of $22,000 and all expenses paid, had more money than he had ever before enjoyed. He talked Browne and Bioff into letting him use their share of the Warner Brothers' shakedown, along with something more than $15,000 of his own money, to begin work on his "dream nightclub."

There was an old brownstone front at 744 Rush Street, once the home of the Selfridge department store family. It was half a block from the Yacht Club. Circella promptly bought it for remodeling. He made of it a plush gambling spa and opened it with much fanfare as the Colony Club. The furnishings and fittings were modern and costly. Nicky Dean liked to think the club rivaled the state casino in Monte Carlo for elegance of appointments.

Circella was successful in persuading Browne and Bioff to invest the first $65,000 of their share of the 1935 theater shakedown money in this enterprise. The gambling profits, when they began to roll in, were shared by Circella with Frank Nitti and the others of the Capone Syndicate. Browne and Bioff got nothing for their money except a home away from home, a club, where they could drink, dine, and entertain.

Warners was only the first of the Chicago motion picture exhibitors approached with the Browne-Bioff shakedown. John Balaban, secretary-treasurer of the B & K chain, was invited to lunch with Bioff "shortly after Maloy's death." Bioff said that for $120,000 he would guarantee that the union's demand for two operators in every booth on every shift would not be pressed. Balaban said it was his understanding that Tommy Maloy had been paid regularly for just that purpose.

Balaban testified that Bioff replied, "Maloy ain't here no more. This is a new deal."

John Balaban conferred with his brother, Barney. They decided that to save their theater empire "from financial collapse" they would pay $60,000, just half the Browne-Bioff asking price.

The money was paid. Browne and Bioff met Frank Nitti and Paul Ricca for lunch that day in the Capri Restaurant's third-floor private room, and Browne counted out $30,000 as the Syndicate share.

With Warner Brothers having paid, and the Balaban & Katz organization having paid, the other theater chains in the city knew they could not hold out. They came across, one by one. Several lawyers and a theater official gave depositions to the federal prosecutors later, telling of acting as intermediaries in these shakedown payments.

Charles W. Schaub, law partner of Billy Parillo and executive of Meadowmoor Dairy Company, said he handled $32,500 which was paid to Bioff. Benjamin Feldman, a lawyer, said he handled $60,000. E. C. Upton, a theater official, said he had been ordered to pay a total of $56,095 to Bioff. An assistant Illinois attorney general handled $32,500 of the payoffs.

One lawyer said under oath that he handled $30,000 for a theater chain; another lawyer said he handled $36,500. All of it was paid Bioff within "a period of five or six weeks after Maloy's death."

This total of $332,000 was definitely traced to the shakedowns in February and March of 1935. There may have been more. As Bioff made each successive touch, Browne delivered half the money to Nitti and Ricca and the others. Browne and Bioff agreed that Nicky Dean had talked them out of only $65,000 of their share.

The motion picture theater operators who paid so readily were simply the guinea pigs for a bigger shakedown that was to follow, although they did not realize it.

Nitti and Ricca, who had been big operators for years and were no strangers to large sums of money, were astonished at the fact they had collected a third of a million dollars in a few weeks from just a handful of theater owners. They reasoned that if this could be done in Chicago, every city in the nation was an oyster waiting to be opened.

Maloy was killed February 4, 1935. The Warner Brothers shakedown occurred within two weeks of his funeral. The other shakedowns took place almost daily after that. Maloy had not been in his grave six weeks when Frank Nitti unveiled the Syndicate's grand scheme. Browne and Bioff were to try the same type of shakedown on motion picture exhibitors of New York City and if it worked there as it had worked in Chicago, the filmmakers themselves—the legendary billionaires of Hollywood—were to feel the pinch. Nitti said calmly, "I think we can expect a permanent yield of a million dollars a year."

21 The man who trusted Willie Bioff

When Frank Nitti met with his council next day at the Capri Restaurant he brought with him a handful of newspaper clippings. He had been busy researching among the financial pages of Chicago newspapers. Several of the clippings covered the positions in the entertainment industry held by the seven Balaban brothers.

Nitti's councilors knew John and Barney Balaban, either personally or by repute, as managers of the Balaban & Katz chain of motion picture theaters in Chicago. Now Nitti showed them other connections of the Balaban family. One of the Balaban brothers headed Paramount Pictures Corporation in Hollywood. Another headed the Hollywood producing firm of Radio-Keith-Orpheum pictures. A third headed a chain of New York exhibitors, the Publix Theaters, Incorporated.

Nitti told his councilors, "By this time all of them know every nickel we got in Chicago. They sure as hell talked it over before any of them paid us anything. So the guys in New York are already softened up for us. They're just waiting for us to walk in the door and ask for the money."

Nitti said he had been on the telephone that morning, talking to Lucky Luciano in Manhattan. By the end of the day a demand for a pay raise for the motion picture projectionists in New York City would have been made upon the exhibitor chains. Harry Sherman, president of Local 306, would personally make the demand while accompanied by Lepke Buchalter.

Nitti told his listeners that George Browne, as president of the AFL International Alliance of Theatrical Stage Employees, parent union to Sherman's local of the Motion Picture Operators, could appear in the role of peacemaker and stabilizer of the industry. Nitti turned to Browne and said, "You fly to New York this afternoon. Talk to Sherman and he'll brief you on it. Get the money tomorrow and fly back."

Before the day was out Browne and Bioff, accompanied as always by Nick Circella, had the story from Sherman's lips. He told them, "I really pressured Major Thompson, in the RKO office. I said I was of half a mind to call the strike right then, in the middle of the afternoon. I said

271

the men were grumbling about the measly wages they are getting. The only thing holding up a strike, I told him, was the fact that you were on a flight between Chicago and New York so I couldn't get hold of you. That guy is really worried."

The next morning Browne telephoned Thompson to ask, "What's all this rumpus that Local 306 is kicking up all of a sudden? Can't I even go out to see my family for a few days without you guys being at each other's throats?"

Browne said he would send Willie Bioff to Leslie F. Thompson's office "to straighten things out."

Bioff later testified that he wasted a few minutes in small talk and then told Major Thompson the strike threat was serious. But he thought the union officers knew just which of the men were grumbling loudest and could soothe these men's feelings if they could "sweeten the kitty" for them with a few thousand dollars each.

Bioff said that Thompson visibly began to breathe easier.

Then Bioff hit him with the strike settlement fee: $150,000.

Thompson immediately began to haggle. He tried, as had the Balaban brothers in Chicago, to settle for half the sum asked. Bioff said he could not possibly go back to Sherman's local 306 with only $75,000. Bioff was a born bargainer. He finally got Thompson up to $87,000 "to guarantee there will be no strike of operators at this time."

Thompson used the phone to check with his principals. He told Bioff he could have $50,000 of the money by noon. Bioff said, "Cold cash. No checks." Then Bioff left.

As Bioff testified later he laughed and said, "A good morning's work."

Browne later testified that he personally went to the RKO office and was paid $50,000 that day. The other $37,000 was paid him at the corporate office in Chicago the next day.

When this $87,000 payment was split with the Capone board of directors, all agreed that the rest of the New York City shakedowns would be just as easy as those in Chicago had been. The first $87,000 had been simply an experiment, to see if the technique worked. Now that they knew, Nitti said it was time to put the grand plan into motion.

Half the top men of the Syndicate were in Florida at the time. Winter was still very much with Chicago at the end of March and the city's leading gangsters were soaking up the sun at the Palm Island estate of Al Capone, in Biscayne Bay off Miami Beach. Capone was then in Alcatraz. His brother, Ralph Capone, was acting as host to the Florida visitors. Nitti told the small group gathered at the Capri in Chicago, "Let's adjourn this meeting and reassemble on Palm Island. I'll call John Roselli and have him fly in from Los Angeles."

Browne and Bioff, a few days later, were guests for the first time on the Capone tropical island. Their fellow guests included Ralph Capone, John Roselli, Nick Circella, Charles Gioe, Louis Campagna, Ralph Pierce, Frank Maritote, Charles Fischetti, and Phil d'Andrea. Nitti and Ricca completed the group.

This was the first time Browne and Bioff met John Roselli, then and now a member of the Chicago group, who acted as West Coast representative for the Chicago interests. Roselli was familiar from telephone conversations with everything the Syndicate had been doing to shake down the entertainment industry in Chicago. Roselli told the others how the major film studios were organized in Hollywood.

Nicholas Schenck, said Roselli, was president of Loew's, Inc., a holding company of which Metro-Goldwyn-Mayer was a subsidiary. Nick Schenck was then considered the most powerful motion picture executive in the world. His brother, Joseph Schenck, was chairman of the board of Twentieth Century-Fox Film Corporation. The Schenck brothers were natives of Russia.

The motion picture industry in Hollywood signed industry-wide union contracts, so that each film studio did not have to negotiate individually. Each year, said Roselli, the representatives of the big corporations sat at one side of a table while at the other side sat representatives of the various unions whose craftsmen worked to produce motion pictures.

The major unions were the International Brotherhood of Electricians, headed by Dan Tracy; the International Brotherhood of Carpenters, headed by William Hutchinson; the International Brotherhood of Teamsters, headed by Dan Tobin; and the American Federation of Musicians, headed by Joseph Weber.

All of these were AFL international unions, similar to the International Alliance of Theatrical Stage Employees headed by George Browne. But Browne's various unions, lumped under this alliance, had always been thought of as having jurisdiction in the exhibiting end of the industry, rather than in the production end.

The big film-industry men each year signed with the big union men a contract called "the Basic Agreement." No one had ever proposed making Browne's IATSE a party to this agreement.

After Roselli had told his story, all sat and digested the information. As usual Frank Nitti put his finger on the keystone to the whole structure. He asked, "What about the studio technicians corresponding to the stagehands? If they're not in Browne's union who has got them?"

Roselli said, "Some are organized in the carpenters' union, and some in the electricians."

Nitti said, "Okay, that's what we need to know. Browne writes a letter to Hutchinson and to Tracy. He tells them he wants those technicians returned to his jurisdiction, where they properly belong. No reason George Browne shouldn't collect their dues, instead of Bill Hutchinson and Dan Tracy.

"As soon as he writes that letter Browne goes to see Nick Schenck and demands that the IATSE sit at the bargaining table with the other unions. No reason why Browne's international should not be a party to the Basic Agreement. How does that sound?"

Everybody appeared to think about it. All agreed that it might work if they had enough leverage. They decided that Willie Bioff ought to accompany John Roselli back to the West Coast to work full time in beefing up union strength among the stagehands, the motion picture operators, the theater janitors and porters and charwomen, the theater ushers, theater treasurers, box office cashiers, and other lesser unions which the AFL considered part of Browne's IATSE.

Much of Roselli's time was taken up with the organization and operation of gambling, prostitution, and other Syndicate activities. Bioff could work as Roselli's lieutenant in the labor field. As Browne's personal representative, Bioff would take control of all local unions and make sure their presidents and walking delegates knew the IATSE meant business when it demanded a place at the Basic Agreement bargaining table. If Bioff had any trouble, Roselli could supply the necessary muscle to iron it out.

The idea was to be prepared for an industry-wide strike should it become necessary.

A full day was spent by the Syndicate board of directors discussing details of this daring proposal to demand a voice in control of one of the nation's largest industries. Browne and Bioff later testified that while Nitti solicited counsel from all and listened patiently as each expressed his viewpoint, Nitti's was the final word.

The meeting was held in the open, at the side of Al Capone's private swimming pool. Eventually everyone had said everything he had to say and the plan seemed firm. Nitti, strictly business, told Browne, "You'd better get right up to New York. Get those letters off and see this guy Schenck."

Browne demurred. Ever since he had been taken into the Syndicate, two years earlier, he had been coining money. He had more money than he ever had thought one man could accumulate in a lifetime. He had bought a luxury farm, actually a gentleman's estate, in the countryside not many miles from Chicago. But he had never worked harder in his life. He seemed to have no time to enjoy it all.

Browne often remarked to Willie Bioff at this time, "These Syndicate guys don't know how to relax. They just work all the time, day and night, and never take time out to spend their money."

Now, at the side of Al Capone's swimming pool, Browne said to Nitti, "Jeez, Frank, we just got here. I haven't had a dozen bottles of beer today. Nobody has been in the pool. Nobody went over to look at Miami Beach. Can't I stay awhile and get a little of this March sun?"

Nitti looked astonished. Browne said Nitti was obviously surprised that anyone should ever want a vacation. But Nitti was generous. He said, "Go ahead. Have a night on the town. Get some sun in the morning. Then be on the noon plane for New York tomorrow."

Browne was busy from the moment he reached his New York office. He wrote Tracy and Hutchinson, as he had been told, and next day got calls from them. They all met and Browne made his pitch. Neither Tracy nor Hutchinson liked the idea. They sought to do some horse trading with Browne, but he had no room to maneuver. His orders were clear. Tracy and Hutchinson, knowing nothing of the Syndicate's grand plan to which Browne was privy, could not understand his adamant attitude.

Browne was in daily touch with Willie Bioff in Hollywood. They talked to each other by long-distance phone each evening. Browne could never get rid of Nick Circella, and Bioff could never get rid of Roselli. The Syndicate's leaders knew that Browne and Bioff talked too much when they drank and so they were watched. Bioff had a firm grip on the West Coast unions in two weeks. Once this was assured, Browne had to make his move. Bioff joined him in New York.

Nicholas Schenck later testified that on April 14, 1935, Browne and Bioff were announced by the receptionist in the New York office of Loew's, Inc., at 1540 Broadway. Schenck quoted Browne, "When you sign the Basic Agreement next year, you will have to sign with the IATSE as well as the other unions."

Schenck asked questions and listened. Since Browne and Bioff set no deadline other than the vague "next year," Schenck heard them out. Then he shook hands with them as he showed them to the door. Schenck returned to his other work. In his effort to keep abreast of everything that went on in the industry, Schenck knew of the Chicago and New York exhibitor shakedowns.

Even so, he later testified, he was shocked five months later when his aides on the West Coast phoned to give him hourly bulletins on a threat by George Browne and Willie Bioff to call out all their Hollywood workers. They were threatening to paralyze the entire producing industry with a strike. One of Schenck's confidential aides was told by Browne that he could head off such a strike for a payment of $100,000.

Schenck told his aide, "Pay the money."

Bioff remained in Hollywood to continue working with Roselli in September, 1935, when Browne collected the first $100,000 from the Hollywood film moguls. Browne returned to Chicago with the cash. He was summoned to meet Frank Nitti at the La Salle Hotel and he stuffed $50,000 in a briefcase to deliver it to the Syndicate leader. Nitti quickly counted the money, laid it aside, and got down to business: "You'll have to put a couple of men on the IATSE payroll. One was a cousin of Frankie Rio's. He needs a job. The other guy is somebody you need. He is Izzy Zevlin, Lou Greenberg's brother-in-law. Izzy has forgot more about accounting than those Internal Revenue Service guys ever knew."

Browne asked Nitti how he could qualify Izzy Zevlin for union employment. As always, Nitti had done his homework. He had studied the union constitution and bylaws. He gave Browne explicit instructions. Browne was to run a classified ad in the newspapers, seeking a man with exactly Izzy Zevlin's qualifications. Browne was to keep copies of these newspaper advertisements permanently in his files. Then, if he were ever asked how he and Zevlin met each other, he could produce the ads.

Browne put Izzy Zevlin on the payroll at $75 a week, later increasing this weekly check to $100. Zevlin continued to handle the accounting chores for the Manhattan Brewing Company, in which Frank Nitti was associated with Lou Greenberg, and for Greenberg's Seneca Hotel at 200 East Chestnut Street.

Zevlin was clearly being put in charge of Browne's books so that Nitti could make sure the Syndicate was not getting short-changed. But Zevlin immediately showed George Browne how to turn a personal profit of $1,000,000 a year without cutting Nitti in for a cent of it.

Zevlin got Browne and Bioff together and told them they ought to levy a 2 percent assessment on the earnings of the 125,000 workingmen and women who were dues-paying members of the IATSE. There were still a few who were working for starvation wages, but most of the members by the fall of 1935 were earning from $5,000 to $10,000 a year.

Browne later testified that in six years this assessment brought in $6,500,000. Not a penny of it cleared through union books. Not a penny of it went to the Capone syndicate. Browne said he and Bioff "split it down the middle."

This net profit of a million dollars a year for Browne and Bioff came solely through their ownership of the IATSE unions and had nothing to do with the film industry million-dollar shakedown.

Zevlin, unlike Browne and Bioff, had not been a school dropout. He knew everything taught in accounting schools. He set up a double set of books for Browne. In one set the union income from dues was recorded.

In the other they kept track of income from assessments. Browne stashed the second set of books in a secret vault.

Then it became clear that Frank Nitti was like Al Capone in that he wanted those around him to profit by their association. While he had no official knowledge of the assessment which Browne was levying on all union members, Nitti apparently was not in the dark as to what was going on. As soon as Zevlin had given Browne the extra set of account books, Nitti told Browne, "From now on whatever money we get won't be split fifty-fifty. You only have to split your share with Bioff, but there's a lot of guys in the Outfit that have to be taken care of. You keep one-third for you and Willie, and I'll take two-thirds for my people."

Browne testified that he tried to dissuade Nitti from this demand. Browne argued. He said it was not fair. He pounded the table as he recalled the original agreement about "any proceeds that might accrue." Browne said they were in Nitti's suite in the Bismarck Hotel at the time. He said Nitti "got so mad he backed me into the bathroom. I thought he was going to push me out the window." Browne agreed to the new division of the extortion profits.

From this and similar reports, prosecutors at the subsequent trial told the court they believed that not everyone in the Capone Syndicate shared in every profit-making scheme. Apparently, 10 percent of all profit went into a mutual fund, the Syndicate treasury. Beyond that, only those privy to or necessary to a scheme's operation—or those who invested in a particular enterprise—shared in the profits.

Out of these shares each individual paid tithes to the Syndicate if he was a member of that loose-knit organization. The Syndicate had a corporate bankroll, as well as the individual members' bankrolls.

In 1935, Browne and Bioff had shaken down the Chicago film exhibitors for $150,000, the New York film exhibitors for $150,000, and the Hollywood film manufacturers for $100,000. They were to carry off one last coup in Chicago in 1935 before they went to New York to confront the biggest men in the world of films for the Basic Agreement showdown.

On December 1 and 2, 1935, a convention of the executives of the Paramount-Publix chain of movie houses was held in Chicago. This was on a Saturday and Sunday. Every important man in the production and distribution end of the industry was present, along with the exhibitors. Browne in Chicago coordinated a squeeze play with Bioff on the West Coast, both of them using syndicate muscle to back their threats.

Browne at the time controlled the stagehands, projectionists, ushers, treasurers, porters, and the hatcheck concessionaires in theaters from coast to coast. Now he demanded control over the studio mechanics, sound technicians, laboratory technicians, and others in the manufacturing end of the film industry. This would add 35,000 union members to the 125,000 already paying dues through the IATSE.

Browne told Nick Schenck, as soon as he arrived in Chicago for the convention, that he intended to take over these other Hollywood unions.

Over that December 1–2 weekend, Browne pulled the projectionists out of forty-six movie houses in Chicago for strikes of only a few minutes duration. As mentioned above, this was on a Saturday and Sunday. The strikes were nothing but a show of strength, a brief interruption of the movies being shown. The patrons were scarcely aware of the hiatus.

The strikes took place in Loop theaters in Chicago and in such suburban theaters as those of Elgin, Aurora, Waukegan, and Joliet. In suburban Evanston, the Varsity Theater was closed for forty minutes, for the longest such interruption in the area. The strikes also took place in such downstate centers as Peoria and Springfield.

Film industry executives could not generate much enthusiasm for that particular Chicago convention. A strike which shuts down a movie house, as Nick Schenck later testified in federal court, cuts off the supply of money which then never gets to Hollywood. Schenck spent the entire day of October 9, 1941, testifying on this and similar matters in the federal district court of Judge John C. Knox in New York City.

Schenck said that as a result of Browne's show of power that weekend in 1935, the film moguls not only gave him the unions he demanded but signed a closed-shop agreement with the IATSE.

Now Browne had a legitimate right to sit at the conference table when the Basic Agreement came up for consideration in 1936. Browne and Bioff did not pussyfoot. As Schenck later testified, they came to the point the moment they entered his office. Bioff said firmly, "Get this straight: I'm the boss. I elected George Browne president of the international for just one purpose. I want to get two million dollars out of the production end of the movie industry. That is, two million dollars a year."

Schenck testified, "I told the man he was crazy. But he said, 'We have shown you what we can do. You'll have to come through with it.'"

Schenck understood that the reference was to the work stoppages in Illinois the previous December. He said that Browne and Bioff left his Broadway office with the words, "Think it over."

The next meeting brought together George Browne, Willie Bioff, Nick Schenck, president of Loew's, Inc.; and Sidney R. Kent, president of Twentieth Century-Fox (of which Joe Schenck was board chairman). Bioff told Nick Schenck and Kent, "I've thought this matter over. Maybe two million dollars a year is too much. I'll take a million."

Schenck and Kent began to protest but Bioff cut them short. He said,

"We'll meet again two days from now. Today is April 16. When we meet on April 18, you say yes or no. That's all."

Schenck told the jury in Judge Knox's court that on the appointed day, "Bioff took Kent and me aside and asked if we had made up our minds."

Schenck quoted Bioff as saying he had decided they should get $50,000 a year from each of the big film-producing companies and $25,000 a year from each of the smaller ones.

Schenck said he took the matter up with the other major movie-producers. They all agreed that they had to yield to the demands or face ruin if industry-wide strikes were called. The industry men involved were Austin Keogh, vice-president and general counsel of Paramount; Major Albert Warner, vice-president and treasurer of Warner Brothers; and Hugh J. Strong, supervisor of personnel for Twentieth Century-Fox.

Schenck said that on April 21, 1936, the film tycoons agreed to pay. Bioff called the next day and asked if Schenck "had the bundle ready." Schenck still hoped for some miracle. He pleaded for "a breathing spell." He told the court that Bioff gave him "one more day's grace." Then, said Schenck, "The following day I said I was ready. Bioff gave me the number of a room in the Waldorf-Astoria Hotel in New York. I got the money from David Bernstein, treasurer of Loew's. All in large bills. Fifty thousand dollars in United States currency."

Schenck and Kent went together to the room at the Waldorf. They knocked at the door. Bioff opened it. A moment later, said Schenck, Browne entered from the bathroom.

Schenck did not then realize it, but Browne and Bioff were much more nervous than their visitors. They were at the most touchy moment of any shakedown scheme, the moment at which the action can go either way. Schenck and Kent might have "come in like gangbusters," as Browne was later to put it, accompanied by police and private detectives and agents of the Internal Revenue Service or the FBI.

Instead, Schenck and Kent entered the room with their hats in their hands to pay tribute to a man once convicted of beating up aged whores. Schenck told the jury, "There were twin beds right there in the hotel room. I put my money on the right-hand-side bed. Bioff took half the money and started counting it. He put the other half on the other bed and told Browne to count it. They said it was correct, fifty thousand dollars."

Then Schenck walked to a window and smoked a cigarette while Kent went through the same procedure with the $50,000 he had brought.

Schenck said that the following year he personally handed over his

$50,000 once again to Willie Bioff. After that they made other arrangements.

Each of the big four companies paid $50,000 a year. These were MGM, Warner's, Paramount, and 20th Century. Each of the smaller companies paid $25,000 a year. These included Columbia, RKO, and other of the lesser producers.

The executives of Warner's and the other firms later swore that they kited expense accounts to cover the payments given Bioff and Browne out of current cash. They had to keep the stockholders from learning where the money went. All the executives testified that they never reported the matter to their boards of directors, their stockholders, their bankers, the police, or the various federal agencies which might have been interested.

Schenck said he worried about juggling the company books so that stockholders could never learn where the money was going. Then he and Willie Bioff arranged a way to disguise the payments.

This was an ingenious scheme. Bioff was to receive "commissions" amounting to $50,000 a year on the sale of raw film to MGM. Once that arrangement had been worked out, said Schenck, he no longer was "scared to death" of Bioff's threats every time the two met. Schenck quoted Bioff, on this "subagent" arrangement: "You'll have to pay enough additional so the subagent can pay income tax on the money supposedly earned. I want my fifty thousand net."

Schenck agreed to this arrangement. He already had given in to Bioff's threats and had paid him the $50,000 for the second year before the subagent plan went into effect. A few weeks later, Bioff got the $50,000 from the subagent for the first time. Schenck asked Bioff to return the "advance" of $50,000 which had earlier been paid. Schenck ruefully added, "Bioff never returned the $50,000 he owed me."

22   Willie keeps his girls in line

Nick Schenck told the court a straightforward story when discussing the way he paid money to Willie Bioff. He recalled names, dates, places, and amounts down to the penny.

But he proved uncertain and forgetful on cross-examination when asked to estimate his personal income. At first he could not even guess. Then he thought, "It might be around three hundred or three hundred and twenty-five thousand dollars a year."

His brother, Joe Schenck, had the same trouble. His loss of memory was so bad that it led to investigation of his income tax returns. He was tried, convicted, and sent to prison for three years for tax fraud.

Bioff took the witness stand to tell something of the financial affairs of the Brothers Schenck. Nick used Bioff as a messenger to deliver bundles of cash to his brother Joe in Hollywood.

Nick was then in New York and Joe on the West Coast. The cash transfers were between brothers and had nothing to do with the industry shakedown. Bioff handled them as a convenience to the Schencks.

Bioff told the court that Nick Schenck was robbing the stockholders of Loew's, Inc., sending cash to Joe for deposit in their joint account.

Bioff said Nick Schenck made a half-hearted explanation, saying the film industry was being "sandbagged by legislation" and the cash went to California legislators who wanted to be corrupted.

But Willie Bioff, the curbstone philosopher, laughed at Schenck's explanation. In court, Bioff told a jury, "These businessmen are nothing but two-bit whores with clean shirts and a shine."

Willie Bioff knew all about the uses of cash to avoid clearing money through account books which might later be audited.

Bioff said one package of cash given him by Nick Schenck in New York for transfer across the continent totaled $62,500. When he got to Hollywood he took it to Joe Schenck's house. He found Joe at the pool. Joe asked, "Did Nick take care of your traveling expenses?" Bioff shook his head. Joe peeled off five $100 bills and gave them to Bioff as a tip, "to cover the two cross-country trips you had to make."

Judge Knox asked Bioff:

Q—How many trips of this nature did you make?

A—About a dozen.

Q—In the aggregate, how much did you deliver on these occasions?

A—More than a million dollars. I arrive at that figure by taking the figures of those who have testified and adding others they forgot.

Browne and Bioff agreed that in six years from 1935 to 1940 they shook the film producers down for a total of $1,827,000. They kept one-third. Two-thirds was divided among Capone Syndicate participants.

In all this time they had occasion only once to question the accuracy of film-producer payments. Warner Brothers once sought to short-change Browne by $15,000. Browne said Bioff was busy that morning and asked him to stop by the Warner office in New York to "pick up $35,000." Browne went to the office. He said, "Major Albert Warner was not in. A girl at the switchboard handed me a package."

Browne handled such sums as casually as most men walk around with a pocketful of small change. He never looked inside the package until he stopped in Jack Dempsey's restaurant "for a corned beef on rye."

Then Browne casually thumbed through the greenbacks. He sensed something amiss. He counted the money carefully. There was only $20,000 in the package, instead of the $35,000 he had been led to expect.

Through the thirties, George Browne enjoyed theatrical extravaganzas. He promoted dozens of benefit performances at which entertainers put on shows lasting four or five hours. Although the casts read like a *Who's Who* of the American Theater, nobody ever got paid. Tickets sold at $10 or $20 apiece. The benefit was solely for George Browne.

One such cast at the Grand Opera House in Chicago at this time included Ed Wynn as master of ceremonies, Vincent Lopez, Leon Errol, Sophie Tucker and Ted Shapiro, Ben Bernie, Amos 'n Andy, Nazimova, Helen Morgan, Eddie Cheney, and Tony Carlo.

Browne always knew such events would be sellouts. Every union member was given half a dozen tickets to sell. Whether he sold them or not, he was charged for them.

The headliners at one such benefit in the Aragon Ballroom included Fanny Brice, Gypsy Rose Lee, the Ritz Brothers, Veloz & Yolanda, and Bobby Clarke.

Every penny from such benefits went to buy blooded cattle for Browne's $250,000 showplace estate of 400 acres at Woodstock, Illinois, a suburb of Chicago. Browne was sentimental about this place. He called it Col-Mar, to combine the names of his daughter, Colleen, and his wife, Marge.

The million-dollar movie shakedown might have gone on forever had not a syndicated newspaper columnist attended a Hollywood film executive's party at which Willie Morris Bioff was present.

The columnist was Westbrook Pegler. Peg had gone to work at the Hearst afternoon paper in Chicago in 1912, when his father was one of the great rewrite men of the profession. The younger Pegler frequented the pre-World War I saloon run by Mike Fritzel—the old Arsonia Café on West Madison Street—where Fritzel's girlfriend, Gilda Gray, would be hoisted to the bar so she could do her inventive shimmy dance.

Pegler, like any good newspaper reporter, had observed the prostitutes in Fritzel's and other night places as well as the pimps for whom they worked. He had covered the police courts of Chicago and remembered some of the less attractive criminals he had seen stand before the judges.

So at this Hollywood party, Pegler did a double-take at a man he saw across a wide room. The man was handsomely turned out in Hollywood style. He was beautifully trimmed. His outstanding feature was his eyes, hard as glass, which seemed never to smile despite the ready laugh on his lips.

Pegler searched his memory, then sought out his host. "Is that man's name Bioff?" The host replied, "Yes, one of our most illustrious citizens. Do you care to shake hands with him?" Peg replied, "Not without gloves."

Pegler watched Bioff and then, as though it were an old movie being shown in his head, his memory took him back to a time when Willie Bioff was regaling several fellow pimps in the Arsonia bar on his technique for "keeping my girls in line."

Pegler remembered other things as he watched the prospering Bioff, whom he had not seen for nearly twenty years. Pegler left the party with a plan in mind. Next day he went to Los Angeles police headquarters and talked to some of the old-timers among the detectives. He found one or two who had worked in Chicago at the time of World War I. They remembered a Willie Bioff who had been arrested for beating up whores but had not connected him in their minds with the Hollywood labor leader.

Pegler returned East, stopping off in Chicago. He looked up Police Lieutenant Make Mills of the labor detail. Mills, the Russian-born cop who knew where all the bodies were buried, remembered Bioff well. He and Bioff had spoken Russian and Yiddish to each other, although Mills had no use for the panderer.

Mills and Pegler together looked through the old police records. They found an "open" conviction in Bioff's dossier. Bioff had served several

brief terms but his record showed one conviction, with a six-month jail
sentence, for which he never had been apprehended.

Bioff owed the state of Illinois six months for slugging a whore.

Pegler knew in that moment that he would one day see the West Coast
labor statesman put away in a cell in the Cook County jail.

Pegler and Lieutenant Mills talked further about labor matters. Make
Mills was a good cop. Like most such cops at the working level, he knew
just about everything that happened on his beat. And Make Mills' beat
for years had been labor unions and all that pertains to them.

Make Mills told Pegler he knew, just as surely as if he had been
present, that Tommy Maloy was killed with the prior knowledge of
George Browne. He had seen how smoothly George Browne took over
Maloy's union after the latter's death.

Mills had known what was going on when the movie projectionists
threatened strikes. He made it his business to learn that the strike threats
had been called off without any change in the wages, hours, or working
conditions of the operators. To Make Mills, that spelled payoff. George
Browne and Willie Bioff were the obvious recipients.

Mills and Pegler talked of other things. When Pegler left Chicago he
went to New York and looked up policemen recommended by Make
Mills. He learned more of what was going on. Then he returned to Los
Angeles, convinced he was on the trail of something big in the way of
labor news. He learned how Willie Bioff had muscled in and taken
control of 35,000 union workers who previously had been paying their
dues to other AFL international unions.

Having finished enough legwork, Pegler was ready to start writing.

Now he launched a series of newspaper columns, citing dates, names,
and places, to show that much of union labor was in the hands of
racketeers. He demanded that Willie Bioff leave his kidney-shaped
swimming pool in Hollywood and return to Chicago to serve six months
for beating up whores. He demanded that Bioff give up the Caribbean
cruises to which he and his family were addicted until he had paid his
debt to the state of Illinois.

Pegler recalled George Browne as a simple labor slugger. He pointed
to Browne's quick rise to the status and life of a country squire after the
untimely passing of Tommy Maloy.

Pegler pointed out that no union whose members have a voice in their
own destiny will return to office year after year the same officers. Others
will inevitably come along equally competent and in whom members
have equal confidence. Pegler cited as an axiom: The union leader in
office five years or more is inevitably corrupt.

The Capone Syndicate sought to hit back at Pegler. Similar crime
syndicates in every major city in the country sought to round up support

for Syndicate union stooges under Pegler's fire. The film industry, the newspaper industry, the preachers and the teachers and the entire "liberal" establishment was called on to repay promissory notes owed the underworld.

Suddenly the radio commentators and the preachers and the "liberal" columnists in the press were labeling Pegler as antilabor. The Communist press took the lead in carrying the ball for the Syndicate in this mass smear. The *Daily Worker* on the East Coast, the *Daily World* on the West Coast, the *Midwest Daily Record* in Chicago blasted Pegler every day. The *New Masses* carried articles and cartoons blasting Pegler every week. Some newspaper publishers canceled their contracts with Pegler's agents.

Mrs. Eleanor Roosevelt in her daily newspaper column and in her almost daily speeches called Pegler reactionary. Pegler responded by citing the unsavory characters of some of the labor leaders and lesser lights who had entrée to the White House during the Roosevelt occupancy.

But meanwhile Pegler never lost sight of his central theme: Willie Bioff, the respected labor statesman, owed the state of Illinois six months of his life because he had been found guilty of beating up whores.

George E. Browne, in a union convention, defended those actions of "my friend and yours, Willie Morris Bioff," as "youthful indiscretions which should be forgiven." But nobody ever tried to deny the police and court records of that 1920 conviction against Bioff.

Finally Bioff had to leave his wife and seven children in Hollywood. He had to return to Chicago to enter the House of Correction on April 8, 1940, twenty years after the original conviction. He was released on September 20, 1940. While in jail, Bioff was given "a private office and a tub of iced beer renewed each day." Bioff and Browne had been buying Chicago politicians for many years and knew how to demand favors.

Pegler's constant digging on the Bioff issue began to disclose to him a pattern. He saw emerging a story of the Capone Syndicate muscling into many different unions to grab the union treasuries, gouge the members for dues, and shake down the employers in the industry. Pegler slowly sensed and followed the trail which led to exposure of the nationwide crime-syndicate conspiracy. This was long before any law enforcement agency at any level had indicated awareness of what was going on.

Pegler did not dig up all the facts himself. He did not have to. Union members across the country, feeling they had a champion whom they could trust, began writing him letters giving him leads. Sometimes they were able to tell him the whole story. Pegler could and did check out every lead before running it in his daily column.

Honest cops in many towns took the same path as union members.

They wrote or phoned Pegler, often with anonymous tips, giving him facts needed to round out some story on which he was working. One story led to another. Pegler never set out to make a career exposing thievery but there was so much of it and it was left so completely untouched by anyone else in the field that he seemed to harp on the subject interminably.

Agents of the Internal Revenue Service began turning to Pegler's column every day for new leads against tax evasions by men in their own communities. And that was the way the federal agents took up the trail which was to lead to indictment and conviction of several top men in the Capone Syndicate.

Browne and Bioff were indicted six months after Bioff got out of jail in Chicago.

When Bioff entered jail he publicly announced that he was resigning from the union because Pegler's attacks had destroyed much of his value "to the cause of union labor." Browne later testified in court: "Willie did not really resign. We agreed that he would not keep up his public affiliation with the union but that privately he would keep acting in the same capacity. His salary would not stop. We even voted him an extra year's pay when he entered jail."

Boris Kostelanetz, the special assistant United States Attorney who questioned Browne in court on October 28, 1943, asked:

Q—Did Bioff, when you visited him in jail, tell you of any other visitor he had had?

A—Yes. He said Louis (Little New York) Campagna had visited him. Willie told Campagna he was resigning.

Q—What did Bioff tell you Campagna answered to this?

A—Willie said Campagna told him, "Whoever quits us, quits feet first."

Kostelanetz drew from Browne, in Bioff's presence in court, the story of Bioff's trial before an underworld kangaroo court.

Browne said that once when Bioff was suspected of "going into business for himself" he was the defendant in a full-dress trial in which his life hung in the balance.

Browne said the vaudeville performers' union, called the Artists and Actors Association of America, then was headed by Ralph Whitehead. Its parent international under the AFL was Actors' Equity. Whitehead felt the Actors' Equity was trying to oust him from the presidency of the AAAA. So Whitehead went to Browne to ask if, in case Actors' Equity threw him out, the IATSE would issue a special charter for his union. Browne said, "Whitehead told me he was sure he could bring most of his members with him into the IATSE. Of course this meant we would collect dues and assessments on them. Whitehead said he was prepared to discuss an equitable split."

Browne took the case up with Nick Circella, his constant companion. Circella himself saw no value in the proposal. But Circella checked with the Capone Syndicate leaders in Chicago and Frank Nitti thought it a good idea.

Browne said that even before mentioning Whitehead's proposal to Circella he had taken it up with Joseph Padway, legal counsel for the AFL. Padway discussed it with William Green, then president of the AFL. Green approved. Just to make sure, Browne double-checked Padway's report with Green's secretary.

Now that the AFL was in favor of it, and the Capone Syndicate was in favor of it, Browne phoned Bioff on the West Coast to tell him about it. Bioff opposed issuance of a charter. And at that time, Bioff's personality was so much stronger than George Browne's that the latter feared to stand up against him.

No charter was issued.

A few days later, Browne continued in his testimony, Nick Circella phoned from Chicago. Circella told Browne, "George, go ahead. My people would like to get hold of that union."

The nationwide crime syndicates then controlled most of the nightclubs and cabarets across the country. They had to hire vaudeville and variety artists. If the Syndicate owned the union as well as the cabarets, the bargaining would be much easier. Browne understood this but he hesitated. Circella said he would come East and they could talk about it.

They met in the Robert Treat Hotel in Newark, across the river from New York City. Circella handed Browne a fountain pen and Browne signed the charter as demanded. Then he called Willie Bioff to tell him what he had done. Bioff became angry at the idea of Browne completely disregarding his counsel. Browne testified, "Willie was shouting at me over the phone from Hollywood, Telling me, 'Revoke that charter!'

"Circella was standing right next to me hollering, 'Don't do it! Don't do it!'

"I was in a bad position. I began to sweat. Finally I handed Circella the phone and said, 'Here Nick, you take over.' But he wouldn't. Nick was so burned up at Bioff he refused to talk to him.

"So I took the phone again and told Willie, 'Calm down. I'll revoke the charter.'"

That opposition to Capone Syndicate orders nearly cost Bioff his life. Bioff's testimony bore out Browne's in every particular. When he took the witness stand, Bioff said under oath that a few nights after this incident he got a call in Hollywood from Paul Ricca in Chicago.

Ricca told Bioff to drop whatever he was doing in Hollywood and catch the first plane for Chicago. Ricca told Bioff, "You're in trouble. But good."

Bioff said that when he reached Chicago he went direct to the Bismarck Hotel, to Frank Nitti's suite. He testified: "Soon De Lucia [Ricca] came in. He said he came early to warn me."

Then came Nitti, Charles Gioe, Louis Campagna, and the others. All were grim-faced. There was no laughter or greeting. Nitti waited until all were seated, then he spoke. "Bioff, you been trying to muscle in. You think you're going to run things for yourself. You're trying to put yourself in front of George Browne. You're trying to take personal charge of this vaudeville actors' union and its treasury and its dues. You're just headed for a hearse."

Bioff recognized that he was hearing a death sentence from which there could be no appeal. But he was saved by Paul Ricca, who took the floor and said, "From now on, Charlie Gioe will run this actors' union. Now let's hear no more about it."

This was in 1939. Both Browne and Bioff agreed that it seems to have marked the definite emergence of Paul Ricca's power at the top of the Syndicate. With those words, Ricca stepped out as Nitti's successor as the head of the Capone hierarchy. Power gravitates to the man strong enough to take it and hold it. Strength of personality is all-important. Ricca's personality won the approval of those present. Nitti from that time on was in second place.

A little more than a year after he got out of jail in Chicago, Bioff was on trial in a federal court in New York charged with the film-industry extortion. This was on October 25, 1941. Bioff's co-defendant was George Browne. Both were found guilty and sentenced.

Browne and Bioff sought leniency by offering to discuss the part played in the extortion plot by the Capone Syndicate leaders. Both appeared as state's witnesses before the federal grand jury in New York which sought to link Nitti and the others to the plot. One of the other witnesses before this grand jury was Lou Greenberg, who had been Nitti's partner in various illegal enterprises as far back as 1910.

The federal grand jury on March 18, 1943, returned indictments naming most of the top members of the Capone group who participated in the shakedown. Among those named was Nitti.

The night the indictments were returned in New York, the little group which had met so often at Nitti's home in Riverside, the Chicago suburb, met once again. News of the indictments was on the radio. None of the little group was happy about the news.

Ricca took control of the meeting at once. He said to Nitti, "Frank, you brought Browne and Bioff to us. You masterminded this whole thing and it went sour. There is no point in all of us going over the road. Remember how Al Capone took the fall for all of us and went on trial alone? That's the way we ought to do it now. Frank, you can plead guilty and we'll take care of things till you get out."

Nitti said, "This is not that kind of case, Paul. This is a conspiracy indictment. Nobody can take the fall for the rest of us in this one. We all have to stick together and try to beat it."

Ricca lost his temper. Harsh words were flung back and forth. The dozen or so men present kept still as the two leaders slugged it out verbally. Ricca was white-faced and panting when he finally said, "Frank, you're asking for it."

There was dead silence after this statement. Nitti looked around the room for support and found none. Each of his erstwhile friends in turn looked away. Nitti realized that Ricca had supplanted him completely as head of "the family" in Chicago.

When Nitti saw the stony faces of these men, with whom he had broken bread for thirty years or more, he considered for a long moment. Then he rose to go and open his front door. It was a wintry March night in Chicago and there was snow on the ground. Nitti said not a word. The fact that he had opened the door to his guests, indicating that he wanted them to leave, was a breach of the Sicilian peasant rules of hospitality in which they had all been reared.

Nitti thus threw down the gauntlet to Ricca and his fellows.

The embarrassed group got up, gathered hats and coats, and went out into the night.

Nitti, who had been born Nitto, outside of Palermo, was fifty-eight years old. He was a small man, diminutive even, but a general in the army of racketeers. Nitti's steps the next day took him along the Illinois Central railroad right-of-way across a prairie in suburban Riverside. There was a drizzling rain falling.

At least two persons halted their work when they saw him, wondering what this well-dressed little man was doing walking along the railroad tracks in the rain. One of these witnesses was a matron at the Municipal Tuberculosis Sanitarium, adjacent to the right of way. The other was the engineer of a freight train which had come to a momentary stop while switching cars.

Thus there were two witnesses able to swear to Nitti's suicide. They saw him draw a pistol from his pocket, about 2 o'clock in the afternoon of March 19, 1943, and shoot himself. Nitti was dead when police reached him.

Nitti's companions in the shakedown were brought to a trial which lasted seventy-three days. It ended with verdicts of guilty on December 23, 1943, in the midst of World War II. Two weeks later, on January 5, 1944, Federal District Judge John C. Bright of New York City read the sentences.

Paul Ricca was to go to prison for ten years and pay a $10,000 fine. Identical sentences were read for Louis Campagna, Philip d'Andrea, and Charles Gioe.

Identical sentences were read for Francis Maritote and John Roselli.

All appealed. The convictions and sentences were upheld in the United States Court of Appeals. All went to prison.

They were to be eligible for parole after one-third of their time had been served. This eligibility was contingent on good behavior, payment of all their fines, settlement of all their tax obligations, and release or settlement of any pending criminal charges.

Three of the defendants at the time were under indictment for mail fraud.

Ricca felt betrayed by the prison sentence. He had been to prison before and he would go to prison again but he never got over feeling that in this case Frank Nitti should have taken the fall for all of them. Ricca had been twice a murderer before he ever left his native Italy. He had falsified information on his application for citizenship, had been in the United States illegally for years, had paid and paid and paid to politicians in Europe and in America. Experience had taught him that if he was ever generous in paying politicians, nothing really bad could ever happen to him. And now here he was in prison.

His lawyers tried to explain to him that politicians are limited in what they can do, even if they have been on underworld payrolls for years. Judges can be bought, United States Senators can be bought, even people in the White House can be bought. But all are powerless when a syndicated news columnist such as Pegler keeps the searchlight turned on a single case such as the film-industry extortions.

Ricca told his lawyers what to do about Pegler. His lawyers tried to convince him that if Pegler were publicly murdered he would become a martyr and public opinion would be such that Ricca and the others could not be paroled in the minimum time.

This was the argument that clinched it for Ricca. He wanted details. His lawyers told him that while technically he could be freed after serving one-third of his ten-year sentence—that is, at the end of three years and four months—the fact was that a parole usually took from six months to a year longer than that.

The lawyers said that nobody in history ever got out of prison on the very day he became eligible for parole. Usually his petition for parole came before the parole board at its first public meeting following the date on which he became eligible. If the petition were granted in minimum time, the prisoner might still serve several months beyond the date on which theoretically he could have walked out of prison.

Ricca heard the lawyers out. Then he is reported to have asked, in the broken English which he never overcame, "Who is the head man, the one who finally has to okay the parole?"

Ricca's lawyers are said to have given him the names of members of the federal parole board, together with the name of the chairman who would probably consider the petition of the Chicago gangsters.

The Congressmen who later investigated the parole and all its ramifications said that they were told Ricca persisted in asking his lawyers questions. He wanted to know how parole board members were appointed.

Ricca is said finally to have drawn from his lawyers the fact that the ultimate authority for such paroles rested with the Attorney General of the United States. Then Ricca, lifelong master of the fix, is said to have told his lawyers, in effect: "That man must want something: money, favors, a seat in the Supreme Court. Find out what he wants and get it for him."

Ricca's lawyers were far less confident than he was. But they said they would try. The proof of the pudding was in the eating. They tried—and they succeeded.

Three years and four months after entering prison, within thirty seconds of the first minute at which they could legally be released, Ricca and the others walked out of prison.

It had never happened before in history, but it happened this time.

And sure enough, President Harry S. Truman appointed Tom C. Clark, who approved all the steps to quick parole for the four men, to the very next opening on the Supreme Court bench.

Before the paroles could be granted, huge income tax claims had to be settled for Ricca and Campagna. Their fines had to be paid for all four of the prisoners. There were mail fraud indictments pending against Ricca, Campagna, and Gioe. Those indictments had to be voided personally by Tom C. Clark, Attorney General of the United States, before a parole could be considered.

While Ricca and the others were in custody they were in Leavenworth. They were regularly visited there by Tony Accardo, Ricca's nominee as executive director pro tem for the Capone Syndicate. Obviously,

Accardo could not walk up to the front gates of Leavenworth and demand to see Ricca so he might consult with him on management problems of the criminal underworld. Accardo needed a disguise.

The disguise which he affected was that of attorney-at-law. The only props he needed were an attaché case and a gray flannel suit. Accardo signed in and out of the prison with the name of Ricca's real lawyer, Attorney Joseph I. Burger (born Giuseppe Imburgio).

Every time Accardo went to the prison he was accompanied by Eugene Bernstein of Chicago, a Twenty-fourth Ward lawyer and tax expert who had once entertained the literati at the Dill Pickle club as an amateur hypnotist.

Accardo and Bernstein eventually were taken to task by Chicago authorities for misrepresenting themselves during their visits to Paul Ricca. But anyone who has read this far knows that nothing came of it. Accardo to this day has never stayed overnight in a cell. He is the only man in the Capone Syndicate revered by underlings as "just as smart" as Al Capone himself. And one of Accardo's sycophants even went so far as to say, "Tony Accardo has more brains before breakfast than Al Capone ever had all day." Accardo and Bernstein went free.

The first step toward getting the paroles for Ricca and the others was to satisfy the income tax claims against Ricca and Campagna. A total of $600,000 was supposed to be paid. Bernstein settled the claims for a paltry $128,000. When asked later in court where he got the cash, Bernstein said, "Men came to my office, strangers to me, bringing sheafs of bank notes. They would throw a roll of bills on my desk and say, 'This is for Paul,' or, 'This is for Louie.' Pretty soon I had enough money."

Bernstein was asked if he knew any of the men who came to his office. He swore he had never seen any of them before or since. He said, "You don't ask such men their business."

So the $600,000 in income tax claims were settled on November 1, 1946.

Even before this, the federal parole board had been presented the cases of Ricca, Campagna, Gioe, and d'Andrea on January 16, 1945. This was the first time the parole board met after the quartet entered prison.

Presumably the minutes of meetings of the federal parole board are matters of public record. Not in this case. Those minutes could not even be subpoenaed by the Congress of the United States. Nobody representing the people of the United States has been able to this day, a generation later, to find out exactly how Paul Ricca worked it.

After the income tax claims were settled, the mail fraud indictments had to be vacated. For the income tax claims the Syndicate had employed Bernstein, the Democratic politician. As Al Capone always said, "Don't look for a smart lawyer, but for a lawyer with political clout." For the mail fraud indictments, the Syndicate leaders approached a friend of Attorney General Tom Clark. This was Maury Hughes of Dallas. Hughes later acknowledged he had been paid $15,000 for his services. He described the services: "I represented these men in the federal court of New York. Some charges were hanging. I demanded they be tried or dismissed. They were dismissed."

With the mail fraud indictments out of the way, the next step was the parole board.

The "lawyer with political clout" in this instance was Paul Dillon of St. Louis. Dillon had been financial manager of the campaign of President Truman in the St. Louis area. Dillon's man, Truman, was sitting in the White House at the time. Dillon represented the men seeking paroles.

Ricca and the others walked out of prison on August 13, 1947.

Two years later the first seat on the Supreme Court bench opened up. Truman nominated Tom Clark and the generous Attorney General donned the long black robes of an Associate Justice on October 3, 1949.

It may be done differently in the Soviet Union, but that's the way it is done in a democracy.

This scandal of the entire government of the United States being thus turned upside down to free four of the most notorious gangsters in the nation brought about a Congressional investigation. But no matter how the Congressmen tried, they could not get to see the minutes of the meetings of the federal parole board. No matter how the Congressmen tried, they could not get answers to their questions from any of the public officials involved.

Two of the Congressmen on the investigating committee, Clare Hoffman of Michigan and Fred Busbey of Illinois, said publicly that Tom C. Clark, then Attorney General of the United States, "did not tell all he knew."

The Chicago *Tribune* on January 30, 1952, spoke editorially of "Mr. Clark's utter unfitness for any position of public responsibility and especially for a position on the Supreme Court bench." The newspaper called for his impeachment for his part in the early paroles granted the Capone Syndicate leaders. The editorial went on: "We have been sure of [Clark's] unfitness ever since he played his considerable role in releasing the four Capone gangsters after they had served the bare minimum of their terms."

Just as in the British Empire there is a tradition that the royal family is immune from criticism, so until just recently in the United States, tradition has prevented linking the name of the President with criminals.

The Congressional committee which investigated the paroles used the term "big money" in speaking of expenditures to grease the skids. In the Chicago underworld the talk was then and is now that much of this big money went "into the White House" as well as into the Attorney General's office.

Since these paroles, several Congressional committees have held inquiries into syndicated and organized crime. Every six years some Senator such as Kefauver or McClellan thinks he can make political hay by appearing relentlessly to pursue the threads of crime and the criminals they lead to. Generally speaking the people who drink beer and eat popcorn in front of their TV sets think it's a pretty good show to watch.

Obviously, asking Jones to investigate the unsavory links between Jones and Smith is not likely to turn up anything derogatory to Jones. Just as obviously asking politicians to expose the links between politics and organized crime is not likely to turn up anything derogatory to politicians. But the people who move their lips when they read are not likely to figure this out.

In this story of the film industry shakedowns only the financial aspects have been explored. The shakedowns were not bloodless. The men who owned the West Coast unions did not without a fight give up their claims to huge treasuries and monthly tribute in the form of dues.

There were millions of dollars in the treasuries of the unions taken over by Willie Bioff and John Roselli. There were 35,000 members paying upward of $10 a month in the form of dues and assessments. This comes to one-third of a million dollars a month, straight income with no overhead. Murders are done for that kind of money. Four murders in 1938 helped convince film studio owners that Willie Bioff meant business.

Louis B. Mayer, who owned one of the studios and thus was of the upperworld, tried to be a holdout. He changed his mind. He later said that the boys from Chicago convinced him he would be killed before dawn unless he changed his tune.

Willie Bioff and George Browne, having turned state's evidence on their Syndicate colleagues, were freed when the others went to prison.

Browne went to his farm in Woodstock to enjoy life. Bioff sought to hide.

Bioff had the $3,000,000 or more which was his share of the $6,500,000 collected in six years through the 2 percent assessment on the earnings of union members. He had carefully stashed the money in safe deposit boxes across the nation, including one in the vault of the Harris Trust Company in Chicago.

When Bioff decided to hide, he adopted his wife's maiden name of Nelson. He called himself "Al" although he still wrote his first name as William. He and his wife settled on a luxurious little farm outside Phoenix, Arizona.

Al Nelson and his wife, Laurie, were popular in Phoenix. In 1952 they made a $5,000 contribution to the political campaign of a department store heir named Barry Goldwater.

Goldwater was then seeking a seat in the United States Senate on the Republican ticket. He won the seat, was reelected, and later ran unsuccessfully for the job of President of the United States.

Goldwater and Bioff—or Nelson as he then called himself—became good friends. Goldwater, a brigadier general in the Air Force Reserve, loved to fly. In a private plane, he chauffeured Bioff and his wife to parties all over the Southwest. In October, 1955, when Goldwater was a member of the Senate, he and Mrs. Goldwater flew Al and Laurie Nelson to Las Vegas. Then Goldwater flew the quartet back to Phoenix.

Two weeks after this trip, on November 4, 1955, Al Nelson came out of his Phoenix home and slid behind the wheel of his pickup truck. When his foot touched the starter pedal, it detonated a dynamite bomb affixed under the hood. The explosion rocked the area. Parts of Willie Bioff and his truck were strewn in every direction under the desert sun.

Exit Willie Bioff, whoremaster and stool pigeon.

23   Nick's lady love dies hard

Besides the four notorious Chicago hoodlums who were paroled in record time with permission of the Attorney General of the United States, a number of lesser men were involved in the film shakedown. The disposition of their cases was interesting.

Browne and Bioff, of course, had become witnesses for the prosecution. For this they earned whatever leniency a grateful government could grant. They were tried, convicted, and sentenced to terms of eight years and ten years respectively.

But Browne and Bioff served their sentences the easy way. Their time in custody was spent in luxurious hotels, their wives at their sides, living the lives to which they had become accustomed—but this time at the taxpayers' expense. The prosecutor told the court that without their testimony the cases against Ricca, *et al,* could never result in convictions.

Nick Circella, alias Nicky Dean, was indicted for his part in the conspiracy on September 29, 1941. He was brought to trial the following spring and pleaded guilty. By doing so he avoided taking the witness stand. Thus he did not have to testify under oath, or refuse to testify when submitted to cross-examination, as to details of the extortion scheme.

Nicky Dean was sentenced to eight years in prison. That was in April, 1942. He went behind the bars with enough money to assure preferential treatment on the part of warden and guards. Nick earned enough time off for good behavior to go free in six years. When he came out he found that the government had instituted deportation proceedings against him.

Although he had been in the United States since 1902, when he was four years old, Nick Circella had never bothered to take out naturalization papers.

Rather than be shipped to his native Italy at government expense, Nicky Dean elected to buy his own ticket—or tickets, for himself and his wife—and go to that South American paradise to which Monsignor Pat Molloy had once been exiled. Circella sailed from New Orleans on April

21, 1955, aboard the SS *Del Norte* headed for Buenos Aires. He and his wife later moved to Mexico City, the most cosmopolitan community in the Western Hemisphere.

Nick Circella, born in Naples in 1898, had started kindergarten in Chicago. He and his younger brother, August, spent their formative years learning the rules of the ghetto.

Nick became expert in the use of a paving block or baseball bat. He learned to wield a shiv and yearned for the day he could pack a gun.

Nick was not yet in his teens when he showed expertise with an ignition jumper. That was in 1909 and 1910, when most grown-ups could not even drive an automobile. Nick Circella somehow learned not only to drive any car made, but to steal any car left unattended on the streets of Chicago. He was a handy youngster. By the time he was fifteen he had realized his ambition to pack a gun and was convicted on a charge of robbery with a firearm.

For the next ten years he was constantly in and out of jail or prison, always on the same charge: robbery with a gun. Nick Circella simply loved to fondle a short gun, pistol or revolver, and was constantly in trouble because of his passion.

One of his earliest companions was Frankie Rio, a bright young hoodlum in his own right although he was later to be overshadowed by his more famous cousin, Al Capone. Frankie Rio always tried to convince Nicky Dean—as the young gunman by now was calling himself—that revolvers were for cowboys. Rio told Nicky that the future for bright young men of the criminal persuasion lay in the field of labor relations. Nicky Dean later quoted Frankie Rio: "No gun was ever a substitute for brains. It's just as easy to make your point with a broken bottle shoved in a man's face. And the cops won't pinch you for picking up a broken bottle when you need it."

Nicky Dean was vain of looks and figure. He had regular features, a swarthy complexion, a mop of somewhat oily hair through which women of a certain type loved to run their fingers. He had a tall and slender build so that when he began earning enough money to buy good clothing he looked good in dinner jacket and Chesterfield. He became something of a dandy. And he had an undeniable appeal for light ladies looking for adventure. It was because the name Circella sounded too Italian that he adopted the alias of Dean.

Both Nick and his younger brother were attracted to the entertainment field. August got a piece of a few South State Street burlesque houses and kept them through the next couple of generations as an anchor to windward, while he picked up a spare dollar wherever he could. Nick loved the nightclubs. When he was just a wild youngster whose horizon did not extend beyond the next stickup, Nick spent all he could steal in the town's cabarets. He loved to dress up, sip bootleg booze in the semidarkness of an upholstered cellar, and make his pitch to the girls of the chorus.

Thus it was that when a few members of the Capone Syndicate pooled their money to open the Yacht Club, at 100 East Superior Street, Nicky Dean got in on the ground floor. He had a little money in the bank and was able to buy into the venture. He not only had a piece of the action but drew a salary as manager.

The Yacht Club, which later was called the Club 100, was a speakeasy in the days when Prohibition was in full flower. The place was glossy and glittering, situated on the edge of the Gold Coast, and it attracted those of the upper-income brackets who in summer could be found sailing skiffs and larger craft in Lake Michigan.

Nicky Dean owned a piece of the cabaret by the time he reached the age of thirty. The place was in the East Chicago Avenue police district, in the Forty-second Ward, a territory which throughout Chicago's history has been a paradise for smart operators. Nicky Dean took care of the cops on the beat, the sergeants in their squad cars, the district police captain and his lieutenants. He took care of the precinct captain, the ward committeeman, and the alderman. On election days he helped get out the vote for the party in power. He became a gentleman of substance.

Prohibition was long gone by the time Browne and Bioff began the local theater shakedowns which were to grow into the film-industry extortion scheme. They had known Nicky Dean as a young thief but had not realized how much he had grown up during the years of cabaret management. They permitted him to con them out of their first $65,000 and use the money to outfit and open his own swank casino across the street from the Yacht Club.

Nick called his new joint the Colony Club. It was at 744 North Rush Street.

For some years before this, Nicky Dean had owned a girl who called herself Estelle Carey. She had been born with the prosaic name of Smith, spent her childhood in an orphanage, was of high school age when she entered the working world with a job as waitress in a Logan Square restaurant. She supplemented her earnings from salary and tips by doing a little semipro work on a mattress, telling current lovers that she was short just a few dollars of enough to pay her room rent.

After Estelle learned the waitress trade in Logan Square she got a job in Rickett's restaurant at 2727 North Clark Street. She quickly picked up enough about serving a higher-class clientele so that she could move up to the job of hostess at the White Horse Inn.

Estelle was working there, at the age of twenty-one in 1930, when glamour walked into her life in the person of Nicky Dean. Nick was then thirty-two. They became lovers, but that is never enough for an underworld dandy. The men of the underworld might well be considered the patron saints of the Women's Liberation Movement, for they were among the first to put the fair sex on an equal plane as far as working for a living is concerned.

Nicky Dean put Estelle Carey to work in the Yacht Club as a hostess.

Estelle was attractive, pleasant, smart, thrifty—and young. She was twenty-one, but might have been thought five years younger. All Nicky Dean's friends wanted to try out his new girl and he shared Estelle with anyone whose friendship or favor he sought. So long as it did not interfere with her work as a hostess in the speakeasy.

Estelle got along from the first with Henry "Sonny" Goldstone, the floor manager in the club. Goldstone was a gambler by profession and the man out front in operation of the club. Nicky Dean was always on the premises, keeping track of the income and making sure purveyors gave honest weight and good-quality merchandise, but he ran things from behind the scenes. To the public he was simply a guest. Goldstone smiled at the patrons, accepted the compliments, handled drunks when they felt cheated, and patted the rounded buttocks of such girls as Estelle Carey.

Estelle's duties from the first included operating the "26" game. This was a dice board about three feet square at which customers were encouraged to "throw for the drinks." A pretty girl such as Estelle could keep drunks entertained at this simple game for an hour, during which they might drop any amount from ten dollars up. The profits for the house were greater than on drinks sold in an equal amount of time.

Estelle was adept at running the 26 game and keeping players happy.

The customer could play for a quarter. He put down his 25-cent piece, picked up the leather cup to shake the dice, then rolled them out in hopes of reaching the magic score of 26. If he did so, he won a brass check entitling him to a dollar's worth of drinks at the bar. But there were tricks to the game as Estelle Carey played it.

The whole idea was to keep the customer drinking and playing, spending the evening on the premises and coming back night after night. The customer was made to feel a part of things in this bar, made to feel that he had found a home away from home. He would come back when he could, spend whatever money he could afford, encourage his friends to join him in the pleasant atmosphere of the club. There is an Estelle Carey in every successful bar in the world.

Estelle proved such a good come-on girl that when Nicky Dean was able to open the Colony Club across the street she was put in charge of several 26 games, each operated by an attractive girl. Estelle taught the girls how to handle customers to build up repeat trade.

The Colony Club had a bar and restaurant on the first floor, the dance floor in conjunction with the restaurant. The casino was on the second floor. The third floor consisted of offices, with a couple of bedroom-and-bath suites for the use of Syndicate leaders who wanted to stay overnight. There was also a single great conference room.

The basement was storehouse for supplies and for the tools of the maintenance crew.

Goldstone hired the help and managed the kitchen and restaurant. Estelle hired and trained the 26 girls. Nicky Dean personally ran the casino, as well as keeping track of the entire day-to-day operation.

While the 26 game was played openly, since there was nothing illegal about this method of selling drinks, the girls were encouraged to send players "upstairs for some real action" when any drunk indicated a compulsion to gamble. The girls got a bonus for every customer they could direct to the roulette, craps, or blackjack table.

The action on the second floor, of course, was against the law. Nicky Dean kept up his payments to the police and politicians so he could operate.

The girls under Estelle Carey's direction were sometimes available to players at whatever price the traffic would bear. On a dull night a girl might be taken to one of the third-floor suites for $50. On a busy night the same girl might cost $100. On her day off, if a man met her at the beach or in another bar, he could have her for ten.

Nicky Dean was generous in his praise of Estelle's qualities. He called her "the best money-girl in the country" and told his friends, "I once saw her steer an oil man from Tulsa to the tables. He lost ten grand in an hour. She kept him happy all the time and after that whenever he came to Chicago he wanted Estelle."

Miss Estelle Carey was living at 40 East Oak Street on September 29, 1941, when the federal grand jury in New York City indicted Nick Circella for his part in the extortion conspiracy. Nick was told of the indictment by a long-distance call from a Capone lawyer in Manhattan. He called Estelle and in fifteen minutes the two of them were on their way to a safe hiding place.

Estelle permitted her hair to grow out to its natural shade of dishwater blond and Nick Circella shed his finery of dress for clothing more suitable to a workingman. They put the glamorous life behind them and holed up quietly in a suburban roadhouse called Shorty's Place, at 147th Street and Cicero Avenue. Neither of them enjoyed the change.

Two months later, on December 1, 1941, Nicky Dean was arrested at Shorty's Place by agents of the FBI. He was flown to New York that same day, just six days before the Japanese bombed Pearl Harbor and brought the United States into World War II.

Obviously someone had tipped off the FBI to Dean's hideout.

Since Nicky Dean was a member of the Syndicate, even if he occupied only a minor position in the hierarchy, he was entitled to protection against such a sellout. A kangaroo court was convened and Estelle Carey was found guilty of putting the law on Nicky's trail.

There is no appeal from that type of court. Estelle's career was coming to an end. Nicky Dean, from New York, asked his colleagues to hold off for a while. But after he had been in prison for a year the boys saw no reason for further delay. They went after Estelle Carey.

By that time she had taken an apartment at 512 West Addison Street. The execution squad found her there on February 2, 1943. Their interest in her was not solely revenge. They had an interest as well in the location of nearly a million dollars in currency which Nicky Dean was assumed to have left in Estelle's care.

So, before Estelle died, she was urged to disclose the hiding place.

The interrogators used an ice pick, a knife, and brass knuckles. No medical examiner afterward was able to figure out in just which order Estelle's nose was broken, several of her teeth had been knocked out, her head was a mass of welts and bruises, while across her throat was a superficial cut made with an extremely sharp knife or a razor.

When she died, Estelle Carey was naked except for a red housecoat. She was known to sleep without pajamas or nightgown, so it was assumed by police that she had been awakened while sleeping late and had gone to the door with the housecoat for covering. The housecoat had been soaked by her killers with lighter fluid and then set aflame.

If they wanted to keep her alive for future questioning, they made a mistake in setting the housecoat afire. Estelle died from suffocation as she burned hands and arms trying to put out the flames. The coroner's physician said her heart stopped as a result of shock and suffocation.

Estelle apparently went to her grave without disclosing the hiding place of any money. This may have been out of loyalty to Nicky Dean. Or it may have been her selfish refusal to give up what she had come to consider her own stake. Or she may not have known of any money.

Exit Nicky Dean and one of the party girls who occasionally get mixed up with leaders of the Capone Syndicate.

24 "The cleanest little city . . ."

Jackson made only one move to flee when the enforcer poked the sawed-off shotgun in his belly. Then the other three moved in with blackjacks ready to swing.

William (Action) Jackson realized he had no choice. He had been to many such parties before but somebody else had always been the guest of honor. Jackson's eyes rolled in fear, showing a lot of white. Sweat broke out on his forehead, despite the basement's air conditioning.

Jackson kept muttering, "Wait a minute. Now, wait a minute." But he did not really struggle as they slipped handcuffs on his wrists. He was passive as they drew his ankles together for the tie rope.

The three who were witnesses later said they could actually feel the big man trembling, his entire body shivering as though with chill, as they lifted his 300-pound bulk. The vanadium steel chain between the cuffs was linked over a meat hook permanently mounted on a steel I-beam in the ceiling. That meat hook, in the spacious meat refrigeration room, is seven feet above the basement floor.

Jackson swung with his feet in the air.

A moaning sound came from Jackson's thick lips as his tremendous bulk forced the handcuff bands to cut into his wrists. The sound was muted as the enforcer tied a rag around his mouth as a gag. Jackson seemed resigned to what was to come.

But when the enforcer used a razor to cut the clothing off Jackson's swinging body, and when that clothing fell to the floor and left him naked, the big man's fear caused him to lose control in every way.

His bodily secretions poured out. The three who were watching later said, "You never smelled such a stink."

Jackson, a huge mountain of muscle, began to twitch and twist and jerk. He was supposed to be the toughest collector on the Chicago loan-shark circuit. There was nothing tough about Action Jackson now. The witnesses, who later were instructed by their masters to talk freely about it, said that Jackson whimpered through his gag each time the enforcer pounded on his testicles with a baseball bat.

The gag held the noise to a minimum. The scene took place beneath a suburban gambling casino and no one wanted to disturb the players above, nor the gentlemen and ladies enjoying their late dinners in the restaurant section. Jackson's torture chamber was the cooling room used for the aging of sides of beef.

The baseball bat, swung repeatedly against his thighs and lower abdomen, reduced Jackson to the animal level at which consciousness is gone but the body still flinches involuntarily away from pain. More urine and feces continued to drop from the naked body as it swung in the air.

The enforcer laid aside the baseball bat and reached for a lighted blowtorch with a humming yellow flame. A quick adjustment of the air pump turned this flame to a hissing blue. Jackson retained enough consciousness to seek to jerk his body back from the torch. Even the hardened witnesses were sickened as the enforcer burned out both of Jackson's eyes.

Jackson may still have retained a shred of consciousness as the enforcer picked up his straight razor to slice two or three slabs of meat off Jackson's heavy hips. Then the razor was used to slash and chop at the victim's abdomen. A knife was plunged into the abdomen three or four times. Sometime during this cutting and stabbing the body ceased to jerk. A coroner's physician later said, "Jackson died of shock. His heart showed he suffered a massive fatal coronary."

At this point the musclemen took photographs of the black shell which once had been a man. Pictures were made with flashbulbs from many angles. They highlighted every mutilation. Hundreds of glossy prints were later made and carried by underworld lackeys to be shown as widely as possible. Action Jackson's fate was meant to serve as an object lesson to others who might get out of line.

The lesson was clear: No thief steals in Cicero!

Jackson's body was finally lifted down. Handcuffs and gag and tie rope were removed. The body was stuffed in the trunk of Jackson's green Cadillac and the car was driven to downtown Chicago. It was parked where it would sooner or later attract attention, abandoned on the lower level of Wacker Drive at Wells Street.

A flat tire on the parked car caught the attention of Patrolman George Petyo on August 11, 1961. Petyo testified at the inquest, "I halted my squad car to investigate. As I walked toward that Cadillac in the heat of the August day the smell almost knocked me down. I called my sergeant."

The medical examiner said Jackson's body had been decomposing for three or four days.

The Capone Syndicate killers could have disposed of the body in quicklime. They could have buried it, as so many others are buried each year, in the limitless prairies surrounding Chicago. They could have poured cement over it and used it as a building block in the construction jobs about the city. They could have wrapped it in heavy chains and dropped it over the side of a motor launch ten miles out in Lake Michigan. But they wanted that body found. Jackson's death by torture was to be told and retold to drive the lesson home: "Nobody steals in Cicero!"

Chicago police detectives told the coroner's jury of Jackson's background. He had once been a fighter. He knew how to put his heavy shoulders behind a few punches to the midriff so as to leave a victim sick for days. He was employed as a collector for the Parr Finance Company at $125 a week and expenses.

The police said that Jackson had been a lifelong thief. Veteran of a hundred street fights, he was picked up by "the sporting element" and given a chance to go three rounds in the Saturday-night preliminaries for $20 or so. That was when boxing was a popular sport. Jackson's heroic size made him a good drawing card.

When twenty years old, with a youthful police record of petty crimes, Jackson was sent to prison in Green Bay, Wisconsin. Assault and battery. At twenty-eight he went to prison in Joliet. Robbery.

When killed, at the age of forty, Action Jackson was under federal indictment in Illinois, charged with hijacking $70,000 worth of electrical appliances in his hometown of Cicero.

That little city of Cicero, entirely surrounded by the larger city of Chicago, has few black residents. Jackson was one of them. With his wife, Marion, he lived at 1215 South Forty-ninth Street.

While Cicero is a city of decent and thrifty families, most of whom are homeowners, it has its share of industry. But it is known to the people of Chicago and to tourists principally for the gambling layouts and quiet brothels along "the Strip" on Cermak Road. The good citizens of Cicero raise their children to avoid that part of town.

Between the good law-abiding citizens of Cicero and the Syndicate which governs the city there is a tacit agreement: The citizens will close their eyes to prostitution and gambling along the Strip and in return they will be assured a city totally free of other types of crime.

When the federal grand jury charged Action Jackson with theft from one of Cicero's leading industries, a dealer in a Cermak Road poker game commented, "A son of a bitch like Jackson could get these Bohunks and Polacks out here so riled up they might run us all out of town. Or string some of us up to the nearest telegraph poles."

Cicero is not especially a city of immigrants, but most of its residents are Czechs, Bohemians, and second-generation descendants of other Eastern European peoples. They know from experience in the old country that a force such as the Capone Syndicate cannot be fought or ousted. They know that police and politicians can be bought and there is little the ordinary citizen can do about it. They accept Ali Baba and the Forty Thieves as a fact of nature but they want their children to be safe on the streets in front of their homes.

The Syndicate made of Action Jackson's death a public spectacle. The purpose was to reassure the people of Cicero, in particular the important business and industrial interests of the community, that lives and property are safe under Syndicate protection. A secondary purpose was to serve notice on the underworld that crime in the Capone Syndicate's own city simply will not be tolerated.

The truck hijacking took place April 13, 1961. The truck, laden with electrical appliances, was driven away from a Cicero loading dock. The city of Cicero is so free of such incidents that trucks are left unguarded every night at every loading dock in town.

Every stool pigeon and tipster in the Midwest underworld was alerted. Turn up those hijackers, and fast, the tipsters were told. The underworld buzzed with rumors of substantial cash rewards, as well as the goodwill of Syndicate bosses. With that kind of organization, the hijackers were quickly caught.

Jackson's companions testified before the grand jury. They named Jackson as the ringleader in the theft. They said he had compelled them to unload the loot. The theft took place in mid-April and even with the delays in federal law enforcement the indictment was returned by mid-summer. Jackson's trial was scheduled before Federal Judge Bernard M. Decker.

But the indictment was not a week old when Jackson was killed. Underworld justice is not subject to upperworld delays.

No policeman or newspaperman speculated publicly as to the reason for Jackson's death. All those who followed Syndicate affairs with consistency knew why Jackson was killed. But Chicago is so self-conscious about having been the stamping ground of Al Capone that police may not talk publicly and newspapermen may not write about such things as deals between the upperworld and the underworld.

Some speculated that he might have gone into business for himself as a moneylender without getting a Syndicate okay. Mrs. June Boniakowski, a blond waitress of twenty-eight, said that he was a loan-shark operator in his own right and that she had helped finance his entry into the business. Her testimony told of excellent profits: "I lent Jackson thirteen hundred dollars to put out at interest in multiples of five dollars.

He quickly returned to me my entire capital investment. From then on he paid me fifty dollars a week. I was pleased with the arrangement."

This was the public speculation. In private, the police and the newspapermen agreed as to the real reason for Jackson's dramatic exit.

The Syndicate in Chicago and its environs has about a dozen men who could roughly be classified as the council or board of directors. Under them, there are about 300 men in supervisory capacities of one kind or another. Under them there are about 3,000 who have some vague connection with the Syndicate, even if it is only as a lowly scratch-sheet peddler or numbers runner or whorehouse towel boy. These 3,000 or so count for nothing except as votes on election day.

The Syndicate's board of directors, and those who work closest with them, are much like successful men in any upperworld enterprise. They live in the best neighborhoods, send their children to fine schools.

Some will be found living on North Lake Shore Drive, some in north and west suburban communities, some, such as Murray Humphreys, in high-rise apartment buildings on the edges of the downtown section. Most are far removed from the thuggery which carried them to the top, except in unusual cases such as the elimination of Roger Touhy or the public punishment of an Action Jackson.

Their children are encouraged to study law, medicine, architecture, to enter upperworld banking in a more respectable capacity than as loan-sharks. Their daughters are encouraged to attend universities or finishing schools. Their social tendencies as well as their interlocking business interests make of Syndicate leaders a close-knit community, so their children almost invariably marry into other Syndicate families.

The Syndicate leaders have the same problems as any other parents. They worry about the companions their children might take up with at school. They fear that their children may drink too much, or start smoking marijuana to prove their manhood or maturity, or take LSD as an experience and wind up on a bad trip and the psychiatrists' couches.

Those Syndicate leaders who live in the suburban communites of clean streets and nicely kept lawns encourage carol singers at Christmastime. They erect Nativity scenes in their front yards. While they avoid involvement publicly in civic affairs, because they are conscious of the nature of their business, they back the community leaders in any effort to keep street crime far from home.

Thus their animus in the case of Action Jackson. The Capone heirs feel proprietary about Cicero. By his theft, Jackson dirtied the nest.

Capone Syndicate leaders can be generous. If a police lieutenant wants to take his wife to Europe, he can always find a top man in the Syndicate happy to pick up the tab. If a judge's wife thinks she ought to have a new car, most likely an air-conditioned Cadillac, the judge is enabled to have it gift-wrapped for her birthday.

But nobody wants to be generous with a deadbeat. The Syndicate men are realists. They know that a deadbeat only understands terror.

If the deadbeat had paid his debts and kept his credit good in the upperworld he never would have had to borrow at high interest rates in the underworld. Every deadbeat on the loan-shark's books would cheat the lender if he thought he could get away with it. The deadbeat understands a sound physical beating. The deadbeat understands sudden death. The deadbeats are killed at the rate of one a month in Chicago.

Here is the record of known deadbeat killings in the few months preceding Action Jackson's death.

On November 15, two gamblers were killed. They were Michael De Marte and Theodoros Sampaniotis. A few days later, three burglars: Richard Fanning, Lester Belgrad, and Frank R. Del Guidice. On June 13 it was an unlucky horse player, L. C. Smith. On June 14, a narcotics peddler, Shelby R. Faulk. On July 29, a burglar, Michael Joyce. On August 1, a petty thief, Carl Wiltse. Then Jackson was killed.

With the exception of Action Jackson, these men were not simply gang victims. They were known debtors of loan-sharks.

Dozens of collectors on Chicago streets made their rounds each day to collect "the vigorish," or interest on loan shark debts. The very first time any man missed an interest payment, the collector "sank one or two in his belly," then said, "I'll be here tomorrow. That gives you overnight to stick up a filling station or pawn your mother's false teeth or do whatever you have to do to get up that interest payment. You're better off giving it to me than having me take you out to see the boss."

A dozen deadbeat borrowers told police what a collector meant when he spoke of seeing the boss.

The deadbeat would be taken to a Melrose Park gambling casino in the west suburb. The place has always operated as a handbook by day, a dice and roulette casino by night, and often there have been excellent restaurants on the premises. The place has had a variety of names.

When the collector took a deadbeat to the casino a kangaroo court would be convened in the basement. A panel of three Capone Syndicate supervisors would sit in judgment. The delinquent borrower might be sentenced to a full-scale beating or to having one arm broken.

The sentence would be carried out right there in the presence of the judges. Then the deadbeat's indebtedness would be increased by an amount sufficient to defray the judges' expenses in attending the hearing.

A former convict who defied a North Side loan-shark was summoned to the court. The loan-shark who acted as prosecutor presented the facts. The judges ordered:

A beating administered on the spot.

An immediate increase in the weekly payments due.

A hoodlum told police of being summoned to the court to explain actions interpreted by the Syndicate leaders as prejudicial to their operations. The man's co-defendants were acquitted. He was found guilty. A bludgeoning was decreed and carried out in the presence of the court.

The underworld holds, as the upperworld once held, that punishment to be effective must be quick and certain. Jackson's punishment was quick, certain, and effective. One of the witnesses to his death, an educated hoodlum, laughed as he said afterward; "The penologists always oppose the death penalty because they have an economic stake in keeping prisons full. With no prisoners, they'd lose their jobs. They tell the do-gooders that the worst problems are caused by the repeaters, the recidivists. There has never in history been a single case of recidivism among people subjected to the death penalty. Action Jackson would never steal in Cicero again."

Interestingly, Action Jackson's employer was Don Parrillo, whose father, Billy Parrillo, had been one of Al Capone's lawyers. Billy Parillo graduated from Kent College of Law at the age of twenty-three. When Parillo hung out his shingle, Al Capone became one of his clients.

In that period in Chicago the lawyer who had Capone for a client was in much the same position as the Renaissance painter in Florence having a Pope for a patron. Parrillo's relationship to Capone was more than that of a lawyer to his client. Frank J. Loesch, president of the Chicago Crime Commission, on March 25, 1932, publicly identified Billy Parrillo as "a known partisan of Capone."

Billy Parrillo became Republican committeeman of the Twentieth Ward in the spring primary election of 1932. The alderman may be out front, but the power and the money are lodged in the hands of the committeeman. In 1934, Billy Parrillo had enough political clout, with the aid of the Capone organization, to get himself appointed a member of the Illinois Commerce Commission.

The truly big money in politics always lies in the field of public works. This was true in the days when the pharaohs built the pyramids and just as true today when the glass waffle known as the United Nations building is constructed on the East River. Or when the hydroelectric projects of the Agency for International Development go up all over the world.

Every contractor always wants a piece of the action when President

Eisenhower announces a vast program of federal highway construction, or President Truman announces a Point Four program, or Mayor Daley of Chicago announces a slum-clearing project. Public works are what a politician's dreams are made of.

One of Billy Parrillo's precinct captains, Andy Flando, testified that Parrillo "spent fifty thousand to seventy-five thousand dollars every election" to get himself regularly reelected to the job of ward committeeman, which pays no salary.

Billy Parrillo was finally defeated in 1944 and replaced in the post of ward committeeman by this same Andy Flando. Parrillo all but apologized to his constituents when he told newspapermen in that election that he could not meet the going price for votes in his ward. He said, "The Flando forces are paying a straight twenty dollars a vote."

Such a price may come as a surprise to those who think Chicago votes can be bought for a drink of whiskey or a cigar. The people of Chicago know the value of their franchise. They will shop around to see who is paying best if they have any sense. The highest prices are paid in the primary elections, where the party elects committeemen.

Any man with money behind him can afford to pay $20 a vote—or five times that sum if necessary—to win election to the unpaid job of ward committeeman.

The ward committeeman in the downtown First Ward of Chicago always values the post highly for it offers open and aboveboard legal profits from insurance. The ward committeeman always handles insurance. And every business in the ward—and every businessman— needs insurance for just about everything.

Billy Parrillo was a Republican. When his son, Don Parrillo, was elected alderman of the First Ward it was as a Democrat. In Chicago, such distinctions are not important.

Nothing criminal has ever been charged against any member of the Parrillo clan. Billy Parrillo was a Capone man and made no bones about it. Such loyalty is part of the legacy.

25 Nobody infiltrates the 42 Gang

In Chicago as in any other city in the world—including those in the Soviet Union or Germany under Hitler—all power is held by about 1 percent of the people. The other 99 percent go each day to their jobs or the little grocery stores they own or to the income property in which they share ownership with a savings and loan association and for which they do their own maintenance work.

The 1 percent with the power is divided into three groups: the upperworld, or Establishment, whose power is rooted in wealth usually inherited; the half-world of politics, whose power is based on service to the Establishment; and the underworld of organized crime, whose power is genuinely rooted in free enterprise.

None of these groups could exist without the others, although the Establishment of inherited wealth could probably come closest to independent existence.

No matter how many films in motion picture houses or on the TV screens at home tell of outsiders infiltrating one or the other of these groups for purposes of "exposure," such a thing will never happen. Once in a while an insider might wash in public the dirty linen of his friends and neighbors and peer-group colleagues but an outsider will always remain just that—an outsider.

The man who becomes chairman of the county central committee of one of the dominant political parties is elected to the post by his fellows on the committee.

He becomes a member of this committee in the first place through election by the precinct captains, the block workers who ring doorbells and get out the vote.

No stranger is going to disguise himself and infiltrate an American political organization. He may come in and work his way up from the bottom, but that is the only route to the top.

All of this refers, of course, to the professional politician. It has nothing to do with the dilettante, the man who inherits a widely known name or inherits or earns a fortune and who enters the political arena at or near the top. Such a man will be elected governor or Senator his first or second time out, owing his election to the professional politicians. He is not himself a professional politician and is not respected by the professionals.

There are only four reasons why anyone becomes a professional politician. He may have been born to the work, born the son of a professional and rise in the profession through nepotism. He may view the work of glad-handing and backslapping as a sort of confidence game by which he can get others in the community to support him.

The only other two reasons for which one enters politics are either to line one's pockets or to wield power over one's fellow men. A Napoleon, a Hitler, or a Thomas Jefferson has ideas of public polity which he would like to impose on his community or nation. He wants to see them adopted by his fellows. He seeks power to put these ideas into practice.

The arena of the professional politician is the half-world of politics. Anybody seeking to rise to the top will be known by all who inhabit this world. No outsider can possibly infiltrate it. But this world could be more quickly entered and conquered by a determined man than could either the upperworld of the Establishment or the underworld of organized crime.

The Chicago upperworld of North Lake Shore Drive, of the Casino, of Lake Forest, is no more exclusive than is the underworld of the Capone Syndicate. The members of the Establishment for the most part have known each other since earliest childhood. Their families have known each other since the turn of the century. If a gentleman or lady moves to Chicago from Boston or Baltimore or Charleston, the introductions will be made personally or by telephone. The newcomer will be vouched for most thoroughly before being accepted.

Just as no outsider could infiltrate the political power structure of Chicago undetected, and no outsider could infiltrate the upperworld power structure undetected, so no outsider could possibly penetrate the underworld undetected. This despite fictional tales to the contrary. The thieves, pimps, whores, gamblers, sluggers, and killers who make up Chicago's underworld may be betrayed by one of their own, but never exposed by an outsider. The Capone Syndicate is safe from infiltration.

The men and women of Chicago's underworld have known each other since childhood. The toughest of them while still in short pants caught and held the arms of blind beggars while their confederates robbed the tin cups. They have been together over the years ever since, except for those brief periods when one or another was sent away to prison. They would never trust any outsider, no matter how good his cover story.

The background of the Fusco family and of the Priolo family already has been traced to the 1895 chartering of the Unione Siciliane. Each leader of the Unione in turn has been a king. Each of his sons is or has been a crown prince. The sons of the old Unione leaders today are members of the Illinois legislature or operate excellent restaurants. They attend church regularly, give generously to charity, are respected and honored by all the Italian and Sicilian communities of Chicago and its environs.

The Unione predates the turn of the century, but is still just what it always was. Members court respectability, seek to do what the Jews have done with their Anti-Defamation League—but the stench remains. After World War I a new crop of thieves grew up in Chicago to take their places among slugging veterans of ethnic gangs and circulation wars.

The histories of some of these youngsters—Dion O'Banion and Bugs Moran and Dingbat Oberta—already have been told. This postwar crowd of Chicago gangsters were the protagonists and antagonists in the machine-gun wars of the twenties. Those who survived to die in bed or to become respected elders in the underworld—men such as Dutch Vogel or Tony Accardo—were simply luckier or more skillful at their professions than the others.

Many of those who survived got their start in the 42 Gang, an organization of the criminally inclined youth in the Italian-Sicilian community. The 42 Gang was just as exclusive about its membership as New York's prewar Four Hundred. Its members were teen-age apprentices to the Gennas of alky cooking and Black Hand notoriety.

One family which served its apprenticeship in crime in the 42 Gang, with each of four sons rising in turn to chieftainship, was the Battaglia clan. The eldest was Paul, born in 1894; the next, Augie, born in 1899; the third, Sam, born in 1902; and the youngest, Frank, born in 1904. All had police records dating from childhood. All were aggressive. All showed tremendous qualities of leadership.

Paul was old enough to be a member of the Genna gang, a pioneer in the 42 Gang, and to be one of the latter's earliest chiefs.

Paul Battaglia was arrested January 24, 1924, in the shakedown robbery of a wholesale commission house on Eagle Street between Halsted and Union. Among those with him on that job were Willie Bioff, Nicky Dean Circella, and Frank Miller. Bioff and Circella have already been introduced. Miller was a cousin of the four notorious Miller brothers who formed the Hirschie Miller gang.

When repeal put the old Genna group of alcohol cookers and runners out of business, Paul Battaglia went into an even more dangerous line of work. He became the finger man for gunmen who specialized in holding up handbooks and horserace betting rooms. The life expectancy of such a finger man is not high.

Paul lived at 831 West Cabrini Street and owned a saloon at 819 West Madison Street, from which he conducted a bail bond business. This saloon was next door to the burlesque house which was the first to which Willie Bioff directed George Browne when the two set out to shake down theater owners.

Naturally, the handbook operators and owners of horse-betting parlors, all more or less organized under the Capone Syndicate by the middle thirties, compared notes about the stickups. They looked for a common factor in all the armed robberies. They figured it out to be Paul Battaglia. A price was put on Paul's head and a torpedo was hired to handle the contract.

Paul was shot to death August 27, 1938, at the age of forty-four. His body was found sprawled in the alley behind 5115 West Monroe Street, where it had been tossed from a car. He had been shot twice through the head. Paul had a lot of qualities but not much commonsense.

There is little to be said of Augie Battaglia. He apparently was well thought of by his peers, for he was leader of the 42 Gang when killed in 1931.

Frank Battaglia had been in fast company on May 23, 1930, when arrested in the fatal shooting of Mrs. Marie Pelletier of 2521 Ridgeland Avenue in suburban Berwyn.

Mrs. Pelletier was forty-nine, the mother of four. She resisted a gang of purse snatchers and one of them shot her. A few minutes later, just after midnight, a cruising squad of police detectives sought to halt a carful of youths for questioning. The car sped away but was caught after a chase. During the pursuit, Mrs. Pelletier's empty purse was thrown from the car. Frank Battaglia was one of the young men in the car.

Frank was twenty-six at the time. The three with him, all twenty-one, were Lawrence Cozzi of 1430 West Flournoy Street, Frank Berardi of 1456 West Polk Street, and John D'Arco of 801 South Bishop Street.

Sam Battaglia, second-youngest of the brothers, proved over the years to have the most staying power. He had risen to the heights in the Capone Syndicate. Now he is proprietor of a luxury horse-breeding farm and country estate in Kane county, northwest of Chicago, near the little town of Hampshire, Illinois.

Sam's police record dates back to the pre-World War I years. He achieved some degree of notoriety on November 17, 1930, when the wife of Mayor William Hale Thompson was robbed of $17,000 worth of her jewels. Sam was identified as having taken the shield and revolver from her chauffeur-bodyguard, Policeman Peter J. O'Malley.

The case came to court two days later. Mrs. Thompson said her jewels had been returned. O'Malley was so surly and angry that he said nothing at all. Sam Battaglia said he had been watching a movie at the time of the holdup, and six witnesses said they had been watching Sam while he watched the movie. Sam went free.

Two weeks later, on December 1, 1930, Sam was picked up while driving a getaway car for a gang of holdup men robbing a poker game in a restaurant at 818 West Randolph Street. A bunch of commission merchants from the Randolph Street Market were in the habit of meeting in the restaurant every Saturday afternoon to end the week with a few illegal drinks and a little friendly poker.

Sam and the rest of the holdup men were tipped off to the game, where there was usually a good deal of cash on the table, and the police were tipped off in advance to the proposed holdup.

Nobody intended any such thing as a shoot-out, but that's what happened. An egg inspector, Leonard Sanor was a kibitzer at the game. He was caught in the crossfire and killed. The holdup was unsuccessful but the police had to bring in somebody so they nabbed Sam Battaglia as he sat in the car outside with the motor running. A lot of money had to be spent to square this rap.

That month was not yet out when Sam Battaglia was accused of shooting Police Detective Martin Joyce of the East Chicago Avenue District. The shooting took place in the C & O Cafe at 509 North Clark Street on New Year's Eve, December 31, 1930.

Sam and some of his friends had been doing a little drinking in the speakeasy to celebrate the passing of the old year and the coming of the new when it was robbed. This was during Prohibition and about half the patrons of the place were armed. When the robbers drew, so did everybody else. The guns began popping like firecrackers and in the free-for-all five men were shot.

In the course of the shooting, Marty Joyce, who was off duty, caught a bullet in his abdomen. Sam was caught while fleeing. Joyce recovered from his wound and on June 16, 1931, positively identified Sam Battaglia as one of the holdup men and the one who had shot him.

In the early thirties, kidnapping became so popular a source of income for the underworld that Congress enacted a Lindbergh law which was supposed to guarantee the death penalty for those guilty of abduction for ransom. Few were ever executed under the law, but Sam Battaglia was accused of at least a couple of such kidnappings.

In the early summer of 1933 Louis Kaplan, who owned an auto agency at 3152 Ogden Avenue, was kidnapped near Kenosha, Wisconsin. He was freed on his promise to raise $100,000 ransom. He positively identified Sam Battaglia as one of the members of the 42 Gang who had kidnapped him.

A month later Sam was using the alias Joe Rock when accused of being a member of a kidnap gang in Houston, Texas. That was on July 28, 1933. He was represented on September 4, 1933, by Sidney Korshak, the Capone Syndicate lawyer. This was the Sid Korshak of whom Charles Gioe told Willie Bioff, "Any message he may deliver to you is a message from us."

Sam was a leader of the 42 Gang on August 29, 1933, when picked up in the machine-gun killing of John Parrillo. Battaglia was said to have held onlookers at bay with a pistol while the machine gun was handled by Ted Virgilio, who then "owned" the union of checkroom workers in theaters and restaurants.

Parrillo was seated on a bench in front of a grocery store at Polk and Miller streets when shot to death. The shooting was witnessed by his father, Louis Parrillo, who positively identified Sam Battaglia as the man with the pistol. Other members of the 42 Gang picked up at this time included Jimmy Belcastro, "king of the bombers" and a cousin of Sam Battaglia; Machine Gun Jack McGurn, whose prowess has earlier been noted; and Jimmy Adducci.

Sam Battaglia's rise in the Capone Syndicate hierarchy was slow but steady. As a child he had been called "teats" because of an unusual chest development. The name stuck. He came to head one of the cells of which the Capone organization was composed in the years after World War II.

In these years, when he was past fifty, Sam Battaglia exercised control for the Syndicate over a network of gambling joints, loan-sharks, and prostitution rings working the city's motels. He looked after a heavy investment in such diverse enterprises as a parking service for hotels and restaurants and an industrial development in New Mexico.

In Sam's cell were Albert (Obbie) Frabotta, Felix (Milwaukee Phil) Alderisio, and Marshall Caifano, younger brother of Fat Lenny Caifano.

The cell is the basic unit in the Capone Syndicate organization today. Sam's cell met every Saturday night in the basement of his home at 1114 North Ridgeland Avenue in suburban Oak Park.

Once a month Caifano, as representative for the Battaglia cell, attended a meeting of the Syndicate's council, of which Sam Giancana was chairman. Although Giancana's home at 1147 South Wenonah Avenue in Oak Park was only a few miles from that of Battaglia, the council meetings were seldom held in the home. Instead they were held after closing hours in a suburban cocktail lounge, sometimes in Forest Park and sometimes elsewhere, in varied locations to avoid surveillance of federal agents.

At these monthly meetings representatives from each of the cells made their reports on projects being handled for the council by their group. They were assigned by the council new projects to be carried out by their cells.

New deals were discussed, disputes among individual gangsters and cells were ironed out, those who appeared by their activities (drinking too much, falling in love with non-Syndicate women, going into business for themselves as loan-sharks) to be skirting Syndicate rules were given a chance to explain themselves.

The cell representative with new deals to suggest could draw on the council's bankroll if the investment required more cash than was available to the cell and its individual members.

Work assigned a cell by the council might include a deal originating in New York City or elsewhere. Testimony by federal agents indicated that one such deal was the disposal of a carload of fine scotch whiskey which had been hijacked somewhere in the East. The New York Syndicate sought to dispose of it in the Middle West. Battaglia's cell was given the chore.

The Battaglia cell took charge of the whiskey after it was trucked into Chicago, according to federal men who had it under surveillance. The whiskey was sold at wholesale through Syndicate purveyors in the Chicago market, and at retail through the bars and cabarets along Rush Street which were owned or controlled by Syndicate members.

The New York Syndicate similarly cooperated with the Chicago council. A legitimate businessman whose industrial plant was based in Chicago might want to burn one of his Eastern plants to collect the insurance. He would get in touch with the Battaglia cell's representative in his neighborhood, who would take the proposition up through channels to cell and council and thence to the East Coast.

Part of the underworld service to the upperworld has always consisted of arson or killing for a price. Few legitimate bankers or industrialists in Chicago know the telephone number of a hit man in a distant city. They must work through the Capone Syndicate when they have need of such talents.

The territory policed by Sam Battaglia's cell was not determined by geography. The parking-service activities blanketed much of Chicago. The gambling activities were confined primarily to the West Side and the west suburbs with the exception of Cicero. In handling projects on a reciprocal basis for faraway criminal organizations, the Battaglia cell's members might find themselves working for colleagues in Los Angeles, San Francisco, Kansas City, Detroit, or New York.

Once, in looking for a place to invest tremendous sums of cash realized from gambling operations, the Battaglia cell sent Marshall Caifano to Las Vegas. He spent several million dollars buying industrial real estate later to be subdivided as a manufacturing development.

Battaglia and Caifano were arrested August 18, 1943, when they stopped a car at Broadway and Montrose Avenue. A cruising squad car came along, the policemen recognized them, and a sawed-off shotgun was found in their car.

On July 11, 1958, Sam Battaglia took the Fifth Amendment when being questioned by Robert F. Kennedy before a Senate rackets committee hearing in Washington.

All four members of the Battaglia cell on January 3, 1961, attended a stockholders' meeting at the Twin Food Products Company, 3250 South Wentworth Avenue. This was one of the cell's investments. An officer of the company identified the four as salesmen.

Sam's wife, Mrs. Florence Battaglia, was asked to testify before a grand jury inquiring into the disappearance of 300 cars from the lot of the bankrupt Sterling-Harris auto agency at 2626 North Cicero Avenue. This was another of the cell's enterprises.

The cell's members supervise investments in real estate, auto agencies, laundries, hotels, motels, resorts, trucking, building supplies, clothing factories, food processors, dairy and dairy products, town clubs and country clubs, cabarets and theaters.

The sociologist ought to be interested in how the investments made by leaders in the Capone syndicate vary, depending on whether their family backgrounds are urban-oriented or rural-oriented.

Fred Evans, whose first wife was Donna Levinson and whose second wife became the owner of a hotel in partnership with one of the wives of Lou Greenberg, was urban-oriented. Besides the West Coast luxury hotel he owned the Chicago apartment hotel at 5100 South Cornell Avenue and a piece of the luxury apartment building at 1263 West Pratt Avenue.

Lou Greenberg owned the Hawthorne Hotel in Cicero, the Seneca Hotel on Chicago's Gold Coast, and a number of motion picture houses in the city. He was urban-oriented. Jake Guzik's father was a city man in Russia and while he foreclosed on many an ex-serf's farm, it was for the purpose of realizing on an investment rather than becoming a farmer. Jake ended up owning half a dozen big apartment houses in Chicago.

Compare the investments of the peasant-background Italians and Sicilians, or the Midwestern American ex-farmboys, Billy Skidmore and George Browne and Dion O'Banion.

Two-Gun Louis Alterie had his 3,000-acre ranch near Glenwood Springs, Colorado. Sam Battaglia had his luxury horse-breeding farm and country estate in Kane County near Hampshire, Illinois. Paul Ricca had his farm and country estate at Long Beach, Indiana. Dago Mike Carrozzo had his 804-acre estate, complete with horse barns, near Hobart, Indiana.

Billy Skidmore had his 1,000-acre estate on Pistakee Lake in McHenry County, just outside of Chicago. George Browne had his 400-acre farm just outside of Chicago near Woodstock, Illinois. Dion O'Banion had his 2,700-acre ranch south of Denver.

26 The Syndicate invokes the Fair Trade Act

The ordinary criminal in Chicago is free to operate just about as he pleases so long as he abides by the rules. He may not interfere with operations of the Capone organization. The attitude of the politicians who take his money is that if caught the criminal is on his own. They will try to help, so far as they can, but if the case has gone beyond their help the criminal might have to "take a fall"—go to prison.

Those are the rules of the game.

This applies only to the ordinary criminal, the purse snatcher, the pickpocket, the jackroller, the shoplifter, the cat burglar who works in homes, the loft burglar who works in stores or warehouses, the stickup man who specializes in filling stations and liquor stores, the highly skilled bank robber who organizes a gang to work in the open with shotguns or enter a vault by digging through the roof or a wall over the weekend.

This does not apply to killers or kidnappers. With few exceptions they are totally independent operators and as such are fair game for any cop out to make a score or get a promotion. If they are killers-for-hire, or professional kidnappers-for-ransom, they will usually try to make a one-time deal with lower-echelon cops right on the scene.

The ordinary criminal pays his dues either through the union (paying a politician to take care of the district police captain and a bondsman), or on his own. In the latter case he makes his deal with the cruising police squads and their sergeants.

Generally speaking the man who thus works on his own is considered a free-lancer, a man without class. The argument goes that if he had any class, if he was a real pro with any intention of making a long and successful career of crime, he could get himself introduced to the proper politicians.

What has been said here applies to pimps and whores when they work in those sections of the city not staked out as territories by the Syndicate through its cells and individual members. There are many such sections still open. In the poorest areas of the city and in some of the black

321

neighborhoods a pimp and his whore—or stable of whores—is a genuine free-enterpriser. He is bothered by nobody except the cops who work the same side of the street.

The fields of organized crime are carefully delineated. If a call girl tries to freelance a motel in which prostitution is Syndicate-controlled, she will be stopped either by the police or by Syndicate enforcers. If she talks fast she may get away simply by splitting her take after proving her ignorance of the rules. More than likely, she will be sent to the hospital for a week with a broken jaw.

The criminals who work with the Capone organization are sometimes on a weekly salary from the city's top Syndicate council, from one of the cells, or from an individual member doing well in his own business. He may hire a freelance slugger to serve as bouncer in his saloon, cabaret, or dance hall. Or a slugger to collect usury interest.

Members of the Syndicate are like members of the old-fashioned church in that they tithe. They pay a flat amount into the central treasury, averaging about 10 percent of their income, for membership in the club.

The services they get for this money include protection from politicians, bondsmen on weekly retainers, and on-the-spot legal services. The lawyers are on annual retainers.

This sort of legal work is almost like first aid in the field of medicine. It is meant to ensure against spending the night in jail. If an individual gets into a long legal hassle over his income tax returns, or becomes defendant in a major criminal trial, he has to raise the money for his own legal counsel.

The protection assured by membership in the Capone Syndicate is not all in the form of straight weekly payoffs to the political party in power. Some of it is almost like institutional advertising, not visible at first glance but taken as a calculated risk in the thought that someday in some fashion it might be made to pay off.

These are the payments allegedly made to federal officials. They are seldom made directly. That is, the bagman for a Senator does not come around every Saturday night for his handout, as does the bagman for a district police captain. Rather, the payments to men in the upperworld whose value to the Syndicate depends upon their retention of respectability are made through involved legal setups.

The underworld has learned this trick from the upperworld. The Establishment even before World War I had mastered the legerdemain of influencing research by setting up fellowships for members of the academic community.

The underworld has several foundations, similar to the Ford

Foundation of the upperworld. They use these foundations as channeling devices to pay regular sums to men who may someday be in a position to help. If a judge accepts money from a Las Vegas gambling casino, he knows what he is doing. No matter how the contribution is wrapped up in pink tissue paper and made to appear in a worthy cause, the recipient knows that it comes from a source which sooner or later will be involved in litigation. The money is paid so the contributors will have a friend at court.

The Capone Syndicate now is so powerful that it can place its friends on the federal bench, can have its own men in various government departments including Justice, and can use the legal forces of the United States to keep its business rivals in check. A clear illustration of this happened in 1957.

A clique of gamblers who tired of paying protection through the Syndicate decided to go into business for themselves just outside of what they thought of as the limits of Chicago Syndicate influence. They set up shop in Terre Haute, Indiana.

Had they simply booked horse bets from Hoosiers of the Wabash River Valley they might still be in business, prospering and with the good wishes of all their old friends up in Lake Michigan country. But this group thought that with long-distance phones being what they are, they could take horserace bet business away from the Chicago people.

The daily count of the gambling take in the Chicago area is a computerized thing. Before each day is over the men in charge know to a penny how much has been bet in all the handbooks of the area. They know there is a fairly regular total, certainly tens of millions of dollars, wagered in the Chicago territory each week. This may have seasonal variations, but those are plotted, too. When as much as 1 percent of this total handle suddenly disappears from view the Syndicate computers ring bells and flash red lights and behave in general like pinball machines signaling tilt.

That happened for several weeks in the autumn of 1957.

The men in charge of the Syndicate quickly located the source of the trouble. The clique of gamblers in Terre Haute was cutting in on Chicago profits. The next question was what to do about it. The old-timers, the veterans of Al Capone's own era, said simply, "Send a couple of dynamite men down there and move those guys across the Wabash Valley."

But the saner heads, Jake Guzik and his assistants, prevailed. Let Washington handle the competition. That was the decision. The Syndicate lobbyists in Washington passed along the information as to the goings on in Indiana.

Agents of the Treasury Department on November 29, 1957, raided the third-floor gambling suite above a restaurant in downtown Terre Haute. They said they had reason to believe that for ten weeks the place had been a clearinghouse for bets on football and basketball games as well as horseraces. They said the gross take of the establishment was about a million dollars a week. When the agents walked in with a search warrant issued by a federal district judge there were clerks at eight jangling telephones accepting bets from callers.

No great fanfare was made about the raid at the time. The newspapers and wire news services reported the affair as though it were just one more knockover of a gambling joint. Every police jurisdiction has such raids periodically to reassure voters that the local police chief or county sheriff is on the ball. Apparently the Treasury Department was trying to collect excise taxes.

Eight defendants were named in the federal complaint of the gambling operations. All were old-timers who had spent their lives in gambling. Nearly all had worked with the Capone Syndicate. On the face of it they had simply moved nearly 200 miles south of Chicago to go into business for themselves.

They were charged with failure to comply with the 1951 federal law which made it mandatory for a professional gambler: (1) To register as such with the Internal Revenue Service; (2) To file monthly statements declaring the gross handle; (3) To pay a monthly tax on this gross figure.

The law never had been invoked against members of organized crime syndicates. The word flashed through the underworld that gambler members of the various organizations in Northern cities had nothing to worry about; that the Capone people were behind this raid and its subsequent trial. Some free-enterprise gamblers had set themselves up as rivals to the Chicago Syndicate. Instead of having them killed out of hand, the latter had decided to teach them—and others so inclined—a lesson by legal means. The Syndicate would permit no fix, no deal, no light sentences, no compromises on the amount of federal tax due.

One of the men caught in the raid, Leo Shaffer, when in Chicago had worked as a salesman for Matt Kolb, gambler and partner in bootlegging of the earlier mentioned Roger Touhy. Kolb, before being shot to death in 1938, had been a fixer for thirty years.

Another, Jules Horwick, had been an associate of Joe Epstein, who had been Jake Guzik's chief accountant and who had introduced Virginia Hill to the Chicago Syndicate. Horwick and Epstein had been partners in handbook operations at 10 North Clark Street and at 720 North Wabash Avenue.

Both Shaffer and Horwick knew everything there is to know about

putting in the fix on any sort of case. After being arrested they got out
on bail, then started around with a bundle of money to put in the fix.
Every door had been slammed against them. They found they were
under surveillance. They could do no more business.

Nine months after the arrest, on August 25, 1958, a federal grand
jury in Indianapolis indicted the eight. They were all named in a
five-count indictment charging conspiracy to evade federal excise taxes
on gambling to a total of $326,297.50. This was presumably the amount
which could be proved.

When the T-men originally had spoken of a gross handle of "more
than a million dollars a week" it was the usual talk of federal agents
anxious to build up a case in the newspapers against defendants. But the
grand jury had been given solid figures considered sufficiently
impressive for an indictment to charge the wire room handled a gross of
$3,263,150 in a three-month period.

The federal district attorney, Don C. Tabbert, said the group had
quietly moved to Terre Haute to "avoid the big crime syndicates" and
the police of New York, Chicago, Los Angeles, Las Vegas, and New
Orleans. The underworld across the nation accepted this statement as
indicating that the Capone Syndicate had blown the whistle on its
competitors.

The gamblers in and around Chicago shook their heads and said
dolefully, "Lucky they didn't wind up in the trunks of automobiles."

District Attorney Tabbert said the group operated a racehorse
handicapping service as well as a points spread system for college and
professional football games, for World Series baseball, and for college
and professional basketball. The grand jury ordered $10,000 bail for
each defendant while awaiting trial. Each count of the conspiracy charge
could be punishable on conviction with a maximum of five years in
prison and a $5,000 fine. The grand jury had studied evidence for
twelve days.

The defense lawyers laid down a barrage of motions to delay
indefinitely or move to another city the biggest criminal excise tax case in
the nation's history. Federal District Judge Cale J. Holder denied all
motions. As to the defense contention that widespread publicity had
created an atmosphere hostile to the eight gamblers, Judge Holder said,
"No evidence has been presented to support this contention that another
federal jurisdiction exists that is a vacuum or utopia where newspaper
publicity has not reached."

The trial opened June 22, 1959, and no trial since that of Al Capone
nearly thirty years earlier so caught and held the attention of the
underworld nationwide. If the Capone Syndicate could show in the

Middle West that it pulled the strings for prosecution out of Washington, every other Northern city operation could be assumed to have similar power.

Five weeks later, on July 30, 1959, a jury found the eight guilty of failure to register, of failure to pay the excise taxes due, and of conspiracy to commit these felonies. The jury had deliberated less than four hours. The defendants did not take the stand. The defense called no witnesses.

On September 10, 1959, Judge Holder fined each of the defendants $25,000 in addition to court costs for their lengthy trial. This was the maximum fine that could be imposed. He ordered each man to serve five years in prison, four years for conspiracy and excise tax evasion and the fifth year for failure to register.

That case is still cited to any underworld gambler who thinks of going into business for himself. The Capone Syndicate took credit for having used its power to have the government put its business rivals on the rocks.

Nobody in the underworld ever thought of Jules Horwick and Leo Shaffer as anything but "stand-up guys." They would never complain to anyone but their closest friends that they had been thrown to the wolves by the heirs to Al Capone. They believed they would have been stuffed in the trunks of their own cars except for the fact the Syndicate leaders wanted them in prison as an object lesson.

As earlier mentioned, money reaches politicians in devious ways. One was that by which a Nevada gambling-site owner arranged for $12,000 a year tax-free to be paid into the hands of Supreme Court Justice William O. Douglas.

The money was paid through the Albert Parvin Foundation. This foundation was financed largely through a mortgage on a Nevada hotel and casino. Albert B. Parvin, benefactor of the foundation and part owner of the Fremont Hotel and Casino, of the Sands, of the Four Queens, and of the Aladdin—all Las Vegas gambling joints—identified Justice Douglas as president of the foundation.

Parvin further said that the foundation's directors included Robert Maynard Hutchins, former chancellor of the University of Chicago and chairman of the think tank in Santa Barbara, California, called the Center for the Study of Democratic Institutions; and Robert F. Goheen, former president of Princeton University.

Parvin said the foundation derived most of its funds from a first mortgage on the Hotel Flamingo and its casino in Las Vegas. The Flamingo was the hotel that brought about the gangland killing of

Benjamin (Bugsy) Siegel on June 20, 1947, in the apartment of Miss Virginia Hill.

A great deal of the Capone Syndicate's money is invested in Las Vegas. Siegel was said to have sought to defraud the Chicago boys. The kangaroo court hearing the case against Siegel was convened in Havana and Lucky Luciano flew to Cuba from his Italian exile for the occasion. Siegel was condemned to die.

Parvin said, "Justice Douglas' acceptance of payments totaling fifty thousand dollars in the last four years was to cover travel expenses he incurred in connection with the granting of scholarships by the foundation."

Douglas at the time was being paid a salary of $39,500 a year by the people of the United States, a salary which would continue for life any time he wanted to retire. The salary has since been increased to more than $50,000 a year.

Douglas' benefactor, Al Parvin, is known throughout the gambling fraternity. He is president of Parvin-Dohrmann Company, which supplies the furniture used by most of the Las Vegas gambling centers. His company paid $11,000,000 for the Fremont Hotel. The money was paid to an associate of Bobby Baker, secretary to the Democrats in the U.S. Senate when Lyndon B. Johnson was majority leader.

When the Fremont Hotel was bought, the seller was a group headed by Edward Levinson, a gambling operator involved with Bobby Baker in various business enterprises. Levinson is a brother of "Sleep Out" Louis Levinson and of Donna Levinson, first wife of Fred Evans. Eddie Levinson was one of the gamblers retained by Parvin at $100,000 a year each to run the Fremont.

At the time Parvin had Justice Douglas on his payroll at $250 a week, the more naïve people of the upperworld said to each other, "Good old Bill Douglas. He's naïve but he means no harm."

The sharpies of the underworld are less kind in their judgment. They have spent their lives buying and selling judges and legislators. They believe Douglas knew exactly what he was selling, and Parvin knew exactly what he was buying.

The men of the Capone Syndicate are cynical about judges on their payrolls. One judge is no different from another in the eyes of the men who pay them. On one occasion Tony Accardo was arrested for a minor offense and taken to a Chicago police station shortly before midnight on a Saturday. The district captain was out of town and the cops who had the Syndicate boss in custody were not on the Capone payroll.

The arresting officers affected not to know Tony Accardo. They indicated they would treat him as they would any other prisoner in similar circumstances: shove him in a jail cell until some judge could set bail on Sunday or Monday. Accardo, who can be smooth as silk or rough as a cob, asked to use the public telephone in the station.

Apparently he knew the number he wanted. On his first call he got Judge George L. Quilici, who was playing bridge with a group including Louis Mariano, a subeditor for the Chicago *Daily News* The card party was being held in a private home. Between the police who listened to one end of the conversation, and Mariano who listened to the other, it was easy to reconstruct the dialogue.

Accardo explained his situation to the judge. Quilici nervously hemmed and hawed, said he was in the middle of a bridge tournament with Italian friends, assured his caller he would get away as soon as possible but explained that it might be some time yet.

Accardo prides himself on the fact that he has never in his life spent a night in jail. He told Quilici, "You understand the situation. They are going to hold me until a judge gets here to set bail. Then I can post the bond and get out. I need a judge and I need one now."

Quilici sought to keep his dignity. He said, "Yes, I understand, Mr. Accardo. I assure you I will get away just as soon as I can. It will probably be a while yet. . . ."

Accardo, once one of Al Capone's top men with a machine gun, has a low boiling-point. He tired of this game. He sought to lower his voice but his whisper carried better than a shout. He told Quilici, "Now you listen to me, you [something in Italian]. You get your money every week. You get your ass down to this station and I don't mean in ten minutes. I mean now. Or else. You understand, you [that same word in Italian]."

Quilici, said his audience, appeared faint at the telephone. He staggered to his hat, did not even excuse himself to his hostess, began to run before he got to the door. He drove off, burning rubber on his car.

In the police station, Quilici sought to regain his dignity but Accardo would have none of it. Accardo said, "Shut up. They tell me you got to set bail. Set it."

Quilici told the police sergeant he would like Accardo delivered to his courtroom. He said he would open night court and hear the charges so he might make a determination. Accardo shut him off. "You're here and I'm here. We don't need no courtroom. Who the hell do you think you're dealing with? Some punk who still needs his diapers changed? Forget hearing the charges. Tell these cops how much. I'll pay the money and get out of here."

Quilici said, "I order the prisoner released on one hundred dollars' bond."

Accardo peeled a single note for $100 from a huge flat packet he carried. He threw this note on the blotter before the desk sergeant and told Quilici, "You sign whatever papers they need. You're my lawyer."

With those words, Accardo walked out into the night, got in his car, and drove home. Judge Quilici, in the presence of a score of policemen who had watched his humiliation, got out with as much grace as he could muster.

As far as the Capone Syndicate is concerned, there is no difference between Tom Clark, who got his Supreme Court seat after Ricca and the others went free; Bill Douglas, who took $250 a week of the gamblers' money; George Quilici, whose seat on the bench was bought with underworld cash; and Judge Cecil Corbett Smith, whose story is now to be told. This yarn opens with a funeral.

Mike Spranze, once bodyguard to Al Capone, was buried April 9, 1963. Among those attending the service at the undertaking parlor, 6901 Belmont Avenue, were such Syndicate wheelhorses as Tony Accardo, Joe (Gags) Gagliano, Jimmy (The Monk) Allegretti, Milwaukee Phil Alderisio, Charles (Chuck) Nicoletti, Leonard (Needles) Gianola, Crazy Sam De Stefano, and Willie (Potatoes) Daddano.

As always, this particular funeral was kept under surveillance by several police squads from the department's organized crime division.

Sam De Stefano drove his 1962 Cadillac. Willie Daddano was his passenger. Upon arrival at the funeral parlor, both knelt at the side of the bier and said their Our Fathers and Hail Marys. Then they rose to go. Detectives Lee Gehrke and John Zitek were assigned to follow.

No hoodlum of any experience can be trailed by one car without being aware of it. De Stefano enjoyed teasing the police. So when he got to Newland Avenue, a one-way northbound street, he entered it and drove south. Gehrke and Zitek might have overlooked the traffic offense, as police do frequently in the case of underworld bosses, but De Stefano was driving so fast they thought they ought to stop him to prevent an accident.

The police went after De Stefano's car, lights flashing and siren moaning. De Stefano laughed and speeded up. He turned off Newland Avenue and turned into Sayre Avenue to go north. Sayre is a one-way southbound street, so once again De Stefano was bucking the stream of traffic with police in pursuit. De Stefano drove right back to the undertaking parlor, pulled into the parking lot, and parked his car. The police squad car drew up alongside.

Gehrke silently wrote out a traffic ticket charging De Stefano with driving the wrong way in a one-way street. He stuck the ticket under De Stefano's windshield wiper. De Stefano laughed at him.

Five weeks later, on May 16, 1963, the case came up in the court of Judge Cecil Corbett Smith. The usual penalty for such an offense at the time was $10, and the case could have been disposed of in two minutes. Instead, De Stefano made a circus out of it and kept the case before the court for two weeks.

The prosecution was handled by Erwin Cohen and Frank Wilson for the city corporation counsel. De Stefano elected to handle his own defense, although he kept at his side Attorney Robert J. McDonnell.

De Stefano had brought to court some of his friends. These included Leo S. Foreman, an ex-convict who was publicly introduced by De Stefano as "a longtime associate of our honored presiding judge." Then De Stefano announced that he too was "a longtime associate" of Judge Smith.

De Stefano did not wait for the prosecution to present its case. He took over direction of the court immediately. He asked a jury trial. Judge Smith said no panel of veniremen was available but that he would be happy to transfer the trial to another court. De Stefano said, "That won't be necessary. I waive my right to a jury trial."

Detective Gehrke was the first witness for the prosecution. He recited the facts, saying that when De Stefano's car came to a halt the man who sat next to the driver was Willie (Potatoes) Daddano. At this, De Stefano—a convicted bank robber and rapist—sprang up and shouted, "I'll not have the names of gangsters mentioned during my trial."

McDonnell, the defense lawyer, whispered something to De Stefano. The latter loudly told McDonnell, "Shut up."

At conclusion of Detective Gehrke's testimony, De Stefano began to cross-examine the witness. The court sustained an objection to a line of questioning regarding Gehrke's background. De Stefano said, "I want to know his background. Joe Stalin may have sent him."

When court reconvened after lunch, Judge Smith told De Stefano, "Confine yourself to the issues." De Stefano clowned and said, "Please don't handcuff me, your Honor."

When the judge denied De Stefano's request that the arresting policeman be held in contempt of court, De Stefano moved for a mistrial. When this motion was denied, De Stefano clowned and asked the court, "Are you trying me—or persecuting me?"

So it went through the afternoon. The newspapers reported the story. When court opened next day it was to an overflow crowed. Everyone wanted to see "the crazy hoodlum" make a fool of the august and dignified judge. De Stefano did not disappoint his audience. He launched into a series of tirades, with Judge Smith the butt of the rawest kind of humor.

Taking a flat wad of bills from his pocket, De Stefano spread them out like a handful of playing cards so that everyone in court could see that each bill was for $1,000. He asked, "Who says it's wrong to have money?" He told the curious in the courtroom, rather than the judge on the bench, that he was in the moneylending business. He said that Fidel Castro had tried to get him to go to Cuba and set up a moneylending operation in Havana. He looked at a young girl in the front row and said, "You ought to go into business as a loan-shark. Right here in traffic court. You would find the judges are your best customers."

Despite strict rules against smoking in courtrooms while court is in session, De Stefano lit a cigarette and blew smoke rings into Judge Smith's face. The implication was clear that the judge was one of De Stefano's loan-shark victims and could not complain. When De Stefano accidentally knocked over a glass of water on the table before the bench he tried to sop up the water with a piece of paper. He told the judge, "I've got a million dollars and I'm scrubbing your stinking court."

Prosecutor Cohen complained that De Stefano did not know the rules of evidence. He told Judge Smith, "He's turning this into a circus."

On two occasions during the trial, De Stefano referred to himself as an "eminent attorney who received his extensive knowledge of law at that great institution in Waupun, Wisconsin." De Stefano in 1933 had been sent for eleven years to the Wisconsin state penitentiary at Waupun after being convicted of bank robbery.

Judge Smith finally told De Stefano that if the case went on as it had been, "we'll be here for a week." The case was continued to May 10, then for another week to May 27. Judge Smith finally found De Stefano not guilty of driving the wrong way on a one-way street.

27   "Sue at the drop of a hat"

In the world of Al Capone, all men were divided into two groups: the squares and the hustlers. A square was any man who could not be bought by the underworld with a girl, a tip on the market, or an outright payment of cash. A hustler was any man who saw the square as a mark to be taken. Capone used to say, "Only two kinds of hustlers I can't stand: a pickpocket and a hophead."

Capone then would explain that the pickpocket does not go out with a pistol as an open and above-board pirate, looking to stick up a filling station or liquor store. The pickpocket works the crowds at ballgames and political conventions, on streetcars or buses. Capone said. "A pickpocket once crowded up next to my mother on the State Street car and took the wallet out of her purse. I've got no use for a dip. They prey on working people, the scrubladies coming from Loop office buildings in the morning and the tired clerks going home at night."

Capone's feeling toward hopheads was never so succinctly explained. He simply had no use for any addict or pusher. He wanted nothing to do with the importation, distribution, or retail sale of narcotics.

A daily newspaper editor calling on Al Capone in his Lexington Hotel headquarters once found all Capone's immediate aides engaged in shaking down the bedroom assigned to one of his bodyguards. The man had been sent on some errand to get him out of the hotel for the afternoon.

Capone's aides were unscrewing the knobs from corner posts of the brass bed, removing electric switches from their insulated boxes in the walls, taking up rugs and hammering at floorboards for hollow places.

Capone explained that the bodyguard, an old friend from the early days in the Four Deuces, was hooked on heroin. When Capone discovered the fact he personally gave the man a beating and then sent him off to the government farm in Kentucky to be weaned. Capone said sadly, "Willie claims to be clean these days. Maybe so. But every month or so we have to shake him down to make sure. I love the son of a bitch but if he ever goes back on that stuff he'll wind up in a cement overcoat."

Capone never explained his feeling about narcotics users. Perhaps it was because, in the hands of police, any of them would disclose any secrets in return for a fix. Capone himself said that his feeling about narcotics addicts, like his feeling about homosexual men, was irrational. He simply could not abide being in the same room with one.

Except for these idiosyncrasies, Capone accepted every man at face value. If the man was a square, Capone accepted the fact. He might try to hustle one, but he frequently numbered squares among his friends. He spent a lot of time talking to such square reporters as Jim Doherty and Harry Read, actually thinking out loud about the philosophy of his business as well as its practice.

If a man was a hustler, Capone accepted the fact. Some hustlers are "heavies," carrying guns and not hesitating to use them. Some are talkers who would not carry guns if their lives depended on it. Capone discriminated against no man because of his race, religion, or nation of origin.

One of his most trusted aides was Jake Guzik. Guzik's chore—one of the chores to which he succeeded—was to sit nightly at the same table in St. Hubert's Old English Grill and Chop House. There he would be visited by district police captains and the sergeants who collected their graft for them, by the bagmen for the various Chicago mayors and their aides, by virtually anyone who had a money problem in connection with the Syndicate and wanted to bring his problem to the attention of the higher-ups.

When Jake Guzik died he was laid to rest with as much pomp and ceremony as could be accorded any financier of the upperworld.

After Jake's death his roly-poly little body was attired in black skull cap, dark gray stole, and brown suit for his last public appearance. The wake was held at Tancel's funeral chapel at 2921 South Harlem Avenue in Berwyn. Jake was in an ornate bronze coffin said, in the whispered tones heard at such festivities, to have cost $5,000. One hoodlum repreated the current joke, "For that money we could have buried him in a Cadillac."

The orthodox Jewish service for the dead was conducted by Rabbi Noah Ganze of the Chicago Loop Tabernacle at 16 South Clark Street. He was aided by Cantor Nathan Taube. The rabbi quoted from the Twenty-third Psalm. He called Jake "a fine husband who was good to his children. Jacob Guzik never lost faith in his God. Hundreds benefited by his kindness and generosity. His charities were performed quietly."

Some of the police captains and politicians who were among those hundreds who benefited from Jake's generosity looked at the ceiling. They hoped Jake's charities had been performed so quietly that they never would come to light in the shape of little black books which might be examined by the income tax accountants for names and sums.

The hoodlums in attendance did not understand the rabbi's subtlety. They looked at each other in astonishment. They thought this was a side of the Syndicate's treasurer to which they had never been treated. Joe Epstein, chief accountant under Jake Guzik, nodded sagely as though he had known all along about the double life of the sixty-nine-year-old pimp.

Jake's personal lawyer handled public relations at the funeral. This was Gene Bernstein, the Twenty-fourth Ward tax expert and amateur hypnotist who had accompanied Tony Accardo on the latter's trips to Leavenworth to get orders from Paul Ricca.

Jake's personal physician, Dr. Israel Ritter, signed the death certificate in the apartment at 5492 South Everett Avenue which Guzik maintained under the name of Jack Arnold. Dr. Ritter certified that the deceased had been stricken with a heart attack at 6:17 P.M. on Februrary 21, 1956, while dining simply on a couple of broiled lamb chops and a glass of Mosel. The place of death was given as the restaurant address, 316 South Federal Street in the Loop.

Jake was at his table, as he was regularly at that hour, in his capacity as collector from all bookmakers and brothel keepers, and paymaster for the police, prosecutors, and political bosses of the eight-county Chicago metropolitan area. He apparently was in perfect health right up to the moment he was stricken.

He maintained a suite at the Pick-Congress Hotel on South Michigan Avenue, where he sometimes caught forty winks of an afternoon. He owned in his wife's name the building at 7240 South Luella Avenue in which he and Mrs. Rose Guzik kept their apartment. Their home had bars on its windows and sheet steel linings on its doors. It might have been a fort—or a prison. Bernstein said of his client, "Jake did not believe in banks or vaults."

Guzik's personal income, according to the annual returns filed with the Internal Revenue Service, exceeded $15,000 a month. Probate Judge James S. Montana issued letters of administration for the estate to Guzik's widow and she listed Guzik's personal property which she estimated at $3,000. A car is worth more than that.

Jake had a thin skin. In later years he went to law any time he thought he was being cheated. He sued any time he though he was being given less than a perfect image by people who wrote about him. He knew exactly what he was doing. He told newspapermen, "I'm paying those judges, so why shouldn't I use them?" Jake never won any of the lawsuits, but that was not their purpose. He knew that just the threat of a suit will cause most editors to blue-pencil anything derogatory in copy crossing their desks.

Jake never intended to win a lawsuit. He was the unofficial public relations adviser to members of the Syndicate, and constantly sought to demonstrate to them how easily the courts could be used to muzzle criticism. He told a gathering of top gangsters. "Sue. Never be afraid to sue. Go into court at the drop of a hat, any time you don't like what some newspaper guy writes. You pay your lawyers a retainer. The judges are on our payrolls. You can sue in Cook County for fifteen dollars. Just the fact that a suit has been filed will cause most people to shut up. They can never be sure that some nutty jury won't award you a million dollars in damages."

One of Jake's lawsuits was against a racetrack. Another was against a daily newspaper and one of its writers.

In 1954 the Arlington Park racetrack hired a new security chief, Kline Weatherford, a former special agent for the FBI. Weatherford's job was to give the tracks a new image. He decreed that known hoodlums were to be barred. On July 29, 1954, Jake Guzik was denied admission to the clubhouse and to the reserved seat section. Jake sued.

In a superior court brief filed on December 10, 1954, Guzik charged that Ben F. Lindheimer, president of the Arlington Park Jockey Club, was embezzling money. Other defendants named included Eugene F. Murphy, secretary; and Peter Brandness, administrative officer. Guzik demanded an accounting.

Immediately after having been barred from the track, Guzik had sued in federal district court under the Fourteenth Amendment, charging that he was being deprived of his civil rights in being denied the right to watch a horserace.

Lindheimer was represented in the superior court suit by Attorney Jack Martineau, who on October 5, 1955, took from Jake Guzik a deposition. Guzik said for the record, "I been in racetracks all over the country, especially in Arlington Park. Any day of the week, ninety percent of the people you see at the tracks are thieves, ex-convicts, and bookmakers."

Guzik told Martineau that horserace betting ought to be legalized "away from the tracks." He said the only people who could get out to the tracks during the racing seasons were "thieves, pimps, judges, and prosecutors, with a sprinkling of their whores and kept women."

Guzik said that honest workingmen who could not get away from their jobs during the day ought to have the same opportunity to place bets on horses of their choice as did "the judges and their whores."

The lawsuit against Lindheimer died with Guzik.

Another of his suits was that which he brought against the Chicago *American,* a Hearst newspaper, as a result of a story printed February 20, 1955. The story had been written by Elgar Brown, a gentle soul and an uncommonly fine writer. Brown would have disdained to shake the hand of a Jake Guzik, an Al Capone, or a Tony Accardo. He had a distaste for pimps and towel boys, coupled with a native gift for invective.

Brown's story, in light vein, referred to Jake Guzik variously as "Old Baggy Eyes," "Mr. Fix," "Dean Jake, of Old Scarface U," "Chief Pander," "a potbellied toughy," and "Gangland's Fearless Fosdick." All who were acquainted with Jake Guzik from his frequent court appearances over the years acknowledged that Elgar Brown had pretty well caught the flavor of the old pimp.

Guzik recited this terminology in his suit charging libel by the Hearst Publishing Company, Inc. Jake's suit was filed in municipal court. It died with Jake and was later dismissed by Judge Quilici.

A lawsuit on behalf of Jake Guzik was filed a few weeks before his death by the American Civil Liberties Union. Charles Liebman, vice-chairman of the Illinois division of the ACLU, apparently thought the time and resources of his organization could be put to no better purpose than vindication of the character of such a man as Jake Guzik.

Liebman went into federal district court in Chicago asking $50,000 in damages on Jake Guzik's behalf. The suit was on Constitutional grounds, holding that Guzik's civil liberties had been denied when the pimp was arrested January 13, 1956, in the company of Murray Humphreys, Lester (Killer Kane) Kruse, and Meyer Sachs, a gambler.

Liebman emphasized that he asked no fee of multimillionaire Guzik, and told the court he felt the arrest had damaged the reputation of a lifelong pimp and thief to the extent of $100,000, and he asked the other $40,000 in punitive damages.

The defendants named in Liebman's suit on Guzik's behalf included Police Commissioner Timothy J. O'Connor, Lieutenant Joe Morris, and Lieutenant Bill Duffy. Morris at that time headed the police intelligence unit, charged with keeping track of organized crime and its practitioners. Duffy was Morris' deputy. The suit was filed two days after Guzik's arrest.

The policemen testified that Guzik and his companions when arrested had been creating a disturbance in front of the Hucksters, a private Syndicate-owned key club saloon at 100 East Chicago Avenue. Guzik when arrested was carrying $9,000 in cash. In three previous arrests he had been carrying $11,000, $17,000, and $21,000. He explained the huge sums: "With a roll like this I don't have to worry about getting kidnapped. I just give the dough to the guys who want to snatch me and they go away more than satisfied."

Guzik was kidnapped for ransom at least once to public knowledge.

On one occasion Jake Guzik went into the circuit court of Judge Richard B. Austin to ask that police be enjoined from bothering him as he went about his business. Austin was then chief justice of the court. He thought Jake Guzik's request reasonable. He granted the injunction and admonished Police Lieutenant William J. Drury.

Drury was one of what has since become known as "the new breed" of policeman. He was a bright youngster, brother of a famed Chicago newspaperman, a natural scholar. He was also an athlete, one of the first to compete in the Golden Gloves boxing tournaments. In the police department Drury studied hard, rose rapidly on merit, and never lost his contempt for pimps and underworld payoff men.

Drury accepted the fact that he could not single-handedly wipe out organized crime in Chicago. He knew that the politicians and the Establishment need the underworld and do not want to get rid of it. But Drury felt that if he could do nothing else he could at least harass the bullies and extortionists who with impunity constantly harass the decent working people of the community.

So when Drury would meet a Jake Guzik or Tony Accardo or a Murray Humphreys walking the streets in broad daylight he would assume they were doing nothing honest. He would ask for their identification. He would compel them to lean at an angle against a Loop office building, legs spread and fingers outstretched, while he frisked them for concealed weapons. The multimillionaire killers fumed at being so treated.

Guzik in particular would get so angry he would literally foam at the mouth. Saliva would fly in every direction as he shouted at the interfering policeman, "You son of a bitch, I'm a millionaire and you know it. I'm no vagrant. I've got more money in pocket right now than you earn in a year. Why don't you get smart and let me give you some of it?" But Guzik had to stand still for the frisk or be carted off in a patrol wagon to the nearest police station. He grew to hate Bill Drury.

Guzik told Drury, "You'd better wise up. Look at the record and you'll see that I always reward my friends and punish my enemies. You can decide which you want to be."

Circuit judge Austin was elevated to the United States District Court and is now a federal judge. Police Lieutenant Drury was shot to death in his garage by gangland killers on September 25, 1950.

In his last years Jake Guzik was outspoken on nearly every subject. He did not place a high value on the gentlemen in black robes. He said,

"You buy a judge by weight, like iron in a junkyard. A justice of the peace or a magistrate can be had for a five-dollar bill. In the municipal courts he will cost you ten. In the circuit or superior courts he wants fifteen. The state appellate court or the state supreme court is on a par with the federal courts. By the time a judge reaches such courts he is middle-aged, thick around the middle, fat between the ears. He's heavy. You can't buy a federal judge for less than a twenty-dollar bill."

Jake's brother, Harry Guzik, was eleven years his senior. While still in his teens, Harry was running a stable of whores on the Levee in the First Ward. He married one of them, Alma, and they worked as a team recruiting young whores off the farm. They sold these girls to Big Jim Colosimo; to Jim's wife, Victoria Moresco, who had her own whorehouses; and to Johnny Torrio.

Colosimo, Torrio, and Victoria Moresco among them had a string of brothels which used up girls faster than they could be brought into the business. The whorehouse customers always wanted girls young and new at the trade. The girls who were used up either went for cheap trade on the streets or were shipped to the South American brothels.

Two newspaper reporters once had occasion to hear a discussion on the recruiting of whores by two men who probably knew as much about the business as anyone in the world. The experts were old Harry Guzik and young Willie Bioff. Both agreed that no girl can be forced into prostitution. The only ones whose talents can be turned in that direction are girls who already are laying anything in pants. Guzik said, "They're so dumb you have to teach them never to give away what they can sell."

Bioff and Guzik agreed that the way to turn "a charity lay" into "a money girl" is first to get into bed with her. Then spend money on her, buying expensive gifts. Possibly get a job as a waitress for her, and arrange for her employer to pay her double what waitresses usually earn. Cultivate expensive tastes in the young lady. Then show her that the way to earn the money to satisfy such tastes is easy. Bioff told Guzik, "I always wake up some morning and tell her I'm broke. Then I hint that if she really loved me she'd lay a friend of mine who wanted to give me a hundred dollars if he could just get in her pants once. She always cries. She always tells me she loves me and she could not possibly lay anybody else. But I tell her I wanted to buy such wonderful things for her—and here we are without even breakfast money. She comes around."

Guzik laughed and said, "You've sure got it right, Willie. And once she's laid one other guy for money, she's hooked. After that you can put her right into a house and she'll turn over her earnings to you every night. If she tries to hold out, you just slap her around a little."

Harry and Alma Guzik were unusually adept at recruiting. They would go out into small towns, in the countryside around Chicago, and separate as soon as they entered the town. Harry would work among the waitresses, the girls who clerked in the drugstore or dry goods stores, the maids in the hotel. Alma would work among the beauty operators, the girls who patronized the town dances, the flashily dressed girls who obviously did not want to work on the family farm. In all their travels, neither of them ever met a virgin.

One way or another they would get the girls, one at a time, to go to bed with Harry. While he was in bed with the girl, Alma would enter the room, undress herself, and get into bed with them. The whole idea was to convince the country girl there was nothing morally wrong with sex, that it was great fun and that everybody ought to enjoy all they could get of it all the time. Later, Alma would take the girl aside and say, "Look, honey, no matter how much you enjoy this don't be a damned fool and give it away for nothing. Harry's got money. Ask him for some."

If the girl would not do so, Alma would tell Harry, in the girl's presence, "Don't be a cheapskate, just because this girl doesn't know the ropes. At least give her ten dollars for a new dress."

When Harry and Alma Guzik left town, they would make arrangements with each of the girls individually to come up to Chicago and spend a weekend. They would tell the girls they would pay the trifling railroad fare and that the girl would not be given a chance to spend a penny while in Chicago.

The girls always came. Once again, each girl found herself in bed with both Harry and Alma. Only this time one of Harry's friends dropped in while the threesome was in bed. And Harry's friend would step out of his clothing and join the fun. When he left he would insist on paying both Alma and the country girl $10. And a day or so later the new girl would find herself working in a Colosimo whorehouse.

For such a fresh girl, Colosimo could get $10 a trick. Harry and Alma Guzik would get $5 a trick from the earnings of each such girl until they had collected $100 on the sale, plus the expenses they had been put to on their recruiting travels. If they could thus recruit ten girls a month they had $1,000 a month clear, over and above their expenses.

Everybody was happy. Colosimo was happy to have a constant source of new talent. His customers were happy to have girls fresh from the country, the hayseeds still in their hair. The girls were happy to finally get away from drudgery on the family farm. Harry and Alma Guzik were happy to be able to live well among their peers, the First Ward thieves.

Once Harry and Alma Guzik spent too much money living high and did not keep up their payments to First Ward police and politicians. The police arrested them on a charge of white slavery. They were tried and convicted. That was in 1922. They got out on bail, worked one country town after another to earn enough money for what they needed, then bribed the governor and got a pardon.

As the three younger Guzik brothers came along, Harry and Alma got them jobs in the whorehouses in the Levee.

In later years, when in reminiscing mood, Jake would tell how policemen and judges came to the Guzik home at all hours of the night. Each would want "a couple of dollars" or "a pass" so they could use the girls at the nearby whorehouse without paying. Jake never cared how many Gentiles were within hearing as he would say, "Those cheap goys never wanted to spend a nickel. Always trying to get something for nothing. I never saw a goy judge after that that I didn't want to vomit."

By the time Jake Guzik was twenty, he was working in his brother's saloon at Twenty-second and State. Harry and Alma had opened the joint, keeping a string of whores upstairs. Jake was a bartender and solicitor for the girls' services.

In a happy mood in later years he sometimes discussed his childhood. "In our neighborhood no shoe merchant would ever let a kid try on both shoes of a pair. The kid got one shoe, and the other one stayed up on a shelf. So we would go into Loop shoe stores, where the merchants were dumb. Two kids would go in together. One of the kids would try on both shoes of a pair. When he had them buttoned up, the other kid would push over a display case to distract the clerk. Then both kids would run out the door with a new pair of shoes."

Jake first came to public notice as a panderer on October 29, 1912, when Miss Kate J. Adams wrote of his activities in her report on crime in the Levee district. Her survey is cited on page 847 of the Landesco Report. At the time Jake and his family were paying off police and politicians so that he had no record except in Miss Adams' papers.

Jake was thirty years of age in 1917 when first convicted of larceny and sent to the city jail. The following year, on November 7, 1918, he was again convicted of larceny. By this time he had remembered the lessons of his youth and cut the local precinct captain in for a share of the loot. With his previous record he could not go absolutely free, but he got off with five days in jail and a $10 fine.

Jake saw the future in beer when the Volstead Act became law. He ventured his savings to take an option on a small brewery at 2340 South Wabash Avenue, a block south of the Four Deuces brothel. At first he simply kept the staff busy in making legal malt products. That paid the rent while Jake waited to see which way the cat would jump. When Johnny Torrio began going in for breweries in a big way, Jake offered the gang boss his brewing facilities on a percentage basis. Through this he came to know Capone.

All these years Jake Guzik had never neglected the teachings of his father, the First Ward precinct captain. Jake automatically had all his pimps, whores, newsboys, saloon hangers-on, and brewery employees registered. He voted them all, every election day. In a small way, Jake Guzik was an independent political power with a bloc of votes he could deliver or withhold.

After Capone killed Joe Howard, he had in Jake Guzik a faithful dog. Guzik would have gone through hell for Capone. With Capone, the loyalty always went both ways. When Jake lay ill in Michael Reese Hospital, Capone visited him daily. Capone stationed his personal bodyguards in a twenty-four-hour watch at Guzik's bedside to guard against possible assassins.

Guzik became the grand vizier to the sultan.

A Barbarossa, a Bonaparte, an Al Capone does not come along every day. Most men would be content to be the favored of such a leader. Jake Guzik gave a lifetime of scheming and effort to the enrichment of Capone and his heirs. Each of Capone's successors—Nitti, Ricca, Giancana, Battaglia, Accardo—gave Jake the widest latitude in exercise of his own judgment, the complete trust of rulers for a favored elder statesman.

Even the writers of copybook maxims would have to concede that Jake Guzik, by his own standards, lived and died a successful man.

28 "We're bigger than the government"

Al Capone in his various interviews with newspapermen liked to envision himself as of an analytical turn of mind. He would say, "A man of action is one who can observe things, analyze them, draw conclusions from them and then act on his own conclusions. Most men can't. They can never make up their minds. That's why most men are ciphers. They will always be losers."

That sounds on the face of it as though Capone scorned the ciphers of this world. That was not so. He apparently thought the ciphers just as necessary to the scheme of things as anyone else. They simply did not count in his reckoning as anyone except consumers of the various things he had to sell.

In this respect, although the entrepreneurs of the upperworld are seldom as outspoken about it, Capone probably did not differ from the millionaire manufacturers of cigarettes, automobiles, or refrigerators. Capone said often that he felt 99 percent of all the men in the world are losers, totally at the mercy of the other 1 percent, who are the men of power.

"The men with power are the men with money or the will to take it. They break down into just two classes: the squares and the hustlers. I am a hustler, but I got respect for squares.

"A square is a guy like Henry Ford or Thomas Edison, a guy with brains and determination and a willingness to work for what he wants. A guy like that you got to respect.

"A hustler in the upperworld is a stock market speculator, a guy who wants to make money out of money instead of producing something people want and need. I got no respect for those people. They are greater crooks than hustlers in the underworld. At least an underworld hustler has the guts to go out and take it at the point of a gun."

Everything Capone said indicated that his sole standard of value was money. Every judgment he made seemed to trace back to money, the lack of it or the possession of it, the gaining of it or the loss of it. He never questioned that money, and the power it could bring, was the dominant value in all life.

Adolf Hitler has been quoted by historians as saying in effect that the enemies of his Nazi party might defeat it, but to do so they would have to adopt the Nazi mentality and methods so that in the end it would be the Nazi ideology which would win. So far as can be learned from any of the published interviews with Capone, he never said this about his own viewpoint but it probably applies. Part of the heritage of the Capone era seems to be that a great part of the upperworld has adopted the methods and standards of the gangster.

After the 1956 death of Jake Guzik, the job of Loop vice and rackets boss for the syndicate fell to Gus (Slim) Alex, a Greek. Alex enjoys skiing. He made annual trips to Switzerland until in 1965 that country, assuming that he was a courier for underworld cash, declared him undesirable. The Swiss banned Gus Alex for ten years from touring, visiting, or entering their country.

Alex fought the order. He had no difficulty getting aid from Illinois' then senior Senator, the Republican Everett M. Dirksen, or the state's then senior Congressman, the Democrat William L. Dawson. Both Dawson and Dirksen wrote the Swiss government on his behalf, saying that Gus Alex was a fine and upstanding citizen. They both said that Alex, while often arrested, had never been convicted.

Gus Alex was raised in the neighborhood of Twenty-sixth Street and Wentworth Avenue, just south of Chinatown, in Dawson's home district. Dawson told the Swiss he had known Alex more than twenty years and that Alex had "a good reputation."

Dawson admitted to Virgil W. Peterson, director of the Chicago Crime Commission, that he solicited campaign contributions from the underworld. Dawson said, "A politician goes where the money is. In my district, that's the underworld. Nobody in his right mind gives a politician a dime unless he expects to get back a dollar on his investment."

In 1962 Dirksen led the opposition against a campaign to regulate the cost and safety of consumer drugs. That year he got heavy campaign contributions from the pharmaceutical industry officials of Warner Lambert Pharmaceutical Company; the Olin Mathieson Chemical Corporation (Squibb); and G. D. Searle and Company, drug manufacturers.

In this and other instances Dirksen solicited financial help from men in the upperworld who had something to gain from friendship with an Illinois legislator. Throughout his career, Dirksen showed that his political friendship and help was available at a price. Gus Alex obviously paid that price.

Capone's view of politicians has been mentioned. Somewhere he had heard or read that some politician had said, "No girl was ever ruined by a book." He would paraphrase it to say, "No pol was ever corrupted by a buck." He contended that an honest man was incorruptible, could not be corrupted if paid a million dollars cash. He said, "But you don't find honest men in politics. If one gets in by mistake he gets out quick. The rest of them cannot afford to have an honest man among them. He would be too likely to blow the whistle on the others.

"A politician may turn down my first offer or even my second. If I need him bad enough I'll meet his price eventually. Then some do-gooder will come along and say I corrupted the bastard. Hell, the way I see it that corrupt bastard just shook me down for more money."

So far Paul Ricca stands out as the one man among Capone's heirs who has gone farthest in holding himself above the law. For several decades the United States government officially sought to deport Ricca as an undesirable alien. He had entered this country by fraud, obtained citizenship by fraud, and had been convicted of several felony charges. When ordered deported, Ricca just paid off politicians to prevent the order being carried out.

Ricca had been ruled an undesirable alien by the courts. He had been ordered deported. After all appeals had been lost, he boasted that he told officials "from the White House down" that before he would leave the United States he would wash all the dirty linen of politics in public.

Paul Ricca was born Felice De Lucia, the son of Antonio De Lucia, on November 14, 1897, near Naples. On May 18, 1917, he was found guilty in the court at Ottavino, near Naples, of the murder of Emilio Parrillo. The principal witness against him was Vincenzo Capasso. Ricca was sentenced to two and a half years in prison.

About the time Al Capone showed up in Chicago, Paul Ricca got out of prison in Italy. The first thing he did, of course, was to look up Vincenzo Capasso, whose testimony had convicted him. He killed Capasso and fled. He was tried in absentia for the killing, found guilty, and sentenced to twenty-one years in prison. The trial and sentencing took place in 1920. Ricca was a fugutive.

Ricca was a member of the Mafia and had the organization's help in his next step. A man named Paul Maglia turned his passport over to a Naples travel agency for use in preparing his papers for emigration. Paul Maglia's passport showed his date of birth as July 10, 1898, and the place of birth as Apricena, Italy. Whether Maglia was a member of the Mafia has never been disclosed.

The Naples travel agency told Maglia his passport had been mislaid. Ricca arrived by steamer in New York Harbor on August 10, 1920, carrying the Paul Maglia passport. He entered the United States under the name of Maglia. The passport was returned to Naples and four months after it had been "misplaced" it was "found" and returned to its real owner.

Ricca's first known murder, at the age of nineteen, had been a vendetta killing for the Mafia. His friends and superiors in the Organization sent him from New York directly to Chicago. He spoke no English and on his arrival in Chicago he went to work as an usher in the Dante motion picture theater at 813 West Taylor Street, just west of Halsted Street. The patrons of the Dante all spoke Italian.

When he had learned a little English, he went to work as a waiter in Diamond Joe Esposito's restaurant, the Bella Napoli Café, at 850 South Halsted Street. In those Prohibition days the place sold dago red wine. When arrested in a raid there on May 31, 1923, Ricca gave the name of Peter Riccio. Years later when he applied for citizenship, another restaurant owner and newspaper photographer, Mike Fish, vouched for him and said he had known him as a waiter in the early twenties.

From that time on he became known as Paul (The Waiter) Ricca.

Ricca became an alcohol distributor for the Genna brothers, who had their manufactory at 1022 West Taylor Street under the protection of Joe Esposito, the restaurant man. Esposito was Republican committee-man of the Nineteenth (now the Twenty-fifth) Ward until he was shot to death in 1928, so he was in a position to grant the Gennas protection from police harrassment.

Ricca rose fast as he learned the business. He and Capone were Neapolitans of the same age, for Capone was born in Castellamare, just outside Naples. They had mutual friends in the old country and became inseparable in Chicago. When Ricca married just after New Year's in 1927, two of those who stood up with him and his bride were Al Capone and Capone's sister, Mafalda.

Three weeks after that wedding, on January 24, 1927, Ricca was arrested for carrying a concealed weapon. He used the name Paul Viela. On July 11, 1930, Ricca was arrested in New York City. On November 4, 1930, he was arrested in Frank Nitti's speakeasy at 901 South Halsted Street. This time he was in the company of three state legislators as well as several members of Capone's Syndicate.

Ricca was arrested April 20, 1932, at the Congress Hotel in Chicago with Meyer Lansky and Lucky Luciano. Another hoodlum arrested with them at the time gave the name of John Senna. He was actually John Capone, Big Al's brother. This was a month before Al Capone was to be taken to prison. Arrangements were being made to keep his empire intact pending his return.

Ricca used the name Paul Rizzio when arrested November 2, 1932, in the Planters Hotel in Chicago with Frankie Rio, Phil d'Andrea, Sam (Golf Bag) Hunt, and Tony Accardo. They were then setting up the ownership of the San Carlo Village, for which space had been rented at A Century of Progress, to open in six months. Ricca became a partner in its operation along with his lawyer, Giuseppe Imburgio, alias Joe Burger.

By this time Ricca was managing three hotels on North La Salle Street between Division Street and North Avenue in the Forty-third Ward. The three were the Carling, the Paxton, and the Marshall. Ricca maintained a palatial home in suburban River Forest. He was an affluent gentleman farmer, with a $75,000 country estate complete with swimming pool at Long Beach, Indiana, near the country home of Mayor Richard J. Daley.

Ricca was another of the gangsters of peasant background whose first substantial investment, when they came into big money, was a piece of land.

Ricca had applied for citizenship September 27, 1928, under the name he used in entering the United States, that of Paul Maglia. In his application he swore, despite two murder convictions in his record, that he never had been arrested for a felony. He asked court permission to change his name legally to De Lucia, the name he bore at birth.

After Ricca and the other Syndicate gangsters were freed from prison August 13, 1947, by the intercession of then Attorney General Tom Clark, honest newspapermen raised a howl. At least four murders had been committed in the million-dollar movie shakedown, of which Ricca was a part.

Shortly afterward, the U.S. Bureau of Narcotics opened a European office in Rome and sent Charles Siragusa, then an agent and later deputy director of the bureau, to manage the new office. When Siragusa left Washington he took with him the fingerprint records of a score of widely known American criminals. He asked the Italian police to see if any of them were wanted for anything.

A few days later the man known in Chicago as Paul Ricca was positively identified as the twice-convicted murderer known in Naples as Felice De Lucia.

When Ricca's lawyers suggested he return to prison to ease the pressure on the politicians he had paid for his parole, Ricca refused. This was when he first threatened "to blow the lid off" politics inside the White House and the Senate if the politicians he had been paying for so many years did not stand their ground against their critics.

Ricca went before Federal District Judge Michael L. Igoe in Chicago with a petition for a writ permitting him to remain at liberty. Igoe sought to avoid granting the writ, but Ricca lost his temper in court and the judge complied. Igoe permitted Ricca freedom. Ricca laughed in the judge's face as he did so. Igoe had been one of the politicians who had marched hat in hand behind the bier of the chief pimp in the First Ward, Big Jim Colosimo.

When the information sent by the Narcotics Bureau went through channels to the U.S. Immigration and Naturalization Service, a move was launched to revoke Ricca's citizenship. Federal District Judge Walter J. La Buy in Chicago, after hearing the evidence, agreed that Ricca had falsified his application. His citizenship was revoked by an order of June 8, 1957.

A year and a half later, on January 29, 1959, a deportation order was signed by Otto A. Eck, special inquiry officer for the Immigration and Naturalization Service. Ricca appealed to the immigration appeals board. That appeal delayed deportation but could not keep him out of jail on other charges.

On July 1, 1959, Ricca entered the federal prison in Terre Haute for evading payment of $99,000 in income taxes for the years 1948 through 1950.

On August 25, 1959, the immigration appeals board dismissed Ricca's request. His lawyers went into federal court to appeal that ruling. On February 17, 1961, Federal Judge Joseph Sam Perry upheld Ricca's deportation order. Ricca's lawyers went to the federal appeals court.

While the U.S. Circuit Court of Appeals pondered, Ricca was released from prison October 1, 1961. On December 4, Judge Perry's decision was upheld by the appeals court. On April 2, 1962, the U.S. Supreme Court denied a review of the decision.

By this time Ricca and his lawyers believed deportation could be avoided indefinitely by assiduously pursuing all sorts of legal appeals.

Ricca quit cursing and began smiling. From then on he went to court or to hearings from time to time, never taking them too seriously.

John M. Lehmann, Chicago director of immigration, responded to prodding by newspapermen and ordered Ricca to seek a country to which he would like to be deported. Ricca had told the immigration authorities that since Italy was holding a murder conviction over his head, to send him back to his native land would be to show him no mercy.

Ricca's lawyers sent letters to sixty countries or more, supposedly seeking asylum for their client. To each they sent great bundles of news clippings, indicating to some extent how undesirable Ricca was being found by the United States. Each country in turn replied, "We don't want him, either."

By this time the newspaper readers of Chicago realized that once again their government had sold them out and that they were being treated to a farce. Ricca and all the other characters on stage would play their parts but nothing would happen.

Director Lehmann made a big thing of ordering Ricca to report monthly to his office, and meanwhile to keep trying to locate a friendly country which would accept him as a resident.

On June 30, 1964, Lehmann issued a fresh deportation order. Ricca's lawyers went into the federal court of Judge William J. Campbell next day and got a stay on the order. Campbell said no country would accept Ricca.

Seven days later, Judge Campbell in a surprise reversal said that Italy would now accept him. Campbell ordered deportation. Within minutes, federal marshals arrested the gang chieftain. Within an additional few minutes, Ricca's lawyers were in the U.S. Circuit Court of Appeals with a petition for review of Judge Campbell's order.

This automatically stayed the deportation.

On September 18, 1964, the immigration board of appeals agreed to reopen the case. This was after attorneys pointed out a technical fault in Otto Eck's original 1959 order, in that Eck had failed to designate the country to which Ricca was to be deported.

On November 18, 1964, a new series of deportation hearings started and Otto Eck issued another deportation order. This order was included in a fifty-seven page opinion written by Eck. Since this was a new order, Ricca's lawyers started a new run through the various courts.

Ricca had played his role before the various Senate committees which from time to time come out of the woodwork to make a little political hay with the voters. Ricca was called by the Kefauver Committee in 1950 "the national head of the Crime Syndicate." He was called by the McClellan committee on July 1, 1958, America's "most important" criminal. Ricca, thin and graying, had snarled properly and taken the Fifth Amendment when called before each of the committees.

Newspapermen of Chicago like to needle the politicians. They asked William G. Fols, deputy district director of the Immigration and Naturalization Service, why Paul Ricca was permitted to remain at liberty while under order of deportation. Fols said that as long as Ricca reported to the local office every three months, told of his activities and gave his address, nothing could be done.

In November, 1966, the U.S. Circuit Court of Appeals upheld another court deportation for Ricca. Once again his lawyers went to the Supreme Court. As long as Ricca's money held out, as long as pimping, gambling, and loan sharking poured money into Ricca bank accounts he could keep the United States government running in circles.

Just to vary things slightly, Ricca petitioned the Tribunal in Rome, one of Italy's highest courts, to declare him "a noncitizen of Italy." Ricca did not ask that action be hurried on his peitition. As long as it was before a legal court, the American officials would be able to drag their feet with an appearance of sanctity.

Ricca kept it up for the rest of his life. He made good his boast. He said nobody would dare carry out the deportation order for fear he would "blow the lid off the White House."

A bit of history is called for.

In late 1890 the Italian and Sicilian community of New Orleans was harboring the Mafia, which ambushed and mortally wounded Police Chief David Hennessy. He lived long enough to identify his killers. Nineteen were indicted. They so terrorized the courts that they were freed.*

The city of New Orleans at the time was the most urbane and civilized community in North America. Its citizens were outraged. All the city's most honorable civic leaders attended a protest meeting at which a public vigilante organization was formed. The vigilantes broke the killers out of jail, shot them to death, and hanged their bodies from nearby trees.

This was public action. No one was masked. No protesting citizen sought to hide his identity. The decent people were proud of their action.

W.S. Parkerson, the prominent lawyer who had been elected to head this "movement to correct the failure of justice" was lifted to a wagon bed. He looked at the bodies of the Mafia leaders, bloody and unrecognizable as they swung in the brisk dawn air of March 12, 1891. Then Parkerson looked out at half the citizens of New Orleans, gathered together. He said, "Today I have performed the most painful duty of my life. It had to be done. It was done, and now it is over. Pray God we never have to do such a thing again. Now go home and God bless you and this community."

New Orleans had given its answer to the rule of the underworld. This is the source of the one fear that haunts leaders of the Capone Syndicate. The New Orleans episode, with its international repercussions, which included the breaking of diplomatic relations between Italy and the United States, is now eighty years past. But it is not forgotten by the Mafia. No matter how boisterously they speak of other things, when the gossip turns to this subject they talk in hushed tones.

*The facts of this case and its international diplomatic aftermath are told in greater detail in a previous book by the same author, *The Madhouse on Madison Street.*

The Capone Syndicate leaders admit among themselves that they do not understand the people of rural America. They speak of them contemptuously as "the apple-knockers" or "the hicks in the sticks." This is not simply the way they speak of farmers and ranchers, but of people in any city too small to attract Syndicate control. They think of all such Americans as "cowboys," a word frequently on their lips, and they always fear the cowboys may get out of hand and start shooting.

The gangsters of the streets and alleys and dark places of American cities really fear—genuinely tremble at the thought—that some day the American people will take the law into their own hands. They know they have nothing to fear from the police, the most honest of whom are kept handcuffed by their political masters. The gangsters do not fear their own kind. But their homes, as was that of Jake Guzik, are fortresses. The doors are lined with sheet steel, the windows barred.

The underworld itself does not realize how far the people of America have fallen since New Orleans' hanging spree of 1891.

Before Capone, the people of Chicago might have handled their serious problem of crime in the streets in just such a commonsense way. But two generations of the Capone Syndicate influence has changed them. Today they would fear being labeled advocates of lynch law by namby-pamby newspaper editors, do-gooder priests and rabbis and ministers, the corrupt leaders of the city's political machines.

Before Capone, decent people in Chicago and its suburbs would not knowingly have lived and reared their children next door to pimps and thieves and murderers. Today decent citizens regularly see printed pictures of the $170,000 or $270,000 or $370,000 homes of these pimps—and think nothing of it. Every citizen has read the killers' addresses. No honest citizen seems capable of personal indignation at the presence of Syndicate leaders in his home area.

Before Capone, a Roman Catholic prelate such as Cardinal George Mundelein could send into exile one of his brightest young priests for so much as praying at the grave of callous multiple murderers. Nobody today can even imagine such a thing. The prelates seem to be of the same mind as the do-gooder fools in priestly habit who parrot the notion that "Not the criminal but society is at fault."

When the Lindbergh baby was kidnapped and killed, an indignant Congress enacted the death penalty for convicted kidnappers. Since then the Supreme Court has ruled that none of the sovereign states of the union can put criminals to death. Instead, the multiple murderers, the child molesters and kidnappers, the multiple rapists, must become the burden of honest taxpayers and either kept in prison or freed.

This type of thinking is part of the legacy of Al Capone and his colleagues, the corrupting criminals across the face of America.

Before Capone, ordinary people had faith in the legend across the face of the Supreme Court: EQUAL JUSTICE UNDER LAW. Since Capone that faith has gone a-glimmering.

There has never been city or county or state accountability in Chicago for leaders in the higher echelons of the Capone Syndicate. A few have been brought to book under federal laws against income tax evasion. Even this has been brought into question.

In the early thirties Frank Nitti, Ralph Capone, Al Capone, Murray Humphreys, and Jake Guzik were sent to prison for income tax evasion. It was clear then that the men of the Establishment in the upperworld had decreed a no-holds-barred fight against the leaders of organized crime. Since then, it has become clear that the income tax laws are more and more used for the punishment of political enemies.

In Chicago, when a Chris Paschen is sent to prison for income tax evasion, the word goes around, "He delivered the Forty-ninth Ward primary vote to Ruth Hanna Mc Cormick instead of Charlie Deneen. When Deneen got to the U.S. Senate he told friends he would see Paschen in prison."

When a Frank Keenan is sent to prison for income tax evasion in Chicago the word goes around, "He delivered the primary vote in his ward to Martin Kennelly instead of Dick Daley. When Daley became mayor and had some clout in Washington he decreed that Keenan had to serve time."

There are no federal laws against murder, robbery, rape. The Mann Act against transporting women across state lines for commercial prostitution has not for many years been enforced against Capone Syndicate leaders.

Before Capone, no lawyer would have gone out of his way to enjoin honest policemen from harassing criminals. The various bar associations took the position that every accused man is entitled to counsel and the criminal lawyer would do his best to represent his client in the courts. Beyond that, the lawyers considered themselves decent people interested in decent communities.

Not until two generations of Capone Syndicate influence had softened up the thinking of lawyers did Chicago witness the spectacle of lawyers going into court on their own—on a non-fee "public service" basis—to protect multimillionaire pimps. When the American Civil Liberties Union went into federal court and got an injunction to prevent police from harassing Jake Guzik, not a lawyer in Chicago raised his voice in protest.

Before Capone, decent people might have demanded that known pimps and criminals such as Guzik, even those who had millions of dollars at their disposal, be driven off the streets, thrown in jail as vagrants, harassed until they left the city permanently. But since 1920 the minds and characters of decent people have been softened by the Capone influence. Daily newspaper editors, like so many of the priests, have lost hope.

Before Capone, a majority of the people and the candidates for public office seem to have had standards of value other than those represented by the dollar sign. They wanted decent communities in which to live and rear their children, communities free of the total depravity and corruption represented by the Capone Syndicate pimps.

Since the beginning of time, no organized society has ever been free of crime and criminals. Some men and women have always sought to live without working, by robbing others of the fruits of their toil. But not until twentieth-century America has the world experienced a criminal organization so interwoven with government itself as to be ineradicable. Never before has government acknowledged itself unable to cope with a criminal syndicate.

The one man in the United States Government charged with fighting this type of syndicated crime was ex–Assistant Attorney General Henry E. Peterson, who until 1975 headed the organized crime and racketeering section of the Department of Justice. Peterson told a convention of the National District Attorneys Association in Los Angeles, "So far all efforts to destroy the multibillion-dollar crime industry have been pitiful, just pitiful. I don't know how we are going to destroy its long-term effectiveness."

Peterson was not a politically appointed hack, but a career man with the Department of Justice.

Peterson said the federal government had not gotten into the anti-Syndicate fight in a major way until 1961. He said that for nearly fifteen years his section of the Department of Justice has been analyzing such Syndicate strongholds as New York, Chicago, Philadelphia, and Miami. He said that until they did so he had not fully realized the power of the Syndicate. He went on: "Frankly, it opened my eyes, and I don't think I'm naïve in this area. I looked over a lot of information that had been uncovered and not disseminated. Believe me, I was impressed with the power of this organization. I think it is subversive and very dangerous."

Before Capone, the honest policemen, the honest prosecutors, the honest judges, and the honest government officials such as Peterson had thought of crime as something that could be successfully fought. Not until two generations of the Capone Syndicate and its allied crime syndicates in other major cities had undermined law enforcement was it conceivable that such a man as Peterson could be quoted: "I don't know how we are going to destroy it."

Peterson meant of course that he did not know how it could be destroyed under America's present system of government, when all public officials from the precinct captain to the President of the United States are dependent on Syndicate help for their jobs. The Syndicate controls voting in the major cities, which control the outcome of national elections. The Syndicate can throw its vote for—or against—any candidate; it holds the balance of power.

When organized crime holds the balance of power as it now does, the laws against crime and criminals will be progressively weakened. Definite penalties for certain crimes will be lifted so that judges, who can be bought and otherwise influenced, will have discretionary powers. Capital punishment will be abolished so that criminals, no matter what their crimes, can be freed as quickly as the public forgets.

For more than fifty years, New York has had its Sullivan Law, which forbids ownership of handguns. The law-abiding citizen has been totally disarmed, and now only outlaws regularly carry guns. The Syndicate has benefited. Organized crime wants such a law nationally. The do-gooders parrot Syndicate propaganda and do not realize they are being used.

Before Capone, the people of the United States were capable of real indignation at the knowledge that an aging justice on the United States Supreme Court bench is in the pay of Las Vegas gambling money. The people were capable of wrath at the thought of a politician freeing four murderers who would later boast that they had bought for him the next vacancy on the Supreme Court bench.

After two generations of Capone influence the apathy—indeed, the despair—of the people is visible to anyone who has eyes to see.

When a Goldwater romps all over the West with a Willie Bioff, when a Dirksen writes a foreign government recommending a Slim Alex, when a Dawson admits his campaign expenditures are paid by organized crime, when an Annunzio has as his partner a John D'Arco, nobody gets excited. Every voter feels there is nothing he can do about it.

This brief look at the Syndicate has been limited to Chicago. No attempt has been made to include in these chronicles all the men who worked with and in the footsteps of Al Capone. This has been a selection of the stories of the men who had most to do with carrying on the subversion begun by the Colosimo-Torrio-Capone complex.

Before Capone the individual name most associated with Chicago was that of Abraham Lincoln, who had been nominated for the Presidency at the Wigwam on Clark and Lake streets. Throughout the world today, it is not the name of Abraham Lincoln that comes to every child's lips when the city of Chicago is mentioned, but Al Capone. Chicago today brings to every adult's mind the thought of organized crime and corrupt politicians—and citizens too apathetic to hang the lot from the nearest trees as did the people of New Orleans.

The people of Chicago and of America seem to have lost their capacity for anger at being constantly hoodwinked by their public servants. A once decent and dignified people appear to have been so softened and subverted as to have lost their capacity for honest indignation and wrath.

This is the legacy of Al Capone.

Index